GEM OF A LIE

IAIN HUGHES

GEM OF A LIE

IAIN HUGHES

GEM OF A LIE

© Iain Hughes

Iain Hughes has asserted his rights in accordance with the
Copyright, Designs & and Patents Act 1988 to be
identified to be the author of this work.

Published by:

Wi/\le Publishing

British Columbia, Canada

Email: info@wibblepublishing.com
Web: www.wibblepublishing.com

First published 1st June 2013

Legal Deposit: Library and Archives Canada, Ottawa, Ontario, Canada.

13-digit ISBN: 978-0-9919266-0-2

Printed in Great Britain

ACKNOWLEDGEMENTS

Thanks to all my friends and family for the help and support. For my long suffering wife Julia, in particular, thank you for believing.

To David Stone, my police adviser and a listening ear. To Glyn, Jane and Jackie Bird, thanks for your help.

I would like also to extend my gratitude to my friend Paul Ison, author of *A Crooked Sign on Albion Street* and *The Path* for all his help and advice.

CHAPTER ONE

Jonathan Harker carefully slid out of bed trying not to disturb his wife Lynda, although as she pulled on the duvet making herself comfortable again, he knew he hadn't quite succeeded. The time was 6:45am and judging by the chill he felt as he crossed the bedroom and out onto the landing it was going to be another very cold January morning. After showering he dressed and went down the back staircase to the kitchen to make himself a large mug of tea, the kick start he always needed before his early morning walk with Jet the family's black labrador. He gazed out of the kitchen window, whilst warming his hands on the hot mug, and looking towards the frost covered fields in the distance where the tall poplar trees were gently swaying in the cold morning breeze, silhouetted by the first slivers of light from the winter sun now appearing over the horizon.

Wrapping up warm his fleece lined coat firmly secured he unlocked the side door and stepped outside, immediately feeling a chilling blast from the north easterly wind. Carefully he made his way across the cobbled courtyard towards the old stable block, his feet slipping on the well worn ice covered surface. Steadying himself he knew he would have to throw crushed rock salt over the yard when he returned home from his walk, and before Lynda made any attempt to take the horses across to the indoor exercise ring. When he reached the stone building he opened the top half of the stable door where he could hear Jet becoming very excited.

"Come on then old boy, lets go." Hearing Jonathan's voice, Jet pushed open the bottom half of the door, jumping up to greet him before excitedly running off across the frozen yard and around the side of the west wing down the drive. He was sniffing the cold air as he ran on and in no time at all he was at of the bottom of the long gravel driveway, waiting impatiently for his master. When Jonathan arrived at the large ornate iron gates, which led out onto the narrow country lane, he stopped to look back and admire their wonderful home, thinking just how fortunate Lynda and himself were to be the owners of such a beautiful grand country house.

Sedgwick House was built around 1785 by William Ireland for Sir Clarence Chesterfield, one of Leicestershire's richest merchants of the time, and had only been owned by his wife's family for the last fifty years, but even on this coldest of mornings it looked so majestic standing there high and proud above the picturesque Leicestershire countryside, its lichen covered sandstone blocks giving off a look of true grandeur in the early morning light. The property had been left to his wife Lynda by her late father two years earlier, including all of 1,500 hectares of prime English countryside with its rolling hills sweeping down to the lush pastures in the valley below, all providing excellent grazing land for breeding beef cattle.

Dotted among the hills were small chestnut copses giving good cover for the many game birds that were bred on the estate purposely for private organised shooting parties. Lynda had been made to fight long and hard to keep her inheritance as her step brother Nigel had contested the will, only then, after a lengthy and very costly legal battle which had finally been settled some ten months earlier was the property and land decreed to her.

"Come on Jet, let's get on." Jet didn't need the command more than once and he was soon running down the lane until he reached the canal bridge and his favourite place to spend a penny. Jet, who was just 18 months old, still had that puppy way about him, but had learnt enough to know when to wait for his master, and he now stood once more with his black rod of a tail waving from side to side as he looked up at Jonathan, as much as to say which way now? Always at this point of the walk they would have to decide whether to turn onto the towpath to the left, which would take them towards the small town of Market Wellen, or to turn right down the southern route of the Grand Union Canal towards Kegworth Wharf.

He stood for a moment pondering his decision, while looking over the parapet of the red brick canal bridge where a covering of frost had dusted the already frozen canal. Looking along the embankment to the right the willows hung heavily with icicles left by the freezing early mist. Walking gingerly back down off the steep humped back bridge he decided they would turn right onto the towpath this morning, although it was usually Jet who made the final route decision depending on his nose and that was the way he had also chosen this morning.

Jonathan really enjoyed this time of day, having the towpath mostly to themselves, especially as there was always a good chance of seeing some of the more nocturnal wildlife still around after an undisturbed night's hunting. Carrying on he called out to Jet, startling a moorhen which was trying to escape by running awkwardly on the ice but without having too much success. Jet stopped to look momentarily before continuing on his way, tail a wagging and sniffing everything around him, he loved the freedom of his early morning walk, probably even more than his master.

The normal routine was to continue along the towpath for around 50 minutes to an hour before retracing their steps and this would give himself and Jet a good appetite for their breakfast when they returned later to Sedgwick House. Jet ran off again this time chasing a white bobbing tail into the bottom of the hedgerow. Two minutes later he was out again and looking back towards Jonathan, reassuring himself that his master was still around.

When Jonathan and Lynda's children are home from school on their summer holidays, they also like to go along with their father on the morning towpath walk. Their two children, Holly and Edward, aged eight and ten respectively, are both at boarding school, Holly at Radisson and Edward at Shown Court, following in their parents footsteps and seemingly getting on very well at that. He was rapidly brought back from thoughts of his children and into the reality of his surroundings by a reverberation that stopped him in his tracks, a tremendous cracking of ice being broken with earth shattering force, the sound echoing along the length of the canal. He turned quickly to look in the direction he had thought the noise had come from, but there was nothing to be seen, his only logical reckoning being that it could have been the pressure of the expanding ice releasing an ear-splitting shock wave of immense proportions? He was quite taken back, confused even.

"What the hell was that?" he found himself saying out loud. Jet had also been distracted by the sound and was standing with his head held high as if he was waiting to see if it was going to happen again, but there was nothing, then, soon forgotten, he was running off again. For Jonathan this was slightly more puzzling. He carried on still wondering about the unexplained resonance as they were approaching the road bridge at Kegworth Wharf.

"Not too far, now old boy," he called out as Jet ran on even further ahead, his dark coat now sprinkled with frosted dust off the hedgerow bottom. The wharf was as quiet as ever apart from an occasional dog barking at the nearby kennels. He carried on passing the row of narrow boats moored up for the long winter, and the old day trip boat with the appropriate name of Summer Song, her tarpaulin now only partially covering the old wooden slatted seats. It's bedraggled sheet now pulled tightly down with the weight from the water it was now holding, a sad sight remembering how she had looked last summer with her gleaming paintwork and a full accompaniment of tourists, but he was sure that's how she would look again when ready for those long summer days.

Moored next to Summer Song there were a group of very smart cabin cruisers, most of them the pride and joy of their owners, although one or two were now up for sale. At the far end of the long jetty, and tied permanently to the bank, was an old black traditional barge called Uncle Sam. It was then he realised he wasn't the only person up and about so early on this morning, as the wonderful smell of bacon wafted across the canal from Uncle Sam, blending in well with the crisp morning air.

Jet turned his head in Jonathan's direction before advancing again. It was another half a mile before they would reach the Felford Arm. At this point, if you navigate off the main canal to the left, the Arm would take you down to Felford and the Wharfside public house where Lynda and Jonathan had enjoyed Sunday lunch on a couple of occasions. Carrying on to the right, the Grand Union heads south-west on its long journey towards London, the next place of importance being Norton Junction around 15 miles to the south. Jonathan enjoyed all the towpath walk, but this part of the system was by far his favourite with its gentle meandering bends, and then after a mile or so a large sweep in the canal to the left bringing you eventually around to the woodlands that lay to the south side of Kegworth road bridge, which in early May would be carpeted with beautiful bluebells spreading deep into the shady forest.

Jonathan looked at his watch. It was 7:40am and they would soon have to turn and head home. He called out to Jet who was now getting much too far in front of him. The Labrador turned and ran back towards his master.

"Good boy Jet. Not too far now, we really have to go back soon." He roughed his head with both hands and Jet ran happily off again and in no mood to go home just yet only wanting to scurry around in the hedgerow as they continued along the towpath. It was then Jonathan noticed movement up in front of him. White smoke was drifting slowly up and around a narrow boat moored to the towpath bank.

"Jet, come here boy?" he called out. The dog turned again and reluctantly ran back making a detour through the hedge as he did so. Jonathan thought nothing of it until he heard his dog barking at something in the field on the other side of the hedge. He called out again only this time much louder.

"Jet, Jet come back here boy?" but the dog was still sounding off behind the thick hedgerow. Just as he was about to seek him out, he suddenly appeared from under the hedge, covered in frost shaking himself and panting as if he had been chasing something or other.

"Rabbits, old boy?" Jonathan asked, while taking the lead from his coat pocket and clipping it onto Jet's collar. He was more than a little surprised to see the barge moored up there that morning, and he thought it must have arrived sometime yesterday before the ice formed as the temperature was well below freezing by 2 o'clock yesterday afternoon. It was common practice for Jonathan, after spotting an occupied barge, to always clip the lead onto Jet's collar, as most of the barge owners have pets of their own. Like most dogs, Jet enjoys chasing cats and snarling at other dogs that are to him on what he deems his domain. Jonathan's inquisitive nature and the sight of the barge moored to the towpath had his curiosity levels raised, so he decided to carry on a little further; he was now approaching the vessel and gently eased Jet close to his side; as he did he noticed the smoke from her chimney was now drifting over branches in the hedgerow causing the frost to melt and drip down onto an old dustbin lid lying on the towpath, and creating the sound of a imperfectly tuned steel band. The long brightly coloured narrow boat was probably all of 65ft, and he could tell right away she was one of the many hire boats with her distinct light green painted top and a gold band which separated the upper deck from the black bottom half of the boat. The rest of the vessel's trim had been painted red and yellow. A metal railing ran around the outside of a seating area at the stern, leaving plenty of room for her punters to sit outside and enjoy those warm summer days. He was now only a couple of metres away; when his cold reddened cheeks cracked into a wry smile, as he spotted the vessel's name, 'The Lazy-So and So.'

He thought to himself rather them than me, holidaying at this time of year in a metal boat where thick ice now encircled them in an almost pincer movement. He then noticed a light shining out from two large port holes, which he presumed to be the galley area, at least that was where the chimney came up and out through the roof. Jet sniffed at the frozen rope that tied the back of the barge to a steel stake which had been driven into the towpath. Jonathan stepped carefully over the line while keeping Jet on a tight rein. The cabin area was now almost alongside them and he was passing the first porthole, his head turning ever so slightly in that very human manner, automatically taking a fleeting glance knowing that you probably shouldn't, but it is where impulsive nature gets the better of us.

He diverted his gaze towards the lit porthole and quickly past the second. Immediately his heart began pounding as he walked on for two or three more paces, before coming to a mind enforcing halt. His legs felt like jelly and his thought process was in overdrive. Had his eyes deceived him in some way? No, he was fooling himself if he believed that, but in reality what the hell should he do about it? He found himself in total disbelief that this was actually happening and his morning walk had been turned on its head from normality to revulsion within a few short moments.

He knew there was nothing else for him to contemplate; he must summon up the courage, turn and face up to the situation he found himself in. Jet was standing wondering what his master was up to; he turned and pulled his dog towards the barge gently stroking his head as he did so, reassuring not only Jet but also himself. Then without noticing he stepped onto a frozen puddle, the cracking sound stopping him in his tracks once more. He waited a moment or two listening, but everything seemed to be quiet inside the barge. He had to take another look so he turned again uneasily wondering if he was doing the right thing, or was he opening up a can of worms for himself? Jet was looking up at his master, eager to carry on with their walk but stayed close to Jonathan's side sensing now something was wrong. He stood nervously to the side of the first porthole, carefully placed his right arm to steady himself, then, gripping the hand rail and with great trepidation he bent forward and peered inside.

The heat from the fire had kept both port holes clear of frost, but his worst fears were confirmed. He lowered his head further then looked again. There was a young woman lying on the cabin bench, her legs had been tied to the bench over the top of a dark green pair of dungarees, the light blue tee shirt she had been wearing was now torn from top to bottom exposing her breasts, her mouth was covered with silver tape and her hands had been tightly bound together above her head to a hook on the cabin wall. She looked to be alive but as he stared across the cabin wondering what the hell to do next, her head fell to one side startling him momentary. He wasn't ready for what happened next as she opened her eyes wide and appeared to look directly across the cabin towards him. Her facial expression changed as if was trying to say something. Curiously, the thin vein of silver tape which covered her mouth creased and he was sure she was trying to smile, it was only then to his absolute astonishment he thought he recognised her, muttering out loud, "For God sake it can't be."

He stood quickly, shocked by her reaction, standing for no more than a second or two before he sensed someone behind him instantaneously sending the coldest of shivers down his spine. Jet growled as Jonathan turned, and as he did so the dog's lead slipped out of his hand and he suffered a tremendous blow to the back of the head, causing him to fall heavily against the side of the barge. His face grazing down the cold metal hull before hitting the frozen ground. Jet barked with some venom, but then whimpered with pain as Jonathan tried to get back to his feet, but another clout sent him crashing down again. The faithful Labrador tried to defend his desperate master, but as he felt his own warm blood trickling down his face, Jet let out another agonising howl, almost at the same time as Jonathan received a kick into the middle of his back, quickly followed by another boot to the ribs. He tried again to get up onto his knees, but whoever his assailant was did not show him any mercy as they brought down a further crushing blow to his skull, the momentum helping to roll his body over onto his back. Through distorted vision he could just make out the prominence of someone standing over him, but by this time his sight was horribly blurred and he found himself in utter despair as he received a further eye watering kick to his crutch, he yelled out once more in anguish before finally losing consciousness.

CHAPTER TWO

Natasha, the Harker's nanny, was usually up by 7:30am, as she was on this morning, preparing breakfast for her employers, Jonathan and Lynda, the couple she had worked for over the last five months. She enjoyed living with the family and looking after Holly and Edward in the school holidays, along with her domestic work. It was altogether much more pleasurable than living in London which had been the case for some of the time in her last place of employment.

Natasha made herself tea and sat down in her favourite seat, the rattan style rocking chair by the lounge window. She looked out onto the cold morning landscape and, ever the daydreamer, she was soon thinking back to the time when she was with the Bromleys, her last employers. Natasha had had a good working relationship and was grateful to Mrs Bromley for helping her secure a job with the Harkers now that the Bromley's two children had gone back to boarding school, and as her services as their nanny were no longer required. Mr Bromley had been a long serving officer in the British Army, retiring just before Natasha started working for the couple. His wife Jackie, on the other hand, was a hard-nosed business woman of some repute. Natasha particularly loved their affluent life style, apart from the summer months the Bromleys spent living in London. As for the rest of the year she was travelling all over the world, staying in top class hotels, and sometimes spending up to three months away from the cold British winter at their holiday home near Cape Town.

Freddy and Jackie Bromley doted over the children, Molly and Alistair, and also made Natasha feel part of their family, but things seemed to change the last time they were in South Africa. It was a Monday afternoon just around six o'clock and she remembered taking the children upstairs to bed when the phone rang. She heard Mrs Bromley pick up the receiver off the small round table in the front hallway. "Hello, Jackie Bromley speaking." Natasha thought nothing more of it and quietly carried on with her duties of bathing the children and getting them ready for bed. After telling them a story she wished them in turn goodnight and crossed the landing to her room noticing that Jackie was still talking to someone on the phone. A good hour later, as Natasha came downstairs, she heard Jackie telling her husband that she would have to return to London the following day. Mr Bromley was trying to persuade his wife to stay, forcefully saying to her, "But Jackie, surely you can sort out this problem with your company from here?" She replied quite sternly,

"Freddy, I worked too bloody hard on this contract to lose it. You know how important this is for us."

"I know that darling but what about the children? They are going to miss you dreadfully?"

"Look Freddy you stay on here for three or four more days, you and Natasha will be just fine."

"Well I can't say I am happy about it, but if your mind's made up then you must do what you think is best. That's if you are so sure your incompetent partners can't manage without you. Would you like me to call the airline to book your flight?"

"Yes, if you wouldn't mind." Natasha went upstairs with Mrs Bromley to help her pack.

"You will be all right with the children and Freddy, won't you Natasha?"

"Yes of course I will Mrs Bromley."

She told her how sad she was to be leaving the children and her beautiful house to return to the cold British winter. At four o'clock the next afternoon, Mr Bromley drove them all to Cape Town International Airport to say goodbye to Jackie. The children were very tearful as she kissed them both, before waving goodbye as she walked off towards the departure lounge. She turned again before she was lost in the crowd.

As a special treat for them all, Mr Bromley drove them back in a different direction along by the coast via Sea Point, where Alistair and Molly were able to play for a while on the beach. After driving for another fifteen minutes further along the coast they pulled up outside a restaurant called Algoma's at Camps Bay. There was a fair sized seating area outside the rear of the restaurant so the patrons could enjoy the stunning scenery. They sat down so that all four of them had a view of the sea, which was some two hundred metres or so in front of them. Beyond that, over the bay they had a magnificent view of Table Mountain to the north, where huge white cumulus clouds were forming around the summit. Natasha and the children waited for Mr Bromley to order their food from the very tall smartly dressed waiter.

"Natasha shall we order hamburgers and fries for the children, with a couple of Coca Colas as a special treat? Is that all right for you two?" he asked.

"Yes thank you Daddy," they both eagerly replied.

"What would you like to eat Natasha?"

After a brief glance at the menu she decided on the swordfish with French fries.

"An excellent choice Natasha. I will also have the swordfish please, only I would prefer salad with mine, Nelson. He handed Nelson the menu back and thanked him.

"This is a beautiful place Mr Bromley," Natasha told him.

"Yes we have been coming here for many years. Nelson the waiter was just a slip of a lad the first time we came. He is one of many thousands named after the great man and they tell me Mandela himself has sat in this restaurant on numerous occasions."

Natasha looked across the table at Fredric and realised that this was the only time he had ever made conversation with her, apart from talking about the children or some domestic situation. She looked across the table towards him and she hadn't realised just how soft his blue eyes were. Occasionally she would be out with Mrs Bromley shopping and they would have lunch somewhere perhaps in the West End which was really special for Natasha, but it felt quite strange with her not being here. Nelson brought out the food and Mr Bromley ordered a glass of white Zinfandel and asked, "Natasha would you also like a glass?"

"Well if that's okay Mr Bromley," she replied.

"Of course it is Natasha, please relax and enjoy yourself."

After dining, Mr Bromley paid their bill and left a substantial tip for the waiter before leaving. They made their way out of the restaurant to the car and, as they were securing the children into their seats, she heard someone calling out to Mr Bromley. "Freddy, Freddy. Well fancy seeing you here old boy." A short man in his late 40s with sharp features and a slightly balding head came over towards the car.

"Harry what the hell are you doing down here?"

Embracing warmly he said, "Well I can't quite believe it, oh sorry Harry, this is our nanny Natasha. This is an old school friend of mine, Harry Bernard."

"Natasha, I am very pleased to meet you." He nodded his head towards her, she returning his gesture.

"Well Harry this is a surprise, I haven't seen you since Shown Court at the last old boy's reunion and that must have been ten years ago now?"

"More like a dozen Freddy."

"Where's Jackie, old boy?" Harry asked.

"Unfortunately she had to fly home earlier today. Seems they have a problem with the company lawyers drafting some huge contract she is involved with in Dubai, so regrettably she is under tremendous pressure at the moment. Apparently her partners are too tentative and can't seem to bring the contract in on time, so she thought it best to return home."

"Are you out here on business or pleasure Harry?"

"Business, I am afraid to say. We have had more than our fair share of problems over the last few months and, to be frank, we have been swimming against the tide for some time now."

"Harry, I have to go now and get the children home. Strict orders from Jackie to have them in bed before eight, ring me tomorrow morning and we will arrange a time and get together. Would tomorrow evening suit you for dinner? Here you are Harry, call me on this number?" Bromley handed him a card.

"I will look forward to it my old friend." After saying their goodbyes they drove away and back to the beach house.

Thirty minutes later, after putting the children to bed, Natasha sat out on the balcony to enjoy the warm breeze gently blowing off the sea. Bromley was enjoying a late evening swim down below her. She thought he looked so much more relaxed since his wife had flown home earlier in the day, and it was very noticeable that she had seemed to have taken all the tension away with her. The next morning around about 10am the telephone rang. It was Jackie.

"Natasha are the children all right, it was dreadful leaving them yesterday?"

"They both fine now Mrs Bromley."

"Natasha, please could you find Freddy for me?"

"Yes Mrs Bromley, I will go and find him for you."

Natasha found him in the garden using the hosepipe to water the flowerbeds under the main balcony.

"Mr Bromley, your wife is on the telephone for you."

"Okay Natasha, I'll be there right away."

She took the children out of the house to play in the pool leaving Freddy to speak to his wife without any distractions. Later in the morning the telephone rang again and this time Bromley answered it himself. After a short time he came outside to ask Natasha if she would be kind enough to prepare dinner that evening for himself, and his friend Harry Bernard, carrying on to say, "Of course Natasha, that is after young Alistair and Molly had been put to bed. Do you remember the gentleman we met yesterday afternoon? He will be arriving about 8:30pm. I am sure there must be something in the freezer. Anyway, see what you come up with Natasha. I have got a feeling you might find the odd lobster or two." He smiled warmly and left them all to play in the pool. As he was walking back towards the house the children begged their father to join them, but he declined telling them he would like too, only later in the day.

Although the house was only used as a holiday home by the Bromleys, it was always well stocked for every eventuality. There was a huge walk in larder, where all kinds of provisions were stored. There was also a very large chest freezer containing every conceivable frozen fare. Mrs Asuito, a local lady, came in three times a week to bring fresh vegetables and top up the pantry with anything that was needed. Down in the basement was Freddy's pride and joy, a large cellar, that any sommelier would have been proud to step into, with its traditional earthen floor to keep the rows of dust covered tilted bottles at the perfect temperature. The rest of the house and grounds were lovingly cared for by an army of contract gardeners, pool and domestic cleaners, so it wasn't a problem for Natasha to cook for her employer. As he said, there would be no difficulty finding something for her to make for their dinner that evening, although lobster was going a little too far, she thought.

Sorting through the freezer, she found two good-sized sea bass. If she cooked them in the oven, in tin foil with herbs she picked from the garden, and added white wine, accompanied by steamed vegetables, then she was sure Mr Bromley would be pleased. Besides that, it seemed to be a safe bet anyway as it certainly made Natasha's mouth water. She hoped the two gentlemen would also enjoy the dish and make allowances for the fact she was a nanny not some gourmet chef.

As requested by her employer, she put the children to bed at 6:30pm, and then went into the kitchen to prepare the fish that she had left on the marble countertop to defrost. She placed the fresh vegetables into the steamer and decided that she would turn the cooker on around 40 minutes before Mr Bromley's friend arrived at 8:30pm. After laying the table, Natasha went outside to relax and take a stroll around the Bromley's beautiful garden with its exquisite perfumes from so many jasmine and honeysuckle plants. She walked over to the children's swing. Sitting down, she gently pushed off and felt like a child again, her mind wondering back to when her father would push her high on the swing he had made for them under the mulberry tree. Breathing in the evening air in this delightful garden was just incredible and so many wonderful plants filled every space available, and her favourite, the honeysuckle, cascaded down from the balcony's above. It was then she noticed the clock through the kitchen window read 7:45pm, so reluctantly she went inside to prepare dinner. She was just in time to hear Mr Bromley walking across the hallway towards the kitchen.

"Ah Natasha, is everything going to plan?"

"Yes Mr Bromley. I found several ingredients in the freezer which I hope you will like." She told him what she was preparing for them and he seemed pleased.

"That sounds absolutely delicious, and really something to look forward to Natasha." He went off to the cellar to choose the wine to accompany the sea bass as well as the port for dessert.

Natasha answered the door to Mr Bernard and was pleased to see that he was a good time keeper. She showed him through to the lounge where her employer greeted him warmly, then she left them and carried on back to the kitchen. On entering, the smell from the fish cooking made her feel quite hungry.

About 30 minutes later she asked Mr Bromley and his friend

to come through to the dining room where they were seated. She placed the covered silver platter down in the centre of the table and lifting the lid she unravelled the tin foil to expose the sea bass.

"Natasha that looks wonderful." Bernard warmly agreed. She served the vegetables and poured them both a glass of the chosen wine, a local bottle of Cape Chenin Blanc, then left the open bottle in the ice bucket before leaving them, to hopefully enjoy their meal.

An hour passed before she returned to the dining room to ensure everything was to Mr Bromley's satisfaction and to see if they would like Stilton cheese for dessert to accompany the port.

"Yes please Natasha, the perfect combination, delicious Stilton washed down with the finest Portuguese port."

"Sounds good Freddy, but where on earth do you buy Stilton on the Cape?" Harry asked.

"It probably came out on the same plane as you Harry old boy. Natasha when you have finished serving, your evening is free to do whatever you please. Leave the table until the morning and thank you for a wonderful meal." She thought his smile seemed to linger as he wished her goodnight.

"Thank you Mr Bromley, and goodnight to you Mr Bernard."

After she had left the room Harry commented, "Cracking looking woman you're Natasha, Freddy?"

"She certainly is and a personality to match her good looks."

Natasha made her way up the stairs, checking on Alistair and Molly as she passed their rooms. Both of them were fast asleep. She closed her bedroom door, undressed, then walked into the large shower cubical to wash away the scent of fish. The warm water felt invigorating on her weary body, giving her a feeling of total relaxation so she stayed there for quite some time. Then, wrapping herself in one of the Bromley's fluffy white bath sheets, she picked up the book she had brought the day before at the airport, a travel paperback called Driving over Lemons. She liked the sound of the title so much she just had to buy it.

Walking out onto her balcony she lay down on the steamer sun lounger and felt the warmth from the late evening breeze waft over her. At first she lay looking up at the clear star-filled night sky before opening her new book to read, aided by the light coming from her bedroom. As the evening went on the two men's voices became louder and she could clearly hear their conversation, even though she tried not to. Bernard in particular was now sounding angry, talking about some deal or other he had been tricked into and just how much money he had lost, also heatedly telling Mr Bromley how his standing and his reputation had suffered.

Then she heard Mr Bromley say, "I just can't believe it Harry, Jonathan Harker was a lovely chap when we were all at Shown Court together, saved my bacon on numerous occasions. He could talk his way out of any situation and a good chap to have on your side," Bromley added before Harry Bernard carried on.

"Freddy I agree, but that's all in the past. I met up with him again at one of our old school reunions, must have been five years ago now, I don't think you were there?"

"Well I believe I have only missed one or two over the years, probably that was about the time of Jackie sister's wedding. Yes, that's it, she was married on the same day as the reunion. I was bloody incensed about that at the time, and that turned out to be a torrid affair which only lasted six strained months. Some sort of gold digger Jackie reckons, broke poor Lidia's heart also her bank balance."

"The swine," Bernard mouthed before he carried on.

"Anyway, after that we had several days out together. Golf, shooting, that sort of thing and we became quite good friends again. Strange really, after all those years." He fell silent as if he was deep in thought, then continued.

"Harker was working for his father-in-law as a lawyer, QC even, did you know that Freddy?"

"I knew he had entered chambers, but not the name of the firm," Harry continued, "Only went on to marry old Cockburn's daughter, Freddy."

"No, really. I had no idea he was mixing in such opulent circles."

"Two years on, old Efran Cockburn snuffs it and he leaves Harker's wife, Lynda, the whole bloody shebang. An estate in rural Leicestershire, the family business and the lucky sod is made for life."

"Good God, Harry. He always was an auspicious kind of chap."

Harry carried on, "But even though Harker has acquired all

this wealth through his wife, there was something she was keeping from him that he will probably never find out about."

"Was she having a relationship, an affair, perhaps Harry?"

"No not that Freddy. Lynda Harker has an astonishing almost bizarre secret she has been keeping from Harker," he carried on.

Bromley was hanging on to every word that Harry was telling him. He was fascinated and was waiting to hear whatever next would come from his old friend's mouth.

Harry looked across the table then continued, "This takes some believing Freddy. You see, Lynda Harker's father's family originally came from Hungary and were very well connected at that, but the intriguing thing about this is that the family heirloom has apparently been handed down over the last couple of centuries."

Bromley couldn't wait for Harry to finish as he was so engrossed by his old school friends story. "What on earth could this heirloom be then Harry?"

"Well, according to Ester it's a piece of fine jewellery, probably a hairpiece or a small tiara of some kind."

"How did Ester find out about Harker's wife's, so called, family secret?"

"Ester had become very friendly with both Lynda and Jonathan Harker." Harry's tone seemed to change slightly, Bromley thought. Harry lifted his glass looked into his wine and took a sip and seemed reluctant to continue. "So over some time, and for reasons I am now aware of, Harker's wife divulged to Ester all about her family and their hidden past. Lynda told Ester that being the heiress to the Cockburn's estate strictly prohibited her to reveal to her spouse, under any circumstances, anything regarding this heirloom until they have been married for at least twelve years."

Bromley half laughed, before blurting out, "Good God, what a peculiar family these Cockburns are to come up with such a farcical ultimatum. They must suffer from extreme paranoia. Tell me Harry, why do you think she told Ester and not Harker about the heirloom?"

"Well, please let me carry on with the rest of the story Freddy."

Bromley opened a third bottle of wine and poured Harry a glass. "You see with all Harker's contacts he had made in the city and at Cockburn's firm, and considering his wife's financial safety net, he decided to try his hand in a different direction and so he became a freelance broker in the city. At first he was making all the right moves. This went on for a while and he would often boast about how well his new business was proceeding then, one day, when we were playing golf at Woburn, he asked if Ester and I had ever considered investing on the stock market."

"So did you take Harker's advice?"

"Sore point Freddy. No, but he persisted on numerous occasions coming up with all sorts of investment opportunities. I suppose you could have called it a kind of bullying."

Harry sat forward in his chair and cut himself a slice of Stilton, then wet his lips by finishing off his glass of wine. "The truth is Freddy, Harker was succeeding in wearing me down. Because of Ester's friendship with Lynda we met regularly. Every time we saw each other at bridge, tennis club, that sort of thing, he never missed a chance. To be honest Freddy it all became a little too much for me."

"Harry, I never realised that Harker was such a bastard, pressurising you in that way, unforgivable."

"The sad thing is I always thought I was quite a strong person until I came up against Harker's cajoling. One Saturday morning when we were shopping in Oxford Street, Ester informed me she had arranged to meet Lynda and Jonathan Harker for lunch, at a wine bar just off the Edgeware Road. When we arrived they were already there. Harker beckoned us over to a dimly lit table at the far corner of what I thought was a seedy looking establishment."

Harry looked drawn and quite pale, Bromley said, "Take your time Harry and try a glass of port."

"Sorry Freddy if I sound more than a little forlorn."

"Not at all, from what you are telling me it sounds like you have good cause to be," Harry carried on, "Anyway, as usual, Harker turned the conversation to his own ends, boasting about how well his company was performing in the market place. It wasn't long before he came round to his favourite subject, our business, telling us he might just have the right investment coming up that would probably suit us both. He added, that's if we were interested, to let him know as soon as we could as he had several people who were attracted to this one. Don't wait too long, he added. I had told him on copious occasions I was not interested, but Harker persisted, and I could see that Ester was being won over by the smooth talking bastard, dreaming of big profits. He told us it would require an investment of around £500,000 or so."

Freddy interrupted, "That's a hideous amount of money Harry, what was your response?"

"I told him, not under any circumstances would we want to move, what in financial terms was our life savings, into some sort of dodgy hedge fund deal."

"Okay, just trying to help you and Ester out was his reply."

"I tried to distance myself from Harker after our frank discussion, and that was the last I wanted to hear about his bloody investment company, but over the next few weeks Ester tried on more than one occasion to influence me and change my mind, telling me Harker knew what he was doing and she thought this investment was built on a sound footing. One night we had a blazing row over who knew best what to do with our savings, which were mostly tied up in high street bank ICAs and other safe investments. Again I told Ester, 'I'll be dammed if I would invest with Jonathan Harker.' I found it most unlike her to even mention finance let alone argue over it, but in the end Freddy, Ester had persuaded me to look into Harker's offer. So, begrudgingly, I went to see him and he assured not only Ester and myself, but also our financial adviser who we had taken along with us, and he was also taken in by Harker's self confidence and by his diverse variety of investment strategies, particularly one of his hedge fund investments."

"Don't tell me Harry, you decided when you were under all this pressure to invest with Harker?"

"Yes, like a bloody fool I agreed to invest, not just five, but £750,000."

"My God Harry that's a bloody small fortune."

Bromley poured a glass of port for both of them and cut a slice of Stilton for himself before pushing the cheese board across the table to his old friend. He couldn't help noticing that Harry's whole persona had changed and that he had seemed to have aged somewhat in the telling of his story.

"Then what happened to make you so melancholy, yet so bloody angry?"

Harry lifted his glass and drank the port back in one swift mouthful and then poured himself another before continuing his harrowing tale. "I haven't told anyone else about this next part and I am going to find it extremely difficult to find the words, but I know I can trust you my old friend, but you must promise to keep this to yourself?"

"Harry, you can have full confidence that whatever you tell me around this table stays here. You must know that old chap."

Harry looked across the table at Freddy with a look of deep revulsion in his slightly glazed blue eyes.

"I'll tell you what happened Freddy, I came home early from a business trip to Rome and thought I would surprise Ester. I picked up a bunch of flowers and a good bottle of burgundy from a late night deli before driving back from Gatwick, arriving home around ten in the evening. I was surprised to see a car parked behind Ester's Alfa Romeo. God I thought, who the bloody hell is that at this time of night. Not Jill, Ester's sister, I hoped, because if it was we wouldn't get her on her way until at least midnight although if it was Jill she must have a different car and I was pretty sure she hadn't changed her old Saab for this gleaming new Volvo. I parked my car outside the driveway on the quiet avenue and walked past the two cars and up to the front door, noticing all the downstairs lights were turned off apart from the hallway. The bathroom and bedroom lights were on upstairs which seemed a little unusual so I hesitated for a few moments before opening the front door and then, regaining my composure, I let myself in and went quietly through to the kitchen, placing the bottle and the flowers onto the counter top. I stood still to listen for a while."

Freddy poured Harry a glass of water but never spoke as he listened to his friend's overwrought story. Harry took another sip of port before nervously continuing. "All I could hear Freddy, was water running down the waste pipe from the shower above. I walked back along the hallway and listened at the foot of the stairs and still all I could hear running water. Hardly daring to put one foot up in front of the other, I slowly climbed the carpeted treads only to hear child like laughter the closer I got to the landing. I stood intently listening, gripping hold of the balustrade, then I then found myself creeping along my own landing to see the bathroom door was slightly ajar. Above the noise of the extractor fan I heard what sounded like Ester's voice, along with someone else's. Hesitating once more just before the open door, my back pressed firmly against the wall to try to stop my legs from shaking, my throat was dry and I could feel my heart thumping hard inside my chest. I had to get closer to see what was going on; knowing what I might find would probably end my world as I had knew it. I moved closer before turning to look inside. The steam was pretty dense but not enough to obscure my view of the woman I had loved for the best part of 20 years. She was standing with her back towards me with water cascading down over her naked body, her legs were spread apart in a very sexual manner with both her arms stretched out high above her head, which was bowed forward resting against the wet room tiles. It was then that I took a sharp intake of breath when I saw there was someone on their knees in front of her, their head pressed snugly into Ester pleasure, and not only was this person enjoying the private places that my wife had to offer, to my absolute horror, this person was another woman." Harry fell silent for several seconds trying hard to gain some self-control; his troubled pale inexpressive face had taken on an almost ghostly appearance.

Freddy asked, "Look if this is too upsetting for you my friend?"

"No Freddy, I desperately need to unburden myself of this nightmare I have been living with and you are the first person I have been able to tell."

"Well if you are sure this will help Harry, carry on?"

"I stared on overwhelmed not knowing quite what to do; a feeling of utter disgust, tinged with a strange excitement engulfed me at the same time. Ester was now gracefully swaying her hips in an arousing manner as the other woman began to slowly move her hands around and over her curvaceous thighs. At this point I had an impression of repugnance, a deep sadness, and disbelief of what I was seeing. Whoever was on their knees then began to stand, slowly caressing Ester's body with their moist lips and slowly rising up until their mouths met kissing each other tenderly." He hesitated again before continuing. "It was then I realised, Freddy, who the other woman was." Harry sat for a long moment with his head hung down looking at the table.

"Come on Harry tell me, who the hell was it?" Freddy said, with some excitement in his voice.

"Freddy, it was Lynda fucking Cockburn, Jonathan Harker's wife." Both men sat there in silence for a few moments before Harry spoke again. "That bitch not only slept with my wife, but that bastard of a husband, Jonathan Harker, took me and my company for three quarters of million."

Freddy was so shocked by Harry's revelations that he rocked back in his chair and turned towards the dining room door, as if to make sure nobody else had heard his friend's expletives. Natasha certainly hadn't heard him; she had dropped off to sleep long ago.

"Harry that's absolutely dreadful. No wonder you are so distressed my old friend. What about Harker, do you think he knew this affair was going on?"

"Oh yes, that bastard knew all right."

"So what did you do that night when you caught them compromising each other?"

"Unfortunately Freddy, there was more to it than just the two of them having lesbian sex in our wet room. It was all so hard for me to take in and as I stood wondering what the hell I should do. It was then I heard Harker's voice call out from our bedroom, in a jovial fashion, come on you two don't be greedy, I'm waiting for you. At that point Freddy, I was so traumatised and sickened by their despicable self-gratification, I moved away from the bathroom door and back along the landing towards the stairwell. Freddy, I thought my world had come to an end and all I wanted to do was go down the stairs take the bread knife from the kitchen block and return to kill them all, but in the end I somehow regained my self-control and I went back downstairs and into the kitchen picked up the flowers and the bottle and left, quietly closing the front door behind me. When I reached my car I looked back towards the house and as I did the light from our bathroom window went off."

"You poor chap, where on earth did you go at that time of night?"

"Well, with a heavy heart I drove out of the avenue and turned left onto the north bound bypass. My head was full of self pity and bewilderment and I was thinking how could the woman I had always loved so much do this to me? I know you hear of this sort of thing happening, but you certainly never expect to be betrayed yourself, do you Freddy? At the Cambridge roundabout I took the Cockfosters Road and then on to Golders Green. I had no idea where the hell I was going, but when I saw a Moat House hotel sign I automatically pulled into the car park and checked in for one night. I found my room on the second floor and, after locking the door, I just lay on top of the bed. It wasn't really until then that the realisation of what had just happened hit me and it was too much to bear. I don't mind telling you for the first time in my adult life I broke down."

"My God, what an iniquitous bastard Harker has turned into, when you think we were all old school pals." He waited a moment before asking. "Did you confront Ester the next day Harry?"

"I returned home around ten in the morning; after leaving the flowers and the bottle in the hotel room for the maid; at least someone would appreciate them. I walked back into the house as if I had just returned from my business trip and, although I was hurting inside, I tried to carry on as if nothing had happened. Ester greeted me as she always did with a kiss on the cheek and, even though I felt like strangling her, the fact is Freddy, I still loved her no matter what she has done to me. I know you must think how terribly weak I have become but I just couldn't bring myself to say anything in the fear I could lose her altogether, so that was that as they say. I do still love her so very much and I couldn't take it if she had left me." Freddy leaned over the table and placed a heartfelt hand on his old friends shoulder. Harry managed a smile before continuing. "Several months later, Harker rang me early one morning to arrange a meeting for that very evening at his club. He informed me that he had just received the latest analysis on our investment. I asked if there was a problem of any sort and he was very vague and sounded more than a little sheepish. He asked if eight o'clock would be a good time for us then, without waiting for an answer and before I had any chance of replying, he put the phone down. That evening Ester and I took a cab to Harker's private club in Bentley Street, Central London to meet up with him and his bitch of a wife Lynda. The atmosphere was pretty tense and, for more than one reason, I thought that even in such grand surroundings there was a sense of trepidation in the air. We met them in the lobby and went through the formal greetings before the concierge led the four of us to our table, which was central to the oak-panelled dining room. Freddy, let me tell you I knew by the way Harker and his wife were behaving there was only bad news for us on this night. They obviously wanted to meet us in their own environment and even the positioning of Harker's table spoke volumes. Along with the fact that Harker was very subdued, his wife also looking shall we say uncomfortable. I was certainly expecting there was a problem of some sort with our investment and that the predictions he had made hadn't lived up to his expectations. Gathering by his tone and body language, I began to worry even more that it was probably much worse than I first feared." Bromley cut himself a slice of Stilton and topped both glasses up again and asked his friend to continue.

"Harker was obviously very nervous and his voice showed that when ordering the wine. The two women were also very quiet and hardly spoke or made eye contact with each other which for them was, to say, at least very unusual. I broke the uneasy atmosphere asking Harker in a politest way possible if there was a problem of some sort and was that the reason he had invited us for dinner this evening? He hesitated before answering, and then looking across the table directly at me and for the first time that evening making direct eye contact said, 'Harry, Ester, there isn't an easy way to tell you this.' I interrupted him, anxious for him to put us out of our misery, and asked him to get on with it man and tell us why he had brought us there for God's sake. "Harry, you must know the futures market is going through a sticky patch at this moment in time and I am afraid to say we have all taken some big hits on our share margins recently, so therefore....."

"Come on man spit it out?" I urged.

"..... I am afraid Harry, Ester, the investment you both had along with my own is now worth somewhat less than we expected." He hesitated again and I turned towards Ester to quickly gauge her expression, and then I knew she had already been told what Harker was about to say. "Early today Harry, I had a call from a broker friend of mine warning me to move quickly and take the bulk of our investments out of a particular hedge fund deposit, as the overnight markets abroad and in particular the TSE in Japan hadn't looked to good at all, so I moved as quickly as I could, but by that time it was too late."

"Are you telling me you have lost everything we invested with you, I raged at him?"

"No of course not old boy. I managed to save a fair percentage."

"How much is left damn you?"

"Please Harry, keep your voice down old boy?"

"I'm asking you, how much of our investment is left?"

"Okay Harry, Ester, but please you are bringing attention to the table. Please let me explain - the figure we have managed to save is around 38,000 or so."

"38,000 fucking pounds is that all that's left of our life's savings you bastard?"

"Look Harry there's no call for insults. I am just so sorry but we never thought; and nobody else expected the market to crash in the way it did; or that it would collapse in this manner and so soon."

"What the bloody hell do you mean so soon. You have taken Ester and myself for a couple of mugs and now you are telling us all you have left only amounts to loose change as far as I'm concerned?"

"If I could have saved your investment Harry, I would have done, surely you must believe that."

"I stared across the table, infuriated by him for making light of our predicament. Harker was now looking around to see if I was bringing attention to his table, then his face hardened as he said, "For God's sake Harry, I am a member here you know, please keep your voice down?"

"Keep my fucking voice down, have you any idea what you have done to us you bastard. I stood gripping my chair trying to control my anger, then I turned to see that the concierge was now looking over in our direction. He saw me standing and decided to walk across to our table, asking Harker if everything was in order?"

Harker smiled at the concierge before saying, "Oh yes Robert, we all fine thank you."

"I turned to Ester and told her we were leaving, then waited for her to stand. She looked at me and saw the rage in my eyes and decided it would probably be best if she joined me. As we were walking out of the club, I stopped and told her to wait in the lobby until I returned. She tried to persuade me not to go back. Ignoring her, I turned and walked into the dining room and over to Harker's table once more. Leaning forward on the table, with both hands firmly planted, I looked straight into Harker's eyes and told him in no uncertain terms that I would be bringing my financial adviser around to his office the next morning at ten o'clock, and that he better have all the documentation showing where he had invested our funds and how he claims to have lost them. He never answered but just sat there hoping that I would leave and save him any further embarrassment. I turned and walked back to Ester followed by the concierge, and we left the club."

"Harry no wonder you were so enraged. Did Ester let on that she knew already?"

"No she remained very quiet all the way home and hardly said a word as I ranted and raved. We are bloody well ruined and if that bastard thought we are just going to except his explanation he thought wrong."

Harry was by now pretty drunk, having polished off the last of the port in the telling of his heart rendering tale. Freddy called a cab for his friend and gave him his telephone number in London, telling him they would have to meet up when he returned home.

CHAPTER THREE

Natasha stayed with the Bromleys for another two months before the family decided to send both children to boarding school. Jackie Bromley was very kind when she informed Natasha that their circumstances had changed and there wasn't going to be a position for her. She thought it was only right to give Natasha the reason for terminating her employment.

"Natasha, Mr Bromley and I will be separating as soon as the children are settled in their new schools and we have started divorce proceedings. I don't want you to think that we have not enjoyed you working for us, because we both have, but our life will be very different from now on."

"Mrs Bromley I am so sorry to hear that, I have really enjoyed my time with you and I am sure I will be able to find other work with another family soon."

"Mr Bromley has spoken to the agency, and the lady who owns the business is an acquaintance of ours and she has found you a job with a family who have two children of similar age to Molly and Alistair, that's of course if you want to take the position. Here is the agent's telephone number. Perhaps you would like to give her a call." In a way Natasha was pleased to be moving on as the last two months had felt very uncomfortable; Jackie seemed to be depressed most of the time and the couple had many arguments over her failing business; she also spent lots of time away from their Kensington flat so it really wasn't too much of surprise that her services were no longer required, but as always the hardest part of moving on for a nanny was of course leaving the children.

A week later, on a warm September Saturday afternoon, and after a tearful goodbye, Natasha found herself standing alone on platform four at St Pancras railway station waiting for the 15:10 East Midlands train to Market Wellen. It was an exciting day for her as she had dreamed of living in the English countryside away from the city and new employers, Mr and Mrs Harker, had assured her Sedgwick House stood in the most beautiful open countryside, set in 1,500 hectares. She didn't quite understand what a hectare was, but it sounded an awful lot of land to her, and they had been very kind at the interview so she felt she would fit in very well.

The train left on time and was soon speeding through the open countryside. London and it's suburbs were left in the distance. It passed fields of wheat, some of which were still being harvested after the inclement August weather. She opened up her small rucksack and took out the lunch that Jackie had provided for her. To her surprise, under the blue plastic box, was an envelope addressed in large print simply saying Natasha. She thought it might be a reference of some sort for her new family, but looking closer she recognised his hand writing. The short message seemed to have been written in a hurry. It simply said that she would be hearing from him soon and was followed by a multitude of kisses. She placed the letter in her pocket, smiled to herself, and sat back to enjoy her ham and salad sandwiches.

An hour later the train pulled into Kettering station and she remembered Mrs Harker telling her the next stop after Kettering would be Market Wellen. She checked to make sure she had all her belongings together as the distance between the two stations was only 15 minutes. She had been told that the Harker's chauffeur, Mr Jones, would be waiting for her outside the station's main entrance. She was to look out for a green Jaguar and a tall silver haired man who would be standing next to it. Mr Jones was indeed tall with the look of an ex military man about him she thought.

"Ah, Miss Natasha is it?" he said as he moved towards her.

"Very nice to meet you Mr Jones,"

"You jump in the back my lovely and I will put your bags in the boot." He took the bypass around the town then turned into a country lane. She was a little disappointed as she would have liked to have seen the town nearest to where she was going to be living. He sensed her disappointment and, looking in his rear view mirror, he said, "Don't you worry lovely, you will have plenty of time now to go into Market Wellen. Lovely little place, always reminds me of my home town back in Wales it does." They were now passing by a collection of very large buildings on their left hand side which Natasha assumed to be some sort of military establishment as the high walls were topped off with barbed wire.

"Mr Jones what is that place over there?"

"Ah well, that's one of her Majesty prisons. Gantry, they tell me there's over 500 villains locked up tight in there, but don't you go worrying now will you, they are in there to stay," he chuckled before saying, "Look now Natasha you must call me Owen, let's have no more Mr Jones. Even the Harker's call me by my Christian name, so must you. Well that's all sorted then; we will be at Sedgwick House in around ten minutes so you just sit back now and enjoy the beautiful countryside."

*

Natasha, she could hear her mother's words deep down in her subconscious calling, 'Come along now stop this day dreaming and get on with your work.' That all seems such a long time ago now and she had settled into her daily routine, really enjoying her new job with the Harkers. It was particularly cold that morning. Even the house felt unusually chilly as Natasha made herself a second cup of tea before pouring the milk over her bowl of rice flakes. She went over to the kitchen radiator to look out of the window, hoping that Mr Harker had wrapped up warm as the all the trees and the hedgerows were covered with frost.

After finishing her breakfast she started to make the table ready in the dining room for the family, knowing Mrs Harker was usually up and around 8:30am for breakfast, with Mr Harker at nine. Their dining room table stood in front of a large sash window which stretched from the floor to the high ceiling, and unusually opened only from the bottom to form an extra door out onto the terrace. It was probably only used for those long summer days, she imagined. Looking outside again made her realise what a beautiful county this was, with its rolling hills and so many different kinds of deciduous trees. Very tall larch and other pines were dotted amongst them. They reminded Natasha so much of her childhood back home in Slovenia. She stood and pondered, remembering her family again before wiping away the start of a tear with the back of her hand and sighing as she took in a deep intake of breath. She was brought abruptly back into reality again by the sound of Mrs Harker calling out, "Is Mr Harker back from his walk yet Natasha?"

She walked over to the foot of the stairs, so as not to shout, "Not yet I am afraid Mrs Harker,"

"Oh goodness me, I hope he hasn't forgotten we have a meeting at eleven o'clock with Peter Reedman."

Natasha carried on with her duties and a few moments later Mrs Harker called out, "Would you keep a lookout for Jonathan please Natasha, I really don't want to miss this appointment?"

"Yes of course Mrs Harker. I certainly will." She glanced out of the kitchen window once more but there was still no sign of him. A few moments later as she filled the kettle, she happened to look up to see Jet, Jonathan's dog at the far end of the drive. He was sitting by the iron gates looking away from the house in the direction of the canal bridge. She waited expecting to see her employer come around the corner at any moment then, thinking nothing more of it, she made the tea before looking up again. Jet was now lying down and still facing away from the house. Natasha thought he must be patiently waiting for his master. Five more minutes passed and curiosity got the better of her. She had to find out why Jet was acting in this unusual manner and, unlike most other mornings, why his behaviour today was different, as he would normally pound up the long drive thinking only of his breakfast. Pulling on her Wellington boots and then wrapping up warm her woollen scarf tied tightly around her neck, with the two loose ends tucked into her coat, she opened the kitchen door and stepped outside, quickly closing it behind her to keep in the warmth. She hastily set off down the long frost covered gravel driveway.

"Jet, Jet," she called as she got closer to him. The strange thing was he hardly turned his head, still intent on staring in the direction he knew his master should have been coming from. There was obviously something wrong, or had Mr Harker just stopped off to talk to one of the farm workers. She looked for herself down the track towards the canal bridge in the distance while bending over to comfort Jet.

"What's wrong Jet. Where's your master?" It was then that Natasha noticed he had quite a swelling on his hind quarters and, more than that, he looked very distressed. In fact he was shaking, very cold, and his front paw was bleeding badly.

"Come on Jet let's take you up to the house." Reluctantly he followed Natasha looking back every now and then towards the bottom of the drive. When they reached the house, Lynda was waiting for them in the kitchen. She took one look at Jet and asked Natasha to take care of him.

"I am going to see why he has returned without Jonathan."

"Do you want me to come along with you Mrs Harker?"

"No you stay here by the telephone in case Jonathan calls. I suspect he's probably looking for Jet as he must have ran off chasing a rabbit or something."

"Please wrap up warm, it is bitterly cold out there today Mrs Harker." Lynda kept her real feelings to herself and was more worried than she showed as this was the first time Jonathan had been late back from his morning walk since they had moved to the house. She reached the bridge over the canal but the towpath was deserted in both directions. She had hoped to see Jonathan walking down the path towards her, but now she was undecided to know which route on the towpath he had chosen that morning. Looking more closely she noticed Jonathan's and Jet's footprints in the frost and quickly realised they had turned to the right. She took the towpath heading for Kegworth Wharf. The further she walked the more worried Lynda became. She had been searching now for at least 30 minutes and still there was no sign of him, nothing but the cold frozen canal and the lonely empty towpath as far as she could see. Now there were many more tracks in the frost coming onto the path from different directions so she couldn't distinguish whether they were Jonathans or not. As she rounded the curve in the towpath she could see far into the distance the road bridge next to Kegworth Wharf.

Lynda trudged on, her imagination beginning to run riot, and before she knew it she was now just a few hundred yards from the road bridge. It was then she spotted a dark patch on the canal surface close to the towpath. Her pace quickened and her eyes were drawn to the conspicuous blemish on this otherwise ice covered water. She came to an abrupt halt and was now looking down at a large hole in the ice, and laying there close to the aperture and partially in the frozen water with its new covering of freshly formed ice crystals was Jonathan's black leather glove. She sank to her knees screaming out his name.

"Jonathan, dear God, Jonathan, please God not my Jonathan." Her cold fingers trembled as she reached into her pocket for her mobile, then instantly remembering she had left it at home. The wharf, dear God I must get to the wharf. She stood and ran along the frost covered towpath distraught by her grim discovery crying out for someone to help her, repeating to herself., "Dear God almighty, not my Jonathan."

*

Harry Shaw was just making himself his first brew of the day when this distraught woman came bursting through his workshop door.

"Please help me, please, you must help me, my husband has fallen into the canal, please, help me please?"

Harry was to say the least taken back by his early morning visitor. "What on earth has happened?" he asked in his broad local accent.

"It's my husband, you must help me please?"

"Try to stay calm and tell me exactly what has happened."

"Please you must telephone the police or somebody."

"Are you sure now he has fallen in?"

"Yes, yes, call someone please before it's too late?"

"Come on now, you show me where you think he has fallen in and I will give the emergency services a call on the way."

Lynda was soon hurrying back along the towpath closely followed by Harry Shaw. When they finally reached the spot where a large aperture in the frozen canal could be seen, Lynda broke down again this time slowly collapsing and falling back onto the ice covered bank, sobbing uncontrollably and constantly repeating Jonathan's name. Her head was now bowed; her knees drawn up towards her chin and both arms wrapped tightly around her knees as she rocked backward and forwards absolutely grief stricken. Harry Shaw dialed 999 and stared down into the inky blackness of the ice splintered hole in front of him, troubled by the thought that this poor woman's husband could be lying under the ice close by.

"Which service do you require please?"

"The police please."

He seemed to wait an age, but it was probably only a minute or two.

"Central police control, could you first give me your name, and then tell me how I can help you?"

"Harry Shaw from Kegworth Wharf, Leicestershire. I have a lady with me who is very concerned that her husband may have fallen into the canal while walking his dog this morning."

"I see, I understand your mobile telephone no is 0773926822 sir?"

"Yes that's correct."

"I am passing you over to Leicestershire Police Control sir."

"Charlwood police station, Sergeant Rigby here Mr Shaw."

Harry filled the sergeant in with the situation he faced and the sergeant informed him they had two officers and an ambulance on their way to Kegworth Wharf, and then asked, "Could you tell me if there is any sign of the gentleman's dog sir?"

"Well that's just it. Jet, that's their labrador, returned home a good hour ago, the lady tells me sergeant."

"I see Mr Shaw, has she given you her name?"

"Yes sergeant, the lady's name is Lynda Harker and she is here with me, now understandably very distressed."

"Could you take her back to the wharf and ask her to call home to see if there is someone who could come over to look after her while we investigate the situation?"

"Right you are sergeant and I'll wait on the road bridge next to the wharf to meet your chaps when they arrive."

"Thank you sir, they will be with you shortly."

Harry Shaw took Mrs Harker back to the wharf, doing the best he could to comfort her. He asked who he could call at home for her as they reached the workshop, but by now she could hardly speak as the tears rolled down her cheeks and it was obvious to Harry that the shock of it all was setting in.

"Mrs Harker can I call your home for you?"

She lifted her head to look at him, and then picked up a pencil which was lying on Harry's workbench and wrote her home telephone number onto its wooden surface. He rang the number and a young woman answered.

"Hello Natasha speaking?"

"Hello is that Mrs Harker's home?"

"Yes." Natasha replied.

"This is Harry Shaw from the wharf at Kegworth." Natasha knew instantly that there was something dreadfully wrong.

"Could you possibly send someone over to the wharf, Mrs Harker's here and very upset." She asked what was wrong.

"We are not too sure yet miss, so if you could send someone over to look after her please?"

"Thank you Mr Shaw. I will be over myself as soon as I can."

Harry sat Lynda down next to his brazier to keep her warm, then rang his wife and quickly explained the awful situation he had found himself in, asking her if she could come down from the village to look after the lady. He then told Mrs Harker to stay by the brazier and that his wife was on her way to look after her. She could only nod her head in thanks. He also told her that there was a lady called Natasha coming over to the wharf from her home, this time she didn't respond. Harry walked back out of the wharf gates and onto the road bridge to wait for the police. The road was unusually quiet for that time of day, except for old Stan Wicks who came down the hill from the village on his bone-shaker of a bike, which was at least the same age as him.

"Morning Harry, what ye doing then, standing here making the place look untidy?" Stan was well known as a bit of a local character who knew everything and everyone in the village and to see Harry standing there on Kegworth Road Bridge instead of being in his workshop was to say at least unusual. Knowing Stan, this could make for good conversation that night in the Red Lion. Harry was quickly explaining what was going on to Stan, and as he was speaking he saw a police car with its blue lights on coming down the hill.

With that Stan said, "I'll see ye later then Harry and I hope to God no bugger has fallen in, cause if they have they're a goner all right." Stan peddled off just as the police car pulled up alongside Harry.

"Are you Mr Shaw, sir?"

"Yes constable, and I'm pleased to see you here so quickly. This is a rum old morning, proper shuck me up it has."

"I'm PC Atwood sir and this is WPC Trout. Could you show us the place where you think this gentleman may have fallen in?" Harry walked quickly along the towpath to the place where the ice had been broken, all three stood peering into the canal, before Trout said, "Is that a glove down there on the ice next to the hole Joni?" referring to PC Atwood.

"Your right Joules, and it looks like there could be blood on it, so I think you better call it in, don't you."

Trout walked away a short distance and began talking on her radio. Harry clearly heard the police officer tell someone that there certainly was a strong possibility that someone had fallen into the canal.

"Roger to that Joules, I'll get in touch with the diving unit at Leicester."

Atwood went back to his car, opened the boot and took out a roll of white and blue tape before returning to secure the area, as it now had the potential of becoming a crime scene. He then asked Joules to go over to the wharf to see if Mrs Harker was with anyone. Harry walked back with her, and she asked him how he had become involved and did he know the Harkers at all.

"No officer, I am afraid not. The lady just ran into my workshop earlier this morning asking for help."

"Okay sir, I will just make sure she is all right and then if I could take a statement from you, perhaps you could get back to your business, and thank you for your assistance Mr Shaw."

Less than a mile away the Grand Union canal work-barge *Lucky Lady* was pushing forwards breaking the ice with some ease and making the canal navigable again to the south west.

"I reckon we'll go down the Felford arm first Paul," Steve Haddon called out.

"Then perhaps we'll take a break and have a brew at Felford Wharf shall we Steve?"

"What, not another one Paul, it ain't bin more than an hour since the last one?"

"Got to keep our strength up on mornings like this you know."

These two had worked this stretch of the canal together for the last 15 years or more and knew every nook and cranny on their patch.

"Okay Paul, bring her around." They manoeuvered the sturdy vessel round the wide sweeping bend, breaking the thick ice as the tip of the steel reinforced bow made light work of the frozen surface. Slowly the *Lucky Lady* disappeared out of sight heading for Felford Wharf a mile to the south east.

CHAPTER FOUR

Harker was just beginning to stir from his unconscious state and cried out with the excruciating pain he felt every time he tried to move. Blood was still trickling down his face from a deep cut on his forehead and his whole body was hurting terribly. He thought, 'This really can't be happening, for pity's sake, someone get me out of this bloody nightmare.' The reality of his situation soon dawned on him and he began to remember the barge moored to the towpath, and the light that shone from the two portholes. Then there was the woman, who the hell was she? Had he stumbled upon some sort of weird ritual with this woman tied up half naked, yet still managing to smile at him in that unnaturally bizarre way.

Struggling, he tried to sit up but his whole body seemed to be stuck fast in what felt like a small metal pit, which stunk of diesel oil and coal dust, causing his eyes to smart. He twisted his cold tortured frame once more trying to get some comfort, but he couldn't part his legs or his arms, soon realising they had been tightly bound with plastic cable ties. At that point he stopped struggling; making himself as comfortable as possible, but for all the pain he felt in his limbs never took away the image of the woman's face and the uncanny smile she gave him as he peered in through the lit porthole. Why on earth would anyone smile in such a desperate situation, this he just couldn't comprehend. Jonathan's thoughts returned to how long he had been secreted in this Godforsaken hole. He tried to lift his tethered arms to see his watch, but his wrists were bared of any luminous time piece and he could only feel the plastic cable ties cutting deep into his flesh. He decided that he had probably been lying there for several hours then he thought of Lynda, my God Lynda she will be so worried, surely she must be going out of her mind; and the children, what about his children? What would they do without him?

The more he thought of his terrible predicament the more frightened he became. His situation became unbearable the more he remembered. There was Jet, poor Jet, what the hell happened to him? His only hope being that he found his way back home to raise the alarm, at least then Lynda would know there was something dreadfully wrong. His only hope being someone out there must be looking for him to bring this surreal situation to an end. As he lay, unable to move in his grim surroundings, he was startled by the sound of the engine as it leapt into life right alongside him. It was immediately followed by the sound of the gears being grated into position. Until then it had been almost unbelievably quiet but now there was lots of activity and the barge was moving off. He felt physically sick by the realisation that there was some violent individual, just a few feet away from him, in control of not only the vessel but also his destiny. For all he knew, he could harm him even further or maybe even worse, a position no man should ever want to find himself.

The barge was moving as he could clearly hear ice grazing along the sides of the metal hull. Seeing how it was locked into the ice so tightly this morning, he was more than surprised they were moving off at all. What the hell had he let himself in for by looking through that porthole? He should have just walked on and ignored what he had seen or gone back to raise the alarm, and if he had he would have been back home hours ago. Yes, he should have called the police and left the situation to them but instead he had been beaten badly, frightened for his own life and was now wondering what else these thugs could do to him.

If only he had turned back earlier! Or had they intended for him to see this half-naked woman and the way she had looked at him, at first as if she needed his help, and then the smile. For heaven's sake why smile? Her unexpected strange actions he just couldn't get out of his mind. That of course was unless all along this had been a trap to ensnare him, and someone had deliberately and unknown to him had somehow guided him and Jet along the towpath that morning. When he reached the barge he couldn't have helped but see what looked to him like a desperate situation and when he thought more about it, Jet had some kind of misdemeanour out of sight of him just before he noticed the barge. Had he seen someone behind the hedgerow? There was also the ear-splitting sound of breaking ice, he had never heard anything like that before, had this been man-made? All these thoughts and others continually played on his mind.

Wincing now as his ribs burned with even the slightest of movement, he tried to relieve the agony to find comfort before returning to his menacing thoughts. Why on earth would anyone go to so much trouble? I could have walked off in the opposite direction, it was only Jet who had persuaded me to turn right on the towpath that morning. No, I had stumbled into this only by sheer chance; this couldn't be anything to do with me; they must have the wrong person.

However, no matter how he tried to convince himself, his thoughts constantly returned to the girl's face. He was sure he knew her and this was playing on his mind so much it brought him to thinking again maybe this was all planned, and if that was the case it could only mean one thing, he had been kidnapped. The terrifying thought compounded by absolute despair that he could lose everything that was so precious to him and most of all his young family.

Having been a prosecution lawyer for many years he was well known to many villains. Maybe it was someone whom he had sent down and now they had decided to ruin his life and get some sort of revenge. His state of mind was all over the place and still he couldn't erase the girl's smiling face from his subconscious. Then it came to him in a flash and he remembered the time he visited Harry Bernard's office for a meeting. There was an extremely good looking young woman sitting behind the reception desk - of course it was Bernard's bloody secretary. Bernard's a wimp of a man and there's no way he could be connected to anything as serious as kidnapping, but if it isn't Bernard who in God's name is responsible for treating me with such malevolence?

As he lay looking up he noticed a chink of light which was coming from the hatch cover above. He lay still, his eyes transfixed on the tiny aperture, just then the light changed and he soon realised the barge was probably passing under one of the many road or farm bridges on this stretch of the canal. Jonathan knew this canal towpath so well and this chink of light gave him some much needed positivity, perhaps a glimmer of hope. If only he could keep count of the bridges then, even if his calculations were slightly out and if he could unburden himself of these cable ties, there may be a chance to escape. At least he would know roughly where the hell he was on the canal system.

His thoughts once more returned to why anyone would want to kidnap him. Surely if it was Bernard, he couldn't possibly put the blame on him personally for the market collapsing, losing us all not just him a packet. No, there must be another reason. Jonathan tried to think back over the years and who would have wanted to harm him the most. There was for instance the Jack Mullard case, now there was a real nasty piece of work, threatening him with shouts of revenge as the police struggled to restrain him as they took him down. He must be coming up for release around about now. Yes, someone like Mullard, he would take delight in kicking the hell out of me he thought, and Jack Mullard's a man who would certainly hold a grudge and perhaps in his twisted little mind he now thinks it payback time.

His mind wondered back even further to other high profile cases he was involved with, and as the names of some of the villains came into his thoughts, he felt a shiver of fear run through his broken body. Stop this and think positively, you must concentrate on what is going on around you now and not in the past. They were now passing under a second bridge and he guessed they were approaching the large bend in the canal approximately one mile from the South Kegworth Road Bridge.

To his surprise he heard footsteps of someone walking around the side of the barge. Listening intently, the noise was getting ever closer. He held his breath as he was sure they had stopped right alongside him. He heard someone turning a key in a padlock and a chain rattled on the hatch above him. He felt his body fill with trepidation as the hatch slid back no more than few inches, then a beam of light shone down into his eyes. He closed them tightly fearing the worst and tried to speak but no words came from his dry mouth. He was horribly conscious that someone was staring down at him for what felt like an age, broken only when he felt a sharp jab from some sort of pointed object into his sore ribs. He yelled out as a second prod dug into his leg causing him to recoil and only to feel more intense pain before they slid the hatch shut again. The next thing he heard was the chain being drawn back through the padlock and the key turning in the lock. Then, whoever this sadistic bastard had been, he walked off again back along the barge.

After his eyes became accustomed to lack of light, he now feared even more for his life than before, trying to imagine how anyone could be so brutal, dishing out unspeakable violence on a man already tied and bound. These bastards had him where they wanted and, for whatever reason, were delighting in his desolation. His only consolation being he was pleased to see that there was still a small gap where the chink of light was still entering his makeshift poke. They must have been checking to see if he had regained consciousness and, if they have to unlock this hatch every time to check on him, this probably meant there was no other way of out the hell hole. This wasn't going to give him much hope of escape. He settled back and tried to rest in the best way he could. Hours seemed to have passed as he lay still, trying to hear anything from his capturers, but all he heard was the sound of the old Lister engine thudding away next to him, the warmth from which at least meant he wasn't cold any more.

He knew he had to stay awake even though his twisted body was telling him the opposite, so he tried to concentrate again on who could be behind his kidnapping and why. He thought back to how Bernard had stormed out the his club after he had tried to explain to him the problems they were all experiencing with the investment markets. Then again, when he met up with Bernard, the following day with his financial adviser in tow, Harry Bernard had tried to blame him personally for the downturn in his fortunes, even when his own adviser tried to explain to him that it had been totally unexpected for the market to crash on that particular day, but there was no reasoning with him. Bernard just ranted on, asking how much had I bloody well lost. At that point I had handed him what was left from the investments in the form of a bankers draft. Snatching it from my hand, he took one look and held it up while shouting, 40,000 pounds, is this all you have left of my life's savings you bastard, 40,000 fucking pounds?

Allan Waters, Bernard's adviser looked across the table obviously embarrassed by the situation, and with the sort of glance that meant it was time to wind the meeting up. The last time Harker had heard from Harry Bernard was through his lawyer, setting out that he would be suing him through the courts for the rest of his investments. He remembered writing back to him not as a friend, but in a professional capacity, stating how and where he had with invested his £775,000 into a hedge fund investment which had folded. This was unfortunately where the largest part of Bernard's collateral had been invested. He also informed him how many other people, including himself, had also lost a great deal, and he should have known there are unfortunately no guarantees in the investment markets.

His thoughts quickly came back to his grim situation as he heard footsteps once again, this time they seemed to be inside the cabin area. He held his breath and listened intently as someone was now moving towards him. He could hear floor boards creaking as they came ever closer, now he was sure they were right next to him just on the other side of the bulkhead. He tried to push away from where he thought the sound was coming from, too frightened to even swallow, then the sound from a squeaking hinge as a door was being opened seemingly next to him and then without warning a tiny hatch slid open, causing him to ready himself and expecting more harsh treatment. Grimacing with pain, he tried to move away further from the hatch. Sweat poured out of his tortured body while waiting for some dreadful violent act to be bestowed on him once again.

Jonathan could not bring himself to look at the small amount of light that was now entering this insufferable place. He was so frightened that he felt ashamed of himself, feeling more like a small child who had suddenly woken from some terrible nightmare and just wanting to scream out for their mother in the night, and not him a 45-year-old male. Still no one spoke. All he could hear was the sound of breathing and the stench of cigarette breath wafting through the tiny aperture. Was this his final few moments or just another piece of mental torture they were now practising on him? Desperation gave way to new found courage as he shouted out in despondency, "Come on you bastards get on with it?" No one answered his rage, just a depressing silence. Worst of all, he knew some malicious individual was menacingly peering at him through the tiny hatch and succeeding to put the fear of God into him.

CHAPTER FIVE

Constable Atwood was speaking to Sergeant Cole on his radio, giving his report from the scene.

"Sarge, it looks like this chap Jonathan Harker may well have fallen into the canal as a couple of hundred yards along the towpath from the wharf there's a fair size hole in the ice, big enough to swallow any man. According to the way the ice is only just reforming it looks to have been made recently, but the most worrying thing is there's a black leather glove lying by the side of it."

"Really, well in that case, make sure you secure the area off?"

"All ready taped it off Sarge."

"Good lad. what about this poor chaps wife?"

"She is being looked after by Joules back at the wharf."

"Right Joni, you and Joules stay there and wait for Inspector Collins from HQ to arrive, and in the meantime see if Joules can arrange for; what's the lady name?"

"Mrs Harker, Sarge."

"Can you arrange for someone from her home to come down and pick her up?"

"Already been arranged."

"Well done lad, but until then keep her well away from the towpath."

Atwood walked back along towards the road bridge to wait for Inspector Collins. As he stood there waiting, a green Jaguar turned into the wharf car park and a young lady stepped out from the passenger side and proceeded across to the workshop door. Trout opened the door and the woman went inside. A few moments later she came back out with her arm around Mrs Harker's shoulders. A tall grey haired man now stood waiting by the car. He opened the back door of the Jaguar and helped Mrs Harker inside before they drove off.

Atwood's radio blasted out: "Inspector Collins here

Constable. I am on my way to Kegworth Wharf now. Could you fill me in with some of the details?"Atwood told him as much as he knew and asked,

"Are the police dive team on their way sir?"

"Not yet Constable. Seems they are on an exercise at Markfield Diving Centre in North Leicestershire, apparently on their quarterly deep dive test. With a little luck they should be with us around about 1300 hours and I should be with you in around 20 minutes or so."

"Okay sir. I will be waiting on the bridge for you. Over and out." Trout walked back over to Atwood.

"That poor woman Joni, she is in a terrible state. We had one hell of a job to persuade her to leave the wharf to return home with her children's nanny, Natasha."

"Yes I saw them leave Joules. Looks like a well heeled family doesn't it, what with the chauffeur driven Jag?"

"Well yes, but it doesn't make the situation less heart breaking does it?"

"Did you take a statement from Harry Shaw, Joules?"

"Of course Joni, you know me, always on the ball."

"Good let's hope Collins won't be too much longer. It's bloody perishing out here but I don't suppose you know that, after warming your pretty backside by the workshop brazier, while I've been here freezing my nuts off, do you?"

"Something like that. Anyway look smart, here's Collins now." Inspector Collins awkwardly clambered out his silver Renault Megane then leaned back inside for his radio, slamming the car door he shuffled across the road to the two waiting officers; this was the first time Joni and Joules had come across the new inspector who, judging by his size, must have weighed at least eighteen stone. He was a man of huge proportions, standing a good 6ft 2ins tall, and one who obviously enjoyed the finer things in life judging by his beer belly.

"Good morning constables, and let us hope for this poor chap's sake it is. Right, let's get on. Constable Atwood, isn't it? I want you to go along to Roxton Locks and speak to the lock keeper there and ask him to temporary close the lock down, although looking at the amount of ice on the canal they may have already chosen that option."

"Right you are inspector."

"Also ask him if there would have been any current or flow of any kind around the Kegworth Wharf area this morning and, if so, which would be the most likely direction the water would have been flowing. By the way, watch that ice down those back lanes. We don't want any more accidents do we lad?"

"Okay Sir, I'll get on my way."

"WPC Trout, I would like you to go back past the incident and carry on along the towpath to check for anything unusual, taking special care not to disturb the ground. In the unlikely event, stop any barge movements on the canal, although with all this ice it looks pretty unlikely. If that is the case, then they must tie up alongside the towpath and stay there until we tell them otherwise."

Atwood drove off along the main road. He came to the turn for Roxton Locks. It was still pretty cold and the lane down to the lock was extremely icy. Leaving his car in the main car park he set off to find the lock keeper, passing the Locks Inn public house on his right over the humpback canal bridge. Turning left he then followed the towpath up the steep staircase of locks, finding it hard get a grip on the slippery surface. As he climbed, he counted each lock off one by one discovering there were 10 in all and at the top lock stood an old red brick cottage. It looked like it had been built around the same time as the staircase in 1814. Slightly breathless now from his slippery walk, he knocked on the cottage's front door. At first nobody came, then he noticed a chap in blue overalls walking towards him from the direction of a row of outbuildings on the end of the cottage.

"Can I help you officer?"

"Yes, good morning sir, I'm looking for the lock keeper?"

"Well that's me, Joe Morton. What can I do for you constable?"

"If I could just say first sir, there is nothing for you to worry about personally but do you think I could have a word with you inside?"

"Yes of course. I was on my way back for a brew, if you fancy one yourself?"

"I won't say no Mr Morton, that's very kind of you."

Atwood explained the situation to the lock keeper and, as instructed by the inspector, asked about the amount of flow on the canal near Kegworth Wharf.

"That depends on the amount of traffic going through the lock system. There's bugger all of course going through at the moment, what with the thick ice making the whole system near impossible to navigate, but normally at this time of year there's not too much flow at all. As you can see, the canal is pretty full at the moment also, that part of the system has been recently dredged so the water would be around two metres deep with very few obstructions. Thinking about it, along from the wharf there are a couple of overflows so there would be a slight current from them and of course the locks themselves create quite a bit of movement."

"Could you tell me when was the last time the locks were opened?" Joe went across the room to check his log book and then turned towards the officer.

"Yes here we are, the last barge went down the lock system at 14:30 yesterday afternoon heading for Leicester, but after that the canal has come to a standstill what with the temperature dropping well below zero as it did last night."

"Thank you Mr Morton you have been a big help. Could I ask you sir to be a little diplomatic as to the closing of the locks as this is a very delicate ongoing situation we are dealing with?"

"I understand constable. You don't have to worry, you can rely on me."

He showed the constable to the door telling him, if they needed any further assistance, he had only to call. Inspector Collins was talking to control when Atwood returned to Kegworth Wharf. He was asking the desk sergeant in charge if he could call for back up from the air support team.

"The problem with your request is the helicopter is out on a shout at the moment, an RTA at Cathorpe Junction. As soon as they return I will get them over to the wharf, Inspector Collins."

"I would appreciate that sergeant, as this chap Harker has now been missing for the last four hours. Because the temperature is still well below freezing some haste is needed. If he has managed to survive a fall into the cold icy water and dragged himself out, he has to be found as quickly as possible."

He turned to PC Atwood, "Right lad what did the lock keeper have to say?"

"Well sir, the last barge went through Roxton Locks at 2:30 yesterday afternoon."

"What about the flow?"

"That was a little more interesting inspector. There is a slight current running towards the locks caused by the lock emptying and also from an overflow system up by Kegworth Wharf, this would allow gentle backflow of water towards the wharf when the locks are closed.

*

At Markfield Dive Centre Andy Flower and his men were packing away their equipment ready for the dash down to the Leicestershire-Northamptonshire border. Although this was a police dive unit, Andy Flower was an ex-Royal Navy diver who had worked for the last three years for the West Midlands Police Authority as their dive-team manager. He was in charge of 16 police officers in all, who were called into the dive unit from their every-day policing duties when they were needed. Andy had a vast diving experience and for the past 20 years had been a senior diving instructor attached to the SBS.

"Right lads, let's get all this equipment cleaned, checked and stowed correctly because my life and yours depend on it. The time now is 11:00am and it's going to take at least an hour to get down to Kegworth Wharf, so let's make sure when we get there every piece of equipment is ready to use. Have you all got that lads, and that includes you Smithy?"

"Come on Alan you heard the skip, let's get this lot sorted." Smithy was the team's longest serving diver and well respected by the other members of the team. Having taken recent recruits like Alan Summers under his wing, this was to be his first operational shout. Smithy knew only too well what an adrenalin rush a shout could generate for these volunteer divers. This was so different from their normal, sometimes mundane, duties as police officers, and they were all primed and ready for a real search. Andy checked all the lockers before slamming them shut, then jumped into their long wheel based transit van and headed off in the direction of the M1 Motorway.

Inspector Collins had organised for two community support offices to stop any movements on the canal coming up from the south and to hold them at the Felford Arm. Even though it was a cold icy winter's day, there was usually some traffic on the

Grand Union whatever the weather. Joe Morton, the lock keeper was talking on the land line to his manager, Phillip Mustoe, telling him why the Police had closed down the canal system from the Felford Arm to Roxton Locks, and that it would remain closed until further notice.

"Thanks Joe for letting me know, perhaps I should get over to Kegworth Wharf myself and see if they need any further assistance from us."

"That's probably a good idea Phil and then perhaps you could let me know how they are proceeding with the search?"

"Yes I'll do that Joe, after I have spoken to the officer in charge."

*

Natasha was trying her best to comfort Mrs Harker, reassuring her that the police would be doing all they could to find her husband.

"Would you like me to call any of your friends Mrs Harker?"

She placed her arm reassuringly around her employer's shoulders. Lynda Harker looked up at Natasha, with heart rending sadness etched into her strained face, and asked her to call her friend Ester. Natasha was slightly surprised she had chosen to call Ester Bernard as she was sure Mr Harker and Ester's husband Harry, had fallen out over a failed business deal they had both been involved in. She had often heard the Harkers arguing, sometimes furiously, over how Lynda thought Jonathan had let Ester and Harry Bernard down. It wasn't that she had been prying or listening in on their conversations, it was just the case they were both vociferous sometimes, so for this reason asking her to call Mrs Bernard was more than a little unexpected. She did as she was asked, and the phone was answered by Harry Bernard in an abrupt, maybe even a drunken manner.

"Yes, Harry Bernard here who is this?"

"Is Mrs Bernard there please?"

Before she could finish her sentence Bernard cut her short. "No she bloody well isn't." With that rebuff the line went dead. Not wishing to upset Mrs Harker any further she opened the Harker's telephone book to see for herself if Ester Bernard had a mobile number she could call, and there it was listed under her Christian name, Ester, in brackets. Natasha rang the number and after a few seconds the phone was answered.

"Hello Ester Bernard, who's calling please?"

"Hello, its Natasha Mrs Harker's nanny here. I am calling on behalf of Mrs Harker who, I am afraid, is very distressed at the moment."

"Goodness, what on earth has happened?"

"I am afraid to inform you Mrs Bernard, there is a possibility that Mr Harker may have had an accident this morning and could have fallen into the canal." There was a gasp of apprehension from Ester as Natasha finished speaking.

"Oh my God." Natasha could clearly hear her tearful shocked reaction.

"Are you okay Mrs Bernard?" There was a long pause as Ester was trying to come to terms with Natasha's revelation!

"Yes dear, but poor Jonathan, dear God."

"Would you be able to talk to Mrs Harker, or possibly come over to stay with her, I really don't know who else to call?"

"Of course I will my dear." Her voice now sounding slightly more positive. Natasha carried the telephone through to the lounge where Lynda Harker was sitting. She sat with one hand gripping a tissue, leaning forward, her heart obviously breaking under the emotional strain as endless tears streamed down her face.

"Its Mrs Bernard for you. Will you be okay to take the call?" She turned towards Natasha and took the telephone from her, telling she would be fine.

*

Andy Flower and his team had made good time in arriving at Kegworth Wharf. PC Atwood walked across the car park just as the team were unloading their equipment from the van.

"Hello mate, I didn't know they were sending the A-team on this one Smithy?"

"Well bugger me, its old Joni Atwood lads."

"Took your bloody time getting here didn't you Smithy?"

"Very funny. Right Joni now cut the crap and tell us how far we have to carry this lot." Andy and his team of six carried their equipment over the bridge and down onto the canal towpath. Atwood walked on in front of them carrying a large bag which contained the teams guide lines.

"How much further then Joni?"

"Around 200 metres or so, it's about time you lot got some exercise."

The team were never quiet. Even though this search would be the first shout for some of the younger members, young Alan, in particular, looked more than a little nervous. Andy thought as he looked at the ice covering the canal. He could sense there was some real tension in the air to match the team's adrenalin pumping through their veins. Andy could see this wasn't going to be a straight forward job by any stretch of the imagination.

"Here we are lads, now be very careful not to disturb the glove that's lying by the hole." They all stood looking down onto the frozen canal and into the gaping hole just a short distance from the bank.

"Okay lads, lay all the equipment on top of the polythene sheet and take care to keep it clean. Right Carl, you will be diving with me once I've assessed the situation; but before that we need to break up some more of this ice around the hole."

He sent Smithy back to the van to fetch the long boat hooks. When he returned he made a start in trying to break the ice by lancing around the edge of the aperture with little affect. After a few minutes it became pretty obvious Andy's plan wasn't going to work as the ice was much too thick.

"Constable!" Someone was shouting from the road bridge. Atwood left the team and went to see who was calling him. When he reached the bridge there was a middle aged chap standing there, he was wearing an oatmeal coloured duffle coat and the breast pocket bore the logo BWA.

"Can I help you sir? Atwood asked.

"Well it's a case of can I help you constable, I'm Phillip Mustoe from British Waterways and I have just been informed of this terribly grave situation we all find ourselves in this morning. I wondered what assistance, if any, the authority could offer you?" Atwood explained they were about to start an underwater search, but because they were having a problem breaking the ice and, for the dive teams safety, they couldn't start the search just yet.

"Excuse me for a moment constable." Mustoe took his mobile from his pocket and punched in a couple of digits.

"Steve, its Phil here, where are you on the system at the moment?"

"Ah morning Phil, we are making our way back up from Felford Wharf."

"Wait a second Steve. Constable, I have got a couple of chaps no more than a mile away with one of our work barges which has ice breaking capability, so they could break the ice up for your dive team if you would like them to?"

"Right sir, that sounds a good idea to me, but I will have to ask Andy Flower the dive team manager, and my boss Inspector Collins first, and he's up at the wharf." Atwood and Mustoe walked into the Wharf workshop to find the inspector drinking tea and warming himself by the brazier.

"Constable there you are. I was just on my way down to see how the dive team are getting on?"

"Right sir, this is Phil Mustoe from British Waterways, and he has a work barge in the area which could be used to break up the ice and allow the divers to search more safely."

"Is that so Mr Mustoe?"

"Yes inspector, I have a crew only ten minutes away on the Felford Arm."

"Have you spoken to Andy Flower constable to ask him if he thinks it is a good idea, lad?"

"Not yet sir, I thought I should seek your permission first."

"Well would you go back down to them and see if Andy thinks it would assist them in anyway."

"Right you are inspector."

Atwood returned to the incident just as Andy was about to proceed into the canal, while young Carl was waiting to follow; they were each tied to separate guide lines which in turn were being held by two other members of the team. Atwood quickly explained Phil Mustoe's suggestion to use the work barge to help break up the ice. Andy agreed it certainly was a good idea, but he told Atwood first of all he would like himself and Carl to do a preliminary search of the immediate area around the hole, to ensure this chap wasn't just under the ice.

"Tell the inspector to have the barge standing by just in case we should require their assistance later Joni." Andy lowered himself backwards using his guide line into the bitterly cold icy water, and before he immersed himself completely he carefully picked up the black leather glove off the ice. Using the end of his safety knife he placed it in a clear plastic bag before handing the bag to Smithy, who in turn gave it to Atwood.

"I better take this up to Inspector Collins. There looks to be quite a substantial amount of blood on it to me. He will want to get it off to the Forensic Lab to check the blood type I suppose."

"Bloody hell Joni, we will make a detective out of you yet."

Atwood found the inspector still talking to Phil Mustoe, both of them holding a cup of something, he guessed tea, lucky sods. He excused his interruption and handed Collins the bag.

"How are they getting on down there?" Atwood's first thought was, why don't you go and look for yourself you lazy sod, but of course he told him of the dive teams progress and asked if he wanted him to return to the incident.

"Yes you do that lad, and ask WPC Trout to come up to see me. I want her to take this evidence back to Warwick University Lab?"

"Okay, will do sir." Atwood left the warmth of the workshop and found Joules having a crafty fag with one of the Community Support Officers underneath the road bridge, their backs pushed firmly up to the wall trying to stay warm and out of the cold wind.

"The inspector has a nice little job for you Joules, and it looks like you need something to do?"

"Less of your cheek Joni, I've only been here a couple of minutes, that's right isn't it Paul?"

"Anyway he wants you to take the evidence, that's the glove we found on the ice, into Warwick University Lab for him?"

"Thank God for that. At least I'll be out of this freezing cold weather."

"Yeh as per usual Joules," he sarcastically said as he walked off and back down the towpath.

*

Jonathan Harker lay anxiously waiting for whomever was watching him through the tiny aperture to make a move. They had been there now for what seemed like an eternity, watching him but saying nothing, but he knew they were out there as he could clearly hear someone breathing. It was as if they were practising some sort of mental torture to make him break, but as frightened and totally intimidated as he had become he needed, for the sake of his own self preservation, to somehow summon up the courage to yell out again, and that's exactly what he did.

"Who the fucking hell are you, what do you want from me?" As before there was no reply, no sound other than the narrow opening being slid shut.

He shouted out again, "Come on, what do want from me you bastards?" No one answered, but he was sure he heard a muffled laugh as they walked away, he shouted again incensed by their actions.

"For God's sake you bastards let me out of here." He instantly felt the pain from his exertions over his whole frame as he tried once more to settle back down again. It was all becoming too much and the tortuous pain he felt in his cramped legs brought out a desperate soul destroying cry from this disorientated, near broken, man. After a while he dropped off to sleep, but was soon woken again by the tremendous pain from his wounds. Looking up he noticed a shadow from yet another bridge. All he could think of doing was to keep counting in the vain hope that if there was to have a chance of escape, at least he would have some reference as to his whereabouts, but deep down he knew he was deluding himself, and the only certainty was the barge chugged slowly on pushing away the shards of shattered ice from its bow.

Jonathan's only consolation was by now his battered frame was at least warming up from the heat coming from the engine, the blood from the head wound had stopped running down his face, but he hadn't eaten or drank anything since nine o' clock the previous evening. It wasn't food he craved for, however, he desperately needed water to soften his swollen lips. Surely these pigs would give him something to drink soon. Again he tried to keep his mind off his despairing situation by continuing to count the bridges and so far he had calculated the barge was somewhere between the A14 road bridge, and Yelvercroft village should be coming up very soon.

Moments later there was the unmistakable sound of a

58

helicopter in the distance. Excitedly, he tried his best to sit up a little, anxiously listening to the whirling rotor blades as it came ever closer, wondering and praying if they were searching for him. According to the amount of noise the helicopter was creating it must have been flying very low, and then the deafening racket was overhead, sounding as if it was just a few metres above him. He shouted out in desperation, but then the disappointment to hear the change in tone from the rotor blades as it carried on and into the distance until the only sound he could hear again was the old Lister engine throbbing away beside him.

Please God, they were looking for him, they must come back this way again. All Jonathan could think of was that Lynda must have called the police after he had failed to return home and this helicopter just had to have been out searching for him. At least that was the hope he would now cling on to, and to think that these bastards could imagine they would get away with a kidnapping on this tranquil canal system just beggared belief, and led him to doubt the intelligence of his captors.

*

Back at the dive scene near Kegworth Wharf, Andy and Carl had now finished searching the area directly around the ice splintered hole. With the help of the team, they had pulled themselves back up onto the bank where Smithy and Alan were ready for the next dive. Andy gave them a short brief as this was Alan's first operational search.

"Listen you two, make sure you keep your personal guide lines taut at all times and do not dive any further than two metres away from the hole. If your search doesn't come across anything, we will have to consider getting the work barge up here to break this ice up into sections. Also lads, don't forget we are looking for a body, so make bloody sure we don't have two more buggers to look for, have you got that?"

"Don't worry Skip I will look after him," Smithy replied.

"Ten minutes Smithy, that's more than enough time for you two and be warned its absolutely bloody freezing."

Smithy was the first to enter the cold murky water followed by Alan; they were each tied to a guide line held by two other members of the team. After checking their lines they slowly submerged under the dark icy water. Andy turned to the rest of his team, telling them just how cold the temperature of the water had been. His teeth uncontrollably chattering as he gave his opinion on the length of time anyone would survive without having the correct protection. He then turned to Atwood.

"When Smithy and Alan surface Joni, would you ask the guys from British Waterways to bring up the work barge and get them to standby just short of the road bridge. I'm sure we are going to require their assistance later, that is, of course, if Smithy and Alan don't have any success on their dive. They can use the ice breaking barge to give the area a once-over, because it's going to be far too dangerous for us to proceed any further away from the opening in the ice. In fact, we should look at tomorrow's weather forecast to see if the temperature is going to lift, since I am not prepared to put my guy's lives at risk any further tonight."

After around five minutes Smithy first, then Alan surfaced. Andy, assisted by Carl, pulled the guide lines in slowly as they made their way out of the freezing water and a couple of moments later they were both safely on the bank. Smithy took off his mask and sat down alongside Andy.

"Have you found anything?" he asked.

"Not really Skip, but did you notice that bloody great rock right under the opening?"

"Yeh of course I saw it but what of it?"

"Don't you think it's a little strange that this bloody great rock is directly under the centre of this hole?"

"So are you telling me Smithy, you think this rock of yours broke through the ice before this chap we are searching for had fallen in, and then he kindly left his glove for us to find? I know you are a copper mate, but that seems a little far fetched to me."

"Well Andy, look at this hole. Do you notice anything unusual about it? Just look how thick the ice is around the edge. I don't know how big this guy is, who is supposed to have fallen in, but think about it. If he had slipped in off the bank wouldn't he have just slid on the ice and more than likely finished up lying prostrate rather than making this defined hole?"

"You're serious aren't you?"

"Yes Andy, I am sure of it."

"Come on let's put your theory to the test then. I weigh around 90 kilos so give me that guide line." Andy tied the line to his harness while Smithy and Alan held the line tight. He walked backwards onto the ice and to his surprise found it held his weight comfortably. Now, with a little more confidence in the strength of the ice, he took a small jump of no more than a foot and still the ice bore his body weight.

"Smithy you may be right. You lads better take a little more care so as not to disturb what may turn into a crime scene."

"It's a bit late for that now," Joni interrupted.

"Okay, Taggart, go up to the wharf and ask Inspector Collins to come down here and take a look. We will let him decide which way we should proceed from here."

"Okay, I will go and see if he is still warming his fat arse over the brazier."

"Joni, I wouldn't let Collins hear you slagging him off or you could be a community support officer by this time tomorrow."

"The rest of you guys go with Alan and Joni up to the wharf and get warmed up. We will wait down here for the inspector."

Thanks Skip was there joint reply as they quickly took Andy up on his offer. They didn't have to wait too long for Inspector Collins to come clumsily shuffling along the towpath, carrying his huge bulk with some difficulty.

"The lads tell me you have some issues about how to carry on with the search Andy?"

"That's right sir. Smithy here has pointed a few things out to me that don't quite add up, and he suggested the ice would have been too thick for anyone to have broken through by just slipping off the bank. Do you want to demonstrate Smithy how the ice holds your weight for the inspector?"

"As you can see sir, it would be near impossible to break this ice by simply slipping off the towpath. Even if I was to jump off, it still doesn't budge. A couple of metres down, and directly under this broken ice, there is a large rock, weighing I guess twice the weight of one average person. Smithy seems to think if that rock was dropped heavily onto the ice, the impact of its mass might just have the capability of breaking through."

The inspector turned towards Andy Flower and Constable Smith. "So you both think there's something a little more sinister going on here, than some chap just falling in the canal?"

"Well sir, I know we have only carried out a preliminary search around the hole, but we both now think it's too much of a coincidence that this rock is lying directly under the aperture. According to Joni, sorry sir Constable Atwood, the canal has recently been dredged in this area. Also sir, I am going to call off the dive for the time being as it is far too dangerous for us to carry on searching at the moment, if that's all right by you?"

"Well that of course is your decision to make, and in the light of your observations, I'm going to bring in SOCO, to take a look."

As the inspector ungainly made his way back to arrange for Serious Crimes Officers to attend and take over the incident, Atwood was approaching Inspector Collins from the direction of the Wharf. "Sir the young lady who came to collect Mrs Harker has been on the phone asking if there is any news of Mr Harker."

"Okay constable, leave it to me. You go and stand by the incident and tell Smithy and Andy Flowers to come to the wharf and get themselves warmed up, while you lad, wait along there for further instructions. Also constable, I will be sending Trout along to you as soon as she returns from Warwick, so make sure you take care not to disturb the scene any further than we have already, or else someone will be getting a bollocking, and that's not going to be me constable?"

*

Jonathan Harker had no real idea of the time, only that the daylight through the small crack above him seemed to be fading fast, so he estimated it was probably around four o'clock. There had been no further sound of the helicopter for at least a couple of hours, but they must be out there somewhere he convinced himself and they would certainly find him soon. For the love of God, how could anyone expect to get away with the madness of abducting someone on such a sleepy backwater as this? They just had to find him, but where are they and how hard can it be to find a canal barge travelling at no more than five miles an hour? He tormented out loud, with real despondency in his voice, "They won't get away with this, the bastards just can't get away with it."

Night fell quickly after that, but the sound of the helicopter never returned again that evening, although he imagined he could hear the whirling rotor blades off in the far distance. He felt sick at the probability that his wife Lynda, and his wonderful children, would never see him again. His heart cried out for them as his tortured mind went over and over this day of unbelievable violence and brutality. He just had to wake from this never ending nightmare soon.

CHAPTER SIX

Detective Inspector Wallace arrived at Kegworth Wharf just as the afternoon light was fading. Inspector Collins had known the detective for many years and so they were comfortable around each other. Simon Wallace was a very intelligent detective in his mid-fifties with vivid steely blue eyes; he was one of those rare people who have that certain charisma about them, not just because of his stature but he had the capability of stealing the limelight when he entered any room. Wallace had been a copper for the best part of his working life and commanded great respect from his fellow officers, including Inspector Collins.

"Hello Iain. What have you got for us then, apart from a missing person who may have fallen in the canal?"

"Well Simon, a couple of the lads from the dive team believe somebody is trying to hoodwink us into believing that a gaping hole in the ice, which we have been treating as the place our missing chap had fallen in, was in fact made by other means."

"Right, lead on then Iain and let me take a look."

"The area has been taped off, but of course with the dive team searching along there, they have disturbed the ground a little, but have managed to rig arc lights so at least you will be able to see the scene for yourself."

"Well thank goodness for small mercies," the DI replied.

"How many hours has this chap Harker been missing now?" Wallace asked.

"He left home around 6:45 this morning to take his dog for their customary walk and never returned."

"I see. What about his dog, did that find its way home?"

"According to Mrs Harker's nanny, the dog returned back to the house around 8:45 somewhat later than was normal and Jet, that's the dog's name Simon, was in a terrible state, in fact so bad that he had to be taken to the vet."

"Okay, thanks for putting me in the picture."

They walked in single file along the towpath to where Constable Atwood was standing, doing his best to keep warm on that bitterly cold January evening. The DI nodded to Atwood as he lifted the blue and white tape to let the two officers underneath. The area was well lit from the dive team's arc lights and the glare reflected off the canals icy surface. You could see the aperture in the canal quite clearly as it glistened from the shattered pieces of reformed splinter like ice covering the cold black water beneath.

"They told me that you found a glove on the ice next to the hole."

"That's right. It had what we thought were traces of blood on the leather so I had the glove sent off to Warwick for forensics to take a look at."

"The fact that it had any blood on it at all, probably meant it should have been left where it was found on the ice?"

"I would have of course Simon, but ...." Wallace cut Collins sentence short for him and said, "Yes it's a pity about that. It would have helped us build a better picture of what happened here." Wallace walked back from the towpath, and was now busy looking at something in the bottom of the hedgerow.

"You better take a look at this Iain; you told me earlier that the divers had discovered a large rock of some kind in the water directly underneath the broken ice. Is that right?"

"That's right; they described it as a big bugger too."

"It looks like we have found where it probably came from. Obviously we will have to wait until we have investigated further before we can retrieve the rock, but going by this piece of relatively bare ground underneath the hedge, makes this place a likely home for the rock. Who is the officer in charge of the dive team these days?"

"Actually he's a civilian Simon, Andy Flower. But one of lads, Constable Smith, I think you probably know him, served for a time with CID, he's pretty sure that no one could have broken the ice by just slipping or even falling off the bank."

Wallace was now testing the ice for himself by using a boat hook belonging to the dive team, at first prodding then using some force in trying to break the area around the hole without a great deal of success.

"Well, after my efforts I tend to agree with them. The problem though is, as you know, we can't be sure."

"What is Flower planning now regarding the search?"

"They are up at the wharf deservedly warming themselves Simon and waiting for your decision on what to do next, but Andy Flower thinks it far too dangerous to dive under the ice at the moment and wants permission to ask the British Waterways chaps to break up the ice with their utility barge. It has a hydraulic arm fitted on the back, so if needed they could reverse along the canal and gently break up the ice in small sections."

"Well, under the circumstances, we are going to have to wait until forensics has investigated the immediate area, aren't we Iain?" The sarcasm in Wallace's voice made Inspector Collins squirm, but he never replied.

The two men walked back along the towpath and Wallace told Atwood he would be sending someone down to relieve him. He told him to take a break and get himself warm back at the wharf workshop. The inspector found the members of the dive team sitting around the workshop brazier. Smithy stood up and went over to his old boss.

"How are you sir?" he asked in an affectionate manner.

"Not too bad Smithy, but I can see you still like getting wet."

"Keeps me out of mischief sir. By the way, this is Andy Flower, he's the dive team manager."

"Hello Andy, I hope you're keeping an eye on this one?" he said looking across towards Smithy.

"Very much so sir, you wouldn't like him back in CID would you?" Wallace smiled before carrying on.

"Andy, Inspector Collins tells me you don't believe that anyone has fallen through the ice, and the hole was probably made by this large boulder you have found directly under the aperture, after it had been dropped heavily onto the ice?"

"Well sir, we know the person we are looking for couldn't have possibly just slipped in or even jumped onto the ice to make a hole of that size. When Smithy found the rock, it all looked a bit suspicious." Smithy interrupted them both.

"Then of course, there's the glove sir."

"Ah the glove, pity you removed it before I arrived?"

"Yes sir, I take full responsibility for that," Andy said, before Smithy carried on again, "You see at the time we were conducting a search for this chap who we believed had possibly fallen in, but when I discovered the rock it was just so obvious that it created the hole. After that Inspector Collins thought it was time he brought you in sir."

Andy Flowers intervened. "At that point I decided it was far too dangerous to carry on with the search until the ice has been broken up and, of course, we were waiting for your decision on how to proceed further."

*

Suddenly there was a definite change in the tone of the engine and the barge seemed to be slowing down. Jonathan listened intently and noticed the sliver of light had now disappeared altogether; he lay there trying to work out what was going on before quickly realising the barge must have entered a tunnel as the sound from the engine was now reverberating off the brick walls. He was shocked at the realisation that this could only be the Crick tunnel. They had travelled much further than he had estimated and now he was miles from home, inside a dark 200-year-old canal tunnel, with God knows who at the helm, moreover in control of his destiny. Then out of blue he clearly heard a woman's voice shout out. The sound seemed to come from in front of him and then a second shout only this time even louder.

"Look out you crazy sod." Her words echoing along the tunnel and it was obvious the barge had hit something hard, causing it to rock from one side to the other, before resuming its original even keel and the vessel seemed to be moving smoothly again. Further shouting resumed, only this time they were the loud gruff tones of a male voice mouthing expletives of all kinds but after a while that soon dissipated into muffled moans. All became calm again and the only sound he could hear was that of the Lister engine once more echoing around the tunnel walls as the barge carried on. It was obvious to him that they must have grazed the tunnel wall.

Suzy Walters was cursing Dean Wilmot to herself for not steering the barge in a straight line. How difficult could it be she thought, the man is a complete moron. Ever since Tony had introduced her to Dean she had taken an instant dislike to this lofty thickset pock faced man. Her first impressions of him were upheld after his despicable actions earlier that morning and Tony would probably want to kill him when he discovers just what that bastard had done to her. Dean looked like the hard man he was with his long black greasy hair tied back into a pony tail, he spoke with a gruff East London accent, and he was the sort of criminal even his own kind disliked. Wilmot had been in and out of prison for most of his adult life; for robbery, grievous bodily harm, and various other crimes; in contrast Tony Miles was a well educated man who like many more of his echelon, had fallen on hard times and instead of making money for the companies he worked for, he had been helping himself from their dwindling profits. Consequently he had been sent down for a three-year stretch for fraud, and it was in Wormwood Scrubs he had meet Dean Wilmot where they had shared a prison cell together. When Tony was approached to carry out the kidnapping of Jonathan Harker, he knew that both brains and brawn would be needed in a equal manner. He certainly had the brains and provided he steered Dean in the right direction, and had Suzy there to keep an eye on him, everything should go to plan. Tony obviously hadn't known Dean quite as well as he thought, Suzy surmised.

The barge was now more than half way through the long Crick tunnel by the time Tony Miles turned off the M1 motorway into the north bound services at Watford Gap. He drove around the parked trucks and then, carrying on up the emergency service exit, turning right, he then drove the short distance to Watford Village before taking the second turn on the left which led him down a quiet lane and into the countryside. He had practised this drive on a couple of occasions and even though it was a dark cold night he knew this lane would take him down to the southern exit of the Crick canal tunnel.

Dean had rung Tony a mile or two before entering the tunnel, approximately one hour ago, estimating that they would be at the mooring point at the southern exit at 7:30pm. In his usual brusque manner he warned Tony that he had better be there waiting for them. Tony pulled up at 7:25pm and as prearranged he reversed the transit into the narrow side track at the top of the canal bank, stopping just short of a five bar gate. He was now no more than 50 metres from the tunnel exit. Locking the van doors he walked the short distance to the kissing gate entrance that led down towards the towpath, then gingerly walking down the steep frozen bank and, trying to gain some grip in the process, he soon reached the red brick arch which formed the tunnel exit. It was bitterly cold as he stood there waiting for the barge to appear from the black eerie void of the long dark tunnel.

At 7:35pm he heard the sound of the Lister engine throbbing away not far from the end of the tunnel. A few moments later she came out into the open and smashed into the unbroken ice sending a shock-wave through the frozen canal. Tony could make out Suzy standing on the bow holding a flash light and then he saw Dean, who cut a sinister figure wrapped up in his long trench coat, standing by the tiller and looking every bit the desperado that he was. Tony could see he was struggling to steer the barge over towards the towpath through the unbroken ice; at the same time Suzy threw Tony a rope. On the previous night he had hammered a metal spike into the bank and was pleased to see it was still there. He quickly tied the rope tightly around the spike, then ran back the full length of the barge and pulled the stern in as close to the towpath as he could, hammering in a second spike to hold her into position as Dean shut off the engine. It was now Jonathan knew that he was about to be transferred and perhaps at last he would see his kidnappers for the first time. Frightened now for his life, he tried to prepare himself for what was going to happen next.

Tony gave Suzy a hug and whispered to her to wait up by the van and to make sure there was nobody else around. She climbed up the slippery path through the kissing gate and onto the track just off the lane, looking both ways along the dark country road and as far as she could tell all was quiet. Dean stepped off the barge and both men stared at each other but said nothing as they had agreed. They walked along to the middle section of the vessel to where their hostage was imprisoned. Dean took a key from his pocket placing it into the heavy padlock, the key turned releasing the two ends of the chain. Jonathan was petrified as the top hatch slid back and slammed hard against the opposite side, a bright light shone down into his eyes and a menacing voice spoke out.

"Get the fuck up Harker?" He never moved for what seemed an age, until the same words only this time more venomous.

"Did you hear me Harker; I said get the fuck up." Jonathan struggled in trying to move grimacing with the pain from his twisted legs after being in the same position all day long, then a freezing cold hand grabbed the cable tie around his wrists and violently pulled him up with such force he hit his head against the edge of the hatch. He yelled out but no mercy was shown. Finally as he was nearly upright the two men slid a large sack of some kind over him and, before he had even realised what was happening, they secured it by tying a cord around his waist and then he felt something pulling tightly around his neck, only to hear the unmistakable zipping sound of a cable tie being tightened. His breathing became difficult and he started to choke. He was sure they were trying to kill him, but then he heard a different voice, well spoken this time saying.

"That's enough; you are going to kill him." Then, once again, the guttural sound of Deans voice barked out. "Okay Harker we are going to lift you out of the barge, you can make it fucking easy for us, or you can make it even fucking harder for yourself." Jonathan mumbled back in a tired weary voice, which was barely audible with the cable tie around his throat.

"For God's sake tell me who you are and what do you want?"

"Keep your fucking mouth shut Harker."

"God almighty, why are you doing this to me?" Jonathan let out a scream that would have woke the dead as Dean punched him hard into his already sore ribs.

"Do you fucking well understand me this time you toffee nosed bastard?" Jonathan couldn't have replied even if he had wanted to. He was in far too much pain and he knew now if he hadn't already realised these were brutal thugs who would kill him if they had to without a seconds thought.

They lifted him unceremoniously out of the barge and then, half carrying, half dragging their quarry, they proceeded to haul his battered body up the icy bank towards the waiting van. Suzy was keeping a lookout, but at the same time she was trying to see what Tony and Dean were up too. They seemed to be making hard work of carrying Harker up the bank she thought.

*

One mile away at the Navigator Inn, Les Parson was swilling back the last of his pint of bitter, before buttoning up his duffle coat, readying himself to carry on with his night's duties, then turning to the landlord he called out, "See you tomorrow night Ben."

"Okay Les, you take care now." He stepped outside, pulled the hood up over his head, before climbing into his old works truck and drove out of the pub car park to continue his rounds.

*

Suzy stared along the uninviting dark lane, eagerly waiting to see Tony and Dean emerge through the kissing gate. She mumbled to herself, 'Come on Tony let's get away from here and back to the cottage, it had been such a nerve racking day.' However, her worst fear loomed as the lane was lit by a vehicle's headlights in the distance, and it was proceeding towards her. She shouted at the top of her voice.

"Bloody hell, Tony there is a car coming down the lane?" The panic was obvious in her voice; the two men were stopped dead in their tracks. Tony told Dean to stay where he was, and scrambled up the icy bank towards the van and when he looked along the lane to the right, he soon realised the vehicle wasn't a car by the formation of the headlights. It looked to him as if it could be a Land Rover probably a local farmer.

"What the hell are we going to do Tony?" she asked now a little more panic-stricken.

"The first thing is stop bloody panicking and get into the van with me and pretend to be fooling around." Tony unlocked the doors and they quickly jumped in, he placed his arm around Suzy shoulders keeping one eye on the approaching vehicle.

"Thank God you're here Tony, that bastard Dean."

"Not now Suzy please, tell me later." The Land Rover was only 200 metres or so away now and seemed to be slowing down, 'please just carry on and go past were both their thoughts,' but it wasn't going to. "My God it's stopping Tony, what the hell are we going to do?"

The Land Rover had pulled up no more than six or seven metres away and someone was getting out and the driver was now staring over the top of the Land Rover's bonnet in their direction as if he was weighing up the situation or waiting for them to move. After what seemed like an eternity, and still looking in their direction, the driver started the short walk along the lane towards them. Tony had to think quickly as he felt the cold breeze hit his face as he wound down the Transit's window, the man came straight up to him and in a friendly manner wished Tony good evening and asked if he wouldn't mind moving his vehicle so he could open the gate to go down to the Water Treatment Works. It was then Tony saw the logo on the drivers coat pocket Anglia Water Authority, at that moment the driver looked across and nodded to Suzy.

"Evening miss." Suzy never spoke but managed to smile; Tony answered him with steely confidence. "No of course not, very sorry to hold you up we didn't realise it was a works entrance, I'm afraid."

"That's all right mate, I'll say good night then." He thanked them again smiled and turned away. The relief that Tony felt was immense as he started the engine and with some difficulty drove the van out of the muddy track. The workman let himself in through the five barred gate and drove slowly off down the track, leaving the gate wide open behind him. Tony drove a short distance along the lane before then pulling over onto the verge and out of sight of the entrance down to the treatment works.

"Stay here Suzy, I've got to get back too Dean."

"What the hell are you going to do Tony?" she asked nervously.

"We must wait for him to finish his work at the treatment works and then get that poor bastard Harker back to the cottage as soon as we possibly can. He must be freezing his bollocks off now and we need to get some heat and food into him as we don't want anything to happen to him, do we."

"Tony wait, listen to me, I must know, did you ask that piece of scum Dean to bind rope around my hands and tie me up to the cabin wall?"

"No for goodness sake, what are you talking about?"

"That bastard told me Tony, you had given him permission to do exactly that, as this would be the best way of attracting Harker's attention, then he would be able to surprise him by attacking him from behind."

"Do you honestly think I would have ever agreed to let that thug do that to you Suzy?"

"Well that's not all of it, after tying my hands together he made me lay on the cabin bench and tied me to it."

"What, I can't believe the bastard did that to you. I am so sorry my darling, but don't you worry he will answer for that." The tears rolled down her cheeks as she continued.

"Tony, then when I was powerless to stop him, he tore my tee shirt and then," she hesitated, hardly daring to reveal to him what happened next, but then managed to carry on,"He then ripped off my bra leaving my top half completely exposed as he stood over me enjoying himself at my expense. I thought for a moment the bastard was going to rape me, he had the look of a wild animal about him as he pulled me up and tied my wrists to the cabin wall, telling me it had to look more realistic."

"What, I can't believe he put you through such an ordeal. Suzy, you just wait until this is all over, he won't know what has hit him, I can promise you that my sweet."

"I was just so frightened of him, also I know how much this ransom money means to you."

"Will you be okay if I go back to see how long this Water Authority chap's going to be?" She wiped her eyes and told him to take care. Tony left the van and walked back along the lane and, looking across the field, he could see the white Land Rover waiting with its lights still turned on and parked up by the treatment works. He couldn't believe he hadn't spotted the works when he was here yesterday. He had assumed they were no more than farm buildings of some kind. He was now approaching the track when he heard the metallic sound of a door slamming; the Land Rover fired up and it was now moving back up the track. Hiding behind the hedge he waited, but only to hear the vehicle's engine stop. He stood slowly and peered over the thorn hedgerow to see what was going on, the driver had stopped right over the top of the tunnel exit and was sitting with his cab light on, he seemed to be looking down towards the barge.

"Bloody hell, I hope he hasn't spotted anything." Then he noticed that the driver was holding what looked like a cup of some sort and realised he was only taking his tea break.

After several minutes the truck was on the move again, it carried on up the track and through the open gateway before pulling up once more. The driver stepped out of the vehicle but left the engine running this time. He walked quickly around the Land Rover to close the five bar gate. Tony watched him from a safe distance as he padlocked the gate and walked back towards the driver's door, it was only then that Tony spotted a shadowy figure coming out through the kissing gate before crouching down behind the Land Rover. What's that stupid bastard Dean playing at, he's going to ruin everything? Tony heard the driver's door slam shut and the engine rev noisily. There was a grating of the gears and he saw Dean move up from his crouched position as if he was about to move from the rear of the vehicle towards the driver's door. Dean was too late. Instead of engaging first gear the driver selected reverse and there was nothing Wilmot could do as he was crushed between the gate post and the offside corner pillar of the vehicle. The driver then selected the right forward gear and drove off oblivious to what had just happened. Tony ran over to Dean and found him lying in a crumpled heap. He fell to his knee's beside him only to see blood tricking from the corner of his distorted mouth, his face still etched with the agony he must have just felt, but there was no breath coming from his twisted frame and Tony knew there was nothing he or anyone could do. Dean was already dead.

CHAPTER SEVEN

Consoling Lynda for most of the day, Natasha was trying her best to keep her spirits up, but now that Mrs Bernard was there her employer had seemed less troubled. They both sat on the large Chesterfield sofa in front of the lounge's open fireplace. The Police were also there. WPC Jane Monroe had been assigned as the family liaison officer, her primary task being one of reassurance for the family and to keep Mrs Harker up to date with how the search for her husband was progressing.

Jet had now returned from the vets but was still feeling sorry for himself as he lay in the warm kitchen next to the Aga range, with his head perched over the side of his large wicker basket. Every time anyone came through the door he would look up, hoping to see his master, before looking away again, his large sad eyes showing disappointment.

Natasha was feeling the strain herself from this eventful day and decided she would try to get some rest; she bent over and gently stroked Jet's head while offering him some comforting words before leaving through the kitchen door and up the back staircase to her bedroom. She must have just dropped off, only to be woken by the front door bell ringing out. She made her way downstairs, straightening her clothes and tidying her hair as she did so, opening the door to see two men standing there.

"Good evening miss, I am Inspector Wallace and this is Detective Sergeant Terry." Wallace was now showing Natasha his warrant card. "Would it be possible to speak to Mrs Harker?"

"Yes of course inspector, please, would you like to come in?" She stood to one side as the two officers came into the wide hallway. "If you could wait here for a moment I will go and tell Mrs Harker you are here." Natasha could see Mrs Harker's obvious anxious reaction when she told her that two CID Police officers had arrived and were waiting to see her. Lynda placed her hands up to her face clearly fearing the worst. Jane Monroe asked Mrs Harker if she would excuse her while she went to speak to the officers herself, as she wanted to know the reason for this unexpected visit from her colleagues. She walked out of the room and into the large hallway.

"Good evening gentlemen, I am WPC Jane Monroe from the family liaison office assigned to this case."

"Well Jane this is DS Terry and I'm DI Wallace from the serious crime squad, there has been a development and we need to ask Mrs Harker a few questions. Do you think she's up to it?"

"Yes sir, she is understandably tearful but I'm sure she won't mind if it's going to help." Mrs Harker stood as the officers entered the room and was trying her best to remain composed.

"Good evening Mrs Harker, we are sorry to disturb you so late. I am Detective Inspector Wallace and this is Detective Sergeant Terry from Leicestershire CID. There has been a development this afternoon and we need to ask you a few questions. As you know there was a glove found on the ice this morning where you thought your husband may have fallen into the canal." She gripped Ester Bernard's arm tightly and was expecting only the worst news. "You see Mrs Harker the forensics lab have discovered two types of blood on the glove. I can only imagine how upsetting this is for you madam, but we need to know your husband's blood type?"

"Is this the time for these sort of questions inspector, can't you see how upsetting this is?" Ester Bernard intervened.

"Yes, I'm sorry madam, but we need this information to forward our inquiries."

"It is all right Ester, I know Jonathan's grouping, is the same as my own. A positive."

"Thank you madam, so that leaves the other type which is AB negative, and I am told is quite a rare blood group. What we would like to know is .... are there any other persons who may have come into contact with the glove who may have this rare blood type in the house?"

She looked across at the detective in bewilderment, and wondered how this police officer could think of asking her such a complicated question when she was in such a delicate state, but she never the less did answer him in a quietly spoken voice, "No inspector. I am afraid I don't know of any person with that blood type."

She sat back into the sofa pondering on this question, then she asked the inspector what he thought this meant.

"We are not sure madam, but there has been a preliminary search of the canal and we can't at this point be sure that anyone has fallen in."

"Inspector, if Jonathan hasn't fallen in, and please let us pray he hasn't," her voice now sounding desperately broken, "Then what in God's name has happened to him?"

"I am sorry Mrs Harker I can't answer that, and I apologise for asking such insensitive questions, but all we can do is resume the search early tomorrow morning."

Natasha showed the two men to the door. As Wallace stepped outside into the cold night air, he turned and asked Natasha if the Harkers were a happy family and if she had noticed anything unusual in the household recently. She was caught off guard by his probing questions but replied, "No Inspector Wallace, I haven't noticed anything unusual, and yes they are a very happy family." Wallace was struck by the young woman's loyalty and wished her goodnight.

*

Tony Miles was trying to come to terms with Dean's death, realising the whole plan was now collapsing around him. All the hard work he had put into the stakeouts, his timing which had been almost perfect, even the weather couldn't beat them, but now because of that bloody fool Dean it was all falling apart. He had to think fast or else there would be no point in continuing. He ran back down the lane to the old transit, jumped in beside Suzy, started the motor and turned the van around.

"What the hell's the matter Tony?" Suzy asked as he drove the van back along the track.

"We have a problem but I can't go into it now. Please just help me get Harker up the bank and into the van."

"Tony you're frightening me."

"Please Suzy, just keep quiet and help me." He stopped the van just past the point where Dean's contoured body was laying. Tony jumped out and slid open the side door.

Suzy asked, "Where is Dean, what has happened?" She was now standing right alongside him and he knew if he told her that

Dean was dead they would have no chance of pulling Harker's near dead weight to the top of the bank, let alone lifting him into the van.

"Deans down by the barge, he has twisted his ankle badly, so you have to help me okay." She went to speak but he stopped her before she could. "Come on Suzy we have to get on with this before someone else comes along the lane."

She never spoke again until they reached Harker. Dean had somehow rolled Harker's hessian cocooned body across the bank and he was now lying next to the hedgerow. Tony asked Harker if he was all right but Harker could barely mumble. Tony thought that hypothermia was setting in as he must have been lying on this icy bank for at least 30 minutes. He took hold of the two top corners of the sack and Suzy tried to lift his legs. He pulled with all his might and slowly they were able to heave Harker's considerable weight to the top of the bank. Though struggling, they made it through the kissing gate, although every time they moved on, they could hear Harker grimace with pain. This certainly hadn't been the way Tony had wanted it, but for that thug Dean inflicting his menacing ways.

Dean Wilmot had led a violent life so perhaps this was a poignant way, for him to have died he thought, although picturing his agonized face again he would not have wished that on any man. The lane was still quiet as the two of them heaved Harker's bruised body into the van. Tony had placed blankets on the floor so at least Harker would not be as cold now and he would make sure that he would not suffer any further, apart from losing his freedom.

Suzy was truly exhausted by the last five minutes of physicality and was relieved when Tony told her to get back into the van; he locked the side door and walked over to the gateway to where Dean's twisted body lay, his next grim task was to drag the hefty corpse down the icy bank towards the canal. He felt as if he was abandoning his old partner in crime and he certainly wasn't looking forward to what he had to do next. There was only one place he could depose of the body to ensure no one would find Dean too quickly. Finally reaching the barge, he jumped onto the stern to look for a heavy object to weigh the sizable body down. Time was now getting on and he was fearful that luck wasn't on his side, until he spotted a metal box filled with old greasy tools. This would have to do he thought as he slipped Dean's belt through the handle of the heavy tool box, then, without a second thought, he pushed Dean's large frame into the ice splintered canal and watched it slowly sink down into the cold black water.

When he returned to the van Suzy asked why Dean wasn't with him. At first he ignored her, keen to drive as far away as possible from the nightmare scenario he had just faced; he never looked in Suzy's direction as he broke the bad news to her.

"Suzy, I am afraid to tell you Dean is dead."

She gasped, shocked by what he was telling her. "Dead what do you mean, how, have you killed him?" she screamed out.

"No of course not, what do you think I am? No, that bloody fool was about to attack the chap from the Water Authority, when he reversed his truck and crushed Dean between the Land Rover and the gate post before driving off without even realising what he had done."

She burst into tears even though she couldn't stand the man and called out, "Tony, what the bloody hell are we going to do?"

"We will carry on with the plan, that's what we are going to do, so just try not to think about it and let us get to Nobottle Wood Cottage and make sure Harker recovers from his wounds inflicted by that bloody moron. He's all we have to think about now."

Harker lay in the back of the transit van, cocooned in the darkness of the cold damp sack, powerless to move or have any control over his trembling body and convinced he was going to die if he didn't feel some warmth soon. The sack chafed against his facial skin at the slightest movement and he was losing the will to carry on, his only thoughts that this hellish day was like an horrific kidnap movie, only this time it was really happening and he was the victim. His state of mind was between delirium and despair as he listened to the muffled voices coming from what must of been the other side of a bulkhead from where he had been unceremoniously thrown. One thing had changed, he could no longer hear the gruff menacing tones of one of his abductors, that psychopathic sadist who had harmed him on so many occasions on this, the most humiliating day of his life.

Tony took the left turn off the A5 into Nobottle Road it was now 10:50pm. They were getting close to Nobottle Wood Lane and as he approached the lane he killed the lights on the van before turning left, carefully negotiating the cattle grid. He continued onto the muddy rutted track, breaking the ice on the frozen puddles as he drove slowly on in the darkness.

Harker rocked backwards and forwards with the motion of the vehicle before it came to an abrupt halt and the engine fell silent. He could hear several doors being opened as he waited for their next move, trying his hardest to hear what was going on through the soaked hessian sack. He heard what sounded like a garage up-and-over door glide on its runners and the vehicle started once more; it drove a short distance and then stopped again. He prayed this was going to be their last move of the day and strangely he hoped it would be the gang's hideaway while they offer him up for ransom, why else had these thugs spent all day beating him, starving him, and not even offering him a drink of water. There was no doubt he was in the company of the hardest of criminals who cared nothing for decent human beings such as himself.

The vehicle side door slid open and he found himself being dragged once more. Someone was struggling to lift him by the shoulders, then he felt a second person lifting his feet. They never spoke but he could hear the efforts from their exertions as they carried his aching body through what seemed to be a narrow corridor judging by how many times his elbows collided with the walls on either side. Finally he was placed down onto a bed of some sort and the next thing he knew they were cutting off the sack which was tied tightly around his body. The cable tie was cut free from around his neck and a voice spoke out, not the menacing one from earlier, but a well spoken man who was trying to sound more vicious than he probably was.

"Listen to me Harker, I am going to take this sack off you and untie your hands and feet. If you behave yourself you will be given food and drink, but make one false move and my friend and I will make you wish you hadn't. I am sure your ribs are hurting enough already, have you got that Harker?" Jonathan replied in a pathetic frail voice that he understood. The sack was then pulled quickly up and over his head and he discovered the blood from his head wound had stuck firmly to the inside of the sack pulling a handful of his hair. Looking up he tried to see but the light from above him made it near impossible for him to open his eyes, then the same well spoken voice, only this time less menacing spoke out.

"Harker I know it's been a long miserable day for you, but if you do exactly as you are told and ask no questions, we will not harm you any further is that clear?" This time the only way he could respond was by nodding his head. His eyes were now began to focus slightly and he could just make out a tall masked figure standing at the foot of the bed and a second person he sensed was behind him. All his shackles were now off but the throbbing pain in his legs was still there.

The tall masked man spoke out again. "This room is completely secure and the only way out is through the door which will be deadlocked and padlocked for all the time you are here. Don't even think about trying to escape because there is no way out. Do I make myself clear?" Jonathan nodded wearily again. "If you want the toilet, there's a bucket over there in the corner along with a cold water tap. Once we leave the room you can help yourself to the sandwiches and drink behind you. One more piece of advice Harker, if I was you I would get plenty of rest and see this through, that's unless you want to upset my impatient partner again."

Tony Miles turned opened the door and stood to one side as Suzy left the room, then, glancing in Harker's direction while peering out from behind his SAS style balaclava said, "For you Harker the nightmare is nearly over. All you have to do is sit tight and pray your family care enough about you to pay our ransom demands." The door then closed and he heard several bolts sliding into place before the room fell silent apart from the humming noise from the strip light that hung above him.

He lay there for several minutes before trying to move his painful aching body; he desperately needed to move and help the blood to flow through his tortured limbs now that they had cut the cable ties off his ankles. He waited at least 10 minutes before attempting to move, but then the thought of food and water gave him the incentive he needed.

He slid carefully around on the bed so that his stiff legs bent and hung over the edge of the mattress, the pain he first felt was unbearable so he waited to allow the blood to flow around his joints. After a while he tried again this time placing his arms behind him, then, pushing hard he managed to sit upright and immediately felt the soreness in his ribs. It reminded him just how badly bruised he was but, needing food and drink, he forced himself to virtually fall the rest of the way off the bed and onto his knees, yelling out in agony as he landed on the hard quarry tile floor. Moments later he was cat crawling across the room with one thing on his mind - water. Forgoing the soreness he felt, he kept his eyes focussed on the small table in front of him which was enough to drive him on. As he came closer he lifted his arm to reach up for the plastic bottle, but his fingers found the edge of the plate of sandwiches. He pulled it down onto the floor beside him then he raised the other arm and reached out again for the bottle, knocking it over. It rolled off the table before coming to rest beside him. Opening the screw top wasn't easy but the first drink quenched his camel's thirst and it tasted like no other beverage he had ever drank before.

Harker ravenously ate the cheese and pickle sandwiches and even though they were slightly stale, he consumed the plate's contents. Looking around his prison cell he realised he was being watched from a small video monitor placed high in the corner of the room and facing down so as to leave no part of his cell unseen by his captors. I hope they are enjoying the show he thought as he made his way back to the makeshift bed, pulling his shattered body up onto the mattress. His mind was full of emotion, self-pity even, and his body was hurting so badly from the soreness of his wounds. Harker was so exhausted that he fell quickly into a deep sleep within minutes.

Tony Miles, or to give him his full name, Antony Wilton Miles had been left Wood Cottage by his late uncle, Edmond Wilton Miles, four or five years ago. The property was in such a bad state of repair that he couldn't afford the cost of the rebuilding work so he used the old cottage as a store for some of the antiques and other contraband from his dodgy dealings. It was also somewhere to stay from time to time when the heat was on. It had been empty for around 20 years and was unseen from the main road, half a mile away, making the perfect hideout. The track was only used by a local farmer three or four times a week. Tony, having the right of way to the cottage, hardly ever saw his neighbour which suited him just fine.

CHAPTER EIGHT

Natasha had managed to persuade Lynda Harker to try to get some sleep. It had been hours since the two CID officers had left, and there had been no further news from Jane Monroe who had likewise left, saying she would return at eight o'clock the following morning. Natasha made sure Mrs Bernard and Mrs Harker had settled in before she locked all the doors and went to bed herself. The night was a restless one for the whole household and Ester lay there for some time thinking about Jonathan and the possibility that she may never see him again. She thought she had loved him almost as much as Lynda, or had it all been just lust. No, it was much more than that. In particular she remembered the time Lynda was out of London staying at Sedgwick House and looking after her sick father. She must never know that Ester had spent so many nights together with Jonathan in his flat as it would probably break her heart. 'My poor darling Lynda please forgive me,' but it was Lynda and Jonathan who had introduced her into their, some would say, sordid lifestyle, especially their sexual adventures together in London. Those long wonderful nights they had all spent making love, as if there was no tomorrow, all seemed so terribly immoral to her now. She lay caressing her pillow for comfort as the tears rolled down onto the cotton sheets. How did an educated, God fearing woman, get herself involved in such a distasteful affair? Although Ester knew only too well, she always had, she just couldn't help herself from lusting after not just the opposite sex but Lynda in particular. This went back a long way to their racy teen years together at Oxford. At that time it really was sex drugs and rock n roll, but not always in that order. Her thoughts of those times always brought her mind instantly back to how terrible she had treated Harry, the man who had saved her from herself. He was a gentleman who she had fallen in love with after a chance meeting at the Oxford union ball. Harry had swept her off her feet, took her away from the drug scene, and only six months later they were married quietly in Scotland.

Some fifteen years later a chance meeting at a business lunch in London brought Ester and Lynda together again and from that moment on their friendship was renewed. Not at first to the same extent, but as time went along they meet up on a more regular basis until familiarity turned into something much more and eventually Ester betrayed Harry in more than one way. Only to break his heart in the way she had; knowing she would have to live with her betrayal for the rest of her life, let alone for the financial deal she had organised with Jonathan, which Harry would never get over. The tears once more streamed down her cheeks soaking the already damp pillowcase as she thought about her 20 years of marriage now gone. 'I am so sorry Harry that I been so weak,' she sobbed quietly to herself.

Ester and Harry now lived completely separate lives, although still married in name only. She knew just how much Harry hated all three of them, and the last Ester had heard of him he was working for one of his former business associates. Then her mind switched again to the realisation of what had happened today. The dreadful thought that Jonathan could be under that ice in the canal was too much to bear so she stepped out of bed, dressed, and went downstairs to the kitchen to make herself tea and spent the rest of the night trying to read.

*

The next morning the dive team arrived back at Kegworth Wharf to await orders from DI Wallace. The weather had changed for the better and the temperature had risen by six degrees which meant the ice was now beginning to melt. Andy Flower and Smithy were down by the canal poking and prodding the ice which was definitely much thinner than the day before. They walked back up to the wharf to see if DI Wallace had arrived and when they walked in, all the team were gathered around the brazier drinking more of their host's tea as usual.

"What is the score then skip?" Carl called out.

"Smithy and I both think we will be diving later this morning but DI Wallace is the only person who can make that decision, so until he arrives, mine's a coffee and the same for Smithy."

"Coming up skip."

"Oh, I am sorry Mr Shaw, that's of course if it's okay with you?" Andy politely asked.

"Yes that's fine. You carry on lads, why don't you call me Harry, everybody else does?"

"I hope this lot aren't getting in your way Harry?"

"No, no, makes a change to have people in the workshop, but this is a rum old do. It's that chap's wife I keep thinking about. I can see her face now when she came running into my workshop." Just then DI Wallace and his side-kick DS Jack Terry walked in.

"Good morning lads, this is DS Terry. He's been released from HQ to help me on this case."

"Morning, I recognise a few of you and especially old Smithy over there."

"Can I have a word with you Andy, and you too Smithy, outside please?" The four of them walked out of the workshop and over to the DI's car.

"Right lads. What's the situation down on the canal this morning, is it too risky to attempt a dive?"

"Well sir the ice has thinned, but I still think we should wait until this afternoon before we attempt to dive again."

"Yes I agree. Please lads keep this to yourselves. We have had the forensics report on the blood samples found on the leather glove, and it came back with two different blood groups. One is the same as Harker's, AB Positive, and the other AB Negative, which is quite a rare blood type they tell me. I don't suppose any of your lads could have cut themselves while handling the glove?"

"No that's not possible sir," Andy said with some confidence.

"I picked the glove up myself using the blade of my divers knife and placed it directly into a plastic bag and handed it to Nathan who then passed it to Joni, sorry sir, Constable Atwood. It was then taken, I believe, straight to Warwick University Lab."

"Okay, that's what I needed to know. The truth is, I think as you two do, I am sure there is much more to this than just some poor sod falling into the cut. Then there's that boulder of course, right underneath the break in the ice, did you find any other debris in the same area?"

"Well sir we haven't had too much success yet searching too far away from the aperture, because the ice sheet makes the water even darker than it normally is."

"Yes, of course, I suppose that's understandable. Well then we will just have to wait until this afternoon. Now where's that chap from the Water Authority? I am supposed to be meeting him here at 8:30."

"That will be Phillip Mustoe sir, I think this is him coming now."

"Right then, I'll catch up with you all later and perhaps you will have some more news for me then?"

"I certainly hope so sir."

*

Tony Miles and Suzy Walters were making the best of their surroundings. They had spent a very uncomfortable night sleeping on two old lounge chairs, pushed together to form a makeshift bed. Although Tony had been awake most of the time watching Harker, and thinking about his old cell mate Dean. He couldn't seem to erase his agonised expression from his subconscious, particularly the bizarre way his eyes opened as he slid his contorted body into the cold icy canal. He would most surely have nightmares about this undignified act for the rest of his life. He now had to telephone Ted and tell him the terrible news.

*

Wallace was standing alongside the works barge, *The Lucky Lady,* talking to Phillip Mustoe.

"Mr Mustoe, taking into consideration the conditions on the canal yesterday, could there possibly have been any movements on this part of the system?"

"Well inspector, I have just had a word with the two men who are in charge of the *Lucky Lady* and they have told me that they came up from the northern side of the Crick Tunnel yesterday morning. Their barge is equipped with a hardened steel bow which enables it to be used has an icebreaker, so in theory it would have been possible to navigate that particular part of the system."

"Are your chaps around at the moment sir, if so I would like to ask them a few questions myself?"

"Yes inspector, they are working along the towpath spreading rock salt. I will go and fetch them for you."

"Okay Mr Mustoe. I am going back up to the wharf, if you could send them along to me I would appreciate it." Half an hour and a couple of coffees later the two boatmen walked into the wharf workshop.

"Right sit yourselves down here lads, Mr Mustoe has told you what happened here yesterday hasn't he?"

"Yes he has sir," Steve answered.

"Well there's nothing for you to worry about. I just want you to tell me if you saw anything out of the ordinary on your trip up from Crick yesterday morning. Things such as boat movements or anyone acting in a way that made you think, 'what are they up to?' that sort of thing?" Steve answered first.

"No, I can't say as we did, but it was very hard going all the way through. Took us about three and half hours to get up to Felford Arm. I have never seen the ice that thick for years sir. Most of the barge owners were fast asleep until we came through, ain't that right Paul? Don't half make them old barges rock and roll when the pressure of the ice pushes against them. We always have a bit of a giggle this time of year, that's right ain't it Paul?" Paul turned his head slightly nodding to acknowledge Steve. "I tell you what though, we were surprised to see that the barge, that had been moored up just past the turning point at the Felford Arm, had moved on when we returned back up to the Grand Union from Felford Wharf."

"Why did you think that was unusual?"

"Well I did say to Paul at the time, they must be in a hurry, because they must have still struggled with all that ice, even though we had broken most of it up."

"So this barge, did you see anyone on or inside it at all?"

"No, not a soul inspector but it's chimney was smoking."

"Okay lads, I want you to remember everything you can about that barge and if possible the name, the colour, in fact any details at all," the DI called over Atwood. "Could you take a statement from these two lads constable, just tell the officer all you can and thanks, you have certainly been a considerable help to us."

CHAPTER NINE

The mobile phone in Ted's pocket was ringing out but there was no way he could answer it. He was sitting at the temporary traffic lights at the top of Park Lane and right alongside him was a police traffic car. 'Just my luck,' he mumbled to himself knowing the call would be from Tony. Finally the lights turned green and they drove off,. He turned left into the underground car park and, after parking his old Renault, he used the escalator. He was soon standing in Hyde Park looking across towards the Serpentine. Ted's phone had rung several times while he was in the underground car park, but he wanted to be away from the noise and fumes. His mobile rang again and this time he answered. Ted instantly recognised Tony's well spoken voice.

"Ted we have a huge problem."

"What the hell do you mean Tony?"

"Get ready for a shock Ted." Tony hesitated under the strain of having to tell him the bad news.

"For fucks sake Tony, what's wrong?"

"It's Dean, he has been tragically killed." Ted looked around and, seeing a low wall behind him, sat down, but he never replied. "Ted are you there, Ted, can you hear me, are you there?" But Ted was still trying to take on board Tony's statement, before eventually replying.

"How, for fuck sake?" Tony told him how everything was going to plan until Dean's stupidity got the better of him.

"After all the planning, that bastard may have ruined everything, for fuck's sake Tony, I warned you about that thug and his ability to habitually fuck up."

"Yes Ted, and I told you he was the only person I knew with the capability to single-handily overpowering Harker, so let us give the poor sod some credit. Anyway, more importantly, what do you think we should do now?"

"Okay Tony, I'm sorry all right. Now what about Harker, is he safely locked up in the cottage?"

"Yes he's here, although a little more battered than I would have liked. Dean gave him a bloody hard time and went over the top shall we say."

"I knew we shouldn't have hired that thug. I did warn you Tony."

"So you keep saying Ted, but do you think we should carry on. I need to know if the next part of the operation still goes into motion?"

"Tony you listen to me, and don't forget who set up this operation, so if you want to reap the rewards, you will continue to carry out my plan to the letter, is that understood?"

"Okay Ted, no need for you to become tetchy. I know what I have to do, so don't worry on that score. I will make the call to Harker's wife and play the recording at 8:30 this evening."

*

Jonathan Harker was eating the remains of the food left out for him from the previous day while Suzy was watching him through the TV monitor wondering what this beaten man was thinking. She remembered seeing him walking towards the barge yesterday morning, then he was an upright good-looking man who cut a figure as he walked his dog along the towpath but now she saw how pathetic he had become, lying there trying his best to eat his food through his swollen lips. The poor sod she thought, he had endured terrible punishment at the hands of, she tried to say his name, but felt quite sickened by the thought that Dean was now submerged under *The Lazy So and So*. What had she got herself into for the love of this man Tony Miles? She would have never been involved, if it had not have been for him? Then she heard Tony calling her from the kitchen.

"Suzy, after Harker has finished that tray of food you left out for him, I don't think we should give him anything else."

"Why on earth not Tony, hasn't the poor sod suffered enough already without starving him again?"

"Suzy just do as I say or he will think we are going soft on him. He has probably now realised that Dean isn't around any more. We don't want him to recover too quickly do we now?"

For the first time Suzy saw a different side to Tony, and the pressure was certainly affecting him now. What with Dean's untimely death, and the way he had dispatched his old cell mate, it must have been playing on his mind. Although she also knew he was far from becoming an angel as he had been in and out of prison several times in recent years, but not for anything too serious: false accounting; petty fraud; receiving and other misdemeanours; but now, with the kidnapping of this millionaire, Jonathan Harker, Suzy believed Tony was way out of his comfort zone.

He hadn't really thought this through. Someone she had never met, only known to her as Ted, Tony's old school friend, now had a strong influence over him. When Tony had first told her what he was planning she had tried to persuade him not to get involved again in any crime, let alone one so serious as kidnapping which could result in his downfall. He wouldn't listen to her, convincing himself that this was a huge opportunity. After all Ted's meticulous planning, along with his own local knowledge, he was convinced it would ensure success. Suzy knew that the thought of so much cash had blurred his vision so there was no way she could change his mind. He was positive that this was his chance to make lots of money quickly, and promised her they could both find a better future somewhere together, but now, for the first time since she had known him, she was beginning to regret her involvement with this ex public school boy and his so called friends.

*

Lynda Harker had spent the morning with her friend Ester by her side and, along with Natasha's help, Ester had managed to persuade her to eat a light breakfast. Ester thought that she looked slightly more at ease this morning as the two friends now walked around the garden together. Natasha was in the kitchen with the Family Support Officer, Jane Monroe, drinking tea and chatting about the Harkers, and why Natasha had moved to Britain.

"Natasha, Mrs Harker and Mrs Bernard seem to be very close to each other don't you think?"

"Well yes, I suppose they are really."

"Have you known Ester for long Natasha?"

"I first met her in London when I registered at her employment agency, after my last employers moved on and didn't require my services any further."

Natasha now had the feeling that the officer wasn't just passing the time of day; this was now becoming more like a gentle interrogation than a friendly chat, so she politely excused herself and carried on with her domestic duties around the house.

*

The day seemed to drag on for the members of the police dive team, although breaking the ice was much easier now, it had melted quite considerably and they were able to search large sections at a time in comparison to the previous day. There was still no sign of a body, just the black empty void of the recently dredged canal. There was not even the odd bike, or any of the other rubbish, they usually found on this type of operation. It was break time back at the wharf and the team were all pretty knackered if not a little despondent. Perhaps they were on a wild goose chase and they were saying as much when Inspector Wallace walked into the workshop.

"How's the search preceding Andy?"

"Okay sir. We have made quite a lot of progress, having now cleared an area of approximately 50 metres each side of the original aperture. But we haven't found anything significant yet, apart from the boulder that is, and we were wondering whether you would like us to retrieve it yet?"

"Well yes, I suppose you might as well Andy, and then at least we could confirm yours and Smithies theory. Yes, do that lads."

"Okay sir. I will organise for a suitable winch to be sent from headquarters right away."

"By the way Andy, I have asked the police helicopter support team if I could go with them to search the canal system further to the south. As you probably know, their base is only up the road at Bosworth Airfield."

"Sounds exciting inspector, I only hope you have more luck than we have?"

"The strange thing is Andy, there was only one barge moving on the canal yesterday morning and that left the Felford Arm just after the British Waterways utility barge came up from the south around 10:30. I would like to see if we can locate it, and eliminate it from our inquires."

"Well sir, we are going back down for the final search of the day in a few minutes, and I'll report to you regarding the boulder later."

It was 3:20pm when Wallace strapped himself nervously into the police helicopter, call sign HX55, and lifted off from Bosworth Airfield on that cold but sunny January afternoon. Within a few minutes of flying they were overhead at Kegworth Wharf, flying around 40ft above the canal and heading south-west. Captain James Timpson had informed the DI that this area had already been searched the previous day using thermal imaging technology. At that time they had been searching for a missing person, rather than a 60ft barge, and to be honest he told Wallace that was all they had been looking for. The helicopter twisted and turned, following the canal as it ran under several road bridges, until they came to the bridge on the A14 dual carriageway, which is particularly wide for obvious reasons. Timpson flew over the top of the bridge before turning the helicopter sharply back on itself, in a 360 degree turn, to take a closer look from the far side. Hovering just a few metres above the canal, which enabled them to see fully underneath the bridges structure, it was at that very point of turning that Wallace wondered if he had done the right thing coming along.

"I am afraid there isn't anything to see there sir." Wallace felt his stomach returning to its old location but made no reply as the helicopter instantly climbed, before turning once more; they followed the canal as it meandered through the open countryside on its way towards the next village and beyond.

Minutes later they were over the small village. Moored up to the towpath were three narrow boats but one look told them that the three vessels hadn't moved recently, as they were still surrounded by thick ice, and only the centre of the canal was broken were the work boat or other vessels had come through. There was a good possibility that the barge they were pursuing had come at least this far. Timpson turned the helicopter to the south and around a sweeping bend in the canal, the racket from the rotor blades startling a couple out for an afternoon walk along the towpath; they carried on following the canal out of the village towards Crick. Timpson informed Wallace that they would soon be approaching the northern end of the Crick tunnel and then asked the inspector,

"Is that where you said the utility work barge began its journey yesterday morning sir?"

"Yes that's right captain, so I would suggest we carry on to the southern end of the tunnel to see if the ice has been broken at that point."

"I'm sure that's a good idea sir," the captain replied. Moments later they were above the northern exit of the Crick tunnel and they could clearly see the British Waterways jetty from where the work boat had started her journey the previous day. The captain hovered for a while before lifting the nose of the helicopter and flying off in a southerly direction.

"We are now just approaching the southern end of the tunnel sir," the Captain informed Wallace. The inspector was gazing down to his left as they flew over the top of the tunnel exit as Timpson offered, "There we are sir, your barge if I'm not mistaken?"

"Certainly looks like it captain." The helicopter was now hovering low over a frost covered field on the opposite side of the canal. As they both looked across towards the long barge, which had been moored up to the towpath, the bow was tied tightly to the bank, the aft section being slightly away as if the rear line was slack. The most striking sight for the two men was that the ice to the front of the vessel continued unbroken and into the far distance. There was no sign of anyone on board as the helicopter now moved and hovered noisily above the vessel.

At that point Wallace asked, "Captain, could you confirm the vessel's name for me?"

"It looks like *The Lazy So and So*. Yes, registered at Blisworth."

"I don't suppose there any chance of you setting the helicopter down over there by the lane Captain Timpson?"

"I'm sorry sir, but the ground is still far too slippery," Wallace anxiously interrupted the pilot.

"Captain, does that look like blood to you on the frozen bank?"

"Unfortunately, it could well be inspector."

"Right then Captain, let's head back to Bosworth Airfield and thank you for letting me come along with you. You have been a considerable help."

"My pleasure, only too glad to help sir."

Back at Kegworth Wharf, DS Terry sat in his car waiting for Wallace to arrive. He had been told by the DI that the suspect barge had been found and to be ready to leave for Crick as soon as he arrived. Wallace pulled into the wharf car park, wound his window down, and beckoned Terry over.

"You're looking a little green around the gills guv?"

"Very funny Jack. Perhaps I will send you the next time. Anyway jump in, we need to get over to Crick with some urgency before dusk descends."

They set off in Wallace's car heading for the southern end of Crick tunnel, via the A5, and then down into Watford village before taking a left turn into Back Lane. When they eventually arrived, Wallace parked on the icy verge, buttoning his top coat from the biting cold he turned to his DS saying, "Come on Jack, let us take a look over the hedge first." They both stood looking over the top of the recently trimmed thorn hedgerow and down a steep bank in the direction of the barge.

"There she is then Jack, *The Lazy So and So*. You better call the boat hire company and give them the registration number so they can inform us who the last person was to hire boat and when."

"Okay, I'm on to it now."

"Also get uniform out here to close the lane off 200 metres each side of the incident. There's definitely something untoward been going on here Jack."

"Certainly looks that way governor."

Wallace proceeded through the kissing gate and carefully down the steep slippery bank, making sure not to disturb the ground. On reaching the towpath, he immediately confirmed what they had seen from the helicopter - an incredible amount of blood staining - not only the towpath but also on the ground close to the rear of the barge. From there the blood trailed off along the towpath and back up the path next to the hedgerow, only now the blood wasn't in defined spots, but smeared.

Terry was on his way down the bank when Wallace shouted up to him, "For goodness sake stay there Jack, it looks like someone has stuck a pig down here. Give forensics a call right away, we are certainly going to need them to make any sense of this mess?"

Wallace followed the trail of smeared blood back up the path and through the kissing gate towards a muddy track. He couldn't believe he hadn't noticed the smears when he was on his way down towards the barge. At the top of the path the blood trail continued to the left and there by an old sleeper gatepost, which hung a five-bar gate, was a pool of solidified blood on the frozen ground. He stood back to observe the scene. It was now 4:30pm and the light was fading fast as DS Terry came across towards him.

"Forensics are on their way guv, they should be here within the hour. By the way, I told them to bring some serious lighting along with them."

"Well done Jack, they will certainly need it. I'm afraid it's going to be like the black hole of Calcutta here very soon."

Jack Terry's attention was drawn in the direction of the lane. "Looks like the boys in blue are here?" Wallace turned to see a patrol car coming towards them.

"Go and sort them out for me Jack will you, then join me down on the towpath." Wallace proceeded to negotiate the tricky path back down towards the barge. A few minutes later Jack joined him where he found Wallace leaning on the side of the vessel.

"You look deep in thought, and I reckon we are both thinking along the same lines, although it seems unlikely that anyone in their right mind would try to kidnap someone on the canal system, I'm right aren't I guv?"

"Got it in one Jack but, if we are right, this started out as a kidnapping, but now it looks more like a kidnap that has gone tits up."

"According to the amount of blood around this boat guv, we could be looking at a murder scene."

"I wouldn't go that far Jack until a body turns up."

"Well it all looks a little too obvious now. First we had a report that some poor sod has fallen into the canal. Now it looks more than likely to have been some sort of diversionary tactic."

"I would have to say, it would now be pretty unlikely for the dive team to find a body over at the wharf, wouldn't you guv?"

"Then, of course, the only barge moving in the area yesterday turns up here abandoned, with more blood around it than an abattoir. Yes whatever is going on here could well be more sinister, but let us hope for Harker's sake he is still alive."

"You'd better take a look inside the barge Jack."

Terry climbed on board via the aft section and, by using his flashlight, he found that the cabin door had been left open. He entered very carefully and made his way down the couple of steps into the cabin. There didn't seem to be anything unusual about it as he continued on through the next door into a sleeping area. The bed was unmade and generally untidy with clothes strewn around all over the place. Carrying on along a narrow corridor, typical for this type of vessel, his way was blocked by a bulkhead which crossed the width of the narrow boat. In the side of the bulkhead was a small door locked with two bolts and in each bolt was a heavy duty padlock. At the centre of the door was a small sliding hatchway. Terry returned back through the boat and out through the small double doors. Stepping up and onto the aft section again, he then climbed back down onto the towpath to speak to his superior.

"I am afraid you can't get right through that way guv as there's a locked area in the centre of the boat."

"Okay Jack, leave that for now. I think you better take a look at this first." Wallace knelt down on the towpath and shone his torch around the rudder and between the broken pieces of ice surrounding it.

"I know that this water's pretty dirty Jack, but tell me if you can see anything down there." Terry's attention was drawn to the splattered blood on the broken ice as he shone his flashlight into the murky canal. "Jack, can you see if you can get a hold of that piece of rope floating up from just under the surface, only I can't reach it myself?"

"Shift over guv and I'll see if I can." Terry stretched his arm out and his hand touched the freezing water, "Sod that, I've got a much better idea. I spotted a boat hook hanging on the wall in the cabin. I'll go and fetch it shall I?" He never waited for Wallace to reply as he stood again and stepped up on board, passing the tiller and down into the aft cabin once more. He shone his torch up onto the side of the cabin wall and there clamped by a bracket was a six foot boat hook.

"Any luck Jack?" Wallace shouted.

"Yes, I am coming out now." He handed Wallace the pole as he stepped back onto the towpath.

"Right let me see if we can feel anything down there."

"Are you expecting to find someone on the end of this rope then guv?"

"Well there is only one way to find out Jack. Here you are, have a good old prod around." Wallace handed his DS the pole, at first Terry felt nothing, so he lay down on the cold icy towpath and stretched out as far has he could, his coat sleeve sodden by the freezing icy water.

"I reckon I have found something, yes it feels like some sort of soft object guv."

"See if you can move it then Jack." He had to pull hard before the object started to move up towards him. He held on to the pole and managed to get up onto his knees while still holding the weight of the object.

"I've got something bloody heavy here guv; can you give me a hand?" Wallace gripped the pole and both the officers tried pulling as hard as they could.

"Whatever this is guv, it doesn't want to give itself up to us easily." They were now both down on their knees pulling vigorously with the boat hook and stretching forward as Dean's frozen head popped up suddenly out of the cold murky canal - they were so surprised that they both let go of the pole at the same time.

"Shit!" shouted Terry, as they finished up lying back on the towpath as the body slowly disappeared once more under the murky water. These two had been police officers for many years but they hadn't been quite as surprised as this for some time. Between them they had seen many murder victims, but this one looked as if it was going to spring out of the water at them. Even with their grim discovery they still saw the funny side of it.

"Bloody hell, he's an ugly bastard isn't he? You don't think this is Jonathan Harker do you?" Wallace wiped the sweat from his brow and replied, "No I am pretty sure of that Jack. I have seen a photograph of Harker and this is definitely not him, but you're right Jack about our swimmer, he reminds me of you."

"Yes, very funny guv." DI Wallace was certainly puzzled as to what had gone on here, but now the forensic team had arrived he hoped to get some answers very soon. He left Jack in charge and returned to Kegworth Wharf where Andy Flower and his team were still searching the canal under floodlights.

"Andy," Wallace called out as he walked along the towpath towards the search area. Andy looked up and saw the DI walking along towards him. He quickly turned to his team, saying, "Look lively lads the inspector has just arrived."

"Good evening Andy, I don't suppose you have found anything have you?"

"Not even the usual load of rubbish sir."

"I am afraid to say, you and the dive team have probably been wasting your time here. Let us walk back towards the wharf. I have something to tell you?"

"That sounds a little ominous sir."

"Well maybe it is. We have just found a body at the southern entrance to the Crick tunnel and I am afraid to say the victim is in the canal." Andy stared at the DI for a couple of moments.

"Really sir, well, well, can you believe it? Do you think it could be Mr Harker?"

"I can't say for certain that it isn't Mr Harker, but I would be very surprised if it was him. We will have to wait, however, for forensics to tell us that and they are at the tunnel now. Do you think you could come over there and help us recover the body?"

"Of course sir, but do you want me to cancel the search? If so I'll tell the lads to make up the equipment."

"Yes you do that Andy and I will wait by my car for you and Smithy. Oh yes, best not say too much to the lads until we have identified the victim, but whoever it is, some poor sod's wife or mother is going to get the knock on the door."

CHAPTER TEN

Tony Miles wasn't looking forward to the next part of the plan. This required him to leave the relative safety of the cottage and travel a distance of 18 miles to play a pre-recorded message from a call box to Harker's wife. It was to informer her that her husband had been kidnapped, and also to tell her to wait for a further message the following day at one o'clock. This would then be followed by a warning that if she involved the police in any way she would never see her husband again.

He stood by the kitchen table ready to test the recording. He pressed the start button and waited for the tape machine to play the message, but when he heard the menacing sound of Dean's voice coming from beyond his watery grave, he sat down as he felt a cold chilling shiver run down the length of his spine. One thing for sure was this tape had the power to terrify anyone who listened to it. He wound the tape back before placing the old fashioned Dictaphone into his bomber jacket pocket, after which he walked into the small back room to tell Suzy he was about to leave.

"How is Harker bearing up Suzy?" Tony looked up to the TV monitor as she answered him.

"He's lay there nearly all day, and most of that time he has been asleep."

"Good, just as long as he stays that way. Right, you know what I have to do now don't you Suzy? Whatever you do, don't open the door to anyone until I get back, have you got that?" Suzy knew by Tony's voice that he was worrying about the next task.

"How long are you going to be?"

"I expect to be at least two hours and I am not looking forward to it I can tell you."

"Two hours, I didn't realise you would be away that long," She replied nervously.

"Ted's instructions Suzy. I only wish it was him who had to travel half way across the county to play this bloody awful message." He kissed her and told her he would be back as soon as he could and left, closing the kitchen door behind him.

He slowly drove off down the muddy farm track, keeping the vehicle lights off. The woods around him were dark and the night sky had clouded over so there was no moonlight to help him on his way. The van wheels were guided only by the deep tractor ruts. When he reached the road he was pleased to see there was no other traffic to be seen on the quiet back-water. Pulling out, he continued driving without lights until he approached Upper Marlstone, a sleepy hamlet at the best of times, so he would have been surprised to see anyone there. He turned the lights on and drove out onto the main road heading for the Framptons, now feeling slightly more unperturbed in the knowledge that he had made it to the main road without being seen.

Ted's instructions were very clear. He had to drive to a small village called Church Hardwick, which was around 18 miles distant from the cottage. He was only to use country lanes where possible, and upon arriving he would leave his van parked up in a old lay-by, on the outskirts of the tiny village, which was only used by the local council to store road chippings. Tony had previously driven there two days ago to check out the area, so he knew he would be able to park his van out of sight, behind one of the mounds of aggregate, and would be unseen from the road and just a short walk to Church Hardwick village.

When he arrived he parked as planned. He locked the Transit van before stepping over a stile by the side of the lay-by. The stile was set between an overgrown thorn hedge with a footpath sign next to it, which pointed towards the sparsely lit village in the distance.

He unzipped his jacket collar and donned the hood, then gingerly walked across the dark frost covered field knowing that he had approximately a quarter of a mile in front of him before he reached the village perimeter. From there, the old style red phone box stood on the green just a short distance away. As he arrived at the far side of the field a car turned off the main road into the lane that lead down to the village. It's headlight beams scanned the field and it's hedgerow. Tony instantly fell to his knees, grimacing with the soreness he felt as he hid out of sight by the double step stile.

The vehicle pulled into the driveway of one of five handsomely built properties that were located around the village green. Two people stepped out of the car and carefully made their way up the slippery drive. As they approached the house a security light illuminated the area and Tony could clearly see an elderly man and woman, the man turning as they entered the front door and the car lights flashed twice. A few moments later the sodium element in the security light softened. He waited patiently and was pleased to see the other properties around the rectangular green were relatively quiet. The centre of the green was dominated by a giant oak tree, which dwarfed the telephone box that stood by the side of the path and under it's branches. He could clearly see into the living room of one of the houses, it's curtains were open and the reflection of a television flickered around the room, but there was no sign of anyone. Choosing his moment he stepped over the old stile while scanning the surroundings as he did so. He then walked over towards the green and was pleased to see the light inside the phone box thankfully still wasn't working. Perfect, they hadn't replaced the bulb he had taken out two evenings earlier. On entering he was nearly overcome by bleach fumes that filled his nostrils, causing him to cough as they caught his throat. 'God that makes a change,' he thought. He looked around to satisfy himself that all was still clear before his thoughts quickly turned again to the task in hand. He took the Dictaphone from his inside pocket and turned it on, then looked around again. The area around the green was still. He nervously dialled Harker's number and the phone rang several times before he heard a woman's voice. He pressed the play button and Dean's guttural sounding tones played out its terrifying message. He couldn't hear any response as the track played on, but he remembered to himself, when Dean was making the recording, how he had then thought it sounded like the ripper tape from the seventies. He listened hard for any response as the tape came to abrupt end. Pressing the stop button, his ear was now on the receiver and all he could hear was the desired effect, a woman screaming and a second person repeating, 'Who is it Ester? Who is it?'

Tony put the receiver down glanced outside before placing the Dictaphone back into his pocket. He then left the call box, quickly walking back across the green, over the stile, and across the field to the parked van. He was constantly checking that the coast was clear, and he wasted no time in driving off quickly, relieved to have the fourth stage of the plan in operation.

*

At the Crick canal tunnel, Wallace was talking to his DS Terry. "Jack, a couple of the dive team will be coming over to recover the body, so we may get some idea who this fellow is."

"I hope so guv, as it's certainly got me puzzled."

"Don't worry Jack, I'm sure something will turn up soon."

Just then Wallace's phone rang, it was Jane Monroe. "Sir, we have just received an anonymous phone call stating Mr Harker is being held for ransom."

"Well I can't say I'm surprised Jane, how is Mrs Harker taking it?"

"I would say sir, slightly relieved to know that her husband's alive, but at the same time terrified what they might do to him."

"Jane, would you tell Mrs Harker I will be over in 30 minutes or so?"

"One more thing sir, Ester Bernard answered the call and she is sure it was a taped message."

Wallace turned to his DS saying, "That explains a few things Jack. Seems Harker has been kidnapped after all."

"Smithy was right all along, no bugger had fallen in the cut at Kegworth."

"Certainly looks that way."

"He'll want his old job back again now, guv?"

"I have enough trouble with you Jack, let alone Smithy. Anyway Andy Flower should be told right away. Can you get Atwood to call him on his radio, there's no point putting his men in any further danger, get the search completely called off."

*

The trip back through the Northamptonshire countryside had been uneventful until Tony was about to cross over the causeway at Richford Water. He hadn't seen one vehicle up to then and he had been pleased how well the evening was going, but no sooner than the thought had entered his mind, he spotted car lights at the far side of the causeway. 'Nothing to worry about Tony,' he told himself, they were only waiting for him to go past before making their exit from the reservoir car park, which was a popular place for courting couples. He stayed calm until he saw the unmistakable silhouette of a police car, its roof lights giving it away instantly. Tony drove by keeping his eyes firmly focussed on the road in front of him, and prayed the patrol car would turn in the opposite direction. It seemed not to move as he looked back in his rear view mirrors, but deep down he knew his luck this night was probably about to change. Sure enough he was right, as the police car pulled out and was now trailing him some quarter of a mile away.

Tony glanced in the Transit's mirrors once again and the patrol car was now gaining on him. He resisted the temptation to go any faster, instead he kept to a steady 50, and drove as progressively as his emotions would allow. Would his nerve hold out as he sensed they were now fewer than 100 metres or so behind the old Transit? He didn't dare to steal a second look, but just kept looking forward as he went by the Dutch barns on the right-hand side, knowing he was close now to Brigham village. Several roads crossed each other at the village so there was a good chance they would turn off at some point. He continued into the village, passing the fire station before signalling in good time to turn left onto the main road. The police car had so far mimicked his every move and he was now getting more worried by the minute wondering whether to alter his route or just carry on. There was little time to think as he approached the next junction and turned his van into Carton Road. The police car followed only now even closer. He drove on passing a small complex of shops and noticed a gang of youths hanging around outside the local supermarket. He was becoming more uneasy with the situation and sweat poured uncontrollably down his face, even though it was so cold outside, and still he didn't dare to look back. At the end of the road he turned his head slightly and the police car had disappeared. The relief was instantaneous as he wiped his brow and hit the accelerator.

Just 15 minutes later he was entering Marlstone village and turning into a back lane. At this point Tony turned off the van lights once more, and drove slowly down the lane until he reached the farm track which lead to Nobottle Wood Cottage. All seemed quiet as he drove the van into the garage, and he was truly relieved to pull down the up and over garage door. He took a last breath of fresh air to steady his nerves before going inside the cottage.

Suzy was waiting anxiously in the kitchen when Tony walked in the back doorway.

"Is everything Okay Suzy?" Tony asked, as he looked up at the TV monitor.

"I suppose so," she replied in the manner of a sulking child.

"What do you mean you suppose so? Have you any idea Suzy how important this is to the both of us?"

"Of course, but I have been sitting here looking at Harker and wondering what the hell has this man done to deserve the abuse he has suffered over the last couple of days."

"For God's sake Suzy, you knew exactly what you were getting into. He's not some innocent nobody you know, he's the bastard who has ripped off so many people. Along with that fancy wife of his, they have conned so many decent people, even their own friends, in some cases consistently pressurising people to invest in one or other of his so called guaranteed investments. Instead of making money, they lost people, like your old boss Harry Bernard and others, hundreds of thousands of pounds."

"I know, you have told me this before Tony, but wasn't that surely their fault for trusting him?"

"That's the whole point. He befriended people he hadn't seen for years, old school friends and others he had worked with, before he became the big shot lawyer at Cockburns. Now, of course, he is the owner after marrying Lynda Cockburn. I tell you Suzy, don't you spare a thought for him. He is a very calculating person who would walk over his own mother to get his own way and I should know." Tony sat down and was now looking across the small kitchen table at Suzy. "If you only knew how that bastard and his rich friends bullied me, and anyone else they considered weak or beneath them, when we were at boarding school together. I was lucky enough to have won a scholarship, so I, and couple of other boys in my situation, was treated with contempt and utter depravity. Sometimes they would drag us out of the junior dormitory in the middle of the night, so the likes of Harker and his cronies could ridicule us in an immoral way. Now you know why I was so eager to put him in his place." She reached out and placed her hand on Tony's squeezing it affectionately.

"Tony what did they do to you, please tell me?"

"I can't tell you Suzy, but perhaps the mental scars from this ordeal will live with him, in the same way as I have had to bear the humiliating memoires of my school days for all these years."

*

When DI Wallace arrived at Sedgwick House he was let in by Jane Munroe and before they went through to see Mrs Harker she filled Wallace in regarding the phone call.

"Jane, can you tell me who it was who answered the call?"

"Mrs Bernard sir, but when Mrs Harker saw her friend so desperately upset she rushed over and took the receiver out of her hand. She started shouting, "Who is this?" understandably very upset, so much so we had to give her a sedative afterwards to try to calm her down. They both described the caller as having a chilling guttural sounding voice."

"Did you manage to hear anything yourself?"

"I am afraid not sir and, unfortunately, there isn't a recording mode on the telephone."

"Okay Jane. Do you think Mrs Harker would be up to speaking to me now?"

"Yes sir, I am sure she would after having had to deal with the possibility that her husband had probably drowned. Now this call, if of course it isn't a hoax, has given her hope."

Wallace entered the lounge to find Mrs Harker and her friend Ester sitting close to each other on the Chesterfield sofa in front of a roaring log fire. They both appeared to be visibly shaken. Mrs Harker stood first, although she gripped onto Ester's hand.

"Good evening ladies, I am sorry to have to ask, but it is important that I talk to you about the phone call you received earlier this evening."

"That's quite all right inspector. We both understand. What would you like to know?" She made herself comfortable again on the sofa next to Ester.

"Thank you Mrs Harker. I need you both to remember everything that was said to you during this telephone call. If it makes it easier you could write it down for me perhaps?"

Mrs Bernard interjected, "Inspector Wallace I can remember quite clearly every word that dreadful person spoke."

Lynda sat back and listened to her friend telling the officer all about the call and how she thought it had been a tape recording they had been listening to. Wallace intervened again.

"What brings you to that conclusion Mrs Bernard?"

"Because inspector, when I answered the call there was a distinct delay, and then an obvious click, before anyone spoke."

"Mrs Harker, are you of the same opinion as Mrs Bernard? Did this sound like a taped message to you?" She hesitated before speaking.

"I don't know inspector, but when I saw that Ester was becoming distressed I went over to see who she was speaking to. At that point I took the receiver off her, only to hear a deep rasping sounding voice threatening me by my name. This despicable person also warned that if the police were involved in any way my husband would never be seen again."

She broke down once again and told the inspector how she had lived for two days, going out of her mind with worry, that she had lost Jonathan. Now there was a chance that he was still alive.

"Mrs Harker I have to tell you that in all probability your husband has been kidnapped and this call is, I should say, genuine. I am not basing this just on the call, but with other evidence we have uncovered today, that I am afraid I can't go into at this moment. Is there any reason Mrs Harker, that you know of, why anyone would want to harm your husband and take him hostage?" She looked up at the inspector as if she was about to reply, but could only motion no with a shake of her head.

"Please Mrs Harker, this is very important, I need to know for your husband's sake?"

Mrs Bernard asked, "Do we really have to do this now inspector surely you can see how upsetting this is for Lynda?"

"It's all right Ester, I will be fine to carry on."

"Well if you are sure my dear."

"Inspector Wallace, my husband is a good man and very well respected. I can't believe anyone would want to harm him."

"I understand that madam, but there is always a motive. Forgive me for asking you so many questions at such a distressing time, but the more information we have the sooner we can resolve this situation."

She replied in a somewhat disconsolate voice, "All I can think inspector, there are numerous people who know we are a very wealthy family and there are also a handful of investors who lost out when Jonathan's investment company failed. Of course, that wasn't Jonathan's fault, but the result of the stock market crash last year."

"Mrs Harker, I won't trouble you any further this evening but if you should think of anything further madam, please let Jane know and she will inform me. I will say goodnight Mrs Harker, Mrs Bernard." Wallace left with one thought on his mind. There were a handful of investors who lost their money, so at least he had something to ponder on. He arrived back at the crime scene to find Jack Terry talking to Andy Flower.

"Everything okay here Jack, Andy?"

"Yes guv. We have just pulled the victim out of the canal and, my God, he's a big bloke. Must weigh 18 stone or more, wouldn't you say Andy?"

"Sounds about right sir."

"So what have forensics come up with Jack?"

"Nothing too much, apart from Doctor Lamont's theory. He seems to think the cause of death was probably some sort of a crushing incident and the victim was more than likely dead before he was put into the water. Obviously there is nothing too definite until they get him back to the lab."

"You call that nothing Jack?"

Wallace thanked Andy for his help and told him to pass on his thanks to the dive team. At the same time he asked him to stand down on the operation back at Kegworth Wharf. The inspector then turned and asked Jack to follow him. They climbed up the bank to where the trail of blood began; the whole area now was flooded in light powered by the forensics team's generator.

"Jack this is certainly a strange one, don't you think?"

"Well, first we have a missing persons call. Then it looked as if someone had fallen into the canal. Then we find a body the next day 10 miles from the original scene, weighted down in the canal by a tool box. Yeah, I reckon you could call that strange guv."

"At least Jack, the last two days of twists and turns finally falls into some sort of order. What, with this menacing call to the Harker's place claiming they have kidnapped her husband, and if that wasn't enough, forensics tell us this chap may have been killed in some sort of crushing incident." Wallace crouched down and was now focussing his attention onto the gate post where the forensics team thought the victim had died.

"I can tell you, Jack, that either this was a plan to confuse us again or we are dealing with a bunch of bloody amateurs, just take a look at these tyre marks."

"They look to me as if a vehicle has entered the field through this gate, before turning at some point and finishing up back out onto the road guv."

"Have you been down the track to see where it goes to Jack?"

"I have and there is some sort of water or sewage treatment works operated by Anglia Water Authority."

"Get onto them and find out the last time they visited the site?"

"Already done that. It was last evening around 8:00pm, the pumps have to be checked every day apparently."

"On the ball tonight Jack, aren't you? Best get someone to interview the operative as soon as possible?"

"I spoke to the manager earlier and the driver is due to arrive here in an hour's time. Chap's name is Lesley Parson."

"When he arrives find out all you can, because Jack, he's probably our best bet to finding out what the bloody hell's happened here."

*

Tony was leaning back in his chair looking up at the monitor as Harker turned on the bed, grimacing with the pain he was still feeling. He struggled to sit up and stared up at the camera. His face was now looking slightly less bruised, Tony thought. Jonathan sensed there was someone watching him as he stood and limped over towards the table to take a sip from the water bottle. He had no idea of what time of day or night it was, only having the glare from the fluorescent light above him which was constantly on in a torturous manner. He stared up at the monitor to let them know they hadn't broken his spirit quite yet, then he sat back down on his bed again and continued to eyeball the camera. He was wondering who the hell was watching him and were these thugs trying to arrange a ransom of some kind for him.

He knew he wouldn't have been in this situation if his abductors hadn't have known that his wife Lynda was an extremely wealthy woman. He imagined they would ask for a substantial amount, and he could only pray that she was coping with these horrific circumstances and that there was someone else at home with her apart from Natasha. Suzy was fast asleep when Tony climbed into the sleeping bag next to her. He gently tapped her on the shoulder and she asked begrudgingly, "What's wrong Tony?"

"Nothing is wrong Suzy, only it is your turn to watch Harker."

"No it can't be already, I only just lay down, for pity's sake."

"Come on now Suzy its one o'clock, and make sure you stay awake. Remember this is hopefully the day when our lives change for the better, so come on please."

"I hope you're right Tony. I never want to go through anything like this again."

"Look, once Ted plays the second tape to them later today, Lynda Harker will have to come up with the jewellery and the cash, the deadline is set for eight o'clock this evening."

"What if she decides not to?"

"She will, believe me. The tape Dean made even frightens the likes of me, let alone Harker's wife."

"Surely after you played the first tape, the police will be listening in to the call?"

"They'll be there all right, but we have planned for that. Don't you worry we are going to make bloody fools out of the lot of them."

*

DS Terry was sitting in Lesley Parson's Water Authority Land Rover taking a statement from the bemused operative.

"So Mr Parson, you arrived here at around 8:00pm last evening, did you notice anything unusual?"

"Well when I drove along the lane, as I do every night of the week, apart from Sundays that is, I noticed there was a van parked in our gateway. But it's not the first time I have had to ask a courting couple to move. I pulled up with my indicator on showing them I intended to turn left into the gateway, but they never moved."

"So what did you do then sir?"

"It was a very cold dark old night sergeant and I was more than a little nervous about asking them to move, but at the same time I had no choice. I had to get out of the Land Rover and politely ask if they wouldn't mind moving their van and, as I thought, they looked like a courting couple all right."

"So did they drive off as you asked?"

"Yes they were okay about moving."

"Would you say there was anything unusual about them sir?"

"Not really, although I remember the fellow did speak quite posh, but that was all."

"Could you describe the vehicle for me, Mr Parson?"

"It reminded me of an old high-top mail van but, like I said, it was a very dark old night, so I couldn't be too sure sergeant."

"Mail van you say, so what did you do next Mr Parson?"

"After they pulled away I opened the gate and drove down to the pumping station and checked everything out, which usually takes me about 18 to 20 minutes."

"What did you do after that, sir?"

"I drove back up the track and over the canal tunnel, before stopping in my usual place to have a cup of coffee from my flask."

"You didn't happen to notice a barge moored up to the towpath just outside the tunnel did you sir?"

"As a matter of fact, it was the first thing I noticed sergeant. I was a little surprised by that I must admit."

"Was there any activity at all around the vessel, or lights, that sort of thing?"

"Well, thinking about it, when I sat drinking my coffee I thought I saw something move on the bank, so I kept looking every minute or so, before realising it was probably just a bush blowing in the breeze and thinking that my eyes were probably deceiving me."

"Something moving on the bank, and that is all you saw Mr Parson?"

"Like I said sergeant, it was a dark old night."

"So then you drove back out of the gate, did you sir?"

"That's right. I drove through the open gateway, stopped the truck, and jumped out to close and padlock the gate. I don't mind telling you sergeant, I am always a bit nervous out there on my own, and the sooner I get back into my old truck and get away from there the better."

"Mr Parson, did you have a problem driving your truck away from the gate last night, only I see the ground has several deep ruts around the gateway?"

"Well, I usually have to rock the old girl backwards and forwards before I get away. I know she's a four-wheeled-drive vehicle, but it's always been a problem to find the right gear. I have booked the old girl off the road on several occasions, but they still can't seem to fix the problem. I have been known to hit the gatepost before now."

"Mr Parson, now I want you to think very carefully about your next answer. Can you remember hitting the gatepost last night?"

"What's this all about sergeant, it's not against the law to hit your company's gatepost is it?"

"Sir, just answer the question please."

"Well I certainly had to rock her backwards and forwards a couple of times, and come to think about it, yes I reckon I did. But like I say, I just want to get away. It's not like this old truck hasn't got a few dents on her, besides, this is always my last job of the night so I am always ready to get back to the depot and clock-off."

"Is this the same vehicle as you used last night Mr Parson?"

"Yes, I only use this old girl."

"Would you wait here for a moment a sir?"

The DS alighted the Land Rover and walked around to the rear. He looked closely at all the dents along the tailgate with his flashlight and there were certainly plenty of them as you would expect on a works vehicle of this age. Jack was now paying particular attention to the offside corner pillar, and there he found definite signs of what he was sure were blood stains, about three quarters of the way up the pillar. Also the light lens was cracked and the metal mesh guard protecting it was pushed hard against the broken glass. He went back to the driver's side and asked Parson to step out. As he climbed out Terry smelled the definite signs of alcohol on his breath.

"Have you been drinking this evening, sir?"

Parson looked taken back by the sergeant's question, then he sheepishly replied, "Just a pint of beer earlier this evening sergeant, that's all."

"Are you in the habit of drinking and driving sir, and had you been drinking last night before you arrived here?"

"Look sergeant, I only had a pint at the Navigator pub, that's all." Terry told him that his vehicle was going to be taken back to Leicester police station for forensic tests.

"Could you tell me for what reason sergeant, I'm sure I haven't done anything wrong?"

"I have got reason to believe sir, your vehicle was involved in an incident here last night."

"An incident, what do mean?" Parson worryingly stared at the DS waiting for an answer.

"We are not quite sure yet, but I am afraid I will have to ask you to accompany me to the station for further questioning. Before I do I must ask constable Atwood to give you a breathalyser test." Parson looked puzzled and was wondering what the hell he had done as they walked over to DS Terry's car where Atwood was waiting.

*

After a restless couple of hours, Tony was up early and talking on the phone to Ted.

"Tony is everything going to plan now, that's apart from your friend Dean fucking up."

"You listen to me Ted?" Tony's voice sounded incensed by Ted's quip. "Ted, let us get this straight, you haven't done any of the dirty work and I know this wasn't what we had planned, but I am the one who's taking all the risks here. Just make sure you get that tape played on time and don't you fuck up yourself."

"Okay Tony, calm down and take it easy. I know this a stressful situation, it is for all of us, but don't you worry about my side of this. The tape will be played as we agreed at 2:00pm."

Tony asked, "Are you sure Harker's bank account has that amount of cash available?"

"Yes Tony, and the jewellery. As I told you, the jewellery is in a safety deposit box at her local high street bank and only Lynda Harker has a key, which she keeps in a safe at Sedgwick House."

"How can you be so sure Ted?"

"Tony you may think I haven't contributed too much over the last few days, but someone had to organise this operation of ours and believe me when I tell you it's there - it's there all right."

"Let us just hope we can stay one step ahead of the law Ted?"

"We will, don't you worry about that. From two o'clock on, our plan must, and will, run like a military operation, so unless you have anything else on your mind, we won't speak again until it's completed. Let us synchronise our watches, it's now 7:30am exactly. One more thing, make sure your girl friend knows what she has to do."

"Ted you don't have to worry on that score. Suzy won't let us down, I can assure you of that."

CHAPTER ELEVEN

Doctor Armin was talking to DI Wallace on the telephone. He told him that the forensic tests on the body, found in the canal, had proved that crushing was indeed the cause of his death, and that the victim's blood was type AB Negative, one of the groups found on the black leather glove at Kegworth Wharf.

"Thanks for clarifying that so quickly doctor."

Wallace turned to Jack Terry, "As we thought Jack, Parson's vehicle was the culprit for our friend from the canal's demise. They still have no idea who the poor sod we fished out of the canal is, until they check his finger prints." Wallace sat back in his office chair looking out of the large steel framed window, while Terry sat on the corner of his desk finishing off the last of yesterdays lunch box, a curled up cheese sandwich.

"Jack this is a complete mess. We now have a body in the mortuary and, after taking a closer look at him, also by the blood type, it certainly isn't Harker. This chap Parson has somehow got himself, more than likely innocently, caught up in some sort of balls up scenario without even knowing about it. It reads like a bloody farce."

"Well guv, its true Parson doesn't seem to remember much about last evening, apart from the van parked in the Water Authority gateway and some posh bloke who was polite enough to move for him. Then there is his description of the vehicle, which he thinks may have been an old high-top mail van."

"So, from that description Jack, we would have to assume it to be red in colour then." Jack chuckled.

"Well yes, I reckon your right there, besides that he's not too sure what the object he spotted on the canal bank was."

"Then after Parson pulled away from the gate in some sort of a hurry, at this point our friend we pulled out of the canal, just happened to be walking behind him."

"All I can think is maybe the victim thought that Parson had seen something when he was looking down towards the barge, while he was taking his break. Maybe the big fellow in the morgue was waiting for him by the gateway to harm the driver in some way, before somehow managing to get himself trapped between Parson's Land Rover and the gate post."

"Surely if that was the case Jack, you would have thought he would have realised when his vehicle ran back that he had hit something?"

"Well, after interviewing him again, he has admitted to drinking a couple of pints that evening. Although he was just under the limit by the time Atwood breathalysed him last night, but in answer to your question guv, yes, I think that it is possible he didn't realise. I am pretty sure he's not involved in anyway."

"Well I tend to agree with you, so ask the desk sergeant to tell him he can go for now, but we may have to speak to him again."

"Come on, let's take an early lunch before we go over to Sedgwick House."

"Okay, Peacock is it?"

"Sounds good to me, give them a call and order two full English and tell them to have it ready in 15 minutes."

"I reckon we'll just call it a late breakfast then guv?"

*

Lynda and Ester were standing in the kitchen drinking coffee, as they peered out of the window. Lynda looked dreadful. Her eyes were sore and puffy but, on the other hand, Ester looked a little better, yet she was still fretting and wondering what would happen when the phone call came at two o'clock. The police were there in some strength setting up their equipment and hoping to trace the call. Jane Monroe was keeping both ladies up to date as to what was going on. She had had a talk with Lynda telling her she would have to be strong and listen carefully to the message the kidnappers gave, and to remain as calm as she possibly could, especially under the dreadful predicament she had to face.

Wallace and Terry both arrived at 1:00pm so as to check everything was set up, and to also run through just what might happen later. The two officers walked into the kitchen. Jack bent down to stroke Jet's head but he hardly moved and still looked understandably distressed. Wallace asked if he could speak to Mrs Harker continuing to say, "Mrs Harker, obviously they will ask for some sort of ransom, and you will have to agree at this point to their demands. We will have to keep them thinking they are in control of the situation, so let's just see what their demands are then take it from there."

She never spoke but nodded her head in agreement. Wallace left them in the kitchen and went to find the technicians who were setting up their equipment in the drawing room.

This was the first time Wallace had found time to look around Sedgwick House, and it wasn't until then he realised just how magnificent a building it was. He entered the huge drawing room, where three large dark red leather Chesterfield sofas imposingly stood on a striking pale green Turkish rug. It reminded Wallace of some London Gentlemens' Club he had once visited in the course of his duty many years before. The paintings that hung on the walls looked to have been painted in the style of the grand masters, giving the room an air of true grandeur, and along with the high ceilings and ornate cornices, were finished off with a large over-elaborate plaster ceiling rose. A dazzling crystal chandelier hung to form the centrepiece of this superb room; surely he thought these spectacular works of art must have been original to the house and had been there since the late 1800s. He was brought back from his pensiveness by Jack Terry calling him.

"Sir, I have spoken to the surrounding local forces and they are on standby should they be needed." Jack never referred to his superior in front of civilian company as guv, even though they had been friends and colleagues for the best part of 20 years and there wasn't much they didn't know about each other, but DS Terry had the greatest respect for his boss as a friend and a colleague, knowing just what a good copper he still was.

At ten minutes to two they all stood in the drawing room anxiously waiting for the call. Lynda was dreading the very thought of hearing again the terrible menacing voice. Her friend Ester stood close by, her arm placed firmly around Lynda's shoulders. Wallace and Terry were both standing by the small three-legged table where the 30s style black Bakelite telephone stood. Both officers had been given headphones by Gordon

Townsend, the sound technician, who sat down alongside the table with his equipment in front of him, hoping to trace wherever the call was going to be coming in from.

You could have heard a pin drop as everyone waited in anticipation for the telephone to ring out, apart from Natasha who stood looking out of the window, her mind seemingly elsewhere. At two o'clock right on time the phone rang startling Lynda and Ester. Lynda had been told to leave it to ring, at least three times, before lifting the receiver. Nervously she answered with hello. Instantly they heard the click of a recording machine, and they all listened intently as the disturbing guttural voice threateningly spoke out.

"We know that the police are there with you listening to this message, but let me tell you Mrs fucking Harker if we see any sign of the old bill, we won't hesitate in slitting you're your old man's throat the minute the filth turn up. You will receive another call in fifteen minutes." Then the now familiar click was followed by silence once again. Lynda was sobbing uncontrollably as she returned the receiver to its station. Jane Monroe placed her hand on Lynda's shoulder and walked back over to the sofa with her, followed by Ester who sat down next to her friend, offering her some words of comfort.

"Did you get anything lad?" Wallace asked Gordon the technician.

"Well I got the area sir, North London, but it's not all bad news though. If they are only moving 15 minutes down the road, I will stand a much better chance the next time they call."

"Let us all hope you're right."

Ted drove the six miles to the next prearranged call box. He had checked both phone boxes several times making sure there were no CCTV cameras in the areas, and that they were positioned in quiet side streets, but with close proximity to the main north circular ring road. He parked his car a good 200 metres away in an adjoining street, and well out of sight of the call box. Rain had just begun to fall as he made his way across the road and around to the graffiti sprayed call box. At 2:15pm he stood inside ready to play Dean's frightening message. The rain was falling heavily now, causing the call box windows to steam up. He took the recorder from his pocket, placing it down in front of him, then checked his watch. It was almost time, almost 2:30pm, and with his gloved hand he lifted the receiver, placed five pound coins in the slot and dialled the number. This time Wallace lifted the receiver and handed the phone over to Mrs Harker, who answered again with, "Hello." Her voice barely audible, she then waited for the click and once more she had to endure the malicious sounding voice.

"LISTEN LADY TO WHAT I AM ABOUT TO TELL YOU, AND CARRY OUT THESE INSTRUCTIONS TO THE LETTER IF YOU WANT TO SEE YOUR OLD MAN AGAIN. YOU WILL GO TO YOUR BANK THIS AFTERNOON AT THREE THIRTY WHERE AN APPOINTMENT HAS BEEN MADE FOR YOU. TELL THE MANAGER YOU WANT TO WITHDRAW ONE MILLION EUROS FROM YOUR JOINT ACCOUNT IN USED FIVE HUNDRED EURO NOTES. ALSO YOU WILL TAKE YOUR SAFEY DEPOSIT BOX KEY WITH YOU AND BRING BACK THE CONTENTS OF THE BOX, YOU KNOW WHAT I AM TALKING ABOUT. THE BANK IS EXPECTING YOU, SO YOU HAVE NO EXCUSES. REMEMBER WHAT WILL HAPPEN TO YOUR HUSBAND IF YOU DONT CARRY OUT OUR DEMANDS. ON YOUR WAY TO THE BANK STOP OFF AT KEGWORTH GARAGE, THERE IS A LETTER THERE FOR YOU, AND THIS WILL TELL YOU WHAT YOU MUST DO FOR THE SAFE RETURN OF YOUR HUSBAND. DON'T FORGET WE WILL BE WATCHING YOUR EVERY MOVE SO YOU BETTER NOT FUCK UP LADY."

DI Wallace looked once more at the technician.

"Got it sir the Met should have a car there shortly."

"I am afraid that they will probably be long gone by then. Never mind, it's not your fault. I'm sure you tried your best."

He turned around to speak to Mrs Harker, who had returned

to the sofa. She looked dreadful and the terrible ordeal was certainly taking its toll on her. Wallace sat down beside her.

"Please Mrs Harker, I know this has been a terrible shock to you having to listen to that unpleasant tape but, if you wouldn't mind, I need to clarify a couple of things. They mentioned your bank and they seemed to know an awful lot about your private banking. If you don't mind me saying, is there any way you can think of how this information could be known to them?"

She thought they must have harmed Jonathan in some way to have known of their account details, and she knew the police officer was thinking the same way, but she answered, "No I am afraid I don't inspector."

Then she turned to her friend Ester for comfort as Ester interrupted the conversation, "Please inspector, could you give Lynda a few moments. I am sure you must realise just how upsetting this is for her?"

"But of course madam, we will leave you both alone for a while, but I must make you aware that time is of the essence." Wallace and Terry walked outside into the garden.

"Is it alright if I have a fag, guv?" Wallace looked at his colleague in his normal disapproving way and replied, "Yes if you must, Jack."

"What the hell is going on here? This once sleepy backwater now resembles some sort of Chicago nightmare scenario, but there is one sure thing, these villains certainly aren't from around here?"

"Well guv let's face it whoever is holding Harker must have forced the information out of him regarding his bank account details, then, of course, there's the chilling accent. East End of London I reckon and if his voice is anything to go by, he sounds a right nasty piece of work."

"Jack, if I was trying to put a face to that bloody awful tone, it would be our old friend from the canal, seems to match him perfectly, don't you think?"

"You could be right about that, with respect he is an ugly sod isn't he."

"However, what if they didn't have to force the information out of him Jack, perhaps they had someone on the inside. Maybe even at the bank itself, but there's one thing for sure this certainly isn't some random snatch. I should think they have been planning this abduction for some time, since they knew Harker walked his dog every morning and they actually knew the details of, not only the Harker's bank accounts and this private safety deposit box, but more importantly I expect they know what it contains."

"Come on I think we need to speak to Lynda Harker again?" Both officers entered the room to find Lynda Harker still sitting on the sofa, with Ester by her side.

"Could we please speak to you in private Mrs Harker, if you wouldn't mind?" Lynda turned to her friend.

"Would you be so kind as to leave us for a moment dear?"

"If you're sure you will be all right darling, I will go and make tea for us all."

"Ester, that would be very kind of you."

"Mrs Harker I am sorry, but I must ask you some personal questions regarding the safety deposit box your husband's abductors mentioned?"

"What would you like to know inspector?"

"I know this will seem a strange question madam, but obviously there is only you and your husband who know of the contents of this box."

She looked up at him somewhat surprised by his question, and turned her head towards the window before answering Wallace, "Well actually inspector, Jonathan doesn't know."

She wiped a tear away with her handkerchief while Wallace and Terry looked at each other trying not to show their feelings. She carried on, "The safety deposit box or, more importantly, the key was left to me in my late father's will. It contains a very valuable piece of jewellery which has been handed down through several generations of our family."

"Excuse me for saying Mrs Harker, but isn't that slightly unusual to keep the contents of this safety deposit box a complete secret from your husband?"

"It may seem strange to you Inspector Wallace, but there has been a well kept family tradition to ensure the heir to the key, and of course the contents of the box, must not divulge its secrets to their partner until they have been married for at least 12 years and only then if the heir decides to. This inspector, is thought to have been the duration that real trust could be established with one's spouse according to my ancestors. As much as I love my husband, I saw no reason to change such a long standing ritual and the conditions of the will."

Wallace coughed nervously, slightly bemused by what he thought to be her strange explanation. "In that case Mrs Harker, how do you think the people holding your husband would have known of this family heirloom if, as you are telling us, you are the only person who knows of it?" She never replied but turned her head away, blew her nose and waited for the next question.

"So Mrs Harker, you must have been very surprised to hear the demands on the tape?"

"Of course I was surprised inspector, but with all that has been going on over the last few days, it was just one more piece of dreadful news."

"If you don't mind me asking madam, what do you think would be the current value of the jewellery?"

"The last time it was valued for insurance purposes only, they put a figure between four to five million pounds as the approximate value considering its history."

DS Terry couldn't help himself from repeating, "Four to five million pounds, Mrs Harker?" Wallace walked around the back of the sofa before continuing, "That's a tremendously valuable piece of jewellery madam to hold at your local bank?"

"Yes inspector, but in effect its worthless to me as the current heir, since it is my duty to ensure this family heirloom is passed on to the next generation of Cockburns. Well, of course, now it will be the Harker family, in other words our children. Could I further explain that this valuable piece of jewellery enabled my great-grandfather to make his fortune when he arrived in Britain, in fact the only items he arrived with were the clothes he stood up in and our family heirloom?"

After keeping her composure while telling the story, and the awful situation her family had to endure all those years ago, the reality of the demands of these ruthless men who were keeping Jonathan captive came back to her and she broke down once again. DI Wallace sat down in the armchair opposite her, and asked if she was all right to continue, she motioned to him to carry on.

"Mrs Harker, the demands of these kidnappers are quite clear, but I must warn you that it is police policy in a situation such as this to let the kidnappers believe they are going to get their demands met, but in reality we will have officers on the ground surveying the situation at all times."

She looked across at the stern faced smartly dressed inspector saying, "What you must realise Inspector Wallace is my family are so wealthy that 1,000,000 euros is of little consequence. Besides, I would pay any amount of money or valuables to get my husband back. I am sorry, but I don't care about your policy. I am going to go to Kegworth Garage, collect the letter and keep this appointment with my bank manager." With that she stood up with a determined look on her face and Wallace knew there would be no stopping her.

"Mrs Harker, I must insist that for your safety, and that of your husband, we must keep you under close surveillance at all times as we have great expertise in this type of operation."

There was a knock at the door and Ester came back into the room, just as Lynda was getting ready to leave. Ester asked anxiously where she was going. Lynda walked out into the hallway and took her coat from the stand, while ignoring pleas by her friend to leave the situation to the police.

"I must do this myself Ester, so please don't stand in my way." She picked up her car keys from the hall table, opened the front door and then left without saying another word.

DI Wallace was already on the phone, setting up a surveillance operation, as he watched Lynda drive off down the long gravel driveway. He contacted Market Wellen Police Station and had them send two plain clothed officers to her bank in the High Street, telling the desk sergeant to make sure that his officers knew they were only there to observe.

Wallace also arranged for an unmarked police car to follow Mrs Harker's BMW, after she had collected the kidnappers' demands from the garage at Kegworth. Over the next half an hour Wallace was able to bring in 16 other plain clothed officers from bordering county forces.

Jack Terry and Wallace were now waiting on the corner of Market Wellen High Street and the Kings Road, ready to follow Lynda's car, after her forced meeting with the bank manager.

A good 45 minutes after seeing her friend Lynda nervously leave the house and drive off in her Z4 convertible, Ester was still very upset. She sat on the sofa wondering whether to go to the bank or not to find her friend, but then she remembered the strong look of determination on Lynda's face and thought better of it.

*

Natasha was in her bedroom and watched her employer drive off from her window. She lay on her bed trying desperately to put the day's awful events to the back of her mind, and her thoughts returned to happier times when she was far away with the Bromleys in South Africa. She remembered in particular the night when Freddy Bromley had invited his friend Harry over for dinner, and how she had fallen asleep on the balcony after showering, only to wake and find the large fluffy bath sheet that once covered her modesty, lying beside her. It felt so wonderful as the warm sea breeze had wafted over her naked body, bringing her senses in tune with the surroundings, and the perfumed air from the jasmine was just magnificent. She had stretched out almost catlike, feeling so warm and sensual, even a little naughty, but God it had felt so good to be alive.

She was startled to hear the patio door open from the dining room down below her, she lay motionless not daring to move even or to cover herself, and all she could do was look up at the night sky and hold her breath knowing someone was down below her only a few metres away. Then the stillness of the moment was broken by the gentle sound of water being parted as if a fish had risen from some tranquil lake. Quietly she sat up trying to see over the top of the clematis bound balcony railing, it was then she caught sight of him.

Natasha had known that Fredric Bromley was a man who looked after himself. In fact, for someone in their late 40s he had a fine muscular body. She had thought this from the first time she had seen him playing tennis with his wife. She watched him swim effortlessly to the far end of the pool, feeling guilty that she was invading his privacy, but finding it hard to take her gaze off him. She then caught her breath as he swam beside one of the underwater pool lights when she realised he was swimming completely naked. His tanned body glistering as he cut through the illuminated clear blue water as she looked on unable to take her eyes away from this serene scene.

Guilt got the better of her again and she tried to avert her gaze as he rolled over onto his back, effortlessly pushing himself along with his powerful thighs. She had already surprised herself by not turning away, and now she felt genuine pleasure gazing down at this handsome man, his muscular chest standing high above the waterline while his firm torso showed off a tight muscular midriff. She found herself filling with excitement, but also knew she must move back into the bedroom before he sensed she was there. Then, stealing one more glance before moving away from the balcony railing, she quietly made her way back towards the bedroom doors. Her heart skipped a beat when the towel she was dragging behind her caught on the corner of the sunbed causing it to make a scraping sound which reverberated around the garden. She hesitated, holding her breath, and was horrified to hear Bromley call out in his gentle well spoken voice. "Hello is there someone there?" Then he asked again, "Hello is that you Natasha?" Guilt ridden with embarrassment she dared not answer him, but after his third time of asking, she hesitated again, but knew she had no escape and replied nervously, "Yes Mr Bromley, can I help you."

"Where are you Natasha?" She walked over to the balcony railings, after wrapping the white bath sheet tightly around her naked body, and stood there with one hand on the railing while the other held the towel, hardly daring to look down. When she eventually did he was standing close to the pool wall.

"Sorry Natasha if I woke you, but I just had to have a swim on this wonderful evening. I suppose, like you, I was having trouble sleeping."

"Actually I fell asleep on the balcony Mr Bromley, so I am sorry if I interrupted your swim."

"I don't suppose you fancy a swim yourself do you Natasha, I could do with some company?" She couldn't quite believe what she was hearing and all the time she was picturing him standing there naked, his modesty only hidden by the pool wall. 'This really can't be happening,' she thought to herself, but then to her own amazement the words that left her lips were.

"Well if you put it like that Mr Bromley, it is such a very warm evening after all, and a swim would be very refreshing."

"You're very welcome Natasha. I will fix us a glass of something chilled." What was she doing she thought, as she put her bikini on and threw her dressing grown around her shoulders. When she reached the top of the landing she could hear him in the kitchen and the sound of a bottle being opened. He heard her on the stairs and called out asking if she would like a drink, to which she replied.

"No thank you Mr Bromley, not at the moment,"

"Natasha why not call me Freddy, there is no need for formality." He had asked her once before to call him by his Christian name when his children weren't around.

"Well if you don't mind Mr Bromley, sorry Freddy," she replied. He was now wearing swimming shorts but she thought that he still looked athletic, although his damp body was in complete contrast to his dry white swimming attire which were held up by a blue pull through cord, the two ends untied and loosely hanging down from the waist.

"Come on Natasha let's go outside into that wonderful night air." She followed him across the patio towards the pool, not quite believing what she was doing. He placed the bottle down on the poolside table and she noticed he had brought two glasses with him.

"Are you sure you wouldn't like to join me in a glass of wine before we take our swim Natasha?"

"Well perhaps just one small glass then Freddy." They sat down opposite each other and sipped the wine while making polite conversation. After 10 minutes or so Freddy stood up.

"Come on Natasha," he called out as he ran towards the pool's edge. He dived in, creating only the slightest sign of a ripple on the surface of the water, and soon he was surfacing at the far end of the pool.

"Why don't you join me Natasha?" he called. Reluctantly, she walked across to the crescent shaped steps that led gently down into the clear blue pool, she then elegantly descended the steps and felt the cool water flood around her warm body. Pushing off, she gracefully swam towards the far end of the pool. He was already on his way back down the swimming pool with his eyes firmly fixed on the beautiful creature coming towards him. They almost touched each other as he cut through the water, carrying on to the shallow end where he walked up the steps and back over to the table sitting down again, before asking, "Would you like another glass of wine Natasha?" She was now by the edge of the pool, her chin resting on her slender elbows and looking up at him.

"I really shouldn't Freddy, too much wine doesn't suit me." He laughed out loud before saying, "To be perfectly honest Natasha, it doesn't agree with me either."

He was still displaying amusement as he topped up his glass and then leaned back in his chair, more relaxed than she had ever seen him. "Well if you put it like that, maybe one more glass then, thank you."

Natasha was still finding it very hard to call him by his Christian name, after calling her employer Mr Bromley for so long. He poured her a generous measure, looking on admiringly as she walked up the pool steps, while running her fingers through her long auburn hair. She continued over to the table and sat down opposite him. They talked for a while about Natasha's upbringing in Slovenia, and how she came to England looking for work. He was surprised to learn that she had a degree in medicine, after having trained to become a pharmacist in Ljubljana before she had left Slovenia.

His mood then changed as he began telling her how, after 15 years of owning this beautiful holiday home in Cape Town, they would soon have to put the property up for sale if his wife's company couldn't secure a particular contract over in Dubai. He told her that this was the reason for Jackie's sudden departure back to the UK. This came as a complete shock to Natasha, even more so when he told her that his wife would be seeking a divorce on his return to England. Natasha wondered if their life was really that bad? Yes, she had heard them quarrelling several times, but she hadn't seen anything to suggest there was a more serious problem with their marriage.

As she listened to him talking calmly about the failure of his marriage, she couldn't help but wonder if he was just giving himself an excuse to try to seduce her. His eyes seemed to glint with excited expectation, rather than one of sadness, as he gazed across at her. She soon found herself drinking a second glass of wine and now Freddy was opening another bottle, but any self-reproach she had about lusting after this man's near perfect body earlier that evening soon left her as they both decided to take another swim. He smiled at her as he took hold of her hand, pulling her up and off the chair, then running the short distance to the pool's edge before jumping in together. Natasha was still protesting as they hit the warm water. She surfaced wiping her eyes, ready to lash out in a splashing manner, but all she could do was watch as he swam off. His powerful forearms pulled him through the clear blue water, leaving her in his wake, laughing in a teasing fashion. She watched him turn at the far end of the pool before swimming back towards her, and for a moment she thought he may not have seen her. He twisted onto his back and glided up close, treading water. She watched as he turned his head towards her and smiled.

"Are you enjoying this Natasha?"

"Oh yes Freddy, it's so wonderful." Although the water was tepid, she found herself trembling with anticipation.

"Can I ask you something Natasha?" Was this the moment she had been waiting for, or dreading?

"Yes of course Freddy, what is it?" she said, wondering what he was about to say.

"This is a little embarrassing for me Natasha, but I must ask. Did you see me swimming earlier from your balcony?" Her throat dried because that was the last thing she expected him to say, and she was totally lost for words as she looked away from him. "You see Natasha, I always swim in the nude and I wouldn't have wanted to embarrass or offend you in anyway?"

She thought very carefully about her answer, probably knowing where this was all going to lead to. She hesitated further before saying, "Freddy back home in Slovenia, it was very common for me and my friends to swim without clothes in the beautiful rivers and lakes around my mountain village." Now it was Freddy's turn to be surprised. "So yes, I also enjoy swimming in the nude as you call it."

As she answered him she was recalling his muscular body as he had swam up and down the pool earlier that evening, the thoughts excited her and the feeling she now had deep down in her loins, had been stirred by this man 18 years her senior. There could be no turning back now, the excitement in his steely blue eyes showed that. Whether it was the wine or pure lust didn't seem to matter as it was obvious they both wanted each other. Slipping under the water she came up beside him, but no words came from her lips as she took off her bikini top. discarding it in a provocative manner. Slipping her hands under the water, she took off her bikini panties. Freddy was overwhelmed by this beautiful creature alongside him, her naked form almost touching his, her firm well rounded breasts partially above the water line allowing him so much pleasure. His jaw had now relocated to its normal position as she stared towards him with lustful melting eyes, then asking cheekily, "Perhaps it's your turn now Freddy?"

This surreal moment he had perpetrated for himself, and he couldn't really believe this young woman of such beauty could fall so easily into his arms. It was as if all his dreams had been answered, although he was now no longer in control as she swam away from him towards the pool steps. Surely she wasn't going to step out of the pool in her state of nakedness. His mind raced at the very thought, and under his breath he uttered the words, "Oh my God," as she walked gracefully up the pool steps like some Greek goddess of old, her moist thighs glistering from the orange glow of the terraced lighting. He swallowed hard and found himself trembling, blissfully overwhelmed with pleasure. She walked over to the table and poured herself a glass of wine before turning towards him and seductively lifting the glass to her lips. He glanced up at her, but no words came from his slightly gaping mouth. Placing the glass back down on the table, she crossed the terrace once more and went over to the pool steps, where she sat down on the top step of the gently descending stairway. Her legs crossed, she leaned back with the palms of her hands touching the wet marble tiles. He excitedly slipped his shorts off and swam towards her, looking almost frightened by the power this beautiful woman processed. It was as if he was being drawn in, like a female spider winding its silk around its unsuspecting mate, but he could see she was more than ready for him as she stretched her long legs down over the stairway before bringing them slightly up again. She was in complete control as he came closer and walked up out of the pool towards her, his gaze transfixed on her wonderful naked form, and she could see that his excitement showed.

Freddy bent forward and gently lifted her up into his controlling arms, his wet muscular torso now touching her soft damp skin as he carried her the short distance over to the round rattan sofa, before delicately lying her down onto the soft fabric cushioning. He lay down, gently moving his body closer to hers, until their lips met and she felt him pushing against her warm thighs. Reaching down she carefully took hold of his firmness, wrapping her slender fingers around his manhood, then lightly squeezing as he moaned with pleasure. Eagerly, his hand felt down for her moist area, his breathing now gathering pace as he found the delight he was seeking. He had never felt desire such as this as she guided the firmness of his manhood eagerly inside her. He tenderly kissed the lobe of her ear as his rhythm gathered pace thrusting vigorously against her warm, soft naked body. She murmured sensual pleasures to him as their love making seemingly lasted forever, before reaching their pinnacle in a vocal crescendo still entwined in unrivalled fulfilment. They lay in the still African night air. Natasha was the first to move, he looked up at her and smiled. She in return kissed him tenderly on the lips, before wrapping her dressing gown around her, leaving him to lie alone, spent on the rattan sofa.

She woke around 7:00am with a tremendous headache, still remembering the night of sheer joy as she stood under the shower. She wondered just how she was ever going to face her employer after their night of passion together. The previous morning this man had been to her a totally different person, she had looked up to him and she certainly had no idea that his marriage was in any sort of turmoil. Although, thinking more about it now, she knew that they had had different rooms on occasions, but it never once occurred to her there was any sort of problem with their marriage. She had thought that this must have been down to the fact Jackie Bromley still worked, and needed her own room to concentrate on her business activities. How naive she had been.

She would have to try to carry on as near to normal as she possibly could. She dressed and went along to the childrens' rooms. After checking they were still fast asleep, she went downstairs to prepare breakfast for the family. All was quiet and there was no sign of Freddy.

She walked outside to fill her lungs with the sweet scented morning air before walking across to the swimming pool area. She instantly noticed his shorts floating on the surface of the pool and on the other side lay her bikini top that she had so seductively taken off the night before. Collecting both items with the pool cleaning pole, she quickly took the offending items inside and placed them into the washing machine. It was then she heard him walking down the stairs.

She began to tremble with a nervous uneasiness of what his reaction towards her would be. Would he carry on as before and not mention their night of sheer ecstasy, albeit one fuelled by alcohol, but she had no time to think. She turned away nervously when he walked into the kitchen. He came over to her and her embarrassment soon disappeared as he took her in his arms and kissed her soft warm lips. Moving his head gently away, still gazing into her dark brown eyes, he thanked her for such a wonderful evening. For the next three days they made love on every available occasion and she had fell madly in love with Freddy as he had with her.

*

There was a knock on the bedroom door and Natasha was instantly back from her daydreaming.

"Are you there Natasha darling?" It was Ester.

"Yes Mrs Bernard, I'm just coming," was her reply just before she opened the door.

"Natasha please could you keep me company? I am so worried about Lynda. The poor woman not only has Jonathan on her mind, but now she has to follow the demands of his kidnappers and she has asked the police not to follow her?"

"Mrs Bernard, please try not to worry. I'm sure that the two detectives will discretely stay close by to make sure she doesn't come to any harm."

"I do hope so Natasha," she replied.

"Come along Mrs Bernard. I will make us a pot of tea."

*

Lynda Harker had parked her car behind the bank in Market Wellen High Street and was asking the young woman on the reception desk if Mr Wicks, the manager, was free to see her.

"Oh yes, here we are Mrs Harker. Your appointment is for 3:30." The receptionist looked up at the clock. It was 3:25.

"Would you like to take a seat for a moment Mrs Harker and I will see if Mr Wicks is ready to see you?" She came back asking Lynda if she would like to go through to Wicks' office.

"Good afternoon Mrs Harker. And what can we do for you on this cold winter's afternoon. Please sit down madam?" She pulled the chair up close to Wick's desk and asked him, in a firm calculated but slightly hurried voice, "I would like to draw out a large amount of cash from our joint account Mr Wicks."

She had Wicks full attention. "Yes I see, and how much would you like to withdraw Mrs Harker?" She knew he would be visibly shocked as she said, "One million euros in used 500 euro notes please?" Wicks slumped back in his chair, before saying, "That's an awful lot of money Mrs Harker, and would certainly take some arranging. When would you like to collect it?"

"Today Mr Wicks, I must have the money today," she said resolutely.

"Mrs Harker, I couldn't possibly arrange for that amount of cash in pounds or euros until tomorrow afternoon at the earliest. Would that suit you, madam?"

"No, I must have the money today."

"I am afraid that is impossible Mrs Harker. We do not hold that amount of foreign currency at this branch, in fact not at any branch. The only way you would be able to withdraw that amount in euros would be for you to collect it yourself from Birmingham." She looked agitated. "What time does the Birmingham branch close?" Wicks replied, "Well Mrs Harker, because the bank is located in the city's business centre they remain open until six o'clock."

"Please could you call them and arrange to have the cash waiting for me on my arrival, and don't forget it has to be in used 500 euro notes, but first I need to go down to the vaults to check my safety deposit box."

"Are you sure everything is all right madam only, if you don't mind me saying, you seem to be somewhat anxious?"

"I am fine. Now could you please take me to the vault?"

"Very well madam, if you would like to follow me."

Wicks led her down the dozen or so stone steps to the locked steel gates. He punched in several digits into a security key pad and the gates slowly opened.

"There we are Mrs Harker." She entered the vault and Wicks closed the gates behind her. In front of her there was row on row of brass numbered boxes. She soon found box 375 and placed the key into the lock, turning it to the left. The heavy door opened, she placed her hand inside, and withdrew a black metal box and laid it down on the table in the centre of the chamber. Using the small golden key she kept on her bracelet she undid the tiny lock and lifted up the hinged lid. Inside lay the two velvet pouches that had been handed down by her ancestors, but now they were her responsibility as the rightful heir. One of the pouches was gold in colour, the other being a deep crimson red. Both were tied at one end by a gold pull through cord. Leaving the cords tied, she picked out the gold pouch leaving the crimson pouch inside before she closed the lid. She then locked it and returned the box to the safe. Feeling the contents from the outside of the pouch was enough to ensure her that the family heirloom was still intact.

CHAPTER TWELVE

Jonathan Harker was biding his time knowing he needed to rest to allow his body time to recover. His wounds were healing although they were still pretty sore but he was still very anxious, even though his kidnappers hadn't harmed him since they had transferred him from the barge. Something had changed though. The brutal pig who had kicked and beaten him was obviously not around any more. They had left plenty of food and drink for him when he arrived but that had all gone now, apart from a couple of bottles of drinking water, so it was in his best interest to stay composed and take rest. Surely then they would bring him more food.

Every so often he would look up at the camera monitoring him, knowing they were still watching, and he couldn't help wondering just who the hell was out there. The room was lit by a fluorescent strip light which had been constantly left on with no sign of a switch to relieve its glare. He could only hope that once his kidnappers had received whatever ransom they where after, they would then release him. He knew that Lynda would pay any ransom demands they asked for. His biggest fear was for her safety in case she was made to hand over the ransom herself. He knew just what brutal thugs his abductors were, especially if that bastard who assaulted him was involved with any exchange. As he didn't seem to be around any more, it was more than likely that he would be involved in the ransom switch, if only to frighten.

*

The two officers were discretely following Lynda Harker's car from a safe distance behind. Wallace turned to Jack Terry.

"Looks like she is on her way north Jack?"

"Yes guv, heading for the M6 junction one I should say."

"I hope you fixed that tracking device securely because if that fails, and we lose sight of her car, there's no way we will find where she is heading for."

An hour later the satellite tracking signal had led the officers to 202 New Street, central Birmingham, close to the Bull Ring shopping centre. At the service entrance, parked on double yellow lines, was Lynda's blue convertible. Jack parked on the opposite side of the road and waited patiently for her to return to her car.

Some 15 minutes went by and the inevitable happened when Wallace spotted a traffic warden walking up the street towards Lynda's car. He was talking on his radio and obviously calling for the clamping vehicle to pick up the convertible. Jack was soon out of his car, crossing over the road, to show the warden his warrant card. With his intervention, the warden walked away from the car and was heard to be cancelling the tow truck. Jack had only just returned to his car when Lynda came rushing down the steep granite steps clutching a large black briefcase in one hand and a large bag in the other. She sped off and a few minutes later she was heading back out of the city and was driving south.

The Rover that the two police officers were in was no match for the BMW and several times they lost sight of her car, but all the time DS Terry was busy tracking the faster vehicle and he hoped this would keep them on her trail. Wallace knew from past experience that the ransom handover in most cases takes place within a 20 mile radius of the place the person had first been kidnapped, so he guessed this would be a similar scenario.

"She is heading towards the M6 guv, turning right now and travelling south."

The traffic on the motorway was quite busy but thankfully, due to heavy traffic, fairly slow. They were now able to stay around a quarter of a mile behind the faster car. They knew that Lynda was an intelligent woman, and that she would probably have worked out that they would be pursuing her from a safe distance. She felt lonely and frightened about what she was going to do. Deep down she quietly hoped that someone was watching over her, just as long as they stayed their distance and allowed her to complete the hand-over without putting

Jonathan's life at risk. 'Please God, I hope they haven't harmed him,' were her thoughts.

The motorway matrix sign read M1, A14 - 10 minutes. She had to drive down to the Watford Gap service area on the M1 motorway to read the second part of the instructions that the kidnappers had left for her at Kegworth Garage. On reaching the services she pulled up and into the furthest corner of the large car park. She looked around her and made sure that the car doors were locked before opening the brown envelope again to see her next set of instructions:

DRIVE OUT OF THE SERVICE AREA BY THE EMERGENCY EXIT ROAD, IGNORING ANY NO ENTRY SIGNS, THEN TURN LEFT AND DRIVE 300 METRES TO THE A5 ROAD JUNCTION, TURN LEFT AGAIN AND CONTINUE TO THE LONG BUCKBY JUNCTION, TURN LEFT HERE THEN DRIVE THROUGH LONG BUCKBY VILLAGE UNTIL YOU REACH THE OLD A428 WEST HADDON TO NORTHAMPTON ROAD, TURN RIGHT HERE THEN DRIVE FOR AROUND FIFTEEN MINUTES TO THE JUNCTION JUST BEFORE MARLSTONE VILLAGE, THEN TURN LEFT HERE TOWARDS CHAPEL FRAMPTON. ON REACHING THE MAIN ROAD THE OLD A50, TURN LEFT AND CARRY ON FOR ONE MILE, THERE YOU WILL SEE A LAY-BY ON YOUR LEFT HAND SIDE, STOP HERE AND WAIT UNTIL EIGHT O'CLOCK, BEFORE YOU GET OUT OF YOUR CAR TO GO OVER TO THE RUBBISH BAG STAND. LOOK BEHIND IT'S SUPPORT POST, THERE YOU WILL FIND A PLASTIC BAG STAPLED TO THE POST, THERE ARE FURTHER INSTRUCTIONS FOR YOU TO FOLLOW INSIDE, REMEMBER ANY SIGN OF THE POLICE AND YOU CAN SAY GOODBYE TO YOUR PRECIOUS HUSBAND, ALSO DON'T FORGET WE ARE WATCHING YOUR EVERY MOVE LADY.

One thing at least was in Lynda's favour, she knew this area very well. Her friend Katy had once lived at Chapel Frampton and they used to ride in the area together, but she didn't know this particular lay-by. She set off and drove with some confidence in knowing the route, but her mind was bursting with trepidation. She looked at her watch, it was now 7:20 so she had plenty of time.

Wallace and Jack Terry were following close behind. They had caught sight of her BMW turning left onto the A5, but waited a few seconds before they started pursuing again.

"Guv, it's a pity we never got a chance to open that envelope at Kegworth Garage before she did?"

"I know that only too well Jack. If only we had had more time." Fifteen minutes later the blue convertible was entering Chapel Frampton village. Terry was turning off the A428 at Marlstone; he looked down to view the tracking device.

"Bloody hell guv, there is no signal."

"What the hell do you mean Jack?"

"She has disappeared off the monitor guv,"

"Well what are you waiting for, get your bloody toe down, we must try to catch up with her."

They arrived at the junction of the old A50 at Chapel Frampton village, but there was no sign of the BMW.

"Which way shall I turn guv?" Terry said handing all the responsibility over to his superior.

"I don't know Jack, just go right, and where the hell did you fix that tracking device?"

"Under the rear bumper on the near side guv, the bloody thing must have dropped off down one of these uneven country lanes."

Lynda had turned left onto the Welford Road, only a few minutes before the police officers arrived at the same junction. She was approaching the layby, which looked very uninviting, to say the least, as she warily pulled in. The wind had picked up now and rain was falling heavily as she sat there traumatized by the next move she would have to make. The car headlights were still on illuminating the long desolate layby and there in front of her, no more than a few paces, hung the plastic rubbish bag holder, supported by its wooden post. There were drinks cans and other litter scattered all around the overfilled black refuse sack. Her only thoughts now being, would she have the courage to carry out Jonathan's kidnapper's demands as she waited for eight o'clock to show on the car's digital clock.

The wind speed over the last few minutes had increased sufficiently enough to rock and buffet the canvas hood of the convertible, also the sound of the heavy rain beating on the flimsy hood only made her task even more frightening. She turned the windscreen wipers on and was able to see again along the windswept layby. She looked down and the red flashing light on the car's clock showed eight o-clock.

Opening the door she stepped out of the car, then, pulling her coat up and over her head, she quickly made her way towards the bin. Puddles of water splashed her legs as she ran the few short paces. Feeling around the back of the post, fumbling, she found the plastic covered envelope. Quickly she ran back towards the car and hurriedly climbed in, locking the door immediately after her. She wiped her face and hands and sat there shaking, not only with the cold, but from the whole terrifying experience she found herself in. She convinced herself that there really was someone out there watching her every move.

Wallace and Terry were completely on the wrong track and had pulled over to try to reset the receiver, hoping the device would pick up the satellite signal again.

"For God's sake Jack, Lynda Harker is out there on her own somewhere. We will just have to leave it and search every bloody lane in the area until we find her, so leave that and drive back towards the Framptons."

Lynda had now steadied her nerves sufficiently enough to open the plastic covered envelope and was studying the instructions inside. It read:

DRIVE FORWARD 100 METRES AND TURN RIGHT INTO MERRY TOM LANE, CARRY ON DOWN THE LANE FOR AROUND 500 METRES THEN PARK ON THE RIGHT HAND SIDE IN THE GATEWAY WITH THE RICKETY FIVE BAR GATE. IN FRONT OF YOU IS AN OLD RAMSHACKLE BUILDING SOME 15 METRES FROM THE OTHER SIDE OF THIS

GATE, YOU WILL ALSO SEE A LARGE
GREEN PIPE ENTERING INTO THE SIDE OF
THE WALL. ONCE YOU ARE SURE YOU ARE
IN THE RIGHT PLACE, TURN OFF ALL THE
YOUR LIGHTS AND WAIT FOR YOUR EYES
TO BECOME ACCUSTOMED TO THE DARK,
DON'T FORGET TO BRING THE RANSOM
WITH YOU WHEN YOU LEAVE YOUR CAR,
THEN USING YOUR MOBILE PHONE TO
LIGHT YOUR WAY, OPEN THE GATE AND
PROCEED THE SHORT DISTANCE TO THE
BUILDING, ENTER THROUGH THE GREEN
STEEL DOOR ON THE LEFT SIDE, WHICH
HAS BEEN LEFT SLIGHTLY AJAR. ONCE
YOU ARE INSIDE, BEHIND THE DOOR TO
THE LEFT YOU WILL FIND A SHELF, ON
THIS THERE IS A BATTERY OPERATED
CAMPING LAMP, TURN IT ON AND YOU
WILL SEE A TAPE PLAYER NEXT TO IT,
PRESS THE WHITE PLAY BUTTON AND
FOLLOW THE INSTRUCTIONS EXACTLY, DO
NOT FAIL, NOW DRIVE OFF AND FOLLOW
THE INSTRUCTIONS TO THE LETTER.

When Lynda eventually found what she perceived to be the gateway, she turned off the lane and parked her car on the wet sodden grass in front of the broken gate. The beam from the car's headlights lit up the gable end of an old single-storey brick building. Hanging off the wall was a broken gutter where the rainwater poured off the tin corrugated roof. She noticed the large green pipe protruding from the ground and entering the side wall of the old building. It looked totally neglected and completely uninviting. The thought that she should leave the relative safety of the convertible to enter this dark abandoned place that looked as if it hadn't been used or visited for God only knows how long, filled her with trepidation. How on earth would she summon up the courage to follow their demands? How could she possibly walk over to this gloomy dilapidated place, open the metal door and step inside? The very thought made her tremble with apprehension. Driven by absolute fear, she had little choice. She must carry out their terrifying demands for Jonathan's sake, God only knows what a terrible time he must be having.

Lynda took a deep breath and, almost without thinking, turned off the car lights and waited in the dark for a few moments. She stepped out with the briefcase in one hand and the bag slung loosely over her shoulder. Leaving the safety of her BMW behind she used her mobile to light the way. She opened the gate and carried on through the long wet grass towards the building. After only a few paces she was soaking wet, her white trousers already clinging to her legs. While the heavy rain relentlessly poured down, all she wanted to do was turn back and run away from this place. She couldn't and the thought of Jonathan's plight somehow drove her on. Now frightened beyond belief for her life, and sobbing uncontrollably, she made her way towards the dark abandoned building. On reaching the green metal door she hesitated and in a soft trembling voice asked, "Is there anyone in there?" No one replied so she found herself pushing the heavy metal door open with her shoulder. Peering inside the dark abyss she could see nothing but shadowy dark shapes as she repeatedly pressed the button on her mobile phone to light her way.

Reluctantly, she walked inside dreading what she would find, but there was only the sound of the rainwater dripping through the broken corrugated roof. Worst of all was the smell from the damp rotting timber mixed with the distinct stench of urine. For anyone alone to enter this place would surely be like walking through the gates of hell. Lynda somehow found the courage and stepped forward and further into the building, immediately screaming out in terror as a loud flapping sound followed by sudden rush of air as something flew by her head. She ducked down, still screaming a natural reaction, as several bats left the comfort of their lair.

Crouching on the floor, now even more petrified than ever, salt drenched tears streamed down her already wet chilled face. She prayed to God to give her the courage to continue her unthinkable task. Moments later her eyes where becoming more accustomed to the darkness and she could just make out the lamp standing on the shelf to the left of her. She turned it on and saw the tape player standing next to it. She momentarily hesitated, terrified of what her reaction was going to be, and wondering what their demands would involve. Unwillingly her finger gently touched the white play button, there was a click and the tape played on for a second or two before the voice she had been dreading to hear spoke out. Lynda felt physically sick, convinced she couldn't take much more of this ghastly man's tones. Her heart was in her mouth as Dean's abrupt guttural voice barked out the kidnapper's instructions,

> "FIRST OF ALL LADY I'M GOING TO WARN YOU AGAIN, THAT IF THE POLICE OR ANYONE ELSE APPROACH THIS BUILDING, YOUR HUSBAND WILL NEVER FUCKING WELL BE SEEN AGAIN. SO FOLLOW MY INSTRUCTIONS TO THE LETTER, THERE IS A LANTERN ON THE BENCH IN FRONT OF YOU, TURN IT ON."

Silence once more descended and only the sound of the wind and the dripping water could be heard as Lynda walked unenthusiastically over to the bench. She stumbled slightly on the rotting debris left on the floor around her. At the bench she found the lantern's switch and the light came on. For the first time Lynda could see all around her. Dust filled cobwebs hung down draping over the pipe work leading to heavy looking machinery and her first thoughts were confirmed. Indeed this was some sort of abandoned pumping station, her attention was heightened by his next demand,

> "NOW GO OVER TO THE METAL DOOR, CLOSE AND LOCK IT WITH THE METAL BAR, PLACING IT ACROSS THE DOOR INTO THE TWO METAL CLIPS EACH SIDE, DO NOT OPEN THIS DOOR AGAIN TO ANYONE, THEN GO BACK OVER TO THE BENCH AGAIN, YOU WILL SEE A GREEN PIPE RISING OUT OF THE GROUND AND UP TO A LARGE GATE VALVE. THE VALVE HAS A RED WHEEL SO YOU CANNOT MISTAKE IT; AT THIS POINT THE PIPE BENDS AND

RETURNS INTO THE GROUND, YOU
SHOULD BE LOOKING AT IT NOW."

The tape fell silent again. She looked up and the red gate
valve was right in front of her. Turning she walked back over to
the door and struggled to place the heavy bar she had found
standing in the corner into the retaining clips, before returning
back over to the pipe which rose up and out of the ground and
up to the valve. Lynda was already physically and mentally
drained as she waited for the next demand. The tape continued
startling her,

"UNDER THE BENCH YOU WILL SEE TWO
CYLINDERS MADE OF STAINLESS STEEL,
THEY ARE TORPEDO SHAPED, PICK UP ONE
OF THEM AND LAY IT ON THE BENCH."

The tape abruptly stopped once again. She saw the two
cylinders and picked one of them up and placed it on the bench
as ordered. Once again the tape crackled for a moment causing
her to think it had broken, but then it carried on,

"NOW TAKE THE PLASTIC DRY BAG FROM
INSIDE THE CYLINDER AND PLACE ALL
THE CASH YOU CAN INTO IT MAKING
SURE YOU SEAL THE END CORRECTLY,
WHEN YOU HAVE DONE THIS PLACE THE
BAG INSIDE THE CYLINDER ENSURING
YOU SCREW THE END ON TIGHTLY, BEING
VERY CAREFUL NOT TO CROSS THREAD
THE SCREW TOP. WHEN YOU HAVE
COMPLETED THIS TASK, REPEAT THE
SAME OPERATION, ONLY THIS TIME PLACE
THE JEWELLERY INTO THE SECOND
CYLINDER ALONG WITH ANY CASH YOU
FAILED TO PLACE INTO THE FIRST
CYLINDER."

These instruction may have been clear enough but, for a
woman who had never carried out anything more practical than

saddling up a horse, made her think this task was going to be more than she could cope with. Even without all that was going on around her in this horrendous place, and especially in these conditions, she was finding this all too much. However, when Jonathan's face came into her thoughts once more, she carried on trying her best to conform to this despicable person who was irritatingly calling out these demands to her, for this man was surely capable of committing any crime. Then the tape played again and his voice sounded even more venomous than before,

"YOU NOW HAVE FIVE MORE MINUTES, GET ON WITH IT LADY."

Lynda was trying as best she could, but was having great difficulties with the second cylinder as the screw top just wouldn't quite line up. She turned it again, her fingers trembling with the cold, and this time it was on tight. 'Thank God,' were her thoughts. There was an unnerving click again and the tape played on,

"OK LADY, YOU HAVE HAD PLENTY OF TIME, NOW TAKE BOTH CYLINDERS OVER TO THE GATE VALVE, THERE YOU WILL SEE THAT A METAL PLATE AS BEEN TAKEN OFF THE FRONT OF THE PIPE, JUST UNDER THE RED VALVE WHEEL, PLACE ONE OF THE CYLINDERS INTO THE PIPE, MAKING SURE YOU LOWER IT INSIDE GENTLY, ONCE YOU HAVE DONE THIS PLACE THE SECOND CYLINDER ON THE TOP OF THE FIRST, DO NOT DROP IT DOWN INTO THE PIPE, LOWER IT SLOWLY UNTIL THEY ARE BOTH TOUCHING EACH OTHER."

The tape stopped once more, she carried both cylinders and did exactly as he had demanded. Several minutes later more instructions followed, sarcastically saying,

"NOW, THAT WASN'T HARD WAS IT LADY?"

The dexterity in Lynda's fingers had diminished to the extent that she was having real problems bending them, but she could already see what her next task was to be. The patronizing tape message continued,

"OK LADY, NOW PLACE THE METAL PLATE OVER THE HOLE IN THE PIPE, MAKING SURE THE RUBBER SEAL STAYS IN PLACE, AFTER YOU HAVE LIFTED IT INTO POSITION SCREW THE SIX BOLTS THROUGH THE HOLES AND TIGHTEN THEM WITH THE WRENCH WHICH IS LYING ON THE FLOOR DIRECTLY UNDER THE PIPE, YOU HAVE TEN MINUTES TO COMPLETE THIS TASK, DON'T FORGET LADY, YOUR HUSBAND'S LIFE DEPENDS ON YOU GETTING THIS RIGHT."

*

Jack Terry was driving down Church Frampton's Sandy Lane when the tracking device began to work again.

"The bloody thing is working again guv."

"Thank goodness for that," Wallace replied, "but where the bloody hell as she disappeared to?"

"Well we now are approximately two miles away from her car, which looks to be parked down a lane off the old A50. Just a minute, yes, there it is in Merry Tom Lane. We will have to turn around and head for Carton, then a mile after Chapel Frampton we should be able to turn right into this Merry Tom Lane. From there her car is parked roughly five hundred metres down the lane on the right hand side."

Five minutes later they pulled into the dark single track lane. Terry parked the Rover on the verge at the top of the lane, and instantly killed the car's lights. They sat for a moment while Wallace thought through the situation.

"Jack before we move, get onto Sergeant Benson and Mills on your mobile and give our position. Ask them to drive to the other end of this lane, which looking at the *Navman* comes up to the A508 just before a village called Brigham. Tell them not to call us under any circumstances and they are to wait there for further instructions."

Lynda was still struggling with the metal plate, when the tape sounded out again,

> "YOU SHOULD HAVE FIXED THE PLATE BACK ONTO THE PIPE NOW LADY, BUT JUST IN CASE YOU HAVEN'T I WILL GIVE YOU FIVE MORE MINUTES."

She was in so much pain from her endeavours that her fingers were now bleeding badly and she was having great difficulty screwing the bolts through the plate and into the pipe. When she heard his arrogant demands, she shouted out angrily, "No I haven't finished you malicious bastard." She looked down, trying to see her watch, while wiping away the constant streams of tears and she saw it read 8:25. Still under pressure, she carried on and a few minutes later she had all the bolts in place. Now all she had to do was tighten them using the large wrench by her feet.

*

Wallace and Terry were making steady progress down the thick hedgerow that lined both sides of the quiet lane. The rain was still falling heavily and they were soon soaked through, their shoes being more accustomed to city streets rather than traipsing around in the long wet grass. However, their only concern tonight was for the safety of Lynda Harker and the danger this distraught woman had put herself in.

They could now make out the silhouette of the BMW which was parked approximately 20 metres in front of them, but as they approached it was pretty obvious there was no sign of her inside. There was only the sound from the unrelenting rain hammering down onto the convertibles roof as they now sheltered together under the nearby hedgerow.

Wallace decided he would try to force his way through the thick undergrowth, hoping he would be able to see more from the other side of the hedgerow. He struggled at first but his persistence prevailed as he managed to push his not so small frame under low branches and out into the field on the other side. Terry followed in a similar vein and now both officers were standing together looking across at an old building of some sort, probably around twenty metres from the road and directly in front of them. Wallace turned to Jack and speaking quietly asked, "Jack isn't that a chink of light I can see coming from the broken roof?"

"You're right guv, but why the hell would they want to isolate themselves out in the middle of a bloody field for goodness sake. They must know we're watching them."

"Well at the moment Jack, I am as puzzled as you, unless there is some sort of fancy pick-up plan, but how they think they could pull it off, I really can't work out."

"What do you reckon we should do then guv?"

"We will just stay here out of sight. We have to consider Lynda Harker's safety first and foremost, so let us wait here and see if we can hear anything before we make our next move."

Both officers crouched down trying to shelter in the best way they could. They tucked themselves well under the thorn hedgerow as the rain fell heavily in front of them, almost forming a curtain of water as they peered out and across the field towards the old brick building. Their coats were pulled up over their heads and they looked like two old tramps down on their luck.

*

Lynda strained using every ounce of strength she had left in her tiny blistered hands to force the large spanner around to secure the plate tight onto the pipe. She had just succeeded when the menacing voice bellowed from the tape machine once more,

"OK LADY YOU HAVE ONE MORE TASK. THAT IS TO TURN THE LARGE RED WHEEL OF THE GATE VALVE IN AN ANTICLOCKWISE DIRECTION. IF YOU HAVE DIFFICULTY TURNING IT, USE THE LARGE WRENCH BETWEEN THE SPOKES OF THE WHEEL TO HELP YOU TO LEVER IT

AROUND, BY 8:30 THIS VALVE MUST BE OPEN. IF FOR ANY REASON IT ISN'T DON'T EXPECT TO SEE YOUR TOFFEE NOSED HUSBAND AGAIN. REMEMBER WE ARE WATCHING YOU, AND IF THE POLICE OR ANYONE ELSE ENTERS THE BUILDING, TAKE IT FROM ME LADY, I WILL PERSONALLY SLIT HIS THROAT."

She screamed out, "No please, don't in the name of God no." She sank to the floor, tears streaming down her cheeks, but relentlessly the tape played on,

"WHEN YOU HAVE TURNED THE VALVE FULLY OPEN, JUST SIT AND WAIT INSIDE THE BUILDING FOR AT LEAST ANOTHER HOUR."

With that the tape came to an abrupt end. She looked at her watch again it was nearly 8:30. She pulled herself back up, clinging onto the bench until she was standing next to the gate valve, then placing both of her blistered hands on the wheel. She desperately tried to turn it in an anticlockwise direction as she had been ordered to do, but to her horror it wouldn't budge. She looked around for the discarded wrench and picked it up. Now panicking somewhat, she placed the handle end of the wrench between the spokes of the wheel and tried again. This time there was some movement, and she could hear the sound of water begin to force its way through into the valve. She continued to turn and now it was getting easier with every rotation, finally the valve was fully open.

Completely exhausted, she looked around for somewhere to rest as all her strength had been drained from her weary body. Finally she stumbled over to the door, turned, pressed her back against the cold metal and slid down, totally drained of all strength and emotion, onto the filthy damp floor. All she could hear was the sound of water rushing through the pipeline. She wiped her face with the sleeve of her coat and prayed that this nightmare would soon be over.

CHAPTER THIRTEEN

Tony Miles left Nobottle Wood Cottage earlier that evening around 6:30, giving Suzy instructions to be ready and waiting for him when he returned at 10:00pm. He told her to clean the place up and check that nothing could possibly lead the police quickly to them or give them any clue of their identification. Although he knew that once they found out who owned the cottage it would be him they would be looking for, but by then they would be long gone.

At precisely 8:30pm he was waiting five miles away from the cottage in the old abandoned pumping station at Duston Mill on the outskirts of Northampton. The Mill was last been used in the late 70s and he had known about this emergency pumping station through his uncle who had once worked for Anglia Water Authority as a civil engineer. At one time he had been in charge of the whole of East Anglia Division. On numerous occasions he would accompany his uncle to work and the civil engineer would show him how the water was moved from one reservoir to another. This particular pumping station was only used in an emergency situation to pump water from the river Nene to Richford Reservoir some 10 miles away to the north-east, and the facility was seldom used, apart from in a serious drought situation.

The pumps had lain dormant now for many years and to Tony's knowledge hadn't been started for at least thirty years. The whole site had been abandoned since then, and had seemed to be forgotten, but he was confident in his ability that his extraordinary plan would work. To him it was a simple plan since the pipeline from Richford Reservoir runs at a steep angle down the hill from Richford Water Treatment Works towards the old intermediate pumping station in Merry Tom Lane. He knew the pipeline had been left in a full state ever since the last day it had been used all those years ago. In fact it was his uncle who had finally condemned the system, shutting down the giant pumps on 12th April 1985. Two days earlier Tony had visited the intermediate disused pumping station to leave the tape player along with the camping lantern and wrench. At the same time he had removed the plate from under the gate valve and loosened the valve wheel to make it easier for Harker's wife to turn the valve wheel and, sure enough, the valve still had plenty of back pressure behind it. So he was confident the force from the back pressure of water would propel the cylinders towards Duston Mill leaving the police no time at all to work out where the hell the ransom had disappeared to.

He checked his watch it was 8:40pm, not too long now he thought as he lay down on the filthy concrete floor alongside the pipeline. His ear was pressed firmly against the cold steel listening intently, and sure enough he could hear the sound of water rushing along the pipe towards him. He allowed himself a huge smile and punched the air calling out loud, "I told him it was possible, I just knew it would work." He had proven Ted wrong who had always been skeptical of his plan. He knew it would work, he was sure of it, and he had been proved right. When the cylinders eventually appeared they would land into the now empty filter tank then hopefully float to the surface as it filled.

Waiting there in the darkness, his only source of light a flash lamp. He thought about his future with Suzy and, lost to the world, maybe somewhere in the hills of Spain. They would buy a house or perhaps even a small farm. At that very moment he could hear the cylinders rattling on the sides of the pipe work, then a tremendous crashing of water as the two objects were spat out like missiles that had been fired from a submarine. The force was so powerful that the cylinders hit the wall on the far side of the tank. Tony was thrown of his guard and worried that the cylinders may have been damaged. He shone his torch into the tank desperately trying to find them, and the stress was soon relieved when both cylinders popped up and were now floating on the surface. He allowed himself another moment of triumph, shouting out loud, "Yes!"

He fished the first cylinder out of the water, and then quickly retrieved the second. He placed both cylinders into his rucksack, mouthing, "Thank you lady, thank you." He had been amazed by the speed the cylinders had been propelled along the pipeline from Merry Tom Lane. He shone his flashlight onto his watch and repeated to himself, "20 minutes they only took 20 bloody minutes." He had thought more like 40 minutes. This gave him even more time to get back to the cottage, pick up Suzy, and drive to Southampton Ferry Terminal to meet up with Ted.

He turned, placing the flashlight down on the floor, and went to pick up his rucksack. It was then that he found himself being forced backwards with tremendous ferocity. He had no time to think but he certainly felt the pole that was being lanced into his solar plexus. As he gripped it with both hands, trying to stop the backwards motion he found himself in, the brightest of lights shone directly into his eyes. There was nothing he could do as the inevitable happened and Tony fell over the edge of the filter tank hitting the cold water while still struggling to free himself. His assailant showed him no mercy and held him down under the freezing water with the full weight of his body onto the pole. His final struggles were futile as the attacker slowly withdrew the pole. He then shone his head torch down into the water only to see Tony's body float up to the surface under the green pipe, which only a few moments before had spewed out the two cylinders giving him so such pleasure. The ferocity and surprise of the attack had meant no one could have possibly survived such a terrifying assault, an assault which had lasted no more than a couple of minutes.

The tall spectral figure calmly lifted Tony's rucksack onto his back, pulled the two straps up tight, and left the dank pumping station. He placed the long pole by the door as he left, and then stealthily moved away across the overgrown yard, through the slit in the chain link fence that Tony had made only a couple of days earlier, and made his way along the river bank. All around him the traffic was busy, but no one would see the camouflaged figure down below the road in the darkness by the river's edge.

Duston Mill lay beside the main road junction on the Northampton Westerly Bypass and was just one mile from the M1 junction, 15A. The balaclava clad attacker carried on under the road bridge and then turned right to follow the hedgerow up to the Rotherthorpe Lane where he had parked his vehicle. Everything, so far, had gone to plan and he felt the adrenalin pumping hard around his body. This night had reminded him so much of Iraq on one of his many missions into enemy lines, his Bergen full of equipment, only this time his comrades in arms hadn't been by his side. No it was just him, he was the only one left and that was the way it was meant to be. He had used Tony, it was always planned that way. They had never been comrades in arms like himself, and as for that idiot Dean, if he had been there he would have gone the same way. When he and his fellow soldiers had been on tour in Iraq, his company had lost so many men out in that God forsaken place, while these two were either giving someone a good kicking or ripping some poor sod off. Yes, this ransom was now his to enjoy.

He had deceived Tony and his girlfriend but at this moment of triumph, as was his military way, he completely disregarded his actions as an absolute inevitability. He was the only one who knew just how valuable this piece of jewellery he had secreted in his Bergen really was, and those two had no idea and now they never would. His mission here had been fully accomplished and now the only thing left for him to do was to get himself and the spoils of deceit back to his car, and then, in a few hours time he would be safely out of the country and into France.

When he reached the field stile just before the Rotherthorpe Lane, he waited patiently for the traffic to ease, then he jumped over the stile and ran over to his Renault. In no time at all he was sitting behind his steering wheel, feeling a huge sense of not only relief, but one of self gratification. His only task now was to open the Bergen and make sure the ransom was not only there, but hadn't suffered any damage on its journey from Merry Tom Lane to Duston Mill. Taking out one of the cylinders he unscrewed the top then tipped out its contents onto the passenger seat beside him before opening the dry bag. Leaving the odd bundles of cash in the bottom he lifted out the gold velvet pouch, undid the draw cord, and took out the exquisite tiara. It's jewels caught the small amount of light there was coming from the industrial site opposite.

He felt totally overwhelmed by the precious stones that made up this delightful headpiece and above all it's real sense of history. This posturing wouldn't do as he had to get on. He quickly placed the tiara back into the pouch and transferred the pouch into his suitcase which was on the rear seat of the Renault. He then quickly opened the second cylinder but the cash had been forced in so tightly he was having some difficulty persuading it out of the cylinder. Eventually it slid out in the dry jacket and he unrolled the cover. There lay the one million used 500 euro notes. He looked down at more cash than he had ever seen before rolling the package back up again and turning to place it next to the gold velvet pouch. He closed the suitcase and set off towards junction 15 and the motorway.

*

Ten minutes earlier, Wallace and Terry had decided to move towards the building in Merry Tom Lane. On reaching the wall nearest to their position they listened intently, but the place seemed deserted the only sound being one of running water, but then Terry was sure he could hear someone. Wallace whispered,

"Jack, can you hear what sounds like someone sobbing?"

"Reckon I can guv."

"Jack come on, let's make our way around to the other side of the building." The two officers made their way by keeping close to the buildings wall, the wet grass was long and brambles pulled against their sodden clothes. Reaching the door, Wallace placed his ear against the cold metal, they were right, there was someone in there, a woman's voice quietly weeping. The sound seemed to be coming from just the other side of the door. Wallace decided it was safe enough to call out as it was obvious to him that no kidnapper would put themselves in such a tight corner and the only person inside had to be Lynda Harker.

"Mrs Harker is that you?"

She was startled by his intervention and screamed out, "Go away, go away?"

"It's all right Lynda, it's DI Wallace and DS Terry."

"Go away inspector, please go away. If they see you here they going to kill Jonathan?"

"But there's no one out here Lynda, we have been here for the last three quarters of an hour and there is no sign of anyone."

"I can't let you in anyway, you don't understand. They have told me they would kill Jonathan if they don't receive the cylinders."

"What cylinders are you talking about?"

"I can't tell you inspector."

"Has anyone been here Lynda, and have you handed over the jewellery and the cash to them?"

"No I have not seen anyone." Wallace urged her to open the door. She looked down at her watch, there was still ten more minutes to go before she could open it.

"Inspector I will open the door in ten minutes time." Wallace turned towards Terry who had been observing the surrounding area.

"It's no good Jack, we will just have to wait a while."

The rain was easing a little when Lynda finally opened the old pumping station door. She explained to the officers all she had been through, how the tape player had given her instructions, telling her step by step what tasks she had to perform to achieve their demands.

"Mrs Harker, you're telling us you have sent the ransom off in some kind of cylinder?"

"Don't you see? I had to, they gave me no choice," she replied still uncontrollably sobbing. Wallace continued,

"Lynda, does the tape tell you where your husband can be found?" Wallace didn't need a reply, he could see by her distorted expression. She collapsed down onto the floor again holding her hands up over her face. Terry quickly got down on one knee and helped Lynda up, at the same time doing his utmost to comfort her in the best way he could. Wallace was calling Sergeant Benson on his mobile.

"Hello Sergeant Benson here."

"Sergeant this is Inspector Wallace, I want you and Constable Mills to get over to Richford Reservoir Treatment Works and see if you can gain any information regarding the old pumping station at the bottom of Merry Tom Lane, better still, get them to send someone down to me as soon as possible?"

"We are on our way now sir." On reaching the treatment works the two officers were having trouble locating anyone, until they spotted a light coming from underneath a large sliding door. Benson hammered hard on what looked like a workshop door, a few moments later the door opened.

"Good evening sir, I am Detective Sergeant Benson and this is DC Mills." He held out his warrant card for the small balding gentleman to see.

"Come in out of the rain please," Joe Tite insisted.

"Now what can I do for you on such a night as this, cup of tea is it?"

"No thank you sir, we are enquiring about the old pumping station in Merry Tom Lane?" Joe laughed.

"That old place hasn't been used for year's sergeant, only by kid's, tramps and such like."

"Could you tell us sir, what it was used for? Better still, would it be possible for you to come along with us now and show us what it was used for?"

"Goodness sergeant, I can't leave the treatment works. There's only two of us on duty at this time of night, but I can certainly tell you all you want to know. It was built in the early 60s after a practically dry summer and has only been used since then when we have had drought conditions. We would pump water from Duston Mill, that's over by Sixfields football stadium in Northampton, out of the river Nene and back to the reservoir to bring the level back up, replenishing stocks."

"Could you tell us sir, if this pipeline runs to anywhere else apart from this mill in Duston?"

"Seeing that I was around when it was constructed sergeant, I can tell you with full confidence it is a single pipeline only linking the reservoir and the two pumping stations to the River Nene. Can you tell me what's going on down there then sergeant?"

"I am afraid I can't say at the moment, but perhaps you could tell us if Duston Mill is still operating?"

"No, it was also abandoned several years ago."

"Well thanks for your help sir."

"That's okay, only too glad to help, and if you want me to, I can call head office and get them to send someone down there to you, or up to Duston Mill?"

"Thank you sir, if you can ask them to call this number." Benson handed Joe his card. "Perhaps we could arrange then, where we would need to meet up."

"Right you are sergeant; I'll get onto head office right away."

*

Suzy was very restless worrying about Tony. She looked up at the kitchen clock and the time was 10:45pm, Tony was due back 45 minutes ago. 'Come on Tony,' she repeated every so often to herself. She was now fearful something had happened to him. Checking the monitor she could see Harker was lying on his bed, and she was wondering how he was staying so calm considering he was at the end of his second day, and seemingly was just waiting for the whole terrible episode to run its course. Turning his head Harker glanced up at the camera, sensing not for the first time someone was watching him. She read the expression on his bruised face as much to say, I know you're watching me you bastards.

Suzy was almost as fed up with this situation as Harker, she never wanted to get involved, but had been talked into it by Tony who persisted to impress on her that nothing could possible go wrong. It was Tony's friend in London, and someone she only knew as Ted, who had been planning the kidnap for several months. He only brought Tony in a couple of weeks ago for his local knowledge, but as far as Suzy was concerned, it was only to carry out Ted's dirty work for him. Tony though, wouldn't have a bad word said about his old school friend. He saw the kidnapping of Jonathan Harker as a means to making lots of cash very quickly, which would help them both realise their dream of living abroad together.

Unfortunately it hadn't quite gone to plan. Tony had brought in that thug Dean who had beaten Harker up really badly. He certainly wouldn't have wanted that to happen and then that bastard had assaulted her, ripping off her top to expose her breasts. She was sure this was only for his own satisfaction and, now he had been killed, that certainly wasn't in any plan. What of this Ted? What has he done to earn himself any of the ransom spoils, apart from planning this bloody awful nightmare for all of us? She looked up at the clock on the kitchen wall again, getting more agitated by the moment, and her desperation showed when she called out, "Tony where are you, for goodness sake, where are you?" He had made it quite clear she wasn't under any circumstances to call his mobile, but he was now over an hour late. Suzy punched in his mobile number, but the only reply she heard was, "Currently this mobile maybe switched off."

There was something dreadfully wrong. He must have been arrested, she started to panic and planned to leave, to get away from this place before the police arrived. She decided that she would wait for a further 30 minutes and she wasn't going to wait any longer than that. But what about Harker? She couldn't just leave him in this cottage locked up, no one would ever find him? Someway she would have let someone know where he was being held.

*

Mrs Harker was being driven back to Sedgwick House near Kegworth Wharf by DC Mills. She was sitting in the back of her own car exhausted by her ordeal, and hardly spoke to the police officer other than to give him directions just before reaching her home. DC Mills' orders were to stay with her and to check if any other messages had been received by Mrs Bernard. Natasha and Ester helped the poor exhausted woman up the stairs to her bedroom, after she had declined anything to eat, all she wanted was a cup of tea and to rest. Ester sat on the bed next to her until she was fast asleep then, gently kissing her brow, she left her very weakened friend to hopefully sleep for the rest of the night.

*

Wallace and the other two officers were now approaching Duston Mill; they had just turned down a lane opposite Sixfields Football Stadium.

"That must be the place sir," Benson informed his inspector. Wallace drove the car off the dual carriageway around a small roundabout, parking the Rover at the top end of the overgrown lane. They then proceeded on foot down towards the relief pumping station which had been built on the site of the old Duston Water Mill. Wallace turned to look back at the orange glow coming from the Sixfields area with it's many fast food outlets and multi-screen cinema complex, but in contrast the lane was dark unlit and very uninviting. Before long they were approaching a large neglected building, silhouetted by the sodium glow of the city's lights. In the foreground were two steel gates covered by brambles which was now obviously being used by fly tippers.

"Bloody hell guv, this place hasn't been used for years."

"Good observation Jack, you'll go a long way," Wallace mouthed with the slightest hint of friendly sarcasm in his voice. He climbed up over the rubbish and pushed at the gates, but there was no movement at all.

"Come on Jack, let's find a way around the perimeter and see if there's any other way in." For the second time on that night they found themselves struggling through wet undergrowth as saturated brambles tore at their clothes once more. Using a torch wasn't an option so they had to feel their way by keeping in close contact with the perimeter fence. Slowly they made their way to the rear of the large barn like building, that had once housed the pumping station.

"Looks like someone gained entry by cutting the fence here guv, there's at least a metre long slit in the chain link fencing over here."

"Okay Jack, stand back and I'll go in first." Wallace parted the fence and stepped through, closely followed by Jack. Wallace turned and in his quietly spoken voice ordered Sergeant Benson to wait outside the perimeter fence. They made their way following a trail of disturbed wet grass swept to one side as if it had been used very recently. Eventually they reached a green metal door which had been left partially ajar, they hesitated to listen for a moment before Wallace pushed at the door with his shoulder. The door dragged on the concrete floor as it opened leaving just enough room for them to enter.

Once inside all they could hear was the sound of gushing water echoing around the large old empty building. Wallace had decided long before entering that they were now unlikely to find anyone here and turned on his torch. Carefully, they both walked in the direction and sound of where the water was coming from, and soon they were standing looking down into a large open top tank. The tank was set in the concrete floor and water was flowing from a large green pipe directly above the tank. Instantly Terry remarked, as the whole kidnapper's ransom plan fell into place before them. "Bloody hell guv, you have got to hand it to them. All they had to do was wait patiently for the cylinders to travel through this pipeline from Merry Tom

Lane to this place, fish them out of the tank, and scarper. You have to admit, that's clever guv."

"You're right Jack it was very ingenious to say the least, but I am afraid this one wasn't quite so fortunate." Wallace was shining his torch down into the water and underneath the pipe that was still expelling its flow.

"Fucking hell! Sorry guv, I hope that's not Harker down there."

"So do I Jack, so do I. You better call for forensics again, they are in for a long cold night?"

CHAPTER FOURTEEN

At about 12:30am Ted pulled into the Ashford Euro Tunnel Terminal and drove up to the ticket office.

"Good morning sir, could I please have your ticket?" Ted leaned over the passenger seat and handed the spectacled woman his reference number.

"Could I also have your passport please sir?" She looked at the passport photograph then glanced across at him. After a couple of minutes she handed him back both his ticket and then his passport, "Please drive to Lane number 167 sir, and have good journey."

Hanging his lane card on the interior mirror he wished her good morning and drove off. Just as he thought he was in the clear he came to a random spot check and a short, stocky Border Control Officer held up his arm and pulled the Renault over into a search bay. He wound down the window as the officer approached and, for the second time within minutes, he was wished, good morning. "Just a random search sir, could you tell me where you are travelling to today?" Ted told him he was on his way to Clermont Ferand, Central France.

"Business, or pleasure sir?"

"I'm on my way to visit friends for a couple of weeks, for a short holiday."

"Could you open the boot for me sir?" Ted stepped out of the Renault, walked around to the rear of the car and opened the boot.

"If you don't mind me saying, you have an odd load on board for a two week holiday," the officer said rummaged among the clutter of boxes. "Are you thinking of opening a shop in Clement sir?" he asked in that sarcastic manner only a British uniformed officer could get away with.

"Yes, it does look like that doesn't it officer, but they are all food stuffs for my friends, you know items they can't buy in

France and can't do without, Marmite, Weetabix that sort of thing."

He smiled and said, "Okay sir, you can carry on and enjoy your holiday." Ted drove off to wait in Lane 167, relieved that he was close to getting onto the train and that he hadn't been asked to open his suitcase with the ransom inside. Best policy he thought, leave it out in the open for them to see and they won't think you are trying to hide anything. His train was due to leave at 1:00am, just ten minutes time he thought looking down at his watch, then he heard a loud speaker announcement being made. Looking to the front of the queue he saw the information board was flashing delayed until further notice. He wound down the window so he was able to hear what the announcer was saying, "Due to industrial action by the French union CGT, all passenger and freight services will be cancelled until o-eight hundred-hours local time."

He felt a knot tightening in his stomach as he closed the window and laid his head on the steering wheel. All this planning, and to be so close, and then thwarted by a bunch of bloody militant frogs. He called on his all of his military background to steady himself, get some sleep, and try to wait patiently until the morning.

*

Suzy Walters had made her mind up to leave the cottage around midnight, her nerve could not hold out any longer. She took her last look at Jonathan Harker, lying on his bed staring up at the ceiling. The bruises on his face were now less blackened, and she thought he must be praying that this nightmare will end soon. Unknowing to him, it probably already had. She left by the back door turning the key in its lock, and placing it under the flowerpot. It was only then it dawned on her, to reach the safety of her own home, which was at least six miles away, wasn't going to be easy as she was only wearing a short jacket, jeans and trainers.

Her only chance of escape without being seen was to walk through the dark uninviting woods. This would help her stay clear of the country lanes until she reached the main road at Marlstone village, from there she would have to cross over the road by the old lodge gatehouse at the entrance to Marlstone Forest. After that, down the long drive she knew so well, as she spent many happy days as a child playing in the forest, but had she got the nerve to go through this forest alone?

Suzy looked back for the last time at Tony's cottage before walking away. She knew she would have to be brave, but there was no other way. She looked up the track towards the road for the final time, hoping to see Tony's van coming down the track towards her, but there was nothing to be seen apart from the shadows from the swaying trees as the breeze blew through the their tops, unnerving her even further.

She couldn't wait for him any longer and her fearsome decision was made. She set off climbing over the rickety moss covered post and rail fence that separated the track from the forest and on into the darkness. Before long she was away from the track and heading deeper into the forest, twigs snapped under her feet, the sound echoing through the canopy of branches that hung down over her. She was so afraid and all she could think about was the bedtime stories her father had told to her when she was a little girl. Just why were all those fairy stories always so frightening? Her mind was behaving in an altogether negative manner and she needed above all to be positive if she was ever going to make it back to her home. She tried to focus and disregard any shadows to stop her imagination from running riot. The forest floor was covered with pine needles and every so often fallen branches would block her way, but still she was making good progress and after the best part of an hour she could just make out the edge of the forest, picked out by the orange sodium glow of the lights from the city.

If she could just reach the main road. She knew the next part of her journey so well, through the forest and down the embankment, over the railway line and into the fields beyond, where she had happily courted and lost her virginity in her late teens.

'Come on Suzy you are doing well,' she told herself. Just keep going and then, tomorrow morning perhaps, Tony will call. Eventually she made it to the garden centre on the old A428 then quickly crossed the deserted road, passing by the long time abandoned lodge gate house. She looked at her watch it was 1:15am so she should be home in roughly an hour she thought.

The track in that part of the forest is often used by courting couples and sometimes the odd vagrant, so she would have to be on her guard. When she was only 200 metres down the tree lined track, a car turned off the main road and into the forest. She rushed into the undergrowth, crouching down waiting for the car to go by, which it did only very slowly. She took a sharp intake of breath realising it was a police car, surely they weren't looking for her already. How could they have known she was here? The vehicle stopped no more than 50 metres away from her. Was this the time to run she wondered? But no, she stayed hidden in the undergrowth hardly daring to breathe. The driver's door opened and she recognised the silhouette of a male police officer step out and walk around to the front of the car. Then the passenger door opened, and she could tell instantly that this was a woman. The female police officer joined her colleague, who by this time was now lighting up a cigarette. Suzy was too far away from them to make out what they were saying to each other, but when they laughed out loud, she was pleased it wasn't her they were looking for. She slipped away unseen into the darkness of the forest, knowing they were only there to take a smoke break, and who knows what else.

She was now well away from the two police officers and feeling more confident that she would make it back to her flat, and relieved it was just a few hundred yards to go before she reached the railway embankment. 'What the hell,' she said under her breath, startled by the sound of something running through the forest towards her. Twigs snapped in the distance and she was sure the unnerving sound was becoming even closer, there seemed to be several people all running together causing mayhem as they crashed through the thick brushwood. Petrified, she crouched down behind a fallen tree pressing her back hard against its sodden rotting bark in a foetal position, scared stiff of what would happen next. Anxiously she waited for her fate, listening to the sound coming ever closer. The smell of decaying fungus infested wood and dampness overpowering everything else around her as the terrorising noise became louder with every second. Then she made out a large dark shape running straight towards the fallen tree where she had secreted herself, she must have turned ashen white with fright as a huge stag jumped over the rotting tree that was protecting her. She sat shaking for some time trying hard to steady her nerves and bring her blood pressure down onto an even keel.

"Whatever next is this night going to throw at me? Please God, let me get home," she mumbled as she moved off once more, this time keeping her focus on the natural surroundings and not imagining the worst at every turn.

It was then she heard the sound of a train in the distance and within a few short moments the *West Coast Virgin Express* sped by only metres away, causing the power lines to illuminate, sending sparks flying in all directions, then silence descended once more in the forest as the express raced away into the night. She had been warned so many times about crossing the railway track by her late father, although unbeknown to him she had crossed this part of the track before on a couple of occasions. She was still understandably worried of the danger this busy line possessed and the fact that a couple of people had been killed crossing at this very spot, but this was her only way to escape. Suzy sank to her knees and looked back into the gloomy forest and the enormity of what she was about to face finally hit her hard. She called out in utter desolation with tears flowing freely down the desperate young woman's face, "Tony, how could you have left me to confront such danger?" Her self-pity lasted only a few minutes before she was brought back to the reality as a second express rushed by in the same manner as the first.

Climbing over the chain link fence was clearly going to be the first obstacle. She waited, listening, and then pulled herself up the fence with some effort, and then over the top. She fell onto the top of the steep bank on the other side, just managing to stop herself from rolling down the embankment towards the track. Waiting once more to recover from her exertions, she knew that she had to be strong, nothing else would do if she was to survive the next couple of minutes. She then heard the sound from another train approaching, travelling at great speed along the electrified line. She clung on to the chain link fence and watched as the express passed at incredible speed. Now it was time to make her move, she let go to find herself sliding down the embankment to reach the edge of the track, looking in both directions there was nothing to be seen or heard, so with great apprehension she decided to make her move by quickly but carefully stepping over the first two sets of lines before reaching the centre of the forth track. The static electricity from the express was still in the air causing the follicles on her neck to rise. She looked again before attempting the second set of lines. It was then she heard the sound of another train approaching fast from the opposite direction. She hurried, stumbling in her haste, to get over the next set of lines, but by then the express was almost upon her. She screamed as she threw herself the last metre grabbing onto the long embankment grass as the train roared on through.

*

Ted had spent a restless couple of hours, his nap interrupted by the noise from the busy freight yard close by. It was out of character for him to worry, but he thought what if the French union decided to carry on with their strike? He would have to find an alternative way of escaping the country, which could certainly throw up other difficulties. The time was now approaching 3:00am and to his surprise he could see activity up in front of him, perhaps they had called off the strike. If that was the situation then surely they would soon be loading. He heard another message being blurted out over a crackly loud speaker system and the matrix sign showed the time table once more.

"We are pleased to inform you, that we will shortly be loading from lanes 165 to 167. We are very sorry for any inconvenience caused. We would like to wish you all a safe onward journey." 'Thank God,' he thought as the cars in front of him moved slowly off. Five minutes later he was parked safely inside one of the shuttles carriages.

Forty five minutes after boarding the shuttle he was driving down the E17 A26 motorway on his way towards Rheims, knowing he had an 800 mile drive in front of him. In addition to that, the ferry from Venice was booked for 3:00pm that very afternoon. Ted realised he probably wasn't going to make it. He had booked his passage with *Minoan Lines* on the internet three months earlier, reserving an open ticket just for this type of eventuality, so it wouldn't be a problem in changing the passage to the following day's ferry.

He was now thinking of breaking his journey and staying in a hotel, somewhere in the Mulhouse region of eastern France, which would give him plenty of time to reach his destination, Venice, the following day.

*

Jack Terry was having a crafty fag by the front gates of the old pumping station when the forensic team arrived at Duston Mill.

"Goodness me Jack, you are certainly keeping the forensic team busy tonight." Doctor James was in charge of the forensic scientists now working on the case, which was beginning to stretch his resources to the limit. Jack Terry replied,

"I am beginning to think we are probably in Chicago, rather than the sticks doc."

"Is Inspector Wallace around Jack?"

"I'll go and find him for you doc." Terry left the forensic team standing by the rubbish strewn gates at the front of the old building and made his way around to the rear of the pumping station looking for his superior, who he found examining the filter tank.

"The forensics team are waiting out the front, guv."

"Okay Jack, I wondered where the hell you had got to, fag was it? Anyway you better show them the best way in, oh yes, and ask them to bring some serious lighting with them."

By 3:30am Doctor James had already estimated that the victim had probably died around one to three hours earlier, drowning being the most likely cause. He also informed Wallace that the only marks he could find on the body were bruising around the lower abdomen. Wallace and his sergeant were examining the victim's belongings.

"Look Jack, he has very conveniently left us his wallet." He emptied its contents onto one of the forensics team's plastic bags and out fell Tony Miles' driving licence, landing face up. He picked up the licence with his gloved hand and walked across to where the body was now lying.

"Yes, this is Tony Miles alright Jack."

"Yes, I'll confirm that, not a bad looking bloke was he?"

"Well he was certainly prettier than the last corpse we found Jack."

"So where the hell are they holding Harker, and how many villains are in this mob guv?"

"Well, seeing as that there is no sign of the ransom or the cylinders Harker's wife told us about, I would say at least three. Anyway, call the station and get a check done on this Miles chap to see if he's got any form."

Wallace was now talking to Doctor James, asking him how he thought the victim had received the bruising around his stomach area.

"Inspector, my guess would be, he was probably hit hard by a sharp pointed object, such as a pole or something similar." Wallace looked around and there in the corner leaning up by the wall next to the door was a dirty wooden pole roughly six foot long.

"What about that pole doctor over by the door?" Both men were now walking across towards the object. The doctor got down on one knee and was in the process of examining the end of what turned out to be, an old brush stale. "I would say this is a very good candidate inspector." With their discovery, he called over one of his team to inspect it more closely and take the pole to the lab.

*

All Saints church clock struck four as Suzy walked the last few metres to the tall block of flats where she had lived for the last five months. She opened the community door and then pressed the lift button to take her up to the fourth floor. She was wet through; cold tired and very lonely. Where was Tony, the man who she had fallen for when working in London? He had promised her so much, and look at her now she thought, where was this new life he had planned for them both? Totally dejected she entered flat 201. First of all she went over to check the phone, but there hadn't been any new messages. She collapsed onto the sofa, tears running down her cold sodden cheeks, mumbling to herself, 'Tony where the hell are you?'

*

Jack Terry came back into the pumping station to find Wallace kneeling down by Miles body.

"Right, I have managed to find out who this Tony Miles is. Turns out he has got form for fraud, serving an eighteen month stretch in the Scrubs."

"Fraud you say Jack, well he's certainty moved on from that, but what's still puzzling me is we have this chap Miles who has more than likely been murdered, then there's the big fellow we fished out of the canal who was crushed by Parson's Land Rover, and then someone unceremoniously dumped the poor sod into the cut, not before they tied a box of bloody tools around his waist, and we still have no knowledge as to the whereabouts of their victim, Jonathan Harker."

"Look guv, this is how I see it, There must have been at least four kidnappers, one to look after Harker once they had moved him from the barge, these two stiffs and then there's this fellow who sorted Tony Miles, before scarpering with the two cylinders that Lynda Harker placed inside the pipeline."

"Well Jack, it might surprise you to know that I've worked that out for myself," Wallace said with some irony in his voice. "No Jack, what I was trying to say, and what is puzzling me is Harker's wife."

"You don't think she is involved do you guv?"

"For goodness sake Jack, give me a chance to explain."

"Sorry, you know I sometimes get carried away."

"Look, Harker's wife is supposed to have kept this family tradition of not telling their spouse about the so called heirloom. Now can you believe that anyone could keep a secret for at least twelve years? Well tell me then, how could this bunch of villains have found out about it if that was the case. No, I am beginning to think that Lynda Harker must have told someone else about her inheritance. Let's face it, this secret of hers, would cause all sorts of problems if the other person, in this case Jonathan Harker, found out that he was not privileged to the fact that his wife's bank account wasn't quite what he thought. I know if my wife was holding back the fact we were millions of pounds better off than I thought we were, I'd be pretty bloody livid wouldn't you?"

"What about her friend Ester Bernard then guv?"

"Now you're on the right lines, let's take a closer look at her and her husband, but we'll call it a day. There's not a lot else we can do here tonight and, I don't know about you, I need to get some sleep before we go over to the Harker's place in the morning."

"Sounds good to me, this has been a bloody awful day and to be honest, I'm glad it's over guv."

*

Harker felt sore as he woke from another restless night, although he had no idea of the correct time, he just presumed it to be so. He looked up at the camera that was monitoring his every move and to his surprise the red led light that showed when the monitor was recording was off. Lying back down on the bed he wondered, prayed even, that this would be the day his terrible ordeal would finally come to a conclusion.

*

At 9:30am the next morning, Wallace and Terry arrived at Sedgwick House and were shown into the drawing room by Natasha. Lynda Harker and Ester Bernard were sitting together on the Chesterfield sofa.

"Good morning ladies," Wallace said in a somewhat serious tone.

"Have you any news about my husband inspector?"

"No, I am afraid not madam, but if you wouldn't mind, we would like to ask you both a few more questions, and if I could speak to you first alone Mrs Harker?"

"Yes, certainly inspector, would you mind Ester darling?"

"Not at all Lynda, if you are sure you will be all right." Ester stood and left the room.

"Now, what would you like to know inspector?"

"Can I first ask if you have recovered from your terrible ordeal yesterday Mrs Harker?"

"Well I am still fairly tired and more than a little sore, but if it helps get Jonathan released, it will have been all worthwhile."

"I am afraid there is still no news as to where they are holding your husband, but I'm sure we will find him soon. The reason I needed to speak to you this morning was regarding your family heirloom, and the fact that you had to keep this a secret from your husband." She was slightly puzzled by his reasoning but answered, "Yes that's correct inspector, for twelve years after marrying."

"Are you sure your husband has no idea about this heirloom Mrs Harker?"

"I am sure he doesn't know, because I have never told him inspector."

"Have you knowingly ever mentioned to anyone else or is there someone in your own family maybe who knows about your inheritance?"

"Can I please explain the situation to you again Inspector Wallace."

"Please do so Madam."

"As I think I told you before, I didn't know anything about this heirloom until my father told me about it just before he died. A few days after the funeral I had a meeting with my solicitor and he informed that I was the sole heir of my late father's estate, along with the code numbered key for the safety deposit box. Inside this box I found all the information regarding its contents." She hesitated and then looked up at Wallace.

"Yes madam you were about to say something?" Wallace asked, impatiently.

"Actually, there is someone else who knows inspector." Wallace looked across the room at Jack who was now standing by the window, waiting for his boss to ask the next question.

"If you don't mind, could you tell us who this person is Mrs Harker?"

"It's my dear friend Ester, but she wouldn't tell anyone else about my personal business, and especially not this."

"If you don't mind me asking, what makes you so sure madam?"

"Ester and I are very close inspector. We have known each other since our childhood." Lynda was now staring up at Wallace. "Look, to be perfectly frank with you, Jonathan and I have a very liberal relationship, one of which we are not ashamed of I might say, and Ester is part of our relationship. I am sorry if I have shocked you inspector, but I would trust Ester with my life."

"Thank you Mrs Harker for being so forthright with us. I would now like to speak to Mrs Bernard so do you think you could send her in please?" She stood and walked towards the door before turning to face the two officers to say, "I am sure Inspector Wallace, Ester would not divulge to a soul regarding the contents of the box." Then she opened the door and left, a few moments later Ester entered the room.

"I understand you would like to speak to me Inspector Wallace."

"Yes if you wouldn't mind, please sit down will you." She sat on the edge of the sofa as Wallace walked around to face her.

"Mrs Bernard, could you tell me what you know of Mrs Harker's family and in particular their traditions?" Ester knew instantly what the inspector was talking about.

"Are you referring to her late father's will inspector, and in particular the handing down of the key which opens the safety deposit box?"

"Yes Madam, so do you know what this box contains?"

"Yes, I have been privy to that information inspector," she answered him with confidence. "But if you want to know what its contents are inspector you would have to ask Mrs Harker."

"Have you ever told anyone else about this safety deposit box Mrs Bernard?"

"Most certainly not, inspector," she answered with some resentment in her voice.

"Not even your husband madam?"

"Harry and I are now separated, and no inspector I have never told him about Lynda's box or her inheritance." Deep down Ester knew she was lying to the officer, she had told Harry, but this kidnap hadn't anything to do with him. She was sure Harry wouldn't know where to start, even though he certainly did have a motive.

"Would you mind giving us Mr Bernard's address madam?" She reached into her handbag and pulled out one of Harry's old business cards.

"I am afraid only the mobile number is currently working."

"Thank you Mrs Bernard, that will be all for now."

Wallace and Terry were walking back to their car when Lynda came back into the drawing room. Ester stood watching from the large bay window.

"Is everything all right Ester?" She turned to look at her friend.

"They can't think I had anything to do with Jonathan's kidnapping could they Lynda?"

"Of course not, don't be silly darling." She placed her arm around her friend's shoulders to reassure her. The two detectives drove down the driveway and out of the gates.

Jack turned to Wallace and said, "That's a bit rich, Lynda Harker has told her lover all about this so called family secret, but not the man she married, but then again, I'm not married guv."

They returned to Leicester Police station where Inspector Wallace had a meeting with his acting superior, Superintendent Pepper. He had brought his superior up to date with the case, telling Pepper that he had refrained from telling Lynda that they had discovered a second body, as he still wasn't 100 percent sure that someone else in the household may be involved. After taking on board Wallace's assessment of the investigation, Pepper decided to make the kidnapping known to the public through the local media, asking for any help they could give in trying to find the whereabouts of a local business man. For the rest of the day every news channel was covering the kidnap story.

*

Harker had lain most of the day listening intently trying to hear his abductors, but there was nothing to hear apart from the sound of the fluorescent light humming away above him. They hadn't brought him any further food and he was beginning to believe that they might just have abandoned him. He had to find out somehow, so he stood looking up at the monitor. The red light was still off so he made up his mind to shout out to see if there was any reaction.

"Hello, is there anyone out there?" Nobody answered, he called again, and there was still no reply. He was relieved at first that his captivity must obviously be coming to an end, but the most worrying thing now was did anyone know where he was being held, if they had indeed abandoned him.

He looked around the room he had been incarcerated in, trying to see if there was any possibility of escaping, but his prison consisted of four stark walls and one heavy looking door, which was most probably a fire door of some kind. He looked up at the ceiling, considering the possibility that he could somehow break through the plaster into the roof space above, and then maybe he would be able to find a way out through the roof itself. He looked around his makeshift prison, but there was nothing for him to stand on apart from a small weak table. Sitting down on his bed again, suddenly it came to him. The bed frame of course. Lying down on the floor he felt underneath and found the bed was constructed of two metal cross members supporting the old sprung mattress, in his excitement at the discovery he stood quickly and threw the mattress off its frame onto the floor, only to grimace with pain as he did so.

He was now convinced that there wasn't anyone out there watching him, because if there had been they would have certainly been in the room by now? The soreness from his wounds was unbearable as he turned the bed onto its side before managing to stand the bed frame up against the wall. Somehow he had to summon up all the strength he had left to climb up and onto the structure, praying it would support his weight. His plan was to use one of the metal supports to break through the plaster ceiling. He had no illusions that this would test him to the limit. He climbed up the ladder like frame, hauling himself into position, before striking forcibly upwards with the metal strut, but to his cost it bounced back off the ceiling. His aching arms taking the shock causing him to loosen his grip and the strut fell to the floor.

Struggling, he climbed down to retrieve the makeshift tool, then climbing up, he once more pointed the strut towards the ceiling and struck up several times, hacking at the ceiling with as much force as he could muster. The sharp end of the angled support pierced through the plaster making a small hole, and almost instantaneously the fluorescent strip light went off without warning and the room was in complete darkness.

Steadying himself he stayed completely still and managed to keep his balance, nervously waiting to see if his kidnappers had returned, but no one came running into the room. After a while his eyes became more accustomed to the darkness.

His only reasoning for what had just happened was probably that they were using a card operated electric meter, so after a few moments he carried on until the small hole became larger with every strike of the metal strut, making an aperture a good two feet long and a foot across, the distance between one joist to another. Jonathan peered up into a dark void now certain that this was the roof space and not another room above. This was apparent by tiny shafts of light penetrating through several small gaps in the roof slates, but how could he summon up all his strength to haul his bruised body up and through such a small opening. He decided he needed to rest a while before he should attempt such a feat.

*

This is *BBC Radio Northampton* with the four o'clock news. Earlier this afternoon the police released details regarding a kidnapping incident that took place last Friday morning near to Kegworth Canal Wharf. They are looking for a gang who are thought to have abducted a local business man. Police believe the kidnappers could be holding the person somewhere in an area to the west of Northampton, and they have appealed to anyone who may have seen anything unusual over the last few days to call Northamptonshire or Leicestershire police with any information regarding this matter.

"Did you hear that Betty? Some fellow's been kidnapped in this area and they reckon he's probably still being held around this part of the county."

"You better take care then Bert?"

"Don't you go worrying about me love; anyway I best get on and feed the sheep up at Nobottle Wood."

Bert Wilkins climbed up into his tractor cab and set off out of his farmyard, turning right along the Duston road until he reached Nobottle Wood, then turning left he headed down the track towards bottom field. It was just getting dark as he passed by the old cottage, where the surrounding tall dark pine tree's gently swayed in the cold evening breeze. Bert carried on to the end of the track listening to the radio, so he wouldn't have heard Jonathan Harker smashing his way through the slated roof of the old cottage. When Bert reached the gateway into bottom field he stopped the tractors engine, climbed down, and took a bale of hay from the trailer before carrying it across to the five bar gate.

There he cut the bale strings and threw the loose hay over into the field, at the same time calling out to his sizeable flock of sheep. He was on his way back for a second bale, when he thought he heard the sound of something breaking, and then what sounded like an object sliding off a roof before dropping to the ground and smashing.

"What the bloody hell was that?" He listened more intently, then again he heard the same sound. He decided to walk back along the muddy track to see where the noise was coming from, and before long he was approaching the old cottage. As he reached the broken wicket gate, a slate came sliding off the roof and smashed on the garden path in front of him. Startled, he quickly moved back across the track, calling out, "Who's there?" But there was no reply. 'What's going on here,' he thought to himself. It can't be the wind, it's not rough enough tonight, probably some bloody kids trying to frighten me, well we will soon see about that. He went back to the tractor to find his torch, and within minutes he was back at the cottage shining his new 1,000 candle powered flashlight up onto the single story apex roof.

Jonathan knew there was someone out there, but waited for them to make the next move. He had to be certain his kidnappers hadn't returned. Bert spotted the small hole in the slates and played the beam around the area. It's got to be kids messing about he thought again, so he decided to call out again, only this time much louder, "What the hell's going on up there?" Jonathan had to take a gamble on this person not being one of his abductors, so he replied calling out, "Help me, please, help me?" Bert was taken aback because he hadn't really expected anyone to answer. "What's going on up there?"

Jonathan called out that he was being held by kidnappers. 'Bloody hell, this is the bloke the police have been looking for,' Bert thought.

"Will you be all right if I go to get some help?"

Jonathan couldn't reply, he was too exhausted. He put down the metal bed support and rested in the best way he could, by straddling his aching limbs across the ceiling joists.

Wallace was back at the station when the desk sergeant came into the detective's office.

"There's been a call regarding the kidnapping sir."

"Thank God for that," was Wallace's instant reaction.

"Yes sir, a farmer reckons he may have found your kidnap victim. I have written the address down for you, some village out near Duston called Nobottle." Wallace thanked the sergeant, and punched Jack Terry's number into his mobile phone as he quickly walked out of the office. "Jack, I think we may have found Jonathan Harker. Meet me at this address."

Wallace explained how to get to Brington Hill Farm, where Bert Wilkins would be waiting for them. Terry was the first officer to arrive, closely followed by DI Wallace. The DS knocked on the farmhouse door and a short stocky man in his late 60s came to the door.

"Good evening sir. I understand you may know the whereabouts of the person we are trying to locate?" Bert told Wallace about the strange activities earlier that evening as he was feeding his sheep at Nobottle Wood. Wallace asked if could take them up to the cottage, asking him to stop before turning into the lane, which Bert had just described. They all climbed into Terry's car and proceeded along the Duston road to the farm track. When they reached the track Wallace thanked Bert, asking him if he wouldn't mind waiting for them at the top of the track.

Nobottle Wood appeared very dark and uninviting as the two policemen walked slowly down the muddy track, trying as best as they could to keep their feet dry.

"Jack is that the cottage down there on the right hand side."

"Well your eyesight must be better than mine; I can't see anything at the moment guv, only trees?"

"Just follow me and watch out for the puddles Jack." Soon they were standing behind a large fir tree opposite the cottage, the place being in complete darkness.

"This is an unusual situation Jack, obviously we don't know for sure if the kidnappers are still inside or not, and there's only one way to find out, we will have to make the first move. If Harker is in there on his own, we can't wait too long, as they might come back, although seeing they have left corpses all over the place, I think it's pretty unlikely. We have no option, we have to let this chap know we are here."

"Well the old place looks abandoned to me guv," Wallace called out in a low hushed voice.

"Are you in there Mr Harker?" There was no response.

"You try Jack?" Terry called out, only this time much louder than his colleague.

"Mr Harker, this is the police are you up there?" Then they heard a muffled reply, "Yes, please help me?"

"Mr Harker, are the people who were holding you anywhere around, as far as you know?" he called back, weakened by his earlier efforts.

"No, I'm fairly sure, they have abandoned me."

Wallace asked Jack to stay at the front of the cottage to keep a lookout, while he went around the back to see if there was any way into the property. Within a few minutes or so Wallace was opening the four bolts that had served over the last few days to keep Jonathan Harker a prisoner. He shone his torch around the room and noticed the bed frame leaning against the wall, and the aperture in the ceiling above. He played his flashlight around the hole where Harker must have crawled through between the joists.

"Are you up there Mr Harker?" There was no reply. Wallace left the room to go back outside to fetch Jack, to help him up into the roof space.

"Right Jack, hold the frame while I climb up." Wallace squeezed his head then struggled to fit his broad shoulders up through the small gap. Using his flashlight he was able to see Harker leaning back up against the gable wall. Harker turned his head away as the beam of light shone into his face.

"Mr Harker are you okay?" He didn't answer, but nodded his head to motion yes.

"Can you move sir?" Again he gave the same reaction.

"Please can you try to move towards me sir?" Harker started to make his way across the rafters towards the detective.

"We have been looking for you for three days now sir," Wallace told him as they eventually came face to face with each other. They both helped Harker down from the roof space; Jack had already called for an ambulance to take him to the local hospital to be checked out. He thanked the two offices as he was being carried out of the cottage by the ambulance crew and asked them to call his wife for him.

"Of course sir, I will go over to Sedgwick House and tell her personally."

Wallace turned to his DS saying, "Thank God we have found him alive Jack, because the way this botched up kidnapping has been going; I really feared for this chap's life, thank goodness his nightmare is over."

CHAPTER FIFTEEN

Ted was more than pleased with the progress he had made so he decided to carry on, bypassing Mulhouse on the eastern fringe of France and the German border. He decided instead to continue his journey to the border crossing at Basel. There he would have to pay the Swiss road toll to enable him to cross through the country, knowing this from previous experience of travelling this way across Europe. He would also have to pass through passport control at the crossing, as Switzerland isn't a member of the EEC; his thinking being that the border would be much quieter after dark as there would be less border control officers on duty and, from experience, those who were seemed to be more relaxed at that time of day. That's how he hoped it would still be, so he would drive on and try to reach Basel sometime around 10:00pm.

*

Wallace now had Nobottle Wood Cottage and the surrounding area locked down and forensic personnel were busy in and around the tiny cottage. Uniformed officers had been given orders to search in the nearby woodland. DS Terry had been left in charge and was now talking to Sergeant Benson.

"Where's the governor gone to Jack?"

"He's on his way to tell Harker's wife that we have just found him."

"I should have thought he would have called her, rather than travelling all the way over there," Benson replied.

"Apparently he wants to gauge Mrs Bernard's reaction."

"Does he think Mrs Harker's friend has something to do with the kidnapping then Jack?"

"You know the DI, he doesn't give too much away, you

should know that. Perhaps that's why he's the governor and we are still sergeants George." They both smiled.

"Yeah reckon you're right there Jack."

Natasha answered the door to see Inspector Wallace standing there.

"Good evening Natasha. Do you think I could see Mrs Harker please?"

"Certainly inspector, please come in. Mrs Harker is in the drawing room. I'll go and tell her you are here."

"Thank you, and by the way, is Mrs Bernard still staying here Natasha?"

"Yes inspector, she is."

"Would you ask her to join us as well then please?" Natasha left to go up the stairs to tell Ester that Inspector Wallace wanted her to come down to the drawing room. When Lynda saw the inspector walk into the room with both Natasha and her friend Ester, she was sure it could only be bad news the officer was delivering, "Good evening Mrs Harker, ladies. I have some very good news for you Mrs Harker. We have found your husband and I'm delighted to say he is now safe." The reaction in the room was one of absolute relief.

"Thank God," Ester called out, hugging her friend Lynda who was sitting on the sofa with tears of joy streaming down her face.

"Where is he inspector, is he all right?" Lynda urged.

"He's at Northampton General Hospital." The mood changed slightly.

"Goodness what's wrong with him?"

"I am afraid I can't say, but there is nothing too serious, I am sure of that. Mrs Harker, could your chauffeur, Mr Jones, drive you over to the hospital as I have to return to the cottage where we found your husband?" Ester interrupted.

"I will drive Lynda, inspector." With that the two friends made themselves ready to leave.

Wallace returned to Nobottle Wood at around 9:00pm, speaking first to Jack Terry and asking if anything significant had been found. "I am afraid not, they must have given the place a bloody good clean up before they left, even using bleach guv."

"Yes I thought they had. When I broke in through the back door it really caught my sinuses."

"What about you guv, was the reaction from Mrs Bernard as you expected?"

"Far from it Jack, in fact quite the opposite. If Ester Bernard is involved in some way, then she's a bloody good actress. No, she was genuinely pleased that we had found Harker, so for the time being I think we can eliminate her from any involvement. It's now her husband Harry who we should be talking to. Anyway Jack let's get some sleep, and then first thing in the morning we will go to the hospital to see if Harker can speak to us."

*

The following morning Wallace and Terry walked into the reception at Northampton General Hospital A and E unit. The young woman on duty told them that there was nobody called Harker in any of their admission wards.

"Are there any other A and E units in the area miss?" Wallace asked.

"Sorry, wait a moment inspector, here we are. Mr Harker seems to have discharged himself at 2:00am in the early hours of this morning."

"He discharged himself, does it tell you where or who he left with?"

"No, I am sorry inspector, it doesn't."

The two officers made their way over to Sedgwick House.

"Jack you would have thought someone would have let us know they had taken him back home wouldn't you? Wasting our time travelling into Northampton."

"I reckon the poor sod just wanted his own bed after his ordeal guv."

"Yes, I suppose you're right Jack." Their car pulled into the driveway, the wheels on Terry's car crunched on the frosted gravel as it made its way up towards the house.

Natasha opened the door and warmly welcomed the two officer's in, she showed them through to the drawing room where Mrs Harker was having coffee with Ester. She stood when Wallace entered the room.

"Inspector, sergeant, thank you both so much for rescuing Jonathan, and please thank all your fellow officers involved and tell them we really do appreciate all their efforts in trying to find Jonathan over the last three days."

"Thank you Mrs Harker, how is he this morning?"

"He's very fragile and still a little sore, but after a good night's sleep, I am sure he feels much better this morning."

"We did travel over to the hospital earlier and they told us Mr Harker had discharged himself?"

"Yes inspector, we tried to persuade him to stay, but all he wanted to do was return to his home. I am so sorry you had a wasted journey, but in the excitement..." Wallace interrupted her.

"No don't worry about that madam, I understand, but do you think your husband would be able to speak to us? You see Mrs Harker, it is vital for him to make a statement as soon as possible."

"Yes inspector, he is anxious to tell you all he can to help you to apprehend his kidnappers."

"Natasha dear, could you ask Mr Harker to come down to his study, if you would be so kind?"

Wallace waited for Natasha to leave the room before asking Mrs Harker if her husband knew what was given to the kidnappers as the ransom, and in particular the family heirloom.

"I have told him about the amount of cash I have handed over to them, as this is what his kidnappers demanded. I also told him I gave them some valuable pieces of jewellery, but at this time of course, I have not been able to tell him of the family custom or about the heirloom. Of course this is a very delicate situation for me inspector and I would be grateful if you did not mention this to him at this time?"

"Very well madam, I will try to do as you ask. Let's just hope it doesn't come up in conversation."

"Thank you for being so understanding Inspector Wallace."

Natasha entered the room and informed her employer that her husband was waiting in the study. The two officers walked into the study, but Jonathan didn't stand to welcome them. His faithful dog, Jet, was sitting with his head on his masters lap, not even venturing to turn to see who had just entered the room. It was also plain to see that Harker was still feeling the effects of his ordeal.

"Good morning sir, do you feel up to giving us a statement ?"

"Yes Inspector, Wallace isn't it?"

"Yes sir and this is DS Terry, you may remember him from last evening?"

"Sorry gentlemen, last night was similar to the last few days, it's all a little blurred I'm afraid, please sit down won't you."

"Thank you Mr Harker," Wallace replied. They sat opposite him and Jack opened his note book waiting for his boss to ask Harker his first question. Wallace sat next to Jack looking across at Mr Harker.

"I know sir, the last few days have been, I am sure, very difficult for you, but we need to know what has happened to you, and in particular how you were abducted. And why you think anyone would want to kidnap you, but more importantly have you any idea who could have done this?"

Jonathan told the officers what had happened and how it was much like any other day, until he walked past a barge that was moored up just along from the Felford Arm junction. He explained how he had been distracted by the sight of a half naked woman in distress, who apparently had been tied up in the galleys cabin, and how this woman seemed to be in some distress. He said he did what anyone else would have done seeing her in such a predicament, and his first reaction was that he should try to help her. Nevertheless, before he could do anything he was knocked to the ground from behind, then kicked several times, before he lost consciousness, only to wake up and find he had been bundled inside what he thought was probably the engine compartment of the barge. He said he was locked in like a caged animal without food or water for the rest of that day and most of the next.

"Mr Harker did you see the person who attacked you at all?"

"I only wish I had inspector, but I clearly saw the girl. At first she looked in some pain with her hands tied up to the side of the cabin wall, then as I was trying to make some sense of the situation, she turned her head towards my direction and strangely seemed to be smiling at me. Incredibly inspector, I thought I recognised her, but I couldn't think where from. It was then I was hit hard from behind."

"Did you see this woman after that morning sir?"

"I may have seen her in the cottage where they were holding me."

"You say may have seen her?" Wallace asked.

"There were two people in the room when they removed the sack that they had tied over me. My vision at first was blurred and I had difficulty seeing, until my eyes became accustomed to the intensity of the fluorescent light which was shining down from directly above. One of them was a tall masked individual, there was no mistaking this, he was a powerfully built man. The other was, in contrast, much smaller and could very well have been a woman, but I could not say for sure."

"You said you thought you recognised this girl you saw in the cabin?"

"Well inspector as I lay there in agony that first day, her smiling face was never far from my thoughts. I knew I had seen her somewhere before and then I recalled the good looking woman sitting behind Harry Bernard's office desk. Yes, I am pretty sure it was Bernard's secretary."

"Can you perhaps remember her name sir?"

"I believe it was Suzy or Susan, but I have no idea what her surname was inspector."

"This Harry Bernard sir, would that be Ester Bernard's husband, your close friend?"

"Yes inspector that's correct." Both officers glanced at each other before Wallace carried on.

"Have you any idea how many kidnappers there may have been Mr Harker?"

"Not really inspector, but something changed on the night they were transferring me from the barge to their vehicle, of that I am sure."

"In what way did it change?"

"One of them had a very distinctive voice, it sounded very gruff, almost put on and because I couldn't see this person. His guttural tones sounded quite terrifying."

"Mr Harker, we believe this man to have been Dean Wilmot, have you ever heard of him?"

"No inspector, and if I had known him I would have given him a very wide berth. I am sure he was the thug who had kicked me with such relish and he even punched me when I was still helplessly inside the sack."

"Well, if it was Mr Wilmot sir, he won't be harming anyone else I am afraid. This man is now dead."

Gauging by the reaction on Harker's face it wasn't too

difficult to see that it gave him no pleasure to hear of Wilmot's death, although deep down he was probably allowing himself a moment of joy that this malicious bastard had meet his come-uppance. Wallace carried on with his next question.

"Sir, do you know a Mr Anthony Miles?" This time Harker was obviously shocked to hear a name he did recognise.

"Tony Miles inspector, what does he have to do with any of this?"

"If you could just answer the question sir."

"Yes I know Tony Miles, he attended the same school as me, although he was a couple of years below me."

"When was the last time you saw Mr Miles sir?"

"Probably six or seven months ago in London, but he's a decent chap, he couldn't have possibly had anything to do with my abduction Inspector Wallace."

"Well, I am afraid to say Mr Harker, Tony Miles was most certainly involved." Harker sat back in his study chair trying to take on board the gravity of what the officer was telling him.

"How can you be sure Tony was involved, you see, I just can't quite believe what you are telling me inspector?"

"I can see you are quite rightly upset to find out that Mr Miles was involved sir but you will also be shocked when I have to tell you we found Mr Miles's body in the early hours of Sunday morning, at the place the ransom money had been collected from." Harker turned very pale as if all the blood had been drained from his face, and was now staring down at Jet while he stroked the labrador's head.

"Good God, poor Tony, he never did have too much luck, but why would he want to harm me? I just can't understand that Inspector Wallace."

"It's true enough sir, but are you sure you are all right to carry on with the interview?"

"Would you mind if we took a break inspector, I am having some difficulty taking all this on board?"

"No that's fine, if I can be so bold, perhaps a cup of tea would be in order."

Harker picked up the internal phone and asked Natasha if she would make tea for him and his visitors. Five minutes later she brought in tea and biscuits for the three gentlemen, placing the tray down on Harker's leather bound knee-hole reading desk.

Jet now sat up in a begging manner waiting for his master to drop one of his favourite Hobnobs into his open salivating mouth.

"Please help yourselves gentlemen." His voice sounded slightly broken.

"Thank you Mr Harker, now sir, are you all right to continue with the interview?"

"Sorry about that inspector, I am not normally as sensitive as this, the fact is, it's been a hell of a few days,"

"I understand totally sir, but if you can tell us when you last saw Mr Miles in London, and what he was doing regarding work?"

"Well I know what he was doing because he used to work for my company." Now it was the turn of the two police officers to be surprised by Harker's revelation.

"When you say he worked for your company Mr Harker, what exactly did he do for you?"

"He was a market runner. You see, even with all the new technology you still need someone who can meet other brokers in person, rather than talking to some faceless chap on the end of a phone or computer screen."

"Did he happen to tell you sir, what he had been involved in since leaving your brokers business?"

"Only that he had been working part time for a couple of the freelance brokers, this really is a terrible shock for me, to find out the person you thought of as a friend, turns out to be someone who put me through such hell. It has just occurred to me that the tall man with his face masked must have been Tony Miles."

"Going back sir, to Mr Bernard's secretary, did you happen to see her again?"

"No inspector, like I said to you earlier, there was one other person in the room when they removed the sack from my head after we arrived at the cottage. That was probably her, although I couldn't be sure."

"Okay sir, I think that will be all for now, and thank you for giving us a statement so soon after your ordeal."

"No Inspector Wallace, I should be thanking you and your colleague here, Sergeant Terry."

The two officers stood, Terry bent forward to stroke Jet but the dog never moved, he just sat with his head resting on Jonathan's lap.

"If you do think of anything else sir, that may help us further with our investigations, please don't hesitate to call the number on this card?" Harker took the card from Wallace, still slightly shaken and a little bewildered by the morning's revelations, and the two officers left the room.

Natasha was in the kitchen reading a letter, that had just arrived, as the two police officers walked in.

"Natasha is Mrs Bernard still here?" She quickly folded the letter and placed it in her blouse pocket.

"Yes inspector, would you like me to find her for you?"

"Yes, if you could please." A few moments later Wallace was asking Mrs Bernard if she knew where her husband was now living, as they could not reach him on the mobile number she gave to them.

"Inspector, although Harry and I have parted we are still in touch with each other, but surely you can't think Harry is involved in Jonathan's abduction, do you?"

"I am afraid we have to speak to anyone who may have had a motive and, until we speak to your husband, I am afraid we cannot eliminate him or anyone else who was involved with Mr Harker's business matters. I would appreciate your cooperation Mrs Bernard?"

"Very well. This is his current address in Cockfosters, that's North London you know." Jack walked over to the kitchen window and peered out. As a born and bred Londoner, he was unable to control his real thoughts about this arrogant woman who must have recognised his accent.

*

The Renault's main beam illuminated the large rectangular sign which read, Border Crossing one kilometre. Ted had made good time driving down through France and he was now about to enter Switzerland at Basel's border control. He drove on passing the row of low modern buildings with their typically cosmopolitan designed entrances. Pulling into the parking area, which was the perfect place in full view of the control office window, he knew he had to keep his eye closely on his vehicle.

He locked the Renault and walked over towards the well lit yellow brick office to pay for the tax permit he needed to enter the country. Three uniformed officers stood chatting to each other as he opened the polished glass pivot door One of them turned to acknowledge him as he walked up to the counter.

"Good evening officer, could I purchase a toll vignette please?" The officer, who had a quietly spoken French accent, replied, "Certainly sir, the cost is 40 Swiss francs." Ted handed him two 20 euro notes.

"Haven't you any Swiss francs?"

"I am afraid not officer," Ted replied.

The quietly spoken man proceeded with the transaction. "Will you be staying in Switzerland or just passing through sir?"

"Just passing through your beautiful country."

"What is your final destination going to be sir?"

"I am on my way to Milano, Italy."

"Could I see your passport and driving licence?" Ted handed over the documents as the officer pushed an A4 size piece of paper across the counter.

"Please will you fill this form in for me, making sure you answer all the questions correctly?" After he had finished filling in the form, Ted waited patiently until the officer came back across to him. He scrutinized the paperwork before handing Ted the vignette.

"Here you are sir. Everything is in order and you can continue through my country," he said smiling, as he finally passed Ted his passport over the counter. Thanking the border guard, Ted then walked back across to the Renault and drove out of the control point, passing through the open barriers where two motorcycle riding police officers sat astride their gleaming motor cycles. He turned towards them and gave them an acknowledgement as he slowly left the controlled area.

A short time later he was driving around the outskirts of Basel, with its seemingly endless tunnels and set after set of traffic lights. Tramcar tracks criss-crossed the wide orange lit streets. About 30 minutes later he was back on the motorway heading towards Lucerne and the Hotel Rigiblick, down on the pretty south bank of the lake.

*

At 8:00am Wallace and Terry were busy chatting to each other as they travelled down the M1 motorway on their way to speak to Ester Bernard's husband Harry.

"It will be nice to see my old stamping ground again guv."

"Well don't get too excited Jack, we won't be stopping, at least I hope not, no disrespect to you but I can't stand the place."

"It's like this, I much prefer concrete to all of the cow shit and wet grass we have been trudging around in over the last few days."

"How well do you know the Cockfosters area anyway Jack?"

"Like the proverbial back of my hand. An old aunt of mine used to live in Warden Way, that's about five minutes from the station."

"I didn't know you were stationed at Cockfosters Jack?"

"No guv the train station, she lived near the train station."

"So you reckon you can find Bernard's address pretty easily then?"

"Well it must have altered quite a bit since I was last down there, so we will just let the *Navman* find it for us guv."

"Call yourself a Londoner Jack?" he joked as he cheekily looked across at his sergeant.

*

At 8:30am a dark blue police car drove into the car park at the Hotel Rigiblick, just as Ted was sitting in the restaurant conservatory having breakfast. He watched the officer climb out of his car and walk around the large car park. He seemed to be looking at the windscreens of the parked vehicles as if he was checking for out of date tax discs or something, then when he approached Ted's car he stopped and peered at the Renault's front windscreen. Ted placed his knife and fork down onto his plate. Watching the policeman's every move, he could see he was now writing in his notebook. What the hell was he up to?

The policeman then looked towards the hotel, before walking up to the reception area with rather a stern expression on his round plump face.

A few moments later a waitress came over to Ted's table, informing him there was a police officer waiting to speak to him at the reception.

He asked, "Are you sure you have the right person miss?"

"Yes sir. If you could go to the reception he's waiting there for you now." Ted walked into the plush red carpeted reception lounge, with a broad smile on his face, and politely asked, "You wanted to see me officer?" The policeman who was standing by the reception desk. The short, well built, officer was wearing a smart sage green uniform. Ted thought it was reminiscent of the 1940s. His hand gun grip was protruding from the chrome leather holster which was strapped to his right leg. On his head he wore a peaked cap, slashed in a military fashion, and the whole uniform was finished off by his expressionless face, which made Ted think he really meant business.

"Your car, this is the one yes?" He showed Ted the registration number in his notebook.

"Yes officer, that certainly is my car?"

"It has no vignette permit needed in Switzerland." Ted felt hugely relieved but did not show it.

"I am so sorry officer. I have a vignette permit, but I have forgotten to place it onto the window screen."

"You will show me," he asked in a manner that matched his uniform. Ted reached into his wallet and pulled out the vignette, apologising in his very best French, this only seemed to get the officer back up. He asked Ted to follow him outside to his police car.

"This is a very serious offence; you will have to pay a fine of 100 Swiss francs." Ted was thinking, 'you really are a bastard aren't you,' but politely told the officer he hadn't any Swiss francs and asked if he could he pay the fine on his credit card. It was as if Ted had just told him what an ugly sod he really was, as his face reddened with anger. He reached inside the police car and then placed the card machine on top of the car's bonnet.

"Why do you English never have Swiss francs?" Ted never answered him as he punched in his four digit code and smiled at the officer, hoping this episode would soon be over. But no, the policeman was now walking back over towards the Renault. Ted followed anxiously a few paces behind.

"Where are you driving to?" He really was an arrogant sod, no sir, or mister, or any pleasantries at all.

"I am on my way to Milano officer." The policeman was now tugging on the car door handles, and coarsely ordered, "Now, you will open your car for me?" Ted obliged and pressed his key fob. After he had looked inside and found nothing, he proceeded to walk around to the rear of the Renault where Ted had, just before breakfast, placed his suitcase back into the boot. 'This can't be happening,' he thought to himself as the officer opened the boot lid. He rummaged around moving the packets of food and the French wine bottles he had brought at the filling station just before crossing the border into Switzerland. Now he really was getting more than a little nervous as the officer lifted out his suitcase and placed it onto the concrete, then he continued to search the Renault's boot. Ted asked if was looking for anything in particular.

He looked up at Ted saying, "Where are your emergency tools and spare light bulbs?" Ted leaned forward and opened the side pocket to reveal the items. The policeman looked slightly disappointed that he had all the legal requirements he needed, even the two obligatory triangle warning signs.

"Okay, everything is in order, you can go now." Ted hoped his relief didn't show as he thanked the policeman and wished him good morning. By the time he was entering the hotel reception the police car had left the car park. He paid his hotel bill realising, this was the second time in a matter of minutes, he had used his credit card in Switzerland and he had to make it the last.

*

Terry was now being instructed by the *Navman* to turn right off the Cockfosters road and into Mount Pleasant before turning left into Ashhurst Road.

"Bernard's place is somewhere up here on the right guv. His house should be coming up now, yes there we are 206."

Standing on the front drive was an old Jaguar S Type in British racing green, although the first impressions of the house didn't match up to the Jaguar. The outside of the house was really quite tatty in places and the paint was beginning to peel off the old wooden sash windows and the fan glass door. They walked up to the door and Wallace rang the bell. No answer. He rang again. This time he heard a voice call out, "All right, I am on my way." The door opened and a slim man in his late 40s stood there. Before he could speak Wallace was showing his warrant card.

"I am DI Wallace and this is DS Terry." He looked quite shocked to have a visit from the police, but answered with, "Yes gentlemen, how can I help you?"

"We would like to ask a few questions if you don't mind sir?"

"No of course not, please come in out of the cold."

He led them through to the sizeable living room, which was very sparsely furnished. It's main contents were a green leather sofa, a table and four chairs, all of which had seen better days. There was a large bay window which looked out onto the front of the house where the Jaguar was parked. Bernard seemed to be a polite enough sort of man Terry thought. He offered both officers a seat on his sofa, to which Wallace declined.

"So put my mind at ease inspector, and tell me what I can do for you two gentlemen?"

"Could you tell us of your whereabouts over the last three days Mr Bernard?"

"Am I allowed to know why you are asking me this question inspector?"

"It will all become clear sir, if you could just answer the question for me?"

"Well inspector, I have been here most of the time, that is apart from visiting my mother in Hendon on Sunday afternoon."

"Where in Hendon does your mother reside Mr Bernard?"

"At the old people's home in Wingate Road, it's just off the high street inspector."

"Could you tell us the name of the home your mother resides Mr Bernard?"

"Quinsy Gardens." Terry noted the information in his shabby notepad.

"What about Friday and Saturday sir?"

"I was here all day Friday, but Saturday I went to the High Street to do my weekly shop."

"Did you meet anyone that could verify your movements on these two days Mr Bernard?"

"Actually no inspector, I am quite new to the area, so I haven't got to know too many other people yet."

"Mr Bernard I understand that you and your wife have recently separated?"

Bernard's expression changed to one of concern with the mention of her name.

"Has something happened to Ester inspector? Is that why you are here?" He now looked extremely worried, and there was real anxiety in his voice.

"No Mr Bernard. Your wife is fine, in fact she is the person who gave us your address."

"Ester gave you my address, what for?" Wallace continued, ignoring Bernard's question.

"Could you tell us Mr Bernard if you know a Mr Jonathan Harker?"

"I know the bastard all right." He showed instant antagonism.

"Who's the poor sod he has ripped off now inspector?" He spoke with true venom in his voice, and he had gone from a mild mannered man, to one with hatred in his heart within a few moments. Inspector Wallace looked across at Terry and gave him a look that meant, carry on Jack.

"Well Mr Bernard it is obvious there is no love lost between you and Jonathan Harker. Could you please give us the reason for your dislike of this man?"

"I'll give you a reason Detective Sergeant Terry, where would you like me to start. The fact is this man and I went to the same school, moreover, I once thought of him as a friend, but that was before he completely ruined my life."

"Could you tell us in what way sir?" the DS asked.

"He invited me to invest in a hedge fund venture, which he sold to me as a guaranteed rock solid investment, only to have it crash around my ears within only a matter of months."

"If you don't mind me asking, how much money did you lose sir?"

Bernard hesitated to take in a deep breath, and then spluttered out, as if he was having difficulty mouthing the words, "750,000 pounds." Both officers were visibly shocked by the shear amount of money Bernard was telling them Harker had lost him. He carried on, "But that's not the only reason I hate that bastard." Wallace and Terry let him continue. "You see I still love my wife very much." His voice now softened, also the anger had almost dissipated. "I would have her back tomorrow, but she won't be coming home any time soon, she has been, as far as I am concerned, brain washed by those despicable people the Harkers. She left me, and I don't mind admitting to you, a broken man."

He sat there for some time, trying to regain some equanimity before he could speak again.

"You see, my wife Ester has been having an affair with Jonathan Harker and his toffee nosed wife Lynda for the last couple of years, so now you know why I hate them both so much. They stole my life savings, but worst of all they broke my heart."

The atmosphere in the room was as if someone had just sucked all the air from inside, but if this was all true then Harry Bernard certainly had good reason and definite motive to be involved in Jonathan Harker's abduction.

They gave him a few moments to recover his self control, before Wallace asked, "Mr Bernard what do you know, if anything, about Lynda Harker's family?"

"All I know inspector, is what my wife has told me about her, and that she is supposed to come from some so-called aristocratic family with the name Vasardicky. I believe they were of Hungarian decent."

"You seem to know quite a lot about her family sir, for someone who detests them so much."

"Inspector, when Ester was in her early teens she went to the same boarding school as Lynda Harker, and they were friends even then, so this is how I know so much of their family history. It's only through my wife and, I can assure you, no other reason."

"Do you have any knowledge of any unusual traditions her family may have sir?"

"Only the crazy story Ester told me of an heirloom which has been handed down through several generations of the Cockburn family."

"Carry on sir." Bernard continued on, in the vein of a man who cared nothing for the people he was talking about.

"Well I don't know why, Inspector Wallace, you would want to hear about their ridiculous family traits but, for what it's worth, this is what Ester told me. Apparently the heir, who of course now is Harker's wife, for some strange reason, was not allowed to divulge to her spouse that this heirloom even exists, at least not until they have been married for a minimum of 12 years. Now what does that tell you inspector about these so called aristocrats?" Wallace ignored Bernard's rant.

"Do you think that Jonathan Harker knows of this secret sir?"

"I don't know that inspector, and quite frankly I don't care."

"Mr Bernard, I am amazed by your knowledge of Mrs Harker's family history."

"I have known all these facts ever since her father, Efran Cockburn, past away. Like I said before, Lynda Harker must have told Ester this mysterious family secret rather than telling her own husband, this is why I believe our marriage is over for good. There must be something more than just sex between them all inspector."

"Have you ever talked to anyone else regarding Lynda Harker's ancestry, or possibly what you have just disclosed to us Mr Bernard?"

"Absolutely not Inspector Wallace, and as much as I hate Jonathan Harker, I haven't even told him."

"Mr Bernard, we are investigating a very serious crime where two people have already been killed, most probably murdered."

Bernard's expression changed again, this time to a look of horror to think that he was being questioned about such a serious crime. He had thought all these questions were about Harker defrauding some other poor innocent sod. This was appalling news and he now wondered if his wife Ester was somehow mixed up in this terrible crime? Perspiration ran down his face as Wallace looked directly into Bernard's eyes and asked, "We believe you and your wife, Mr Bernard, were the only two people who knew about the heirloom, apart from Lynda Harker. We don't believe your wife is involved so that just leaves you sir. I will ask you to think again, are you positive you haven't told anyone else about this heirloom?" Bernard seemed uneasy and never spoke for at least a minute, twisting uncomfortably on the sofa, he then looked up at the two policemen and eventually said, "There was one night I let my emotions get the better of me inspector." He carried on. "I was on what turned out to be my last business trip to South Africa, when I bumped into another old school friend of mine. We had dinner together at his house where I became very drunk, ranting on about how that bastard Harker had ruined my life. So I may have mentioned the heirloom then to him, but I could not be one hundred percent sure inspector, because I remember very little of the evening after drinking so much alcohol."

"Who was this old school friend of yours sir?" Bernard felt as if he was about to betray his friend when he told the inspector, "His name is Fredric Edward Bromley, but let me assure you, Freddy is no criminal. In fact, quite the opposite. He was a Lieutenant Colonel in the British Army, served for over 20 years with great distinction, decorated even."

"Which regiment did Mr Bromley serve with sir?" Terry asked with some interest.

"Special Forces sergeant, although he never spoke about it too much."

Wallace asked, "Do you know if Bromley is still living in South Africa?"

"No inspector, he's back in the UK now I believe."

"You wouldn't happen to have his address by any chance Mr Bernard?"

"No, although my wife must have it. She knew Freddy's wife quite well, even though they are also separated I believe. According to Ester, it was not long after they returned to England. His wife took their children out of boarding school one evening without telling Freddy, and left the next day for America, breaking his heart in the process." Wallace looked across at his sergeant and then turned towards Bernard once more.

"Could you tell us the name of the secretary you last employed Mr Bernard?"

"Why would you want Suzy's name inspector?"

"If you don't mind Mr Bernard, could you just tell us?"

"Her name is Susan Walters."

"Would you still have her address by any chance sir?"

"Not her current address inspector, as the last time I saw her she was moving to, where was it now, oh yes, Northampton I believe."

"Mr Bernard, you won't be going out of the country any time soon I hope, will you?"

"Certainly not, I have my mother to care for."

"Right then sir, we will be in touch with you very soon, after we ratify your movements over the last three days. Until then, there are no further questions for now."

Harry Bernard showed the officers to the door. The two policemen left, leaving him to ponder on his morning's unexpected visitors.

"What do you think now guv?" Terry asked his superior as they drove out of Bernard's street.

"Well, he's given us so much food for thought Jack, but there is one certainty. I think we can disregard him as one of our prime suspects, even though he has more than his fair share of motives. I doubt very much if he's involved with Harker's kidnapping, apart from his loose tongue to his South African friend."

"That's unless he's pulling the wool over our eyes of course."

"No Jack. If they confirm that he visited his mother at this Quinsy Gardens old people's home on Sunday, then I think he's probably in the clear. That's not to say I won't be keeping a close eye on him. DS Benson will be tracking his every move. Get him down here now Jack, and ask him to meet us at Muswell Hill police station around 4:00pm, and tell him to bring enough clothes for a couple of days."

"His missus is going to love you."

"Just get on with it Jack."

"This army chap, Fredric Bromley, he's got to be in the running surely?"

"Well now, he more than interests me. After you have spoken to Benson, ring Bernard's wife and see if she has an address for Bromley." Mrs Bernard answered her mobile and sounded a lot more cheerful than she had the last time DS Terry had spoken to her. She told the sergeant she was unable to give him Mrs Bromley's address, as she had recently moved to America.

"Did her husband go with her, as far as you know madam?"

"I really don't know sergeant, I am afraid I have lost touch lately."

"Very well Mrs Bernard, thank you for your help." Terry relayed his findings to Wallace.

"Ah well, worth a try. Okay Jack, let's drive over to this old people's home and check out Bernard's story. After that we'll go up to Muswell Hill station, Fortress Green."

"Here we are Quinsy Gardens - home for the elderly. Suit you this place would Jack, sitting around all day drinking tea and playing bingo."

"Yes, well thanks for that, but I reckon you have a head start on me already guv. I will have a word with the matron when we are inside if you like."

*

Ted was having to make up time and found himself travelling much faster now than he wanted to in order to get back onto his schedule. He had to arrive in Venice at least two hours prior to the ferry sailing, and even at this rate his timing was going to be tight.

It was now 11:00am and he was only just driving past Montichiari Airport, east of Milan on his way to Padova and then onto Venice, which was still another good one hour drive after that. Keeping a sharp eye on the rear-view mirrors, Ted increased his speed even further and, judging by the amount of crazy Italian drivers overtaking him, any thought of the police pulling him over lessened. He had been very lucky so far as this motorway was usually snarled up on a regular basis, and after a few hours of hard driving Ted was almost there. He could see the matrix sign up in front of him which read, Venice Port and Commercial traffic only, albeit in Italian, but quite easy to decipher. He knew the way so well, the only difference this time was that he wouldn't be taking the car onto the ferry.

He drove off the port road, passing the commercial dock entrance, and then onto a rough potholed track that led down towards the sea. Thank God for *Google Earth* he thought to himself as he parked up on the grass verge just off the track. Looking around him he could see at least 20 other abandoned vehicles, left there to rot away in the salt filled atmosphere in this neglected Venice backwater. Taking a screwdriver from the boot he took off both number plates, followed by the Swiss permit and the Renault's tax disc. He needed to get away from this place as quickly as possible before he was seen so, with some haste, he lifted Tony's rucksack and the suitcase from out of the boot and donned his old duffle coat, making sure he hadn't left anything of importance. He then slammed the boot lid shut, and placed the number plates into a carrier bag. Finally, he locked the car and left.

The track was still deserted as he walked towards the footpath that he knew would eventually bring him to the main road, which leads down to the Venice Lagoon, via the causeway. Fifteen minutes later and he was standing by the dual carriageway hailing a cab, that was travelling at some speed, but the driver just ignored him, probably not wishing to stop on such a busy road. Three or four others did the same, until finally someone took pity on him. He opened the back door, pushed his suitcase in and over to the far side of the rear seat, then quickly jumped in next to it, while still holding on tightly to the rucksack. The driver started off before Ted had time to close the door, saying something in unmistakably angry Italian.

"Ferry port, *Minoan Lines* Senor?" The look on his face in the rear view mirror said it all. "Minoan?" he repeated. "Si Senor."

Five minutes later they were crossing the causeway and Ted was leaning forward looking over the driver's shoulder pointing directions into the ferry terminal. The ferry and cruise terminal were bustling with their usual vibrancy, coach after coach load of expectant tourists waiting in the canvas covered white tented shelters alongside their ships demarcation areas. His driver was becoming ever more frustrated with the lack of progress he was making, sounding his horn whilst waving his arm out of the window like some demented child, rather than an adult. In the distance Ted could see the Minoan lines ticket office, and there was no mistaking the huge hoarding above the new concrete building with its giant red arrow pointing down towards the ticket office.

When they arrived he paid the driver and pulled the wheeled suitcase over to the terminal door. Before entering, he looked across at the massive super ferry, the *Ickories Palace*, which would not only be his home, but sanctuary for the next 24 hours. As usual the terminal building was full of agitated people, in row after row of disorganised chaos, and they were pushing and shoving in preference to any over politeness. It was as if the ship was going to leave without them, their demeanour only changing when they eventfully reached the ticket office window.

Ted had seen this so many times and was very aware that this is the place where relatively organised northern European life melts into the less structured east. After queuing for half an hour he stood at the kiosk window, waiting for the raven headed young woman to serve him. As usual the staff never seemed to be in any sort of hurry, even though the ferry was due to sail in just 45 minutes time.

"Kalimera," was her Greek welcome as she approached him and smiled.

"Kalimera," he replied. He handed her his reference number, she hit the keyboard several times and then asked for his passport, glancing at his picture before handing it back. She asked where his final destination would be.

"As my ticket implies. Kerkyra."

"Your ticket is to Igoumenitsa?"

"No I'm sorry, I have paid for a ticket to Kerkyra."

"I am also sorry to inform you sir, because there are only 10 passengers travelling to Kerkyra on the ship, you will have to disembark at Igoumenitsa port."

It was then he remembered his friend Mary telling him many years before that this had once happened to her, and how when the ship docked at Igoumenitsa port on the mainland of Greece, she had to disembark and find her own way to Kerkyra by means of a local ferry company.

"Surely there will be a refund of some sort?"

"No sir, it is not possible." Then with the look of some apology she smiled and handed him his ticket.

He pushed his way back across the busy terminal dragging his suitcase behind him and hanging on to his rucksack as if his life depended on it. He then squeezed through the door, after asking the obese poker faced man to move. When he was clear of the queue he stood for a moment contemplating the best way across the congested ferry port parking area as trucks, cars, motor-homes all edging forward in a chaotic manner, like grains of sand trying to force their way through an egg timer, in the hope of reaching the ferry's narrow entrance and finally disappearing into the bowels of the ship. It was so unlike British ferry ports he thought, with their organised lane systems, where no one would dare to venture over the line or disobey the signs, but this is why he probably loved this place so much. He walked up the ramp and then onto the escalator which took him up to the purser's desk on B deck. After some small talk the purser issued him cabin number 412 on C deck. He was then shown to the cabin by a silver-haired elderly gentleman who couldn't have been far off retirement age, and who never spoke a word to him on their way through the several hundred metres of red carpeted corridors.

On reaching the cabin he opened the door for Ted, at the same time giving him just the slightest of smiles, as Ted handed the old timer three euros for his trouble. He instantly felt a huge sense of relief as the door was firmly shut and securely locked behind him. His first action was to take out the ransom money from the suitcase and lay it out onto the bed cover. Unrolling the bundle he was filled with excitement, so much cash and to think this was like loose change compared with the fortune he had been promised for the tiara. Then, for the first time, Tony's horrifically traumatised face came into his mind. He pictured him struggling as he gripped the pole with both hands as he tried to lift his head above the waterline. Had his conscience finally kicked in. But he wasn't some shrinking violet and it didn't take long before he secreted the thought deep into his subconscious once more.

Taking out the tiara he placed it on the bedside cabinet. He then sat back to admire its truly serene beauty, as the light danced around the gem stones causing an almost magical affect. His next concern was to make sure the cash and tiara would be safe for the long sea journey in front of him. He realised they had to stay with him at all times, so he placed the euro notes inside the rucksack again and then wrapping a Minoan lines hand towel gently around the tiara. He then placed it carefully on the top of the cash. Now he would be able to go up to the boat deck to see the huge ferry slip it's berth from what had to be one of the greatest departure points on earth.

He left the cabin and made his way back along the corridor and took the stairway to the boat deck finding himself a viewing position between two of the large white life boats that were hanging suspended over the deck. The crew of the giant red and white ferry were already lifting the hydraulic ramps to make ready for the voyage, at the same time the dock team scurried around some 40 feet below him slacking off and then releasing the thick ropes from the dock bollards. The ship's bow thrusters then took over to gently push the *Ickories Palace* away from the dock wall.

The earlier hustle and bustle of the dockyard had now subsided and it was now relatively quiet with only a few people waving goodbye to their loved ones on this typically cold Venetian January day. Soon the *Ickories Palace* was steaming up the Canele Della Giudecca with most of the ship's passengers waiting to view, surely the one of the world's greatest sights. Saint Marks Square and then Doge's Palace appeared where hundreds of tourists were milling around and enjoying the magnificent sights.

Ted left the boat deck and made his way down to the bar, he had seen Venice many times but its magnificence never failed to amaze him. He ordered a glass of Mythos, his favourite Greek beer and then sat down over by one of the large picture windows, just in time to see the well known sights of Venice slowly slipping away into the distance.

Twenty minutes or so later they were leaving the Venetian lagoon passing the Opera Santa Maria then continuing through the Canale Dei Petroli Aiberoni as Venice disappeared from view and the *Ickories Palace* sailed out and into the Adriatic Sea.

CHAPTER SIXTEEN

After quite some time talking to the staff nurse at the Quinsy Gardens rest home, and trying to make sense of what Bernard's poor old mother had told them, Wallace and Terry made a visit to the local police station at Muswell Hill to await the arrival of DS Benson. It was 8:00pm by the time they left the station and they arrived home late in the evening. Wallace decided they would visit Northampton sometime the following morning in the hope of tracking down Bernard's secretary, Suzy Walters.

Early next day Wallace was on the phone to Northampton Borough Council Housing Department in the vain hope that Suzy Walters had registered with them. The lady in the Housing Department was not very forthcoming and asked DI Wallace if it was possible for him to come into the office personally, as it was against their policy to give out information regarding tenants' addresses over the phone. He told her he understood and said he would be over later that morning. He asked if she could look into the files regarding the matter. Terry then walked into the office looking like the cat that had just got the cream.

"God what's up with you Jack, won the lottery or something?"

"I wish, no, do you remember when we went through Tony Miles pockets and found that scrap of paper in his trousers."

"Yes, what about it?"

"Well, forensics have been able to decipher a 10-digit number that makes up an STD code and telephone number somewhere in Northampton. I have just been on to BT and guess who the phone is registered to guv? Susan Walters, at an address in the centre of Northampton's Sanders Estate."

"Well done Jack. That will save us a hell of a lot of legwork." An hour later the two officers arrived on the estate as arranged and found Mrs Howell, the estate housing officer, waiting outside one of the several tall tower blocks. She was ready to let the two police officers into Paget Block via the communal door. Wallace showed the lady his warrant card and both officers were let into the building. She took them up in the small lift until they reached the fourth floor, Wallace asked, "Mrs Howell, do you know the tenant we are looking for?"

"No I am afraid I don't inspector, I have only worked on Sanders Estate for a short time; anyway here we are flat 201."

Wallace asked her to wait for them by the lift before trying the door. Much to his surprise it opened, so he pushed it gently and peered inside. There was a long corridor with two doors going off to the left and one to the right so he made his way inside closely followed by Terry. The flat appeared to be empty as they continued along the corridor, carefully opening all the doors in a controlled manner, and they found all the rooms to be clear. Wallace peered around the corner and into the lounge which was also empty. He turned to Jack to gesture to him to follow and now they were both standing in a medium sized, sparsely furnished lounge. In the far left hand corner there was one further door, where Wallace was now listening with his ear pressed firmly onto its veneered surface. He beckoned Jack over to him before gently opening the door and as he did so he could hear someone breathing. Peering into the room and saw that there was somebody lying in bed, asleep, with the covers pulled up and over their face. Pushing the door open a little further he motioned to Jack to follow him. Now both officers were standing inside the small bedroom and alongside a double divan bed. Wallace looked up at his DS, nodded, then bent slightly forward to lift the covers, and with some speed pulled off the blue duvet cover. This was followed by a piercing scream as the occupant sat up quickly squealing obscenities as if she was fighting for her life. The young, fully clothed woman was still screaming as the two officers held her down. Terry managed to secure his handcuffs onto her small wriggling wrists.

"Susan Walters, I am arresting you under suspicion of being involved with the kidnapping of Jonathan Harker. You do not have to say anything but anything you do say may be taken down and may be used as evidence against you, do you understand?"

When she realised it was futile struggling, she calmed down slightly but never spoke a word as Wallace asked, "Has anyone else been living here with you Miss Walters?" Still, she didn't answer him.

"Right Jack let's get her back to the station."

Just as Jack was leaving the bedroom he opened one of the wardrobe doors. It was full of men's clothes. He asked, "Miss Walters, do these clothes belong to Tony Miles?"

Again no reply, but a definite response Terry thought. Later that afternoon DI Wallace, and Terry, accompanied by WPC Trout, were interviewing Suzy Walters. The now tearful young woman was sitting bent forward, looking down onto the Formica topped table, as the inspector was asking her if she could tell him where she had been over the last few days. As before, she chose not to answer.

"Miss Walters, I don't think you realise the gravity of the situation you find yourself in."

"We are investigating two very serious crimes. In fact, the most serious, murder." She looked up at Wallace like a rabbit trapped by the glare of a car's headlights, and with anguish etched into her sore tearful eyes she answered, "Murder, I never had anything to do with any murder." She broke down begging, "You have to believe me inspector."

"Miss Walters, for your own good, you should tell us all you know, because we have a witness who can place you at the scene of the abduction of Jonathan Harker at Kegworth Wharf, last Friday morning." Suzy wiped her eyes before blurting out, "This wasn't our idea. It was that Ted, who put him up to this inspector."

"Put who, up to what Suzy?"

"I can't tell you."

"Do you mean Tony Miles, Miss Walters?" Again she lifted her head and peered up at Wallace saying, "Yes, and now he's left me in this mess."

"Suzy," Trout stood up in anticipation to what the inspector was about to say. "Suzy, I am afraid I have some very bad news for you."

She waited for Wallace to carry on, her eyes flooding once more with tears, "I am sorry to say Miss Walters," she was already screaming before Wallace could finish the words, "Mr Tony Miles is, unfortunately, dead."

Trout was now standing behind Miss Walters with her hands placed on her shoulders trying to comfort the young misguided woman.

"I will go and get some tea for her, shall I sir."

"Yes, let's take a break lass." He closed down the recording device after giving the correct time and information, and then as soon as Trout returned with the tea for Miss Walters, the two detectives left the room. Wallace asked Terry to go back and search Suzy Walter's flat to see what he could come up with. After a couple of hours, Jack was talking to his boss on his mobile.

"Found anything interesting, Jack?"

"You could say that, looks like they were planning to leave the country on Sunday night. There are two tickets here from the Brittany Ferry Company, for a sailing from Southampton to St Marlow, and their suitcases were already packed guv."

"Any indication pointing to anyone else who could have been involved?"

"I am afraid not guv."

"Okay Jack you better get back here when you've finished over there?"

"I should be with you in around an hour; I'm going to get some lunch first if that's all right with you?"

"Any chance you can pick up a cheese roll for me, oh yes, and make sure it's crusty.

*

At Sedgwick House Jonathan Harker was feeling stronger and was sitting in the dining room having dinner with his wife and Ester Bernard.

"Are you sure you are all right my darling?" Lynda asked as she poured him a glass of red wine.

"I am fine believe me, it's you I am worried about Lynda, those unspeakable people making you perform dam near unachievable tasks."

"We must both take it easy over the next few days darling, in fact, once we have completely recovered, I think we should go away, perhaps to the Florida Keys or California for awhile."

"We will have to see Lynda. I really don't want to make a decision like that at this time."

"Well I think that's an excellent idea of yours Lynda," Ester politely interrupted.

"Perhaps you could come also darling?" Lynda interjected.

"Let us just get this over and well behind us first," Jonathan somewhat tetchily chirped in. Natasha then entered the room.

"Excuse me for intruding while you are all having your dinner, but I have something very important to ask you and I am afraid it can't wait?"

"Whatever is it my dear girl, you look dreadful," Lynda said.

"I have just received a text message from my sister, in Slovenia, informing me there is a family problem and so I must go back to help her."

"Natasha you must tell me what the problem is my dear, we may be able to help."

"Thank you madam. It is my mother and father who are getting too old to run our small farm, and my sister, Silencer, cannot manage on her own because she has two little ones to look after, so she has asked me to return home."

"Well you must go back to help, if that's what you want to do Natasha, but how long do you think you will be away for my dear?"

"I have decided to go home to stay for good. I am so sorry to have to let you down as you have been so very kind to me but, under the circumstances, if I don't go back my family will lose their farm." Lynda looked quite taken back, but could see just how upset Natasha was feeling.

"When were you thinking of leaving Natasha?"

"Tomorrow Mrs Harker. I am so sorry I could not give you more notice."

"Tomorrow." Lynda was surprised she would be leaving so quickly. Ester stood up and put her arms around Natasha, telling her not to worry and that she must do the right thing for herself and her family.

"Yes dear of course you must," Jonathan interrupted.

"Thank you sir, you are so kind." She then again repeated how sorry she was, before leaving and closing the dining room door behind her. Lynda was looking across the table at Ester and her husband.

"Well, what a shock. I thought she would be staying with us for years, she seemed so happy."

"Perhaps I should go and help her to pack darling."

"That would be kind of you Ester."

"Yes, I wanted to have a word with Jonathan in private and this will give me the opportunity, that's of course, if you don't mind darling?"

"Lynda you carry on, and I will go and comfort the poor girl." With that she left Jonathan and Lynda sitting at the dining table to go and find Natasha.

"Jonathan I know that this is going to be somewhat of a surprise to you, but I have something very important to tell you that may make you very unhappy with me."

"For goodness sake Lynda, what is it, and is this night to be full of surprises?"

"Well my darling it is about the ransom those terrible people stole from us, in fact it, was much more than I first told you."

"How much more Lynda?" he said with his anger directed at them.

"It was as I told you, one million euros, but there was something else."

"What else for God's sake?" his frustration now beginning to show.

"Jonathan what I am about to tell you my darling, will probably infuriate you."

"What is it woman?" his patience now strained to breaking point.

"Please bear with me darling, this isn't easy for me." He sat back in his chair, folded his arms and looked across the table waiting to find out what was so important. Lynda carried on, "Jonathan ever since we first meet I have been longing to tell you something about my family, and a secret that I have had to keep from you all this time." Now he looked more intrigued, saying. "What secret could you have possibly kept from me Lynda?"

"Please my darling, let me carry on. You see my ancestors originated from Hungary as you know, but what you didn't know was they were related to the old Hungarian aristocracy, and these aristocrats were direct descendants of the Hungarian Royal Family." Jonathan's expression was one of sheer disbelief as to what his wife was telling him. She sat back and waited for her husband to take on board the enormity of her revelation.

"You surely have to be joking of course Lynda?"

"Believe me Jonathan when I say, it is the truth."

"You never thought to discuss or tell me about this Lynda?"

"I am afraid there is more darling. I know it will be hard for you to understand Jonathan but this second secret I am about to disclose to you has been held by every heir to the Cockburn's fortune for many generations of my father's family."

"Get to the point for goodness sake Lynda." he said with even more irritation in his voice.

"Please Jonathan, this isn't easy for me you know."

"Just tell me what it as to do with the ransom you paid out?"

"All right Jonathan. There is a family heirloom that has been handed down through the years to the sole heir and, as you know that is now me, the heirloom is an impeccable piece of jewellery in the form of a tiara, thought to have belonged to a Hungarian Princess who lived some 400 years ago."

Jonathan sat there in utter disbelief at the story his wife was telling him. It sounded more like a fairytale that had once been told to him has a child. As unbelievable as this story sounded, somehow his own wife had kept this a secret from him. Now he looked even more incensed, as he asked, "How in God's name could anyone keep what you are telling me a secret, let alone hidden from the person you are supposed to love?" His voice was now much softer but still retained the anger.

"Of course I love you, if I hadn't I would not have given in to their demands."

"Lynda are you saying you gave those bastards this tiara?" The tears were rolling down her cheeks as she replied, "Yes Jonathan darling, I had to." He reached over the table placing one hand on hers, and with the other he wiped a tear from her cheek.

"You did that for me, gave up this precious heirloom of yours to save my life, thank you my darling," he said as he kissed her sore blistered hands.

"I don't care about the jewellery Jonathan, I just wanted you to come back to me and be safe."

"How much, out of interest, was this tiara of yours worth?"

Daddy informed me about the tiara just an hour or so before he died, and he said that it was going to be left to me. It was then he told me it could be worth between four to five million."

Jonathan's jaw dropped at her revelation, totally flabbergasted, and he found himself repeating four to five million pounds.

"You can't be serious Lynda?"

"I am afraid to say, yes I am."

"How the hell did my abductors know of your family's secret heirloom, if I didn't know myself Lynda?"

She replied, "I have no idea Jonathan, but I am sure no one would ever touch such a valuable piece of jewellery and they would never be able to sell it."

"Lynda, is there anyone that could have found out about the tiara?" Just then there was a knock on the door and Ester asked if it would be all right for her to come in.

"We will talk about this later Lynda," Jonathan uttered with some irritation in his voice.

"Yes come in Ester," Lynda called.

"So sorry to interrupt you two, but Natasha has just received another text message asking if she could leave tonight. I told her I would come and let you know."

"This is all happening so quickly, isn't it Ester?"

"Well, I suppose if she is ready to leave then it is probably best for her to go home as soon as possible, don't you?"

"Yes you are right of course. Shall we ask Mr Jones to take her to the airport Jonathan?"

"Yes that's the least we can do."

At 7:30pm Natasha was standing at the front of the house saying her goodbyes to Jonathan, Lynda and Ester. Mr Jones loaded her two suitcases into the boot of the car and waited for Natasha to finish saying farewell to her employers.

"I hope everything turns out well for you and your family Natasha."

"Thank you Mr Harker, and to all your family for being so kind to me." Jonathan placed an envelope into her hand and told her, "This is for working so hard, especially over the last few days. Lynda could not have managed if you and Ester had not have been here for her."

"Thank you again Mr Harker that is very kind of you sir." She kissed them all and walked over to the car and climbed in. Mr Jones set off down the drive leaving the three of them to wave goodbye as the car turned right at the end of the gravel driveway and disappeared into the night.

CHAPTER SEVENTEEN

As the enormous ferry sailed out of the Venetian basin and into the Adriatic Sea, the wind began to pick up from the south. Ted had been on many rough sea journeys in his time, and the direction the wind was blowing from this evening made him think that this might just be another. The bar on C deck was quite busy with a mixture of truck drivers and tourists trying to find a decent seat to while away a few hours. Two men who looked as if they could have been truck drivers came over and sat at the table next to him, the larger of the two took out a backgammon board from his duffle bag and placed it on the table. Almost immediately they started to play.

Ted glanced across towards them, guessing they were probably Bulgarians because of their dark features and the fact that both of them were wearing well worn leather jackets and half woollen leather caps. In their country is almost the national dress code for a truck driver, at least that was his opinion. He watched them play as they chatted and drank back glasses of ouzo, sipping water in between each swallow to dull the effect of the alcohol. Picking up the heavy rucksack that had been firmly trapped between his legs, he stood to fetch himself another bottle of Mythos before returning to his seat again. The two men quietly continued with their game, one of them looking up briefly at Ted as he made himself comfortable again. He had only just sat down when the loud speaker system blasted into operation, first in Greek and then in English, informing the passengers that the self service restaurant on C deck would be opening at seven o'clock and to ask everyone to alter their watches by putting them one hour forward to local Greek time.

After a while Ted became a little restless so he swilled back the rest of his beer, before picking up his rucksack once more and made his way out of the bar and along the corridor into the self service restaurant. Queuing wasn't one of Ted's preferred pastimes but the food was well worth waiting for. He tucked into the hot plate of pastitsada and a glass of chilled Makedonikos then pressed his back firmly into the chair as he looked around the restaurant. He noticed the two Bulgarian drivers carrying their trays away from the checkout and over to the table opposite him. He couldn't help making eye contact with the larger of the two, but no smile, or any sort of gesture came back, just an uncomfortable stare. He thought no more of it and stood, lifted his backpack over his shoulder, and made his way back up to the boat deck.

Opening the watertight doors, he stepped outside onto the now soaked deck. The wind was blowing strongly from the south as he walked along the starboard side of the ship, 'it's going to be one hell of a night,' he thought, even the gigantic ferry was lifting her bow high out of the water before rolling and then crashing back down into the heavy swell. 'Time to get back inside,' he thought as he found the next available door. The heavy door closed automatically behind him nearly trapping his rucksack in the process. He alighted the two flights of stairs and proceeded to follow the direction signs back to cabin 412. He continued to walk along the passageway, its plush dark red carpets covering the width of the long corridor, a huge contrast from the soaked deck he had just come from. He also felt that the captain must have just deployed the stabiliser as the ship was much steadier now. On reaching his cabin he placed the plastic card into the brass electronic lock and the green light flashed as he withdrew it, at the same time pressing down on the handle and the door opened.

As he entered, he was sure he couldn't remember leaving the light on. He turned to close the door and sensed someone else was in the cabin. He turned quickly and saw a man lying on the his bunk bed with his feet up resting on the bedside cabinet. He instantly recognised him as the smaller of the two Bulgarians.

"What the fuck is going on, this is my cabin?" Ted angrily shouted. The driver stared up at him, grunted something under his breath and never flinched. "Do you understand this is my cabin?" Ted repeated, and again the same reaction. "We'll see about this."

Picking up the telephone off his bedside table, he pressed 1 for service and waited for someone to answer. It was a few minutes before a woman's voice answered his call, with one solitary Greek word, "Ela?"

"Hello, I am in cabin 412 and there is some other person in my cabin, will you send someone down to explain to him that he is in the wrong cabin please?"

"You share your cabin sir."

"Share, I'm not bloody sharing with anyone miss."

"Look carefully at your ticket sir." The Bulgarian looked bemused as Ted open his wallet and took out the ticket.

"I can't see where it says shared cabin?"

"Look in the bottom right hand corner sir." There in small print were the words, shared cabin, in both English and Greek.

"Well I am not happy about it, I would like another cabin."

"I am sorry sir but there are no other cabins available."

With that he slammed the receiver down onto its station. 'This can't be happening,' he thought to himself as he glanced across towards his now angry looking cabin mate.

"I am sorry; I didn't mean to offend you." The driver gave him a look of sheer displeasure, mumbling under his breath, "British heh."

Ted knew he could not spend the whole night guarding his rucksack in such circumstances as these as the cabin was no more than three by five metres. Living with a total stranger who he knew nothing about was to say the least, risky. No, this was an impossible predicament and one he certainly hadn't planned for, but one thing was clear in his mind, he wasn't about to spend the next 24 hours, keeping an eye on the smiling Bulgarian. First he had to get out of the cabin to clear his head and plan his next move.

The rucksack he had been gripping onto ever since he entered the cabin was once more slung over his shoulder. He turned to try to make amends, offering polite conversation to the driver, telling him he was going to take a walk, but the only reply he offered back was to raise his arm from his chest in a gesture of dismissal. Ted then made his way back up to the boat deck wondering what the hell he was going to do. He hadn't took to these two men from the first time he had laid eyes on them, and now he had to share his cabin with the smaller of the two. He had a bad feeling deep down in the pit of his stomach that it wasn't just the sea that was going to be rough on this night.

Checking his watch the time was 10:35pm. He decided to go up onto the top deck which was the home of a line of metal dog kennels, with their barking inmates, and the ship's discotheque. It was set up high so as not to disturb the passengers who would rather sleep than drink and dance the night away. He climbed the spiral staircase and entered the dimly lit room. Walking around the outside of the small circular dance floor, the music was pounding out an Ibiza type beat and the disco's spotlights were keeping to the rhythm. Three or four couples danced while others sat around drinking and laughing with each other. Ted approached the bar and swung his rucksack onto one of the tall barstools, he leaned forward to gain the attention of the smartly dressed barmaid who was chatting to one of her punters. She walked along the bar towards him and he couldn't help but notice just how attractive she was. She had long jet black hair, a natural olive complexion, melting brown eyes and a voluptuous body to match.

He ordered a bottle of Mythos and sat up onto the leather padded barstool. As she turned and opened the beer cooler, Ted asked, "Miss could you please tell me if the disco stays open all through the night?" She answered, "Until 4 o'clock sir." She took the top off the cold bottle and poured it slowly into a tall chilled frosted glass, placing it down in front of him, then noticing the rucksack. She asked, "Have you had a cabin allocated to you sir, only I see you are still carrying your luggage around with you? This threw Ted somewhat and he surprised himself when he answered her with a hesitant, "No I am afraid not, all the cabins seem to be taken."

"So you will be staying here to keep us company through the night then?"

"I might just do that." Someone at the other end of the bar called out, "Ela, Katarina."She pushed a white receipt slip towards him and smiled before walking back along to the other end of the oval shaped bar, he sipped his beer while twisting the stool around to watch the dancers. It was then he spotted the two drivers sitting on the other side of the room looking across in his direction. God there was something very strange going on here, who the hell are these people, and what was it with them, why the menacing looks, or was it that they just don't like the British? Even more concerning was that they had cottoned on to the fact that his rucksack stayed by his side wherever he went, pre-empting them to surmise he might be carrying valuables around with him.

This was going to be a good time to return to the cabin and retrieve his suitcase before his happy Bulgarian share partner returned. Picking up the rucksack, he made his way around the bar and left the disco through the side door out of view of his admirers. Quickly he descended the two decks and was soon entering the corridor leading to the cabin. As he placed the card into the security slot, he spotted one of the drivers entering the corridor, the green light flashed and he quickly entered the cabin turning the lock to prevent anyone from opening the door. The suitcase was where he had left it and looked intact. He heard them outside the door as he stood listening, and they were mumbling something in Bulgarian whilst trying to gain entry. He was trapped, but he had been in much tighter situations than this, and a couple of foreign truckers were not going to intimidate a past Special Service Officer who could put them into the next world very quickly if he so wished to do. Making sure his rucksack was secured tightly to his back, and knowing he would need at least one of his hands free, he then lifted the suitcase in his left hand and unlocked the cabin door. The two men now fell silent as he slowly opened the door, then, giving the first of them a resolute stare that seem to say, in anyone's language, try you bastards if you have the bottle.

By the look on the face of the taller of the two men, he knew he had a fight on his hands. He didn't hesitate in bringing his knee sharply up into his first opponents groin at the same time catching him with a right uppercut to the side of his jaw. The big man's knees buckled and he lay squirming on the floor holding his bollocks. Within a matter of seconds Ted had wrapped his index finger and thumb around the shorter of the two men's throat, holding him just long enough in the sleeper position before letting him go. The man stumbled backwards and finally slid slowly down the corridor wall. He pulled the telescopic handle up on his suitcase and walked casually away without looking back knowing it would be some time before they recovered their composure, and just maybe reflect on who they were messing with.

Making his way up the two flights of stairs, and entering the disco through the main door, he then walked around the outside of the dance floor once more and took up his original position on the barstool admiring the gorgeous Katarina, satisfied his new friends wouldn't want to bother him again.

*

Mr Jones was heading back up the long gravel driveway approaching Sedgwick House when he noticed his employer, Jonathan Harker, walking Jet back up towards the house. He stopped the car to speak to him.

"Good evening sir, are you feeling any better?"

"Yes I am fine thank you Owen, Jet is still a little shaken up, but he will get over it in time I am sure."

"Natasha got off all right then Owen?"

"Yes Mr Harker, but it's a real shame she had to leave us, such a lovely girl."

"We all feel the same way and we are all going to miss her dreadfully, including Jet."

"What a week it has been sir?"

"You can certainly say that again Owen. Let us just hope we can get back to some normality soon."

"All right then sir, I will say goodnight, unless there are any other duties for me?"

"No thank you Owen, you get yourself home and I will see you in the morning."

"Right then Mr Harker, I'll wish you a goodnight."

*

DI Wallace and Jack Terry were interviewing Suzy Walters for the third time. She was still crying as she told the two experienced officers how she and Dean Wilmot had waited for Jonathan Harker last Friday morning. She explained how Dean had tied her and then gagged her against her will, before tearing off her bra and exposing her breasts, making the excuse that it would attract Harker's attention if she was, in his words, just showing a little flesh.

"Could you tell us how Dean Wilmot died Miss Walters?"

She became a little excitable again. "Inspector I had nothing to do with his death."

"So how did Mr Wilmot die then Miss Walters?"

"It was an accident. I was waiting in the van when Tony ..." Suzy stopped speaking. Wallace told her to take her time, and to carry on when she was ready. "Tony told me later that day Dean had been killed when he walked behind the Water Authority Land Rover, and was crushed when the driver reversed, trapping him between the vehicle and the gatepost."

"Did Tony also tell you, what Wilmot was doing behind the vehicle at the time?" She thought about her answer, and then said, "Tony was sure he was trying to harm the driver in some way, and Dean must have thought he had spotted him lying on the towpath bank with Harker."

"Are you sure you didn't help your boyfriend drag Wilmot's body down the bank, and then tie weights onto his belt, before you both threw him into the canal?"

She screamed at Wallace, "No, no, inspector, it was Tony not me. I didn't know anything about what had happened until he told me after we had left the area. We were on our way back to Nobottle Wood, you have to believe me."

"Miss Walters, did Tony Miles mention where he met this chap Ted, that you told us about?"

"He told me he had known him since his school days."

"I don't suppose you have any idea which school Mr Miles attended Suzy?"

"No, only that it was a private boarding school, somewhere in this area, near Banbury I think."

"Okay Miss Walters, that will be all for today. We will speak to you again tomorrow so try, if you possibly can, to remember as much about all that happened when you took Jonathan Harker to the cottage. For your own sake Miss Walters you must tell us everything."

*

Ted was sitting on one of the barstools with his precious belongings next to him. He asked, "Katarina, would you be kind enough to keep my suitcase behind the bar for me?"

"Yes of course, but you will have to wait until my boss finishes work in around twenty minutes time."

"Thank you Katarina, I am forever in your debt."

"You English have so many smooth words to charm, but this is a new one to me."

"Please Katarina, will you have a drink with me?"

"Maybe later, what is your name anyway English man?"

"Well you can call me Ted, Katarina."

"Okay, I'll call you Mr Ted, now I must go to wash glasses before my boss goes off duty."

"You will grace me with your company at this end of the bar later, won't you Katarina?"

"You will have to wait and see Mr Ted." She smiled and then carried on with her work.

He was wondering about the two Bulgarians when the tallest one walked into the disco holding a tissue of some kind up to his mouth. He was scanning the room, obviously looking for him. Ted was a little surprised to see that the man who he had just pole-axed walk into the disco at all. He had to give it to him, he must have an incredible amount of bottle or was he just plain stupid. Then he saw the reason for his courage. Behind him he had two other truckers, both of them big burly guys wearing similar well worn brown leather jackets and both sporting the round pudding face look. They looked over in Ted's direction and spotted their quarry. The one with the smacked mouth made his way across towards the bar, followed by the two heavies. They sat down no more than three uncomfortable metres away from Ted who was still perched high on his stool next to the bar.

For the entire world he looked as if he was ignoring them, but he was primed and ready to strike at an instant. The only concern he had was for his rucksack, he would need both arms this time or his booty could soon go astray. The big guy holding his mouth came up to the bar standing quite close to Ted and called Katarina over, using her name. He ordered four beers which meant the cabin-share guy would soon be joining them. Katarina served him and then went over to speak to Ted.

"Do you know these three men Katarina?"

"Why do you ask Mr Ted?"

"Well, earlier this evening I had a run in with two of them."

"Oh my God, you must stay clear of these men Mr Ted, they

are very bad people. I can tell you they have only just been allowed to travel again on board *Minoan Lines*, after a two year ban for causing all sorts of trouble, including theft."

"Well I think they are about to cause a little more tonight Katarina."

"You must come with me into the kitchen. Please make out you are going to the toilet then, when you get to kitchen door, I will be waiting for you. I must call my friend Spiradoula first, she will meet you at the bottom of the service lift and take you to my cabin. You may stay there for the rest of your trip, you can sleep on the bunk opposite mine tonight."

"But Katarina you hardly know me, and I am not too worried about these Bulgarians truckers. Besides, I know how to look after myself."

"Believe me, these men are not Bulgarian truckers Mr Ted, but Hungarian gangsters on their way to Athens." Ted was taken aback by Katarina's revelations, his mind filling with the thought that in his rucksack there was part of the Hungarian dynasty, he started to perspire and his face gave him away.

"Mr Ted, are you okay?" But he was deep in thought, Hungarians, surely these men couldn't know what he was carrying, it just wasn't possible.

"Mr Ted, are you sure you are all right?" she asked once more.

This time he replied, "Yes I'm fine thank you," although he was anything but.

"Do you want to go and stay in my cabin tonight?"

"That would be very kind of you Katarina, but I don't want to get you into trouble on my behalf?"

"It is no problem; please wait here until I call you?"

"Okay, thank you again Katarina."

The three men hadn't taken their eyes off him ever since they entered the disco, and now he had to leave this place as soon as possible. Picking up his glass, he empted the last of the liquid and waited for Katarina's prompt. The three men sat watching him, waiting for him to make a move. He saw Katarina out the corner of his eye, she ever so slightly tilted her head as a gesture towards him. The Hungarians looked anxious as he stood, motioning to make their move. He walked quickly around to the other side of the bar and into the kitchen holding the rucksack tightly in front of him. Katarina quickly closed the kitchen door behind him and locked it. She led him across to the open service lift doors, telling him that her friend would be waiting for him down on the crew deck. She told him not to worry about her as she had called for security and they were on their way up to the bar. He heard a tremendous hammering noise as the Hungarians tried to gain entry through the kitchen door, just as the service lift descended from the kitchen storeroom.

Spiradoula beckoned him to come quickly, the attractive young woman took him swiftly along the crew's quarters corridor before opening a cabin door at the far end. She told him he must please stay in the cabin, and that Katarina would finish work at four in the morning. "Until then you must try to sleep, English man." Katarina's cabin could only be described as petite, with just enough room for the two single bunks separated by a narrow gap. At least there was a decent sized shower incorporated in the pod type bathroom.

"This is okay for you, yes?" Spiradoula asked.

"Yes this will do fine. It is very kind of you both to help me, Spiradoula." She warned him to stay in the cabin and not to venture outside under any circumstances, as she and Katarina would lose their jobs if anyone was to see him. He thanked her again as she left. After locking the door he pushed his rucksack, followed by the suitcase, tightly under one of the bunks, thinking at last he had a chance to relax a little and take a hot shower before trying to sleep, although he was still very worried for Katarina's safety.

The massive ship rose and fell, and every so often shook after being hit by the enormous seas whipped up by the strong southerly wind. Ted was so fatigued after his drive, not to mention his exertions earlier that evening, that nothing was going to wake him from his sleep. That was until the early hours of the morning when he was woken by someone knocking hard on the cabin door. He sat up realising he had not unlocked the door after taking his shower. Quickly, he jumped out of bed and stood by the door, asking who was there?

She whispered, "It is Katarina." He turned the key and let his new found saviour in.

"Are you all right?" he asked with real concern in his voice.

"Yes I'm fine Mr Ted, once the Hungarians knew that

security had arrived in the disco bar they soon disappeared." Turning on the light she asked, "Mr Ted, my handsome English man, what have you done to these terrible men to make them so angry?"

"Just a slight misunderstanding Katarina, that is all."

"Well, if I were you, I would stay here with me until the ship docks at Igoumenitsa."

"Are you sure that's okay Katarina, I don't want you to lose your job over my predicament?"

"It is no problem, you just relax Mr Ted while I take a shower and then we will take some ouzo together."

It was at that point he looked down and realised he was standing there talking to her in his boxer shorts, so he quickly got himself back into bed. She giggled saying, "Surely a man of the world like you cannot be shy Mr Ted?"

"Sorry Katarina, I wasn't thinking when I jumped out of bed." 'This night was certainly improving by the minute,' he thought, although why would this total stranger want to help him? After all, he was much older than her. Of course he was attracted to her, any man would have been, or perhaps she would finish showering and climb into her own bed. One thing was for sure, he did not expect to be lying in one of the female crew quarter's cabins that night; especially while a gorgeous creature was showering right next to him; this certainly beat sleeping with the cabin-share guy. He heard the shower start to run followed by the sound of Katarina humming to herself and he felt a little guilty listening to her. After all, he was a complete stranger to this woman and hadn't really spoken more than a few sentences to her. Now, because of his dilemma, he found himself in her cabin, waiting expectantly for her to emerge from the shower.

The water suddenly stopped running into the shower tray and the door handle turned. He swallowed nervously in anticipation of what would happen next. The door opened and out of the steam she appeared draped in a red trimmed white *Minoan* towel, which barely covered her otherwise naked olive skinned body. Adrenalin fuelled excitement pumped through his veins as she came over to the bedside cabinet and leaned forwards to take out a bottle of ouzo from the bottom cupboard. Her hair was still wet and several drops splashed his bare chest as she half filled two glasses with the spirit, before topping them up with water. Turning towards him she said, "I hope I am not embarrassing you Mr Ted." Nervously he tried to reply, but found in this surreal moment he was totally lost for words. She continued, "Only the shower room is much too small to dry off with all the smoke." Of course she meant steam.

"No you carry on, after all Katarina, it is your cabin," he managed to say with a warm expectant smile.

"Drink your ouzo Mr Ted and I will dry." 'She will dry,' he thought, as absolute disbelief entered his mind. Surely she wasn't going to get dried off right next to him. No, she walked the three short paces to the cabin door and began to pat herself with her towel. Ted may have been fast asleep a while ago, but he was wide awake now and unable to overt his gaze away from this beautiful voluptuous woman drying herself as if she was alone.

"Are you sure I am not making you feel uncomfortable Mr Ted?" she said when she caught him looking at her.

"No, not at all Katarina," he answered as he turned away from her and sipped his ouzo.

When he looked again she was drying her head and leaning forward rubbing her jet black hair with the towel but then, even more incredible, when she had finished drying she casually threw the towel over the top of the bathroom door and walked over towards the bed opposite and sat down.

"Ha, that feels much better now I am without my uniform." Ted had no answer, he was totally overwhelmed, and in a state of excited gratification as she sipped her ouzo while sitting on the edge of her bed across from him, her stunning bronzed legs now crossed. How could he make conversation with this beautiful naked woman, when he couldn't take his eyes off her large dark ringed nipples, which centred her sumptuous breasts. She stood again and poured another glass of ouzo topping up his at the same time.

Now she was standing right next to him and his body yearned for this raven haired beauty who, for all the world, was making an excellent job of seducing him. He knew he couldn't resist her much longer and he didn't have to as she sat down next to him taking the last drop from her glass before placing it down on the bedside cabinet. She leaned forward placing her arm around his burly shoulders pulling him up towards her until their lips touched as one orgasmic tongue twisting melt; he threw back the sheets and moved over as she lay beside him. Her body was still damp but warm as he drew her firmly towards him, his manhood stiffening as he glided his hand over the curve of her warm naked body to stroke her magnificent firm buttocks. Thrillingly, she drew her finger nails across his broad shoulders as he floated his hand around and under her to find her softest of places. Her breathing gathered pace as he gently touched her pleasure, his hand continuing over the softness of her inner thighs. She kissed him zealously while her slender fingers ran wildly through his thick head of hair. The other hand was seeking out his excitement, at the same time groaning with euphoric pleasure as his fingertips continued to tease. Finding his stiffness, her soft tender hand now wrapped firmly around his hard girth, she then gently steered him into her warm place, groaning with relish as he gently pressed against her. Leaning his head forward he tenderly nuzzle her delightful dark nipples while enjoying the fullness of her ample breasts, their hands now locked together as entwined as their excited bodies. She called out in the pinnacle of uncontrolled passion, "Fuck me, fuck me, Mr Ted." Her cries thrilled him with excited fulfilment as she felt the full strength of his rhythm, her instant reaction being to squeeze him firmly, as she drew her fingernails down over his board muscular back. There was no love here, just pure unadulterated animalistic sex, two people lustfully enjoying a wonderful moment together, kissing passionately just before they found their peak in a verbal crescendo. He lifted his muscular body and rolled over onto his back, exhausted, but utterly fulfilled, as she mouthed, "Thank you that was wonderful Mr Ted."

"No, thank you, Katarina. This night as been absolutely incredible, you are such a beautiful woman, and I can't thank you enough for coming to my rescue, and at the same time giving me so much pleasure." He placed his arm around her and she lay with her head on his chest as they fell into a deep exhausted sleep.

Two hours later, Katarina woke and slipped quietly out of bed, trying her utmost not to disturb him. She crawled along the floor on her hands and knees, feeling under the bed, hoping to find where he had hidden his rucksack. With her arm at full stretch, she froze as Ted turned in his sleep, waiting for a few moments, before continuing. Finally her fingers found one of the shoulder harness straps on the rucksack. She gently pulled, but it wouldn't budge as the weight of his body on the springs made it impossible to move, so she gave up. She knew that she would have one more chance in the morning when he took his shower. Disappointed, she used the bathroom before returning to her own bed, lying there, wondering just what this Englishman was guarding so closely. Whatever it was, she was determined to find out. Ted woke a few hours later to see Katarina lying face down on top of the other bed her head turned away from him. Her beautiful olive skin was catching what little light there was entering through the cabin porthole. He certainly wasn't going to forget this voyage in a hurry. He decided to take a shower, leaving Katarina to enjoy her sleep. Making his way silently, he opened the door to the bathroom. Before entering he stood for a while to admire this beautiful Greek woman lying naked in front of him. Sighing, and now slightly aroused, he took his last look before closing the door.

When she heard the water running into the shower tray, Katarina saw her chance to search once more under his bed. She was desperately searching for the rucksack lying inelegantly on the cabin floor. When she found what she was looking for, she franticly began dragging it out and up onto her bed, stopping to listen out for the sound of the shower. She was just untying the pull through cord on the top of the rucksack when she heard the water stop running. Panicking now, she was in a state of extreme anxiety to tie up the bag, before lying down once more on the floor to push the rucksack back under the bed to its original position. It was then the bathroom door opened.

"Katarina, what the hell are you doing on the floor?" he asked in an astonished voice. She mumbled her words visibly trembling with the fear of being discovered, before finally saying, "Oh, it's nothing Mr Ted. I lost one of my earrings when we were making love in the night, so take care not to get the spike in your feet."

"Well please carry on Katarina, don't let me stop you." He sat on the end of her bed and watched her going through the motions of searching for this none existent earring, while he continued to dry himself off. He knew she was lying to him as she nervously excused herself to go to the bathroom. When she closed the door behind her, Ted got down on his knees and dragged out his rucksack. The first thing he noticed was the top had been tied up in a different manner, but the second pull through cord was still tied at it's end with a knot only known to him and other members of his old regiment. He placed the rucksack under the bed again wondering if Katarina was somehow involved with the Hungarians, or had she done this Good Samaritan act solely to entice him by using her gorgeous body as a method to deceive him? That, he would probably never know.

Ted drew back the curtains and looking out of the tiny porthole he could see the coastline of Albania with its tall snow capped mountains rising up out of the sea. He allowed himself a smile knowing precisely the ferry's position, having seen this magnificent landscape so many times previously, and he knew it wouldn't be to long before the vessel entered the Kerkyra channel, which separates the Island of Kerkyra from the Albanian coast. The shower room door opened and a sheepish looking Katarina came out. It was like a carbon copy of the small hours, only now he knew a different side to this serene beauty.

"Is everything okay Mr Ted?" She waited for his answer while pinching the two sides of the small white towel with the red trim, that barley covered her stunning naked form. Ted was almost lost for words but managed to respond, "Yes everything is fine Katarina, and can I thank you once again for the courage you shown towards a total stranger, and the wonderful night we have just spent together. I really can't thank you enough." Katarina stared across the cabin towards him, seductively smiling as she moved closer. He took the towel from around his waist and, as he began to dry her long raven hair, she turned to kiss him full on his mouth, gently biting his bottom lip as her towel fell to the floor, as they lay on the bed in a state of pure unadulterated excitement. She took hold of his firmness, squeezing it hard between her damp fingers, and he felt the desired effect as he rolled her over. Placing his hand under her, he lifted her warm body as she forced her buttocks towards his waiting stiffness. His hand slid down under her voluptuous curves, finding her moist exquisite place, their hands touching, as her fingers felt his weight before steering his excitement into her soft silky pleasure. He pulled her up towards him as he stood by the bed. Her warm thighs gently pushed against his thick hardness as he gathered pace until they both found their apex in a vocal climax. After the exhilarating frolic that had lasted no more than a few minutes they lay completely spent, until Ted was startled by the ships public address system.

"Ladies and Gentlemen," the ships public information service sang out, "The ship will be docking at Igoumenitsa in 45 minutes time, thank you." As the message was being read out in several different languages, Katarina slid off the bed urging him to hurry as she stood by the open bathroom door ready to take her second shower of the morning.

"You must hurry Mr Ted?" she said with some urgency.

"There is plenty of time Katarina don't worry." He rolled over in almost a dismissive manner.

"No, you don't understand Mr Ted, your car, you must get to the car deck in time or else you could hold up the trucks from unloading?"

"Katarina, I don't have a car. I am travelling as a foot passenger." Somewhat surprised he was on foot, she walked into the bathroom and closed the door. Ten Greek minutes later Katarina was out of the shower, and told him she would have to go to her friend's cabin so they could arrange for him to leave the crew's quarters without being seen. He thanked her once more telling her he would get ready to leave immediately.

Ted pulled his rucksack from under the bed and then retrieved his suitcase. He took both items into the tiny shower room with him as a final precaution. He was showering when he heard someone enter the cabin, he wondered for a moment if she had betrayed him, but then he heard her call out, "Hurry, you must hurry Mr Ted, while all of the crew are getting ready to unload the heavy trucks?"

"Okay Katarina, I'm nearly ready, don't worry. I will be out soon." She never asked why he had taken his rucksack and suitcase into the shower with him. She knew he had suspected her and he was right to do so. Old habits are hard to break even when you really like someone.

"Will you be coming back from your travels any time soon, Mr Ted?"

"I'm afraid not Katarina, but when I do I will certainly be booking the *Ickories Palace.*"

"If you are ever in Athens you will please come to see me?" She handed him a piece of *Minoan* note paper with her address written down. "I would really love to Katarina." They kissed passionately, before reluctantly leaving the cabin together. They walked quickly along the corridor and into the service lift, which took them up to the top deck and the kitchen, then into the disco bar. Katarina unlocked the heavy door at the main entrance to the disco making sure there was no one outside. The disco itself was empty apart from a female cleaner over in the far corner sweeping the floor. Ted placed the suitcase down and turned to lift Katarina off her feet as he kissed her sweet soft lips before drawing back to thank her once more for looking after him. As they said their final goodbyes, she kissed his neck and whispered into his ear, "Signome, sorry, Mr Ted." He knew what the apology meant and returned her kiss, saying, "Katarina, I will never forget you, my beautiful Greek lady."

The *Ickories Palace* swung slowly around in the chaotic port of Igoumenitsa, churning up the sediment and turning the harbour water a muddy brown in the process, as she prepared to make ready to berth. At least six or seven other vessels were already docked in this the gateway to Greece. Lines of trucks queued on the quay waiting for the giant ship to dock. Ted looked over the railings and down onto the deck below where a few of the foot passengers were looking on in great admiration for the captain, pilot and his crew while wondering just how this massive vessel was about to enter such a small area, astern.

The weather had improved slightly but the sky was still grey and overcast as Ted made his way along the top deck, passing the line of wire mesh kennels. He was startled by a loud bark from one of the interns as he walked by the last of the brightly painted pens. When he turned he saw a large German Shepherd angrily snarling in his direction. Ted smiled back at the hefty Alsatian and carried on making his way along the deck, all the time looking around and being very aware of his surroundings.

There was one thing he knew for sure, they would be waiting for him somewhere on his way to the embarkation deck. Then he spotted the taller of the Hungarians standing on the deck below him, checking out the foot passengers as they walked past. The second man, the shorter of the two and his old cabin-share friend, was hiding in a doorway some 20 metres or so further on from his comrade. The others, he thought must be down on the embarkation deck as they were bound to have every possible route off the *Ickories Palace* covered.

After assessing the situation for a moment or two, Ted returned along the deck towards the kennels. He could see most of the pens were empty, apart from the not so friendly Alsatian and, as he approached the kennel, the dog barked again and then gave a couple of agitated turns while continuing to growl and snarl at him as he came even nearer. Ted spotted a card slotted into the kennel frame. It read Zorba, Cabin 376 owner embarks Patras. Ted knelt down in front of the kennel door and spoke in a soft friendly voice as the dog looked on bemused, "Hello old boy, come on then, I am not going to hurt you. There's a good old boy, I am not going to hurt you, come here then, come on then Zorba." Zorba was reluctant to take any notice of this mad stranger, but Ted kept on talking to him calmly with real serenity in his voice, until he had the large dog thinking that this man just might be friendly. It was then Ted played his trump card by using the universal word that every dog on the planet recognises whether in British or Mongolian, "walkies," or something that sounded like walkies.

Ted had taken no more than five minutes to have big old Zorba eating out of his hand. He took off the belt from around his waist and then unbolted the kennel door while continuing to softly talk to his new found friend. Subsequently placing the belt firmly through Zorba's collar, the dog became so excited to be leaving his windswept home that his first action was to piss up Ted's leg, leaving his new owner with a warm sensation trickling down his calf. "Thank you Zorba, that's all I needed." he mouthed out loud.

Ted made his way down the steps and along the boat deck with his new friend following closely by his side. The first of the Hungarians was craning his neck and appearing to search even harder as fewer and fewer passengers walked by him. He had to make a decision whether or not to leave his suitcase behind or struggle to fend off his would be attackers. He would certainly need both arms if he was going to escape these uncompromising men and his left arm was otherwise preoccupied by a very large dog. Dropping Zorba's temporary lead, his foot firmly pressing the belt onto the deck, he pulled both of the rucksack's harness straps up as tight as possible and pushed the suitcase to one side. Gripping Zorba's makeshift lead again, and twisting it around his hand, he stepped down the outer steel staircase and walked along the embarkation deck, ready for anything they could throw at him. The tall Hungarian spotted him and turned to attract his comrade's attention, but now he didn't look quite as confident when he saw Zorba between himself and Ted. He was now no more than two metres from his bruised mouthed friend, and it was at that moment the Hungarian decided it was time for him to confront this Englishman.

Bad idea Ted thought, as Zorba launched himself at Ted's attacker, he stepped back quickly shocked at the ferocity of this animal and so was Ted as he pulled Zorba back using all the strength that he could muster. "Good boy Zorba, good boy." Ted carried on but now his first assailant was walking closely behind him and waiting for his comrade to try his luck. The funny thing was, much to his friend's disgust, he never even left the doorway. He could only wait for Ted and Zorba to menacingly walk by then, joining up with his comrade, both men were seemingly arguing with each other. They were three or four metres behind Ted and Zorba, who agitatedly kept on twisting his head around and snarling at his followers.

Ted and Zorba approached the two open sea tight doors that led into the disembarkation area where the ship's officers would be watching and assisting the passengers as they left the ferry. He walked through the doors and stopped, he couldn't see his would be attackers, so he hoped this was where he said goodbye to his Hungarian playmates. As he looked around again, there they were standing just the other side of the doorway. He guessed he was probably the last passenger to leave the deck apart from these unfriendly Hungarians. Crouching down beside Zorba he spoke softly whilst stroking his wiry fur along his strong canine back. The two Hungarians stood watching and waiting for their chance, then without warning Ted rose up and shouted at the top of his voice, "Right you bastards, go for them

Zorba." Zorba was standing on his hind legs when Ted slipped the belt from around his neck. The large Alsatian resembled the look of Conan Doyle's Hound of the Baskerville as he chased the two terrified men along the deck and the last Ted saw of the tall bruised mouth chap was five minutes later. He was standing on the top deck shouting down Hungarian obscenities to him, while waving his arms franticly. Ted's only reaction was to return his rant with a Churchillian salute, before making his way across the dockyard and losing himself between the heavy trucks, and trying his best to find the quickest way to the ticket office.

CHAPTER EIGHTEEN

DS Terry was busy taking a statement from Suzy Walters, the time was 2:30pm as they had allowed her to rest, giving her plenty of time to contemplate the gravity of the situation. She looked totally distraught as she sat across the table from Jack Terry, realising perhaps that she was the only person who was under arrest.

"Miss Walters, have you remembered anything else regarding what happened last Friday morning at the Felford Arm, on the Grand Union Canal?"

"I have told you all I know sergeant," she mumbled trying to avoid eye contact with the officer.

"Can you remember Miss Walters where Dean Wilmot went to after he had tied you up and tore your top off? According to your first statement he, in other words, sexually assaulted you?"

"Tony had planned the whole thing, telling Dean to follow Harker from the field side of the towpath, and then to break the ice in the canal so that anyone searching for him would assume he had fallen in."

"So how could your boyfriend be so sure the canal would be frozen on that particular day?" The very word boyfriend had Suzy Walters in floods of tears again and WPC Trout handed her a tissue. After a while she regained some composure before answering Terry's question.

"You see sergeant, if the canal on that morning had been free of ice, the plan was to take Harker's coat smear blood onto it and leave it draping from the bank and partly in the water." She fell silent for a moment and sipped the water from the glass in front of her.

"Carry on Suzy and tell us what you remember happened next?"

"Tony and Dean had been over to Kegworth Wharf on the previous two Fridays, and had followed Jonathan Harker from his home along the towpath knowing roughly how far he was likely to travel before turning and heading home again. We moored the barge on the Thursday afternoon near to Kegworth Wharf. What Tony hadn't expected was the sudden change in the weather conditions and that night the temperature dropped to minus seven degrees. I tried unsuccessfully to persuade Dean not to go through with the kidnapping as the canal had completely frozen over, but he took no notice of me and carried on with Tony's plan, regardless of the weather. It was only the fact that the ice breaker came along, or else we would have been stuck in the ice and unable to move. Then when that bastard Dean...." she hesitated before taking another drink, and then continued, "Like I said, after Dean had rendered Harker unconscious and bundled him into the barge, he then took one of Harker's gloves, smeared some of his blood onto it and took it back to where he had made the hole in the ice, placing it down beside his handy work so it could easily be found."

"Miss Walters are you sure you don't know this man that you refer to as Ted?"

"I have told you sergeant, he was Tony's friend and not mine."

"Tony must have told you something about this mysterious friend of his?"

"You have to believe me, when I tell you I didn't know him."

"Did Tony Miles tell you where you were all going to meet up with each other after the ransom had been paid?"

"No sergeant, Tony never told me any of the arrangements, only that we were leaving on the ferry to France sometime that weekend." Wallace was tapping on the glass from the other side of the screen, in the way he always did, when he wanted his officers to wind up an interview.

"All right Miss Walters that will be all for now, we will speak again in the morning. Take her back to her cell, would you please WPC Trout?"

*

Wallace had been talking to DS Benson on his mobile and was asking him if Harry Bernard had been out of his house, or up to anything unusual.

"Far from it sir, he's a boring sort of chap, he just visits his mother at the old people's home, then does a little shopping before returning back to his house, always looks quite sad, if you ask me."

"Okay sergeant, I think another couple of days then you better come back from the bright lights and do some real police work, don't you?"

*

Lynda and Jonathan Harker were having dinner with their mutual friend Ester when the front door bell rang out.

"Oh dear, who could that be at this time of the evening?"

"I will go darling," Ester said as she rose to her feet.

"Thank you Ester," Jonathan replied. She saw two familiar faces standing there when she opened the solid oak door.

"Good evening Mrs Bernard."

"Good evening to you Inspector Wallace, sergeant, won't you both come in please?"

"Thank you, madam."

"Has there been a further developments inspector?"

"No I am afraid not Mrs Bernard."

"Come through into the hallway please gentlemen. I will just go and tell Jonathan and Lynda you are here. If you wouldn't mind waiting in the here for a moment." The two officers waited until Jonathan came out of the dining room. He wished them good evening and asked what he could do for them.

"Could we go into your study sir, we would like to ask you a few more questions if you don't mind."

"Of course inspector, please follow me gentlemen." Harker closed the door behind the officers and sat down, inviting them to join him.

"Now what can I do for you, and by the way we can't thank you enough for all you have done for me and Lynda."

"That's okay sir, just doing our job, now could you tell us if you know a Mr Fredric Bromley?"

"Bromley, of course I know him inspector. Ted Bromley went to Shone Court around the same time as me, although I never had anything much to do with him apart from being in the school rugby team together. One thing I do remember about him though is he hated being called Fredric, which was always a bit of a mouthful, so hence his nickname Ted. This came of course from Edward, his middle name. But why do you ask Inspector Wallace?"

"We need to find Mr Bromley sir, so we can eliminate him from our enquiries."

"Good God inspector, it was bad enough to know Tony Miles was involved in my kidnap, but Ted Bromley! I haven't seen the man for 20 years or more, in fact not since he joined the army."

"So you wouldn't have any idea as to his whereabouts then sir?"

"I am afraid not inspector. Anyway if Bromley was involved, how the hell would he have known about my wife's family heirloom?"

"I take it then sir, your wife has divulged her secret to you?" Harker's face said it all as he answered, "Yes and it looks like I was the last person to bloody well know inspector"

"You do know that Mrs Bernard's husband was a friend of Bromley, don't you sir?"

"Well he probably was way back in our school days, but I never heard Harry Bernard ever mention Bromley's name since those times."

"Apparently, Mr Bernard met up with Bromley last summer when he was on a business trip to South Africa and, according to Mr Bernard, Bromley and his wife owned a holiday home just outside Cape Town."

"So what is the significance of that inspector and what if anything does this have to do with my kidnap?"

DS Terry carried on, "Well Sir, Harry Bernard told Bromley all about your wife's family heirloom." Suddenly Jonathan's whole demeanour seemed to change at what the DS was telling him. He stood up momentarily as if he was about to leave the room, then thought better of it, turning to make sure his leather padded chair was still behind him. He slumped down, shocked that he had only just found out about this heirloom from Lynda.

"Are you all right to continue Mr Harker?" Terry asked.

"Yes, it's just the magnitude of what you are telling me sergeant, and the fact that Lynda must have told Ester and she in turn has told Harry Bernard. It really is hard to take in that Lynda took Ester into her confidence rather than me."

"I realise this is upsetting for you sir, are you sure you want to carry on?"

"Yes sergeant, I want to know if you think Harry Bernard is involved in any way."

"Off the record sir, no we don't, but we are very interested in your old school friend Fredric Bromley. He seems to have parted from his wife a few months ago and apparently, according to your friend Ester, Mrs Bromley has now moved to America. Nobody knows what has happened to her husband so we need to find him. If you can think of anyone you might know who could steer us in his direction, perhaps one of your old school friends Mr Harker, we would very much appreciate your help."

Harker stood saying, "I can't think at this moment inspector, but if anyone comes to mind I will certainly let you know."

"I believe that will be all for now sir, you know where you can find us if you need to." Harker showed the officers to the front door.

"Thank you Mr Harker, by the way where is Natasha this evening? Having a well deserved night off?"

"Actually, no inspector, I am afraid to say she has returned home to Slovenia, where her mother is gravely ill."

"Oh dear, such a pleasant girl, well we will wish you goodnight then sir."

The next morning Chief Superintendent Bendery walked into Wallace and Terry's office, to find them discussing the kidnapping case. Their superior wasn't too pleased with the progress his officers were making.

"So what is your next move then Inspector Wallace?" George Bendery was much younger than his two fellow officers, he was also a stickler for protocol and he would never call any of his officers by their Christian names, only by their rank, and he was known to his men, as old 'Bendover.'

"We are waiting for the passenger lists from ferry ports and airlines Chief Superintendent."

"So you think this chap Bromley we talked about is our most likely suspect then inspector?"

"Well it would seem that way sir and, according to Miss Walters, the ringleader was called Ted, and Bromley's middle name is Edward. He certainly knew all about this family heirloom of Lynda Harker." DS Terry intervened, "At the moment sir, we are planning to take a trip down to Hereford to speak to the camp commander of Bromley's old regiment, but we are still having some difficulty getting permission to ask questions about any of their former officers."

"We will see about that DS Terry."

"With the greatest of respect Chief Superintendent Bendery, and if you don't mind, I would rather you left it to me and DS Terry." The Chief Superintendent's face reddened with anger, but before he could speak Wallace carried on, "Detective Sergeant Terry sir, was formerly a soldier himself and he knows how these people work."

"Very well inspector, but just get a move on will you," he said begrudgingly.

That afternoon Terry was studying the passenger lists from the previous Friday, Saturday and Sunday's outbound flights and the movements from all the ferry port terminals. They were coming in thick and fast and he had to ask WPC Trout to help him sort through all the information. He was covering the ferry terminals, leaving Trout to deal with the airports. After hours of searching, there it was, Bromley's name, booked onto the 00:15am train leaving Ashford Eurotunnel Terminal late Sunday night, and the early hours of Monday morning. There was a correction stating that the train never actually left until 3:00am later that morning due to a French rail strike.

"Take a look at this guv." He slipped the edited list over the top of his desk to Wallace.

"He has to be our man Jack, get onto Eurotunnel and see how he paid for his ticket and, if it was with his credit card, take the details and then we can hopefully trace his movements before and after he reached France. I am pretty sure he will have no bloody idea we are onto him already."

*

Ted was queuing once more in yet another ferry agent's office, waiting to buy a ticket from Igoumenitsa to Kerkyra on one of the smaller slipper ferries that was due to leave roughly on the hour, give or take the odd Greek ten minutes. After paying cash for his ticket he gingerly made his way back across the busy dockyard to find the slipper ferry, the *Ionian Lady*, the small car carrying ferry was due to leave in a few minutes or so.

He was well aware that he hadn't seen the other two Hungarians and was proceeding with care as he wound his way between the huge trucks, caravans, and hundreds of cars. He was keeping a low profile but, at the same time, trying not to look too suspicious. He spotted the blue and white ferry with its ramps still down in the loading position. The unhurried crew were waving their arms in a seemingly nonsensical manner while directing what little traffic there still was to load. He looked around him before leaving the relative safety of the parked vehicles then, crossing quickly to the passenger walkway, he climbed up and onto the deck, offering one of the crew his ticket when he reached the top. The sun was low in the winter sky and he soon felt the chilled sea breeze as he made his way along the top deck to find himself somewhere to sit for the hour long journey to the island.

When he reached the row of wooden slatted seats on the top deck he sat down, relieved he was now nearing the last leg of his long hazardous journey. Looking across at the ferry that was moored next to the *Ionian Lady* and sitting with their feet up on the ship's railings smoking cigarettes, were the other two men from the disco. He stood instantly and made his way around to the other side of the vessel, sitting down once more and he prayed that the *Ionian Lady* would soon cast off and leave the mainland on time. He knew that ninety percent of ferries leaving Igoumenitsa were bound for Kerkyra and that meant the Hungarian's ferry was probably also going his way.

What was going on here? Surely they couldn't know about the tiara. No it had to be a coincidence, but he would have to be on his guard until he reached the safety of the hilltop village. There, he thought, no one would ever find him. The crossing was uneventful but as he disembarked heavy rain began to fall and the wind was now blowing strongly across the ferry terminal. He walked briskly around the wet dock passing the port police HQ and out through the large steel gates to the waiting row of taxis.

"Kalispera, do you speak English?" The taxi driver gestured like most Greek people do by twisting his hand backwards and forwards, and answered, "A little." Ted asked if he could take him to Porsey, Sinies and he placed his wet rucksack on the back seat and climbed in beside it. Like all other taxi drivers throughout the world this driver also gave the impression he had to get back, even before he had left the port, and the next 50 minutes was just like a crash course in how not to drive. Mediterranean drivers in particular seem to take the whole road as theirs, even on a blind spot, or a hairpin bend, until they meet a vehicle coming from the other direction. It's only then they take evasive action. He checked several times to make sure his seat belt was secured. The road up to Ted's retreat was steep and very twisty with many hairpin bends, some having the Greek equivalent to Armco barriers on the drop side, but then again others did not.

When they finally arrived he was more than pleased to get out of the car, and probably thought the driver should pay him for scaring the living daylights out his passenger, rather than the other way round. Even so, he was pleased he had made it, so he paid for the journey and wished the driver goodnight, watching him speed off and into the night.

The last three hundred metres or so were very steep and he knew if he had asked the driver to take him right to the door he would have refused once he had caught sight of the uneven stony track. The wind howled through the tall olive grove as he gripped his rucksack harness and headed off up the steep track. The heavy rain soon drenched his clothing as he leaned forward into the wind and he trudged on until he reached the top of the hill, from there it was only a short walk to the old stone cottage.

A violent storm had now engulfed the mountains that surrounded the tiny hamlet of cottages, and lightning lit up an otherwise murky sky, instantly followed by a tremendous clap of thunder directly above him. Carefully he negotiated the wet slippery steps which brought him down onto the village path that circled the hamlet of six or seven cottages. 'What a night to return,' he thought and wished he had taken his head torch out of the suitcase before he had abandoned it. A few more steps further on and the cottage came into his focus. After a few paces he was standing under the low pitched roof of the traditional Greek cottage and he couldn't wait to get inside, but first he had to find the key.

It had been ten years or more since Ted had last been there, at that time he was on leave of duty, when he came over from Cyprus to stay for a couple of weeks. It had been such a long time, but if he remembered correctly he had slipped the key up onto the beam and under the roof pan tiles which entailed him having to stretch his arm up onto the beam that ran across the width of the cottage. Feeling up he slid his hand into the hole and under the pan tiles, then felt around for the key and, amazingly, there it was just where he had left it all those years ago. He couldn't see too much as he felt around trying to get the key to fit into the old lock, but eventually the lock gave up its ten years of inaction and he pushed the door slowly open to the sound of stiff, rusty hinges squeaking as he did so.

Stepping inside, bending forward slightly, he remembered just how many times he had hit his head on the low door frame. His nostrils were soon filled with the smells of a combination of stale air and an overpowering mustiness. He carefully walked across the dark kitchen knowing the pine table would still be in the centre of the room, and reached out until he found its round form. Once around the table, he only had to reach the wall that lead to the kitchen stairwell. Stretching out once more, his fingers touched the coolness of the damp rendered wall with some confidence in his ability to find his way down the stone steps that led to the living room below. He took hold of the iron banister rail and successfully made his way carefully down a dozen or so uneven steps instinctively then, crossing the quarry tile floor, he passed the large Welsh dresser. His knee caught one of the cupboard door knobs which stopped him momentarily as he felt down to rub away the slight soreness. He then continuing to feel the wall again and eventually the door to the small electric switch box.

He felt inside and pushed all the switches up; the lights flickered and then came on. He looked around to see the sheets still covering the furniture where he had left them all that time ago, but nothing seemed to have changed. He left the lounge and dining room and returned back up the stone steps to the kitchen. Standing at the large double sink he turned the tap on and rust infused water began to run in a stop-start motion, before eventually clearing itself several minutes later. Taking the kettle from its long time hiding place in the top cupboard he made himself a cup of black tea using one of the tea bags he had left in the caddy some ten years earlier. He sat at the dusty table, staring at the rucksack that lay at its centre and he felt a sense of tremendous relief to know he was safe. Providing he lived here in the manner he always had done in the past he thought he would be just fine. Finishing the stale tea he picked up the rucksack and climbed the five stone steps up and out of the kitchen, along the dusty corridor to the main bedroom, which he found was in the same state as the rest of the house. Ignoring the dried up small lizard skin that lay on the rug beside the bed, he pulled the dust sheets off the half tester. He shivered as he rolled his wet clothes off onto the floor, before falling onto the cold sheets. He dragged the moth eaten duvet over him and was soon fast asleep.

The combination of a dog barking somewhere on the mountain and the shaft of sunlight, which was entering through the broken shutters, woke Ted around 7:30am. He stretched out on the bed and was thankful he had made it safely to the cottage. Climbing out of bed he opened one of the French doors, then the green slatted shutters. The air was cold and he felt the chill from the wind which was blowing across the sea from the snow capped mountains of Albania, no more than a few miles across the blue Kerkyra channel in front of him. He quickly slammed the door shut again and found himself a robe from the insect ridden wardrobe, turning it inside out and shaking it vigorously before reluctantly wrapping the garment around him. Trembling uncontrollably, he made his way down the stairs determined to try to get some warmth into the old stone cottage walls.

Somehow he would have to light the range in the kitchen and keep it alight for the next few days to air the old place through. Reluctantly, he went outside to the wood store only to find it padlocked and, for the life of him, he had no idea where the key was. The catch looked weak and rusty so he was sure it would break easily. Subsequently he picked up a small part of an old broken millstone and hit down on the lock several times until the catch gave up its resistance and fell to the ground. He pulled back the rotting door. All his labours had made it worthwhile when he saw that the store was full of tinder dry olive logs, which were accompanied by the odd scorpion or two.

An hour later and the range was blazing, the old iron saucepan was steaming away when Ted came up the steps from the bathroom after taking a tepid shower. He made himself tea, which tasted even more inferior this morning than the previous evening, and he promised himself he would never drink the stuff without milk or sugar again. He sat down in front of the open range door watching the blazing logs spit and sizzle as he sipped the hot tea. On the wall next to the tiny recessed window he noticed the telephone lead hanging loosely down, minus it's receiver. It was just one more job, he thought, to see if the telephone was still connected. He recovered the blue plastic telephone from under one of the kitchen wicker baskets and slotted the plug into the socket. To his absolute astonishment the dialling tone could be still be heard. On the window sill, which was covered in fly spots, lay a dusty yellowing list of local super markets and tavernas. He saw his old friend Nikos' number, dialled the six digits, and waited for a reply.

"Ela, Kalimera," a loud and slightly bad tempered voice answered.

"Nikos my friend, it's Ted from Porsey." The line went eerily quiet for a moment before the man replied.

"Ted, ha Ted my friend, where have you been all this time? We thought you were dead maybe." Nikos laughed out loud to his own humour.

"It's a long story Nikos, but how are you my friend, and your family?"

"Very well and better now for my business, now you are back on Kerkyra," he said laughing out loud again.

"Nikos, could you make up a shopping basket for me, a few bottles of wine and get it up to Porsey sometime today?"

"Of course, I will send my best wine to welcome you back to Kerkyra my friend, on the house as you say."

"Thank you Nikos, that's very kind of you."

"Yanni will be there in half a Greek hour my friend, bye bye."

Two hours later Yanni delivered Ted's supplies and he was soon getting back into the Greek way of life. He was frying goat's cheese whilst trying a glass of Nikos's wine and after lunch he went from room to room uncovering the furniture by pulling off the encrusted dust sheets with their multitude of infestations. He was realising now he had an awful lot cleaning to do if he was going to make his time spent at the cottage more comfortable. He found a bucket and mop in the tall kitchen cupboard and the rest of that afternoon he spent cleaning away a decade of grime. Later that evening, the old cottage looked a little more like home and that was what he hoped it would become, at least for a while.

Ted couldn't understand why his wife had never visited the island with him, he had asked, no begged her on numerous occasions to come and see for herself just how beautiful the Ionian Island and his cottage really was. She had never shown the slightest interest, dismissing the only thing he owned in his own right. It had been left to him by his parents, but only after he had paid the death duty on Padstone Hall, his childhood home. It left him virtually impoverished and with no other option but to follow in his late father's footsteps and become a commissioned officer in the British Army.

South Africa was Jackie's first and maybe her only love. Perhaps, with hindsight, it was probably for the best, since not even she knew where the cottage was located. When he thought more about it, she probably doesn't even know on which Greek Ionian island. 'Nobody knows,' he thought to himself. This was why this tiny house in Porsey was the perfect location for him to arrange the transaction with Frakas, and it within striking distance of Athens, or the less crowded Thessalonica. Wherever the transaction was going to take place he knew he would have to be constantly vigilant at all times, knowing just how ruthless theses Hungarian gangsters could be, if their antics on the *Minoan* ferry were anything to go by. Frakas's hoodlums would certainly think brawn, before brain.

*

Wallace walked into his office looking tired and asked Jack if he wouldn't mind making him a strong cup of coffee.

"God, that's not at all like you guv, coffee first thing in the morning?"

"I know Jack, but I haven't slept a wink since waking up around two. Something struck me like the proverbial bolt out of the blue."

"Had another row with the Mrs again then?"

"Very funny Jack. No, can you remember the time we were talking to Natasha over a cup of tea in the Harkers' kitchen? Well, I am sure she mentioned that she had worked in South Africa before she was employed by the Harkers."

"Can't recall that, maybe I was playing with Jet or something, anyway what had you thinking so hard that you couldn't get back to sleep?"

"I'll tell you what Jack, Natasha's not around any more is she? So I believe we should get back over to Sedgwick House and find out a little more about our sweet Slovenian lass."

Ester Bernard opened the door to the two officers and asked them to come in. She told them that Jonathan and Lynda were both out but asked if she could be of any help.

"Actually Mrs Bernard, it was you we wanted to speak to?"

"Oh, I see inspector," sounding somewhat surprised she led them into the lounge and sat down on the large Chesterfield sofa and waited in anticipation for Wallace to speak.

"Could you tell us who Natasha worked for before she came to work at Sedgwick House?"

"Actually she worked for my agency inspector." Wallace gave Jack one of his surprised stares.

"Your agency Mrs Bernard, she worked for you?" he asked.

"Yes Inspector, that is correct. You see, I still have my business, an employment agency in London's New Cavendish Street."

"So you would be able tell us if Natasha has ever worked for Fredric Bromley then Mrs Bernard?"

"Well yes she did, for his wife certainly, inspector."

"Had Natasha ever been to South Africa with Fredric Bromley?"

"Yes inspector, several times in fact."

"Have you any idea where Natasha is now?" Wallace asked, looking ever more serious.

"Yes inspector. She had to return to her own country, Slovenia, to look after her mother who is seriously ill."

"So as her previous employer you would have her address in Slovenia wouldn't you?"

"Well I could certainly get it for you, but I am afraid there is nobody in the office at the moment. I can, however, let you have that information some time tomorrow."

"Very well madam, but you must understand that it is very important that you let us have this information as early as possible tomorrow morning."

"I most certainly will inspector." She hoped the questioning was over, but Wallace continued.

"So the reason Natasha had been employed by the Harkers, was through your own agency, on your recommendation Mrs Bernard?"

"Yes inspector, once the Bromleys decided they had to let Natasha go, I told Lynda about her. But you sound, if you don't mind me saying, that you suspect Natasha of being in some way involved with Jonathan's kidnapping. Surely you can't think she had anything to do with this terrible episode do you?"

"I am just trying to eliminate her from our enquiries madam, like anyone else who may be involved. Well, if you could speak to me in the morning Mrs Bernard, the earlier the better?"

"Yes of course, Inspector Wallace." With that she showed the two officers to the door. They sat in Terry's car, talking for a while before leaving Sedgwick House.

"What do you make of that then Jack?"

"Well, you have to admit the fact that Natasha worked for our prime suspect Bromley, who left the country via the Eurotunnel in the early hours of Monday morning, heading to God knows where in Europe. Then a few days later his ex-nanny hands in her notice and leaves the country. It's suspicious to say the least."

"Do you know Jack, I thought Natasha was such a lovely young woman, and she gave the impression she was really concerned for Jonathan Harker. She was also very supportive to the whole family, so much so, that the family liaison officer Jane Monroe made a point of telling me how much she had helped. I would still be surprised Jack, if she is involved."

"I agree guv, but there again perhaps we were both taken in by her pretty smiling face?"

"Yes okay Jack, let's get back to the station. I need to talk to Inspector Dryker at Interpol and see if they have come up with anything on Bromley yet."

*

Sergeant Mills was busy interviewing Harry Bernard under instructions from DI Wallace, and was questioning him further about his trip to Cape Town.

"Mr Bernard, when you were out in South Africa with Fredric Bromley, did you happen to see Bromley's nanny Natasha at all?"

"Well yes, I met her for the first time at the restaurant with Freddy and then again when I had dinner with him at his house."

"What do you think their relationship towards one another was Mr Bernard?"

"I don't understand, what do you mean sergeant, their relationship?"

"Well In your opinion sir, did they seem close, more than friendly, flirtatious, that sort of thing?"

"I really don't know what you are suggesting sergeant, but as far as I could see Freddy and his nanny Natasha, had nothing more than a professional working relationship with each other."

"Mr Bernard, did you see Mr Bromley again after you had dinner that evening?"

"No sergeant, and I haven't seen him since." Bernard looked up at the clock on the living room wall.

"Well, if there isn't anything else sergeant, only I have to be at my mother's nursing home this evening?"

"No, I think that's all for now Mr Bernard, but Inspector Wallace may need to speak to you again soon."

The next morning Ester was giving the information about Natasha to Inspector Wallace over the telephone, explaining to him that all the paperwork on Miss Natasha Privsek was very vague and, in fact, all she had was the young woman's name and nothing more.

"I am sorry to say inspector that my manager has just told me that she was waiting for Natasha to send her work permit and other relevant paper work." Wallace was to say the least furious and it showed in his reply.

"You do realise Mrs Bernard, it is criminal offence to employ a migrant without their correct documentation?"

"Yes. I really am so sorry but my manager deals with recruitment and obviously I have told her I am not at all happy with the situation."

"Are you telling me that your company employed Natasha Privsek for the last couple of years and you are still waiting for her paperwork? At least I thought your company would have her address in Slovenia or a mobile number for her of some sort?"

To which Mrs Bernard replied, "I am afraid not inspector ..."

"So am I madam, so am I." Wallace looked and sounded still annoyed when he asked, "By the way Mrs Bernard, would you ask Mrs Harker if by any chance she has Natasha's mobile number?" You could hear real sarcasm in Wallace's voice.

"Yes of course, I will go and speak to her now inspector." He waited a couple of minutes before she came back to the telephone.

"I have spoken to Lynda inspector, and she only has the mobile number from the phone that she herself gave to Natasha, and that phone was taken from her before she left."

"Very well Mrs Bernard, I will speak to you again soon."

Wallace hung up and turned to Terry saying, "You can't believe these people Jack, they act so prim and proper, but when it comes down to it, they are as bad as anyone else."

"Bloody hell, what did she say to you? At one point I thought you were going to bust a blood vessel"

"Jack she hasn't any paperwork at all for Natasha, only her full name, which is Privsek and that she came from Slovenia. That probably means she has been working in the UK illegally all this time."

*

The Acharavi branch of the Alpha bank was very busy as always, the long queue almost reaching out the door and onto the square. Ted had to make sure there had been sufficient funds in his account to cover the all the utility bills over the last decade. Fifteen minutes later he was standing waiting behind a tiny old lady dressed in black and a white lace trimmed bonnet. The old woman was finding it hard to hear what the clerk was trying to say to her. Ted was frustrated with the situation but tried his best not to show it. He stayed relaxed as he pulled the straps on his rucksack up tighter and hoped that his turn would soon come.

Eventually, after many moments of arm waving and chatter by the clerk, the old woman, finally understanding her account, walked slowly away from the counter. She leaned heavily to one side on her twisted wooden stick, still shaking her head in a confused manner. Ted slid the blue bank book under the glass window and wished the clerk good morning. He wasn't ready for the abrupt response as the clerk pushed the book back towards him in a manner of contempt whilst saying, "No good, this Drachma." Then the penny dropped, his book hadn't been made up for years, so all the accounts inside were in the old currency. He looked at the clerk and hoped he would understand him when he told him it was the only book he had, so could he check to see how much money was in his account now? You would have thought that Ted had asked him if he could sleep with his wife, such was the look he gave him back. He said something in Greek that was above Ted's understanding of the language but, to gather from the queues response of mumbling and the uneasy shifting of their feet, he was going to be here for some time.

Finally he came out of the bank and walked across the square to Yanni's car and apologised to him for the long wait. On the drive back to the cottage he thanked Yanni for taking him to Acharavi and he asked if they could go along the old coastal track on the way back. He wanted to see just how much it had changed over the years. When they drove along the rough stone chipped road he was sad to see his favourite wild beach at Almiros, which he had fondly remembered so well, had now been in his eyes almost taken over by a development of apartments and a huge all-inclusive hotel. Albeit, now closed for the long winter and not a tourist in sight, only the foam topped waves crashing onto the beautiful deserted sandy beach could be seen. He turned to Yanni saying, "My goodness this is so sad Yanni?"

"Why do you say such a thing my friend, this is good for the island, we need progress, can't you see this?"

"Sorry Yanni, it is just me being selfish and remembering how things used to be."

"Ah, you English, as romantic has ever and always wanting to live in utopia." They soon arrived in the village of Kassiopi where they stopped off at the local kafenion. Ted drank his

Greek coffee as he sat staring down the quiet street that led down to the picturesque harbour. He felt more relaxed than he had for years and all the pressure of the last few days had seemed to drain away. The tranquility of the moment was abruptly ended by a fume choking moped as it rode by, loaded to the hilt, it's rider was hanging on precariously to the grass cutting strimmer as his elderly female passenger sat side-saddle in a manner that could only happen in this lenient island culture. They arrived back at Porsey where he thanked Yanni again and tried hard to bestow some money for his time, but Yanni told him it was enough reward just to see him back on the island. He then told Ted that he would have to go, before Nikos would think he had disappeared and flown off to find Athena.

With the knowledge that the utility bills were up to date, Ted lifted up the old fashioned looking phone, wiped the thick layer of dust from the receiver, and took a card from his wallet. He dialled the Hungarian mobile number and waited for a response, which seemed to be an age, before Frakas answered.

"Frakas, I have what you are looking for."

"You have done well Englishman, we will meet up soon, yes?" he replied in his rich Hungarian accent.

"Frakas we will, although I will tell you where we make the exchange."

"Englishman, give me your telephone number, and we can talk about this."

"No Frakas, I will call you at midday tomorrow."

"You do not trust me, Englishman?"

"I don't trust anyone Frakas. Let me tell you, I want the changeover to take place in a public area such as the old Olympic Stadium in Athens. You know the amount of cash we agreed for your precious antiquity?"

"Yes Englishman, and you know I must have the tiara authenticated before I hand over any cash, so it will be impossible to exchange such valuables in this stadium you talk of."

Ted hesitated, then once again said, "Frakas, it is the old Olympic Stadium or nothing, I will call you tomorrow." Before Frakas could reply Ted placed the receiver down, knowing he needed to keep the upper hand, and Frakas in his place.

That evening he sat warming himself in front of the range, thinking about the jewellery and the exchange with Frakas, who sounded as mean as his men looked. Perhaps the changeover wasn't going to be as easy as he first thought. One thing was for sure though, he hadn't gone through this dark place in his mind, blocking out his despicable acts, even surprising himself of just what he was capable of for the combination of greed and the love of a woman. There was no going back, the cash was there for the taking and he desperately needed it. Then he could buy a house worthy of his new found wealth, but for the time being he would live in the village again and mix with the friendly locals who knew him only as the soldier, a nickname given to him by the local mayor who knew he was a serving officer in the British Army. He was so Christened when he first came to the island to find his parents mountain house.

The following morning Ted called Frakas, who sounded more than a little offish with him and even more so. When Ted described to him the old Olympic Stadium, telling Frakas in no uncertain terms where they would make the exchange, Frakas tried to interrupt several times. Ted ignored him, and carried on.

"Frakas, you will enter through the main stadium entrance, where you will buy a ticket at the kiosk for the midday stadium tour. Once inside you should leave the tour party and then continue to walk directly down the centre of the arena until you reach the barrier at the far end of the track."

Frakas protested again, "This is bloody crazy Englishman; everyone will see us making the exchange?"

"Frakas, you have no choice, you must do as I say or the deal is off?" Again some sort of Hungarian expletives were shouted down the line, but Ted stopped him in the only way he could by putting down the receiver. He would let Frakas stew for a while before calling again. After he had made himself some tea he casually dialled Frakas' number.

"Englishman you better be aware of who you are dealing with. Do not insult me again by hanging up your telephone on me, do you understand?" Ted never bit and continued.

"As I was saying Frakas, you will continue to the far end of the arena where you will wait by the barrier at midday this Sunday coming, and don't forget to leave your honchos at home, make sure you understand, be there alone or the deal's off?"

"Where will you be Englishman?" "Don't worry yourself about me Frakas, I will be there with the tiara, so make sure you bring the cash with you."

Ted once again put the phone down on his angry Hungarian counterpart.

*

The rain was falling heavily as Ted entered the airport car park on a typically wet late January morning. Grey leaden skies had closed in around the airport and a northerly wind was blowing the rain almost sideways, so much so that he wondered if his 07-20 fight AG401 to Athens would be cancelled due to the extreme conditions. When he saw the rows of taxies parked outside the terminal building, it said it all. The drivers were huddled under the airports over hanging canopy, most of them smoking while swinging their worry beads from finger to thumb. One or two glanced at him as he dragged his small suitcase past them and into the departure terminal. At the Aegean desk the smartly dressed young woman told him that the flight would be at least 30 minutes late due to the adverse weather conditions so he walked over to the kafenion and brought himself coffee and one of his favourite feta cheese pies. It was not what you would call breakfast food but Ted could never resist this Greek speciality whatever the time of day.

A woman's voice spoke out over the loud speaker system gaining Ted's attention: "Aegean airlines flight 401 from Athens has now landed. Would all the remaining passengers make their way to the departure lounge, we apologise for any inconvenience caused."

After he had checked his small suitcase into the antiquated security system, he then made his way towards the departure lounge, carrying his rucksack with the tiara secreted inside. Continuing on through the door to the hand luggage security check just inside the air-side departure lounge, he was met by a female police officer who asked him to remove his coat and place the rucksack into the plastic tray. He did as she asked and lay them on the conveyor belt and then proceeded through the security arch to retrieve his belongings on the other side. The police officer controlling the conveyor belt and monitor screen was busy talking to one of his fellow officers as Ted's rucksack came through the system. He causally walked over and took his bag and coat out of the grey plastic tray and made his way into the air-side lounge. The Airbus 320 was standing within sight of the terminal lounge and the ground crews were busy unloading freight from her hold, while others were running around keen to get this flight away as quickly as possible. Fifteen minutes later he was running across the rain soaked tarmac and up the steps to be greeted by the smiling air hostess.

"Kalimera." She took a quick look at his boarding pass and pointed to the right hand side of the aircraft. He sat by the window and was pleased to see he had all three seats to himself. Moments later the Airbus was taxiing out onto the wet runway and heading for the southern end of the airfield, reaching the white spot turning point before the Airbus made a 360 degree turn and came to a stop. Ted wiped the porthole window and looked out across the rain sodden airfield as the plane waited for clearance and hopefully a decrease in the wind's strength that was now buffeting the plane quite violently. His thoughts once again returned to his military days, where he had had his fair share of rough Hercules transport flights and judging by the extreme weather conditions this may be another.

You could feel a real tension in the air as the Airbus revved its enormous Rolls-Royce engines before the pilot released the brakes. The thrust forced the Airbus instantly forward as it sped along the bumpy Kapodistrias airport runway. He knew this airport so well and when he saw the terminal building flashing past on his right hand side he knew this baby must leave terra firma. Within the next few seconds and that's exactly what it did. It was now climbing while the robust winds continued to place pressure on the plane's wings and fuselage, causing swirls of turbulent air to form on the tips of the aircraft's wings, but this was all in a day's work for these well respected Greek island pilots.

Once the cabin crew were freed from their seats, there was, as always, a sense of relief from the 50 or so passengers, and in no time at all the crew were busy pushing their trolleys seemingly uphill in a race to feed everyone with a snack and a drink. Only 50 minutes later they were being told to buckle up again before making the final approach into Athens. Ted took a sweet from one of the pretty air hostesses and pulled his belt a little tighter, ready for the landing at the new El Venizelos airport, Athens.

The time was 9:30am as he stood waiting for his luggage to arrive at the carousel. His rucksack now firmly strapped to his back and he knew that once he had exited the terminal doors, there was a good possibility that Frakas and his men could be watching him ready to pounce, even though they had no idea from which direction he would be entering Athens. It wouldn't take a genius to work out that the airport would be the first place to set up surveillance. The automatic doors slid back and Ted stepped into the arrivals hall pulling his suitcase behind him. He made a beeline for the taxi rank, with its lines of new and near new Mercedes cars, and walked to the front of the rank and the driver reluctantly stepped out of his warm dry car to open the boot.

Ted climbed into the back seat with his rucksack and told the driver he wanted to go to the Hotel Aphrodites in the Old Placker. The journey was normally around 40 minutes but today it took the 'I'm lost' looking taxi driver 75 minutes. Ted jumped out and paid a hefty fare of some 60 euros but he never quibbled with the young driver, eager to get inside the hotel's swing doors hoping he hadn't been spotted by his Hungarian friends. The hotel Aphrodites had a four-star rating but in reality it was probably more like three, although the marble floors and tall majestic columns made it seem grander than it actually was. He checked in and then proceeded to find room 270.

The old fashion lift creaked as it took him up to the top floor where a wide corridor, with its well worn carpets, guided him along to his room. He opened the door to be surprised by how spacious it was and was impressed by the large queen-sized bed draped in a red satin bedspread. On the bed lay two quality white dressing gowns made up into a swan-shaped display. There was also a good size bathroom with a spacious walk in shower. At the far end of the room was a recessed area where a huge trebled-mirrored door wardrobe stood. He then went across to the window and looked out through the rain splashed pane of glass. The view was reminiscent of the front cover of a European city breaks brochure the Acropolis and Parthenon. they were no more than a few hundred metres in front of him, the only thing stopping this scene from being spectacular was the sight of so many tall tower cranes, their huge jibs covered with company logos.

Looking at his watch he hadn't realised the morning had passed so quickly. It was now 12:30pm and he needed to eat before setting off to survey the old stadium. Picking up the bedside phone he rang the reception and asked them to send up a light lunch to his room. Ten minutes later there was a knock on his door. He opened it to see a small stocky middle-aged man who had the look of, not a waiter but more like one of, a doorman. He was holding a silver tray but Ted couldn't help but notice he wasn't wearing a hotel uniform. He had seen the other staff dressed in on his arrival so he was now on his guard as the waiter motioned to pass Ted the tray with one hand. Ted was looking into the balding man's eyes and could see that not only was he tetchy, he was also more than a little nervous. Ted held out his hand as if he was going to take the tray from the man, then smiling, he quickly grabbed the man's forearm from under the tray causing him to drop whatever he was holding in his right hand. He brought his knee sharply up to the surprised waiter's groin and he fell forward and down onto his knees. He then quickly dragged the unsuspecting man into his room, closing the door with the sole of his shoe.

The so called waiter now lay in a ball, his legs pulled up tightly into his stomach and he was groaning in agony. Ted rolled the man onto his back, making a sound reminiscent of a pig having a brass ring squeezed through it's nose, then exerted pressure down onto the stocky man's barrel chest with one of his size 12s, and asked, "Frakas sent you, yes?"

There was no answer, irritated now by this short-arse, he stood with both feet on him whilst holding onto the corner of the wardrobe. His heavy brown leather brogues were digging into the man's chest and neck. He started to cough and splutter by the weight that Ted was applying, until he uttered the word, "Yes okay, yes Frakas."

He stepped off leaving him for a moment to regain some equanimity, then he dragged him up towards the bed headboard and, using his belt, he tied it around the now helpless man's neck and then through the metal strut between the bed and the headboard. He pulled it just tight enough so as not to choke him, unless of course he moved. Without delay he packed his suitcase again and strapped the rucksack over his shoulders, gave the ex-waiter a little smile and told him to tell Frakas that he wasn't the sort of man to mess around with. He was about to leave and issued a further warning to Frakas that if he wanted to play rough, then he was his man.

The now red faced man watched as Ted walked across to the door, but Ted then spotted the blade of a flick knife resting up and against the skirting board. He bent over, picked it up and stared into the frightened man's eyes. He smiled once and then threw the knife hard towards the pathetic Hungarian gangster. He had a look of sheer terror in his eyes as the knife stuck between his legs piercing his trousers to the plush carpeted bedroom floor. The little man sobbed, and Ted was sure he could see steam rising from his crutch as he left.

He caught one of the local articulated type buses he had seen on his journey from the airport. It had an illuminated sign indicated 'Centre,' along with many other stopping points. He made himself comfortable and paid the ticket collector five euros. This allowed him to travel anywhere around the city for the rest of the day. He stayed on the bus for 10 minutes and then alighted at a place called Kallithea where he checked into a small seedy backstreet hotel. After unpacking his suitcase for the second time on the day, he looked around the room he had paid just 40 euros a night for, and hoped he had given Frakas's men the slip for now.

Returning outside, he then walked down the hill towards the central railway station. After turning right in front of its façade he then headed for the old Olympic Stadium. At every location he noted just how long it was taking him. When he arrived there were, as usual, masses of tourists milling around. Chinese, Japanese, Americans, you name a nationality and they were there, which was from his point of view a good thing, at least they would give him some cover. He bought himself an entrance ticket and made his way into the arena, taking photographs so as to mingle in with the rest of the crowd. He carried on through the open wrought iron gates, his eyes with now transfixed on the gap in the barriers at the far end of the old Panathaneiko Stadium.

Behind the stands he could see the large Olympic rings which stood high above the impressive arena which had been refurbished for the first modern Olympics in 1896. It was then he noticed there were two people standing up on the top row of the seating area, and directly behind the place he had chosen to hand over the Hungarian antiquity to Frakas. One person in particular caught his attention and seemed to be watching him walk the length of the arena and he began to wonder whether he had done the right thing to come here and expose himself in this way.

Ted had assumed the tourists would help him to blend in to the background, but by the time he reached the barrier at the end of the arena he knew he had made a terrible mistake. He turned immediately and, hanging on to his rucksack straps tightly, he quickly walked back in the direction he had just come from and out of the stadium gates.

Nothing was going to make him turn, or look back to see if he was being followed. He crossed the large paved terrace with it's many fountains expelling water showing some spectacular displays. Walking quickly now he twisted through and tried to avoid the hordes of tourists who had just stepped off the several tour coaches. They were now forming a long line to queue for tickets. His rucksack caught an Asian man, knocking him to one side as he was taking a photograph. He never turned to apologise, then finally he was out into the open again heading for the bus parking area a couple of hundred metres from the stadium. One of the articulated buses was ready to pull away from the bus stop and he ran as fast as he could for the last few metres before jumping on as if his life depended on it, and he thought it probably did. As he bus pulled away he saw two men running out of the stadium gates, one, he was sure, looked like his old friend from the *Minoan* ferry who he had last seen being chased by big old Zorba. 'My God,' he thought, I was right, they were working for that bastard Frakas all along, and he certainly knew now that this exchange with Frakas, and his Hungarian heavies, was going to be much more difficult than he had first anticipated.

*

Inspector Wallace was sitting at his desk talking on the landline to Jack Terry. "So you confirmed Jack, that one of the passengers leaving Stansted Airport last Tuesday night on flight EYZ 3245 was a Natasha Privsek bound for Ljubljana?"

"Yes, that was her all right guv."

"Okay Jack, now what about Bromley? Has there been further news from Interpol?"

"None at all I am afraid."

"Jack I think you know as well as I do that there is something that doesn't quite add up here. This girl Natasha, who you wouldn't have thought butter would melt in her mouth, leaves the country two days after this Bromley chap; and then Ester Bernard, tells us she once worked for Bromley's wife, just can't be coincidental, surely?"

"I think you will find that's what I told you guv. She has taken us all in, including the Harkers, and without doubt those two are planning to meet up somewhere in Europe, but where, that's our problem."

"I know I must be going soft Jack. Get on to Interpol again and see if they can trace Natasha Privsek in Ljubljana and tell them they are probably now looking for a couple. It's our best lead and we will have to run with it, at least for the moment. If they can locate her, I am certain they will also discover where this Fredric Bromley has disappeared to."

CHAPTER TWENTY

Ted lay on his single divan bed, looking up at the hotel bedroom ceiling with its yellowing cracked plaster and cobwebbed light fittings, trying to figure out how and where he could find to make it safer for him to complete the exchange with Frakas and his mean looking bunch of modern desperados. He picked up the hotel information booklet and found a map of the Acropolis which looked ideal. After studying it, he located the Theatre of Herodes, a fascinating piece of Greek architecture with its tall stone arches which link the walls circling the old amphitheatre, but most importantly the site stood opposite the Spanish Embassy. From his experience of working along with the diplomatic core, he knew there would be at least one armed guard standing in the front of the official Ambassador's residence which, if the guidebook was correct, should be directly facing the theatre. Ted waited for darkness before venturing outside on the cold winter's night, but he had to check the area around the embassy to work out some sort of escape route as he was sure he would most probably need it.

At 6:45pm Ted was looking up at the Acropolis. Four giant tower cranes stood, with their jibs stretched out over the Parthenon, seemingly crossing each other at different heights. The whole area was lit up in an orange glow of sodium light. He walked around the area methodically working out a plan to make the exchange which, for his sake, had to be completed quickly and above all else safely.

The magnificent Theatre of Herodes was lit in a similar way to the Acropolis which showed off the huge red stone blocks that make up the walls. To the left-hand side of the main facade stood an archway which was at least 50 feet tall and a good 12 ft across. This facade was the main entrance to the Amphitheatre. It had iron gates which were firmly locked with a large chain, which had been pulled around the ornate centre bar and then attached to a considerable size padlock which linked the two chains together.

Next to the gateway was an ornately decorated metal bench, the back of which was butted up tightly to the arena wall. He sat down on the cold metal, noticing immediately that he could see the Spanish Embassy, directly across the road in front of him, some thirty metres away. The rest of the extensive area was clear of bushes and any other shrubbery so Frakas's men could not secrete themselves anywhere to lay in wait for him. 'This was the perfect place' he thought and, with the Spanish guards standing across the road at the embassy, they would certainly see and hear if there was a disturbance of any kind. He knew that if there was, they would be over there quicker than you could say paella. On the way back to the hotel he stopped off at one of the many Greek specialty food outlets and brought himself two cheese pies and a bottle of coke, then quickly made his way back to the hotel.

The morning broke with a tremendous thunderstorm, not unusual for Greece at any time of year, and the rain was falling heavily and bouncing off the pavement at the front of the hotel. The clock on the bell tower in the centre of the wet square read, 8:15am and it was time to ring Frakas to notify him where they would meet and make the exchange at 11:00am that very morning. He waited for Frakas to answer, which he did with some sort of ignorant grunt.

"Frakas, pay attention to me, and make sure you understand that you are not dealing with some sort of British unintelligent thug. I have in my procession what you and I, dare say many of your fellow countrymen, would desire to own. As you know, the tiara is priceless to your countrymen so all you have to do to own the Keszthely Tiara is to give me the 3,000,000 euros as we agreed."

"Englishman your money is here, but you won't be getting your hands on the, how you say, cash, unless I can authenticate that the tiara you are claiming to have is a genuine antiquity, and that it once belonged to the Hungarian royal family."

"Frakas, it's genuine all right. You just make sure you keep your side of the agreement. Now listen to me, this is what's going to happen this morning. You will travel alone by taxi to a destination that I will give you by means of a mobile phone call at 10:40am and you must bring the cash in a wheeled suitcase. When you arrive at the exchange location I will be watching your every move, and if anything looks untoward I will leave with the tiara. That will be the end of any understanding we previously had, do you understand this time Frakas?"

"Englishman, do not try to push me around with your condescending English arrogance or you will regret your words ..." Once again, Ted disengaged the call and hung up before Frakas stopped speaking.

Ted left the hotel, his rucksack firmly strapped to his shoulders for what he hoped would be the last time. It would take him 10 minutes to walk the short distance to the Theatre of Herodes. The time was 10:25am which would give him plenty of time to get there before calling Frakas. As he walked up the wide avenue which was lined with many lime trees, now bared of any foliage, he was pleased to see standing outside the Spanish Embassy two armed guards, smartly dressed with their white gaiter belts and side arm holsters standing out on their otherwise dark blue uniforms. Proudly in their hands, they held automatic sub-machine guns in that relaxed manner that only Mediterraneans can get away with. He managed to find himself a high vantage point to the left-hand side of the metal ornate bench, which was some fifty metres away. He called Frakas at 10:40am exactly, and he answered immediately.

"Frakas, take a taxi and tell the driver to bring you to the Theatre of Herodes. Get out of the car and tell the him to turn the cab around and wait for you, saying you will not be more than 10 minutes. As you get out of the car you will see a metal bench standing by the theatre wall, opposite the Spanish Embassy. Walk over to the bench, sit down and wait."

"Where is this Theatre of Herodes?" Frakas asked angrily.

"Your taxi driver will know where, now get on with it."

He ended the call and placed the mobile back into his pocket. Ted watched the guards walking up and down in front of the embassy, at the same time he was gazing down the long tree lined avenue. Looking at his watch it read 10:48am. Fracas was late but as he looked up again a silver Mercedes rounded the corner and drove up the avenue, but then it turned off the into the road that runs down between the embassy and the Acropolis Museum.

Ted was now getting more than a little anxious that Frakas wouldn't show, until a second silver Mercedes drove up the avenue and stopped opposite the embassy. The two guards looked on as a large man wearing a gabardine raincoat and a brown trilby hat stepped out from the back door of the car. The driver also got out and walked around the back of his car, opened the boot, and handed the man a dark blue suitcase. Frakas looked around and acknowledged the guards by touching his trilby in a polite manner before spotting the metal bench. He walked across the flag stoned pavement, pulling the suitcase behind him, so far obeying Ted's instructions.

On reaching the bench he leaned forward and wiped the wet seat with his gloved hand before sitting down. He looked more than a little tetchy, nervously scanning the area and looking for Ted. After several minutes had past, Ted decided that Frakas was probably on his own although, with the enormity of the now tense situation he was about to face, he knew he would have to remain observant until he was well clear of this place. Frakas stood, obviously agitated, but then he spotted the Englishman walking towards him. Ted stared at Frakas as he got closer and was a little surprised that he wasn't at all how he had pictured him. He had imagined a middle-aged man, not the tall handsome bronzed faced person that was now standing before him.

"Sit down Frakas. We don't want to draw attention to ourselves now do we?" He sat down, unhappy at being told what to do by this arrogant foreigner.

"Where is the tiara, Englishman?" he asked in an unpleasant way.

"I have your precious headpiece Frakas, but first I want to see the cash." Frakas lifted the suitcase onto the bench between them and stared menacingly into Ted's eyes. "Show me the antiquity?" Ted released the straps on his rucksack and placed the bag beside him holding firmly on to the handle with his left hand. He looked across the avenue and saw both guards going about their duties, oblivious to what was going on between the two men. Then he opened the gold velvet bag which was still inside the rucksack and gripping the tiara tightly he offered Frakas a look at the exquisite headpiece.

Frakas took a small mirror from his inside coat pocket and within the confines of the rucksack drew the mirror across the top row of diamonds before he withdrew his hand. Placing only the slightest amount of pressure onto the mirror he snapped the glass into three or four pieces. Ted never spoke and he wasn't about to loosen his grip on the tiara. Now Frakas took what looked like an old photograph from the same pocket. Ted opened the bag a little wider so the Hungarian could get a better view at the tiara, and he couldn't hide the look of satisfaction when the object Ted was gripping on to was identical to Frakas's photograph. Ted asked him if he was satisfied that this was indeed the lost Hungarian Royal Family's tiara.

"It is too soon to say, I will have to complete more tests somewhere else away from this place." Ted's face tightened with rage, his steely eyes burning into the Hungarian as he said, "Listen to me you bastard, if you don't hand over the cash now, not you, or any of your countrymen will ever see this fucking headpiece ever again, do you understand?" Frakas looked down again into the rucksack at the tiara, only to see Ted was now holding in his hand a pair of metal cutters, the blades open as if he was about to snip off the top row of diamonds. The look of horror on Frakas's demented face was the exact reaction Ted was aiming for.

"Don't, you crazy bloody Englishman, I have your money, it's here in the suitcase, look I will show you." He opened the zip and folded back the lid, saying, "There, there's your cash." Ted, still keeping the metal cutters in his right hand, leaned across and lifted out one of the bundles from the bottom of the suitcase. He flicked quickly through the wad of euro notes before laying the bundle on the bench and behind his rucksack. Taking a pen from the inside the rucksack, he scribed across one of the notes and was satisfied at least this one bundle was genuine. He then replaced it before slipping his hand into the suitcase again and randomly pulled out a second bundle, again it was authentic. Finally he took one of the notes out of its wad, and ripped it into pieces inside the rucksack, before turning to Frakas saying, "Okay Frakas, it looks like we have a deal?"

"Good, you mistrusting English bastard, now hand over the tiara."

Ted reluctantly handed over his now well worn rucksack into Frakas's outstretched hand, then immediately gripped the suitcase and moved it onto his side of the bench. Ted stood first, the two determined men stared at each other, both wanting to end this fraught situation. Frakas also stood but Ted spoke first.

"Frakas, you will stay here until I have left in your taxi." Frakas looked furious again, but before he could speak Ted carried on, "If you or any of your men make any attempt to stop me, I will shout out as loud as I can, 'bomb, terrorist,' in my best Spanish and I will be pointing towards you. You just watch our two machine-gun carrying friends from the Spanish Embassy aim in your direction." Frakas said nothing but his body language said it all. Ted walked over to the waiting cab and placed the suitcase on the back seat, while still firmly holding on to it. He climbed quickly in the Mercedes and drove off, but not before he gave Frakas a royal goodbye wave, leaving him still sitting on the wet metal bench enraged and incensed that this foreigner had got the better of him.

The cab pulled up ten minutes later and Ted paid the driver for both journeys. He dragged the heavy suitcase and made his way along several side streets and back towards his hotel. As he peered around the corner of the street where his hotel was situated, he spotted two suspicious characters in a shop doorway next to the hotel. He instantly changed his mind and withdrew back along the street. He was soon well away from the area.

His belongings at the hotel were insignificant compared to the wealth he was now carrying in Frakas's suitcase. His plan was now to hire a car and leave Athens that day, knowing that Frakas wouldn't let him get away so easily without trying to take back the 3,000,000 euros. Above all, he knew they would be waiting at Athens airport and the ferry terminals at Piraeus hoping to catch him before he disappeared from the city. They will have a long wait he thought, as he would simply drive out of Athens and into the Greek countryside, heading as fast as he could back to Igoumanitsa. From there he would go on to Kerkyra, but first he had to find a backstreet rent-a-car hire company though that might be a little tricky as he would probably have to show his passport and driving license, and that was one thing he wasn't about to do.

A few minutes later he spotted a flashing neon sign emblazed 'Petros Car Hire - best prices.' He looked through the grimy office window and saw a plump man sitting at a desk with one foot perched up and onto a chair opposite him. He held a cigarette in one hand while swinging a string of silver worry beads around in the other, catching them every second turn. Ted walked into the smoke filled room hoping to pull the wool over Petros's eyes. He smiled at the man who had now stood to greet him and asked if he could hire a car for 24 hours, the man looked disappointed, probably because it was such a short hire, but answered saying, "Sixty euros my friend." But if you had the same car for one week, then only 200 euros, this bargain yes, best price in Athens." Ted wanted the short mustached Greek on his side so he thought he would make his day and asked, "How much it would cost for two weeks?" Now the man's eyes lit up.

"Three hundred and ninety five euros, good price, yes?"

"Well that does sound very reasonable, yes that is an excellent price, Petros isn't it." Ted held out his hand and Petros responded gripping Ted's hand firmly and smiling warmly at his new customer.

"Would it be possible to take the car now Petros, if that's all right with you?"

"No problem my friend, yes of course." With that he shouted, "Ela," and a greasy looking kid came into the shop. Petros issued the young man, who couldn't have been more than 16, orders and he left again mumbling something under his breath. Ted took out his wallet and lay 400 euros on the desk in front of Petros, who asked, "Please my friend, your passport and driving licence?"

"Ah, that is my problem Petros, I had all my documentation stolen yesterday, and I am now waiting until my new paperwork arrives from England next Monday."

"This big problem for me, I can't let you take one of my cars without these documents?"

"Look Petros, what if I pay you a deposit of 500 euros or more if you like, you see I must have a car for my business. The thing is Petros, my company, Weir Enterprises, are opening a branch in Athens and we are looking for small businesses to work along with us. Now back in England my company hire probably 200 cars every year, so we will be looking for the right car hire company to form a partnership with, here in Athens."

Now Petros was seeing the paperwork side of things in a different light and insisted Ted took the car without a deposit, telling him he looked forward to meeting him again next week when he could take all the details off his licence and passport and then talk some more about Weir Enterprises.

Ted waved goodbye to the gullible Petros and drove off with a full tank of petrol and it wasn't long before he was leaving the city behind him. Some 20 minutes or so later he was on the motorway and heading north-west on the national highway 8A E94 towards Korinthos. He expected the drive to Igoumenitsa would take him a little over six hours. From there he planned to take the local ferry service as a foot passenger to Kerkyra, leaving Petros's hire car in one of the maze of back streets in the coastal town of Igoumenitsa. He knew that once he was back on Kerkyra he would feel a little safer in the knowledge that he had hopefully seen the last of Frakas and his gangsters.

CHAPTER TWENTY ONE

Wallace sat at his desk going over Jonathan Harker's case files when the telephone rang out, startling him.

"Hello, serious crimes office, Inspector Wallace speaking."

"Inspector Wallace this is Mrs Harker from Sedgwick House."

"Good morning Mrs Harker, what can I do for you?"

"I thought you would like to know inspector, we received a post card this morning from Natasha."

"That is interesting Mrs Harker, would it be possible for me to take a look at the card madam?"

"Yes of course inspector. We have an appointment in town this morning, so we could pop it into the station if you would like us to." He told her he would be in his office until 12:30pm and he looked forward to seeing the card. Jack Terry walked into the office carrying two cups of coffee and placed them down on the desk.

"That's a turn up for the books Jack, Lynda Harker has just received a post card from Natasha Privsek."

"Well thank God for that guv, maybe the tide has turned at last." Terry sat on the edge of Wallace's desk and told him that Interpol had also managed to locate Natasha Privsek's address in Slovenia. The airport had also confirmed that she landed on the flight from Stansted to Ljubljana on Tuesday, 27th January.

"So, have they checked out this address then Jack?"

"Yes guv, it's a small village by the name of Murska Sobota, apparently the village is quite close to the Hungarian border."

"I suppose it would be too much to ask if they have caught up with her Jack, wouldn't it?"

"Well no, the place was deserted, and according to the locals the Privsek family moved back to Hungary three or four years ago. They moved after most of their farm was destroyed by fire. The locals believed it to have been an arson attack."

"So Natasha Privsek is Hungarian then?"

"No guv, she was born in Slovenia but it looks like the family's origins are from Hungary."

"What about the fire then Jack, was that a sectarian attack of some kind?"

"Well, the local police have told Interpol, that no one in the immediate area seems to know or wants to talk about it." They both stood up as Chief Superintendent Bendery walked in to the serious crime office.

"Good morning Inspector Wallace, DS Terry."

"Good morning," They both replied in agreement.

"How is the Harker case coming along inspector?"

"Well sir, we are pretty sure that the body we found in the canal, which was dumped their unceremoniously by Tony Miles, is that of Dean Wilmot and we believe that, according to Miss Walters' statement, Wilmot was killed when he was crushed by the Water Authority Land Rover as forensics had first thought."

"So if that's the case inspector, how do you think this chap Tony Miles was killed at Duston Mill?"

"We believe, along with forensics, that he was held down under the water, in the old filter tank, until he drowned sir."

"So who do you think is our chief murder suspect then Inspector Wallace?"

"At the moment we are looking at the possibility that it could have been a friend of Harry Bernard's, that's the chap we interviewed in London, he's the person I wrote about in my report."

"So why isn't this Bernard chap a suspect then Inspector Wallace?"

"I haven't ruled him out completely, but I believe his old school friend, Fredric Bromley, is the man we should be concentrating on. According to Miss Walters, the person who organised the kidnapping was known only to her as Ted and Bromley's middle name is Edward as you know sir."

"Have you any idea inspector to the whereabouts of this chap Bromley?"

"Only that he left Ashford on the Eurotunnel service to Calais in the early hours of the morning, in his Renault. This was after we found Tony Miles' body at Duston Mill and we believe he escaped with both the cash and the Harkers' family heirloom."

"So you think this Bromley chap, murdered Tony Miles then inspector?"

"Well it looks that way at the moment sir."

"What's you're next move then Inspector Wallace?"

"We have an arrest warrant out for Bromley with Interpol sir, and are continuing our inquiries locally of course."

"Make sure you keep me well informed Inspector Wallace won't you?" With that command ringing in Wallace's ears the Chief Superintendent left in his usual abrupt manner.

"Thank God for that, but why didn't you tell him about Natasha Privsek?"

"We have to keep something to ourselves Jack and personally, I would be surprised now if she wasn't involved with Bromley. So we will now proceed along those lines, and don't worry Jack I will tell the super in good time if we need to."

"So have you still got a soft spot for our Slovenian lass now guv?"

"Get out of here Jack, and get back onto Interpol to see if they have come up with anything else, keep pushing them, they must know more than they are drip feeding us."

*

It was three weeks since Ted had returned to Kerkyra, and he had begun to settle back into the ways of the Greek mountain village life again. He began to feel more confident every passing day; he was getting to know his old friend Spiro again, someone he remembered with great fondness after he had first arrived on the island. Spiro was the owner of the local kafenion where he spent most of his evenings when he was there on leave from the armed forces all those years ago. He had also met up again with Harris another old drinking partner of his from Acharavi.

Harris was an estate agent, using the term loosely, and for the want of a better word, you wouldn't say he was dishonest. Certainly not, but most would declare that he sailed a little too close to the wind. Harris knew just about everybody on the north coast of Kerkyra and most of his business was conducted with local people he already knew. In a funny sort of way, they trusted him to get the best prices from the incoming wealthy British, Germans and whoever else had enough spare cash to buy the odd stremma of land; or maybe their old grandmother's house on the mountain that none of the younger generations would ever want to live in again.

Ted had arranged to meet Harris the next day at his office in Acharavi. He arrived a little early so decided to have coffee at the bakery in the centre of the small seaside town. The weather was improving everyday now, and this was the warmest he had felt in months as he sat outside eating a warm goat's cheese pie and watching the locals going about their everyday business. He was just finishing off his cappuccino when Harris pulled up on the opposite side of the road, directly outside of his double fronted shop. He looked across the street as he stepped out of his Z3 convertible and waved to Ted to come over.

Harris was now standing on the pavement, holding both arms out in front of him, and took hold of Ted in a warm Greek welcoming embrace, kissing him first on one cheek then the on other. Ted felt the roughness of Harris's Greek style horseshoe moustache. After the niceties were out of the way, he invited Ted into his office and sat down behind his expensive oak desk beckoning Ted to sit opposite him.

"It is so good my friend that you have returned to the most beautiful island in the whole Mediterranean Sea, let alone the Ionian, will you stay this time?"

"That depends on you Harris."

"On me my friend, well what can I do to make you stay apart from buying you wine in my cousin's taverna next door?" He laughed, then stood up opening the top drawer of his desk. He pulled out two glasses and a bottle of ouzo and continued to pour them both a generous measure, then he lifted his glass calling out, "Yamas, my friend, Yamas."

"Thank you Harris, I can see your hospitality has not changed over the years."

"Of course not Ted, now what can I do for such a friend as you?"

"Well firstly, I need to buy some sort of transport, probably just a small car?"

"You have come just in time my friend, my mother is retiring her donkey, it is only 42, would you like to take a look, yes?" Harris laughed so much tears rolled down his face and Ted could see his friend still retained his wonderful sense of humour.

"I'm sorry Ted, I couldn't resist that. No, I have a very beautiful car out the back of my shop, my old car, just right for my old friend."

"What type of car is it Harris?"

"My old British Lotus sports car, very nice for you in the summer, with the top down."

"You really are kind Harris to offer me such a lovely vehicle and I know just how much this old car of yours means to you, but I need something less conspicuous my friend, more like a Fiat Panda."

He laughed out loud again repeating, "Fiat Panda, it's a woman's car you want my friend, you may be better off with my mother's donkey after all."

"No Harris, some other means of transport, that doesn't shit and gets me around the island, so I am able to shop, that sort of thing."

"Endaxi, okay I will get you're Fiat Panda, no problem."

"Now Harris, I am also going to be looking for a villa, somewhere near here on this beautiful north coast?" Ted now had his friend's complete attention.

"A villa, well my friend look at the walls of my shop, they are covered in pictures of beautiful villas."

"Yes I can see that Harris, but I am looking for something very special. Not to say there is anything wrong with your selection, no, I need a villa that is totally secluded, away from prying eyes and preferably with its own mooring."

Harris never spoke at first, then he looked at Ted and laughed saying, "Are you sure you wouldn't like a pool as well, you English and your sense of humour?"

"Harris I have never been more serious my friend." He stopped laughing.

"But this type of villa would cost at least, one and half million euros maybe more."

"Harris I was thinking around about that figure."

Over the next two days Harris picked up Ted each morning and showed him at least a dozen properties along the north coast, but none came up to Ted's precise specification, apart from one that was well over two million.

"If you are not satisfied with the properties I have shown you my friend, would you consider living off the island?"

"Where exactly off the island do you mean?"

"Erikoussa."

"Where the hell is Erikoussa, Harris?"

"Come please my friend, I will show you."

They were soon driving high into the mountains beyond Acharavi when Ted asked, "Where the hell are you taking me?"

"Please wait one moment my friend, you are too impatient, trust me we are nearly there." Harris pulled over, just off the twisting country lane and Ted found himself following him through a small olive grove. When they eventually came out into the open, they were standing in a meadow filled with wild flowers, their blooms expelling a warm fragrance into the afternoon air, and the view across the field was spectacular.

"Look my friend, there is Erikoussa."

"What am I supposed to be looking at Harris?"

"There, the beautiful island of Erikoussa." He was pointing towards the north and over what seemed like several miles of crystal clear turquoise sea.

"Goodness that looks truly magnificent, have you any properties on this island to show me?"

"I think maybe we have just found your dream villa soldier."

"When can we go over to take a look?"

"Tomorrow my friend, no problem. I will pick you up at 1:00pm, but come now I will buy you a late lunch at my favourite taverna, the Mono Leif."

"Sounds excellent Harris."

The next afternoon Harris drove Ted along the north coast to Sidari, a bustling holiday resort in the summer months, but the town was relatively quiet on this late February afternoon. They turned off the main road into the small harbour quayside car park. Harris had arranged for his brother Yanni to take them across to Erikoussa on his speed boat, *Athena*. After introductions and a good 10 minutes admiring the boat's sleek lines and the 90cc Mercury engine., they set off, slowly at first. Once out of the harbour, Yanni opened up the throttle and now *Athena* was lightly skipping over the slightly choppy water heading for the small island in the distance.

Twenty minutes later Yanni reduced speed as they entered Erikoussa's tiny crescent shaped harbour.

"What are your first impressions my friend?"

"Harris, if the rest of this island is as striking as the harbour, then I could soon fall in love with your Erikoussa." They left Yanni with his boat and arranged to meet him in a couple of hours at the quayside kafenion.

"My goodness Harris, how is it I have never visited this beautiful island before? The whole place looks like some Grecian film set from the 50s."

"I thought you would fall for this idyllic place my friend, most people do, but let's hope you also like the villa as much."

They walked together admiring the surroundings as they climbed the steep hill towards Tantoulis village. Harris told him they would have to go through the village, as this is where the villa is situated.

"So the villa hasn't a mooring then Harris?"

"Ted please, have patience my friend." They climbed up and the hill became even steeper. After a further 10 minutes of walking they turned towards the right and started to descend through what could only be described as a narrow alleyway. This led them through a small hamlet of houses onto a tiny cobbled square where many attractive pastel washed buildings stood, most of them painted in a diversity of colours, some more faded than the others and showing their longevity.

He followed closely behind Harris as they turned off the square and down a lane between two of the houses. A few minutes later Harris stopped and he was now leaning over an old stone wall. They were looking down a dirt track that meandered through the well cultivated countyside and in the distance you could just make out the top of a large yellow coloured building, partially hidden behind several rows of tall olive trees.

"There my friend, is hopefully your villa."

"Wow;" was the only word that came from Ted's mouth as he listened to Harris's description.

"The villa my friend stands in its own grounds of approximately six stremma, that is roughly 10 of your acres I believe. Most of the land is laid down for olive production from some 500 well cultivated trees which produces many hundreds of litres of prime virgin olive oil."

"Harris this place is truly magnificent and exactly what I am looking for, come on what are we waiting for? Let's get down there."

They walked down the lane, where the knarled olive trees hung heavily with their fruits. Harris pointed out the black netting that lay on the ground, carefully placed to catch the olives as they fell, allowing them to accumulate in the nets. He told Ted that the olives were a gift from Saint Spyridon and they must be left to fall from the trees and are never to be picked by hand. Ted wondered cynically if this was just another reason to sit in the local kafenion, drink copious cups of Greek coffee and the odd ouzo.

When they got to the entrance gates Ted was almost stopped in his tracks by the site of the villa that Harris had brought him to see.

"Harris, this place it's just so outstanding, you have really excelled yourself."

"So am I to take that as a complement my friend?"

"You most certainly can, this is the sort of place I have been hoping you would bring me to."

"But can you afford it my friend?"

"What are they asking for the property then?"

"Two million euro's, but the villa has been empty now for three years although it has been well maintained over that time. As you can see the olive groves are in wonderful condition."

"Yes Harris I can see that, okay then, offer them one and a quarter million."

"Come on my friend, you know that figure is much too low?"

"All right then, let's say one million, four hundred thousand cash, no complications and as soon as they like."

"Cash, you can't be serious my friend." Harris was truly shocked that anyone could produce so much paper money.

"I am very serious, please give your clients a call."

"But Ted, you haven't even seen inside the villa yet?"

"Okay, I will look inside while you ring the owners." Harris opened the door and let Ted into the villa, he was smiling yet still looking a little bewildered as he pushed open the impressive door and invited Ted inside.

"I will give them a call now my friend and leave you to look around. I think you will fall in love with this impressive building, yes?"

Impressive, yes it certainly was, with it's huge lounge looking out onto a sky blue infinity swimming pool. It had views out to the sea with the mountains of Albania in the distance and to the rear of the lounge were five double bedrooms, all with en suite facilities. He walked along a wide marbled tile corridor and found a kitchen the size of his old mountain cottage. His eyes were drawn to the black granite counter-tops and it was equipped with every conceivable gadget. He loved it, not just because it was incredibly beautiful, but knowing that this was his perfect hiding place. He believed no one would ever find him, it was everything and more that he could have ever dreamed of.

A good 15 minutes later he walked back outside and saw that Harris was still talking on his mobile phone, to whom Ted assumed to be his clients. As he got closer he realised Harris was speaking in fluent German. Ted was impressed by the speed of his conversation so he waited for a few minutes, passing the time admiring the grounds and the pool.

He then heard Harris say auf wiedersehen and returned his mobile to his pocket. Harris walked over towards Ted, but he wasn't smiling so Ted thought the worst.

"Come on then Harris, don't keep me in suspense, what did they say?"

"Well my old friend they thought the price was much too low, but when I told them the full amount would be paid in cash and could be completed quickly, they accepted your offer, under the proviso that the contracts must be completed within one month from today."

"Thank you Harris, that's fantastic, now let us go back down to your brother and start celebrating."

Harris delivered the Fiat Panda the next day. Ted was happy with the funny little white car, although it was far from new.

"I don't mind telling you my friend, I wore my dark glasses and baseball cap driving your Panda from Acharavi to Sinies."

"Very funny Harris, you could have started a trend." Ted thanked him telling him that it would be just fine for getting around the island, sun glasses or not, and then asked, "Perhaps you could keep the Fiat for me somewhere in Sidari after I have moved to the new villa on Erikoussa?"

"No problem my friend, you will find plenty of parking areas around Sidari. Now tell me Ted, do you want to sell your old cottage now you are moving off the island?"

"Well to be honest I haven't thought too much about that, but it's unlikely Harris and perhaps I would be better off renting the cottage out in the summer to tourists."

"Well if you change your mind, I should think the cottage would probably be worth something like 200,000 euros, for such a beautiful old place as this."

"Harris I will just wait and see for the time being."

At the same time Ted was thinking how much commission Harris was already making out of him from the villa deal. A friend Harris certainly was, but first and always a very good business man. Harris surprised Ted by telling him he was taking a business trip to Athens the following day, and if his meeting finished on time, he was hoping to fly to London.

Ted replied, "London, what the hell are you going to England for Harris?"

"My sister and brother-in-law live there and have a restaurant on Southwark Bridge Road. It is their wedding anniversary and so I promised I would try my best to make it."

This was the opportunity Ted had been waiting for. Without hesitation, he asked Harris if he could post a letter for him when he arrived in the London.

"No problem, yes of course I will take your letter."

"I will come over to your house in the morning with the letter if that's okay Harris?"

"Like I say, no problem my friend."

Now that he had his little Fiat Panda and was independent for the first time since he arrived on the island. That afternoon he decided to drive down to Kerkyra town and visit his Greek banks main branch on the island. He also wanted buy himself a new Greek mobile phone and, if he had time, wanted to look at new furniture for the villa.

When he arrived he paid the three euros and parked his car in the old port, before walking through the oldest part of the town. He wound his way up the narrow streets where the shops sell anything from bread to fine art and jewellery. He bought himself a basic mobile from one of several small electrical outlets and then proceeded to walk up and onto the main street at the top of the hill. There he turned left and after a few metres he entered the bank through the main door. As usual there was a queue and he had to wait for the best part of 15 minutes before conducting his business with the Demis Roussos look alike behind the security window, who was about as polite as every other Greek bank teller he had ever met.

Leaving the air conditioned building behind, he ventured out into the spring like warmth of the bustling old town streets, and weaved his way on towards the Liston building and his favourite restaurant, The Rex, for lunch. The restaurant was situated just behind the Esplanade of the famous old Liston building with its many cafés and restaurants, under a cloister of walkways and it's arches. As he walked on he prayed The Rex would still be open after such a long time. He needn't have worried, it was there all right and the restaurant was near to full. A smartly dressed young male waiter showed him across to one of the tables near the bar area of the restaurant. He was pleased to see that some things never change and there, standing at the kitchen pass, timelessly was the owner, Alexander. He glanced at the menu, before ordering fresh bread, tsatsiki, and a Greek salad. This was to be followed by Alexander's wife's home made moussakas. He felt so relaxed and was salivating by the thought of the moussaka. He gazed around the restaurant but his whole demeanour suddenly changed when he spotted two well built men. One was slightly taller than the other who was entering the restaurant. His heart sunk when he recognised the shorter of the two as his cabin-share friend from the *Minoan* ferry.

They sat down just inside the door, facing out and onto the street. Ted never hesitated in getting to his feet and walked towards the back of the establishment, nodding politely to Alexander as he walked by. He then went through the glass beaded curtain and passed the toilets and out of the back door into a narrow alleyway. Within minutes he was moving quickly back down the busy main street on his way to the old port car park, not quite believing what had just happened. They must somehow have known that he was on the island, and he was now realising, if he hadn't already, that Frakas wasn't going to let him get away with 3,000,000 euros that easily.

CHAPTER TWENTY TWO

Ted was relieved to see the town way off in the distance as the Fiat rounded one of the many hairpin bends as the road climbed higher into the mountains. It would certainly be some time before he would visit the town again, if ever, he thought. The sun was setting and the night air had a distinct chill about it as he arrived back at the cottage, but 20 or so minutes later he had the range roaring away and the kettle was now beginning to sing. He made himself coffee before placing the new mobile phone battery on charge.

That evening, after a belated dinner, Ted was busy sending a text message, when his landline rang out, "Kalispera my friend how are you?" Harris asked.

"I am fine Harris." he said, knowing his words were far from the truth.

"Well soldier, earlier this afternoon I heard from my clients and I have good news for you regarding the villa. They will be arriving in Kerkyra on the 25th February."

"Bloody hell, that's a lot sooner than I thought Harris."

"Are you sure everything is all right my friend, only you sound a little stressed, maybe there is a problem?"

"No I wouldn't say it was a problem, but it is just that I am buying the villa for someone else, and I don't know whether they will arrive on the island by the 25th."

"My God, I know you are a generous man, but that's a hell of a present you are giving away."

"No Harris, I want the villa contracts to be made up in my partner's name."

"I see, so when do you think they will be here to sign the paperwork?"

"I am hoping by the weekend, but I can't say for sure I am afraid. I will know more later this evening Harris, so I will tell you tomorrow morning when I bring the letter around to you."

"Okay soldier we will speak tomorrow, now maybe you should have an ouzo and you will feel more relaxed."

Standing now by the Greek equivalent to an Aga and warming his backside, he was waiting for a response to his earlier text message. He recalled the afternoon events, and the sight of Frakas's men had shocked him, he really found it hard to believe that they knew he was on Kerkyra.

Of all the islands he could have chosen to disappear, why Kerkyra? Was it just a coincidence that he had stumbled on them? Perhaps Frakas has other business on the island, but whatever the two heavies were up to, they had certainly unnerved him and the sooner the contracts were signed for the villa on Erikoussa the more secure he would feel. At last his mobile vibrated and turned in a circle on the table where it was lying, he picked it up, it read, "Can't wait my darling to be together again. I will be leaving in the morning and the journey will take me two days, love you xxx." The message had revitalised Ted's spirits and he was now looking forward to planning the move to Erikoussa, where they would be able to start living the lifestyle he had, until now, only dreamed of.

*

Inspector Wallace was on the telephone talking to the Interpol officer who was dealing with the case at their Netherlands HQ. He asked his counterpart if they had been able to trace Miss Natasha Privsek or Fredrick Bromley yet.

"Unfortunately not Inspector Wallace, we are having difficulties tracing Miss Privsek. As I told DS Terry, we know she landed in Ljubljana and that the family once lived in Slovenia, but I'm afraid we haven't been able to find out where they moved onto from there. As for this Fredrick Bromley there is no news, but rest assured when we have more news for you, I will be in touch again."

"Thanks anyway Inspector Dryker, and let's hope its sooner rather than later."

DS Terry wasn't having much luck himself. He was interviewing Lieutenant Colonel James Blackstock, the commanding officer at the Hereford based army barracks. Terry had the greatest respect for the officers and men from the

Special Forces and that wasn't about to change as he asked, "Sir we are looking for one of your fellow retired officers, Fredric Edward Bromley, and any help you could give us would be very much appreciated." Lieutenant Colonel Blackstock eyed this policeman who stood before him and asked, "Could you tell me Sergeant Terry why you are looking for Lieutenant Colonel Bromley?" He stood up from behind the well polished mahogany desk and walked over to the large sash window, appearing to stare outside while waiting for DS Terry's reply.

"I must first ask if you know this gentleman sir?"

"As a matter of fact Sergeant Terry, I know Lieutenant Colonel Bromley very well."

"I see sir; well I am afraid to say we think he may be involved in a very serious crime." Blackstock turned away from the window and walked towards the policeman, giving the DS a steely look that would have made most men want to avoid eye contact with the officer. Terry was made of sterner stuff, but that wasn't to say he hadn't been unnerved a little.

"Can I tell you Detective Sergeant Terry, that the man you are telling me you suspect of committing a serious crime was one of the finest officers, not only in this regiment, but in the entire British Army and was decorated on many occasions." Terry knew he was going to ruffle a few feathers, but he had only asked his third question and he had seemed to have angered the Camp Commander already.

"Well sir, with the greatest of respect, I have been told of Mr Bromley's record and his services for his country but, I am afraid, I still need to ask you if you knew anything about his private life?"

The Lieutenant Colonel once again looked deep into the detective's eyes and politely said, "Look Detective Sergeant Terry, I know you have an important job to do, as we all have, but you are wasting your time."

"I am sorry you feel like that sir, but again, with the greatest of respect to you Lieutenant Colonel Blackstock, I am investigating a kidnapping and at least one murder." Blackstock sat down again.

"All I want to know sir, is do you or any of your men possibly know if Mr Bromley for instance, had relatives living abroad, or whether he has owned properties himself in another country?" Blackstock gave the impression he was considering Terry's question, before saying, "I can only speak for myself Sergeant Terry, in telling you I am sorry I don't know if Lieutenant Colonel Bromley had properties either here or abroad. As for the Lieutenant Colonel having relatives living anywhere apart from the UK, I really have no idea. If you were to question other serving offices and men in my company, or the Lieutenant Colonel's old comrades in the regiment, well I imagine they would give you the same answer sergeant." Terry knew this conversation wasn't going any further, so he stood and begrudgingly thanked the Lieutenant Colonel for his help, even though all he had achieved was to waste the police officer's time. As he was about to leave Blackstock stood, and said to the sergeant, "I am sorry I couldn't have been more help to you Detective Sergeant Terry." Terry thought there was more than a hint of sarcasm in his well-spoken tones, and replied, "So am I sir, so am I."

Terry left the Barracks feeling as if he had been put in his place and knowing this avenue of investigation was closed.

"Any luck Jack?" Wallace asked, as Terry walked back into the office later on that afternoon.

"As I thought, Bromley's old commanding officer Lieutenant Colonel Blackstock made me feel as welcome as a skunk in a tart's bordello."

"Well I think we were both expecting that, weren't we Jack?"

"The thing is, we are ninety percent sure that Bromley is our man, and we have known that now for at least three weeks. Then of course, there's our Natasha guv. I know you didn't want to think that she was involved, but to me Natasha Privsek has to be implicated in some way with Bromley and the post card the Harkers received from Ljubljana was just one more deception to make us think exactly that."

"Well the more I hear about her movements from Interpol, I am tending to agree with you. But there is one person we can certainly eliminate from our enquiries Jack."

"Who do you mean?"

"Harry Bernard. Apparently he had been visiting his old mother at Quinsy Gardens nursing home and was on the way back to his house in Cockfosters when some bloody kid, high on drugs, jumped the lights in a stolen car and crashed into him from the opposite direction. He hit the poor sod side on and killed him instantly." Jack sat down as if the wind had been taken out of his sails.

"Bloody hell, if that poor sod hadn't already suffered enough."

"My thoughts entirely Jack, Mills rang about 20 minutes ago. He was the first on the scene."

"He was still tailing Bernard then?"

"Only since yesterday. I thought I would take one more look at Harry Bernard before I ruled him out completely."

"What about his wife, has she been told yet?"

"God, give us a chance Jack. I have only just put the phone down as you walked into the office. The chauffeur, Mr Jones, answered and told me both ladies and Mr Harker left for London last evening. I asked him if they had left him a telephone contact number and I was about to ring them when you walked in."

Wallace asked Jack to make them both a cup of tea, before he lifted the receiver and punched in Harker's number.

"Hello, Jonathan Harker here." Harker sounded buoyant. Wallace thought and he could hear music in the background and people laughing, as if a party was in full swing.

"Sorry could you wait a moment while I make my way outside?"

A few moments later Harker replied, "I do apologise, whose speaking please?"

"This is Inspector Wallace sir, is Mrs Bernard with you Mr Harker?"

"As a matter of fact she is inspector."

"I am afraid I have some very disturbing news for her."

"Inspector, surely this is not about Ester employing Natasha without the relevant paperwork?"

"I only wish it was, no sir, much more serious I'm afraid. It's her husband, Harry, I am sorry to tell you he has been tragically killed in a road traffic accident." Wallace waited for a couple of seconds for Harker to take the news on board.

"Good God, poor Harry, when did this happen inspector?"

"This afternoon sir, quite close to his home in Cockfosters. He was then taken to the Royal Free Hospital in Hampstead but unfortunately was found to be dead on arrival."

"Thank you for letting me know so soon inspector. Oh yes, and I am sorry I jumped to the wrong conclusion."

"That's okay sir, so shall I leave it to you to pass on the sad news Mr Harker?"

"Yes, Ester's inside. It's Lynda's birthday you see, and we were enjoying ourselves with a few friends around at Ester's flat. Now somehow I will have to break this terrible news to her inspector."

"I will say goodnight then sir, and please would you give Mrs Bernard my condolences?"

"Yes I will Inspector Wallace, I will, goodnight."

*

Ted stood admiring his new look in the bathroom mirror, the six days of beard growth and the woolly hat he had found in the bedroom wardrobe made his disguise complete. He checked the new mobile again to see if he had missed any text messages while he had been in the shower. He had, and it read, "Ted the Ickories Palace is just entering the Kerkyra channel, can't wait to see you my darling xxx."

He rushed outside from the bedroom onto the balcony and stood looking down towards the sea which was approximately a mile in front of him. He quickly ran back into the bedroom to find his binoculars and then returned to the balcony to wait for the *Minoan* ferry to pass through the straights between Kerkyra and Albania. The view towards the sea on this sunny afternoon was just breathtaking. Grove after grove of olive trees clung to the sides of the steep slopes, intermingled among them were the occasional Cypress trees, their tall pointed branches swaying in the late February breeze. A shiver ran down his spine when he saw the sun glistening on the bow of the huge white ship as it came into view from his left.

This was the moment he had been waiting so long for and soon they would be together again. He remembered the warmth from their last tender kiss, and the softness of her beautiful body in his arms. This would now make the last few months all worthwhile. Just to have her safely with him again. She was a wonderful woman who had swept him off his feet and he had missed her so dreadfully.

She would be looking up at the mountain he thought, as he had asked her to, and in the vain hope he would see her as he trained his binoculars onto the ship. There were lots of people milling around but any one of them could have been her. Then he remembered Katarina, sweet Katarina, and without her help he may not have been standing here today. She had risked her job and had given him so much pleasure that he felt more than a tinge of guilt for lusting after this woman, but pure lust, that's all it had been. His mind was quick to square his thoughts, knowing the person he was hopefully going to spend the rest of his life with, his true love, was on the *Ickories Palace* the same ship where he met Katarina. Banishing those thoughts deep once more into his subconscious, he looked on until the stern of the giant ferry disappeared behind the rocky headland at Agios Stefanos.

Ted drove off down the mountain filled with excitement, but with a slight feeling of anticipation of their coming together again after such a long time apart. His Fiat rattled and bumped over the rough track until he reached the main road at Kentroma. He turned right to put him on course for Kerkyra town once more, but he was going to have stay on his guard and keep a low profile even with his new disguise. Just 40 minutes later he was entering the gates of the new port, but instead of driving along the dock towards the ferry terminal, he parked the Fiat right outside the Port Police Station. The *Ickories Palace* had already entered the port and was slowly turning around and making ready to go astern, her bow thrusters churned up the dock sediment as she gently glided back towards the quayside. Her huge hydraulic ramps were already being lowered as she slowed and she was almost at her berth. Two crew members deployed balled lines from the stern and the massive ramps were gradually bringing her to a standstill as they ground into grooves on the concrete surface of the dockside.

Within minutes trucks were rolling off the ferry and the usual chaos of an any Greek ferry port unfolded. There must have 200 vehicles, all seemingly wanting to choose to get through the port exit at the same time. There were no police, or anyone else for that matter, only the ferry crew franticly waving their arms in an almost frenzied way and giving the indication of, 'come on get the hell off the ship, we have a tight schedule to keep!'

Some foot passengers were by now carefully making their hurried way across the busy port, much to the disgust of more than one horn blowing truck driver. As he stood by a pile of old ropes, trying to be inconspicuous and observing what was going on, there was still no sign of her or the red duffle coat she said she would be wearing. Twenty minutes passed and he was getting worried as most of the foot passengers had already disembarked by now, leaving just the last of the stragglers towing their wheeled suitcases down the ramp and then across the hectic dock.

Trucks were waiting to load for the outbound journey and had starting revving their engines in anticipation that the ferry crew would soon be calling them to begin loading, but where was she? His heart was now sinking ever further. He had waited for months for this moment, surely nothing could go wrong now, it was then that he saw her over on the opposite side of the dock, looking totally lost and standing there with her suitcase by her side.

He quickly walked around to the outside of the dock until he was no more than 20 metres from her. She turned and saw a tall rough looking man in a grey woollen hat approaching her, but then she got caught up in the emotion of the moment when she realised it was him. They moved towards each other, embracing warmly, and he told her he would never let her out of his sight again. He kissed her tenderly once more and told her just how much he loved her. Then, as heartfelt tears streamed down both of their cheeks he said, "Oh my beautiful darling Natasha, how I love you and I have missed you so very much."

"Me too Freddy, it has been so long my darling but now we are together again."

Holding her hand tightly as if he would never let go, they walked away from the dock, Ted pulling her suitcase back towards the old Fiat.

Soon they were on their way driving along the busy coast road happier than they had both been in months and talking about their future together. Natasha's hand firmly gripped Ted's right knee and soon after they had left the town behind them. She fell silent, admiring the mountainous scenery to the north of the island.

"What do you think of the Kerkyra, Natasha?"

"It is so wonderful Freddy, and so green for this part of the world."

"You're right Natasha, and that's what makes Kerkyra so breathtaking, but you must remember that the local villagers and my friends call me soldier or Ted."

"But it sounds so silly to call you soldier."

"I know Natasha, but that's the Greek way. You see, I was in uniform the first time the Greeks caught a glimpse of me. Well I say uniform, actually I was wearing a pair of old military dungarees, so that's the reason I am called soldier and for that reason darling so must you."

"Surely not when I am alone with you Freddy, please?" He laughed out loud.

"No of course not darling, you can call me whatever you want to then." She leaned over, placed her head on his shoulder, and he in turn squeezed the top of her thigh.

Thirty minutes later they arrived at the cottage. She smiled excitedly at him as they walked down the stone steps towards the old pan tiled roofed cottage.

"Freddy it's so beautiful. I love it. I love your pretty cottage." She especially liked the way the bread oven bulged out from the back of the cottage.

"Freddy that shape reminds me of an Eskimo's igloo." She was referring to the traditional bread oven.

"Yes, me also darling, and tonight we will light the oven for the first time in probably half-a-century in your honour."

"Oh that will be wonderful making bread together Freddy."

He laughed again and said, "Well I was thinking along the lines of the pizza that I brought from Nickos' supermarket earlier today."

She nudged him and smiled as they walked over towards the paved terrace where a small round table stood next to two wicker chairs. The cottage appeared to be tiny to her from the outside, but when Natasha entered the kitchen she was surprised that there was much more room than she had first thought. This wasn't at all as she had pictured it after Freddy's description, it was far more beautiful than that. She was like a child running from room to room calling out, "I love it Freddy, I love your gorgeous house." He found her standing on the bedroom balcony looking down the mountain at the Ionian Sea below.

"Oh Freddy this view is unbelievable my darling." He kissed the nape of her neck and wrapped his arms tightly around her and they stayed there, blissfully happy to be together again. After a wonderful evening together accompanied by a bottle of local wine and the pepperoni pizza, they lay in bed together, her head resting on his muscular chest.

"Freddy, please never leave me again will you my darling?"

"Natasha, my sweet lady, this is where I shall be every night holding you."

He leaned over and kissed her soft warm lips and their bodies were soon locked together as one making love endlessly until they drifted off to sleep still entwined in each other's arms.

The next morning the wind had picked up again, causing the shutters on the French windows to rattle and waking them both from their slumbered sleep. Ted was up first on this chilly morning and fetched in some dry olive wood from the wood store. With the help of a couple of fire lighters, he lit the kitchen range and then made them both breakfast, before calling Harris and asking him if they could meet up in Perithia at Spiro's Taverna around 11:00am for coffee. He told Harris he had a surprise for him, eager to show off his beautiful partner.

When Natasha had finished showering she came up the stone steps into the kitchen, and stood watching him stoke the fire in the old range.

"Ha, there you are Natasha. I hope the water was hot enough for you darling and you are feeling refreshed after your journey. I am taking you to meet a Greek friend of mine this morning."

"Oh really Freddy, but isn't it a little too soon to meet your friends when I haven't become used to calling you anything else but Freddy?"

"Natasha it is quite simple, just call me Ted or Soldier as Harris and my friends do, you will soon get used to it." She sat down next to the warm range and finished off drying her damp hair. It appeared to him that she was deep in thought before she spoke out.

"Freddy, I know you asked me not to mention the kidnapping, but please tell me you weren't connected in any way with the terrible violence I read about in the newspapers."

His mood quickly changed, she had hit a raw nerve, one he wasn't proud of, but she could never know of the terrible crimes he had committed just to be here with her now. He wasn't going to let anything spoil the day he had planned for her. He sat down next to her and placed his hand on hers and spoke softly but with only the slightest irritation in his voice.

"Natasha, you must realise there were some very unsavoury characters involved. As I explained to you, sadly it didn't quite go to plan, but I wouldn't harm anyone surely you must know that darling?"

"But what about this Tony Miles, who the police were saying was murdered at Duston Mill." Ted stood again and took a deep breath before carrying on.

"Look Natasha, I wasn't going to discuss this, but if it satisfies your conscience I will tell you what happened at Duston Mill. When I arrived to collect Tony, I found him face down in a water tank, so I concluded that he more than likely fell into the tank and drowned. This was very upsetting for me Natasha, as Tony was a long time friend of mine. Could we please not speak of this again and put this whole episode behind us? Also don't you forget Natasha, that is the reason we are here together now."

He turned away from her, not able to square his own conscience and the deep seated guilt he now felt. She was visibly upset by Ted's rebuff as this was the first time she had seen him quite as angry. He walked back around the table and lifted her to her feet kissing her tenderly before saying, "Please don't cry my darling. I'm so sorry if I upset you, only I have waited for what seems like an age for you to arrive, so can we just look forward now to the future and our whole new life together which starts here today?" Now with her arms firmly around his broad shoulders, she kissed him and told him how much she loved him.

"I am so sorry Freddy, of course you are right, please forgive me."

"There is nothing to forgive my darling."

Harris sat talking to Spiro as the Fiat Panda came around the corner and pulled up outside the taverna. Harris was indeed surprised when he saw that an auburn haired young woman with stunning good looks was sitting in the passenger seat. The couple walked hand in hand into Spiro's smart taverna.

Both Harris and Spiro were deemed speechless as they came over to the table. The two men were standing. "Harris, Spiro, I would like you to meet Natasha, my partner." They both came forward to greet the young woman, welcoming her to Kerkyra and inviting her to sit down. They were near to squabbling as to which one of them could pull the chair out from under the table first. Now ignoring Ted completely, Harris was in full flow using all of his Greek charm. He asked Natasha if she had ever visited his beautiful island before, as if he owned Kerkyra all to himself. She told him she hadn't, but said how beautiful she had found it so far, and how much she was going to enjoy living there.

Harris looked up at Ted as if he was about to ask his friend a question. Ted was now standing behind Natasha's chair with his index finger up to the centre of his mouth, and he was giving him that look which seemed to say, 'don't say anything about the villa Harris.' Spiro left the table to go off to make coffee for them all.

"Well my friend, you are a very lucky man to have such a beautiful woman by your side, tell me what your secret is?"

"Okay Harris, enough flattery. I was wondering if your brother was free this afternoon, as I was hoping to take Natasha out on a boat trip later. Harris instantly knew what his friend was up to and took his mobile from his pocket and called his brother Yannis. He stood and walked over to the doorway of the taverna, a few moments later he was having a typically Greek conversation both with voice and hands, before returning to the table.

"Okay my friends, all fixed for this afternoon at two o'clock."

"Thank you Harris, but I hope you haven't bullied your brother into taking us out on this trip, if he was busy doing something else?"

"No no, my friend, at first he said he was busy, then I told him how beautiful Natasha was and he agreed to take us, no problem."

"Stop it Harris please, you are embarrassing Natasha."

They ordered a light lunch of sardines with a small Greek meze consisting of tsatsiki, small cheese pies, octopus, freshly baked bread and a complementary bottle of Spiro's wine which was brought out by the lovely Dena, Spiro's cook. This is so wonderful Natasha told Harris, who was wiping the olive oil from his plate with the fresh bread.

"Ha Greek food, the best my friends, yes," then lifting his glass he wished them good health,. "Yamas," they replied.

After lunch they left Ted's car outside Spiro's taverna and set off in Harris's Z3. Ted was sitting on top of the convertible's collapsed hood, with his feet forced inside and pressing against the front seats, where Natasha was still being charmed by Harris.

"For God's sake Harris, slow down, are you trying to kill us all?" Ted's words fell on deaf ears. Harris only having time for the beautiful Natasha on this short trip to Sidari.

They arrived just after 1:30pm and found Yannis was busy playing around as usual with his speedboat, *Athena*. When he spotted his brother's car pull into quayside car park, he rushed over to meet Natasha with a similar look of pleasure on his face to that of his older brother, only Yanni, thank goodness for her sake, was a little shier than Harris.

She held Ted's hand tightly and turned to ask him where he was taking her, but all he did was to lift his finger and touch the side of his nose, smiling broadly as the boat skipped across the clear blue sea and towards the north. He raised his voice so she could hear him over the sound of the engine and he asked her to look at the island way out in front of them.

"Is that where you are taking me to Ted?"

"Yes my darling, I want to show you something on this wonderful island."

"Now you have me intrigued, please tell me what it is."

"You'll see soon enough my darling, but I will tell you the island is called Erikoussa."

Ted went back to the wheel housing and asked Harris if Yanni could take them first to the villa's mooring rather than the village harbour. Erikoussa didn't disappoint, looking the gem it was on that sunny late February afternoon. As Yanni's boat came ever closer to the island, she turned to Ted and said, "Ted, this island appears to be just incredible, look at those pretty houses among the hills."

The boat rounded the headland and there on the hillside stood the yellow painted villa surrounded by its attractive grounds. Natasha was still admiring the view as the boat slipped up to the small jetty. Harris leapt off to tie and secure Yannis's boat as Natasha turned to Ted and whispered, "This house looks truly amazing. Does it belong to your friend Harris?"

"No my darling, Harris lives on Kerkyra," He helped her off the sleek speedboat, and they all walked up the steep steps towards the villa.

"My God, this house is absolutely unbelievable Ted, and look at the swimming pool."

"Yes I thought you would like that darling."

"But why have you brought me here Ted?"

"Why of course Natasha, to show you your new home."

"What on earth do you mean my new home?"

"It's all yours darling." She looked across at Harris.

"Yes it's true. The villa is all yours Natasha."

To say she was surprised would have been an absolute understatement, she flung her arms around Ted's shoulders and he lifted her off her feet into the air and swung her around. She held him tightly telling him how happy he had made her.

They stayed at the villa for at least another two hours, Harris showing them all their fantastic home had to offer and before they left she insisted that they walked around the beautiful olive groves. The look of sheer overwhelming joy on Natasha's face made him think that maybe he had been justified in his terrible misdemeanours, but deep down somewhere in the heart of his soul he was ashamed of himself. All the glory he had achieved in his military days now seemed to count for nothing, and he knew he would have to live a lie for the rest of his life.

Natasha oblivious to his thinking looked incredibly contented as Yannis's boat slipped its moorings. They were now both looking back at their wonderful new home, he placed his arm around her and she kissed him again before tucking her head into his shoulder and holding on to him tightly for the rest of the journey back to Sidari.

On 28th February the villa was officially theirs, although the last few days had been anything but easy. Kerkyra operates the notary system like the majority of other European countries, this is where the solicitors from both parties sign the contracts in the same office in front of a notary and at the same time. This is normally quite straightforward, but in this case there were more than a few complications with the paperwork. Ted had left

Natasha to sign the contract in her name only, so in law she was the rightful owner, but because Ted was paying the whole amount in cash, several flags popped up. It was nothing that the Greek solicitors couldn't sort out along with the notary's approval, and after all, they were making lots of money out of the deal. The German couple who had owned the Villa for the last ten years had to tie up a few loose ends themselves, but at 5:30 in the evening of the last day of February, the Villa belonged to Natasha.

*

Wallace had just walked into his office when his landline rang out.

"Hello, DI Wallace speaking."

"This is Inspector Dryker from the Central Agency of Interpol, Inspector Wallace," the female voice informed him.

"Ha, good afternoon Inspector Dryker, have you any news for me?"

"We have received information regarding one of the people you are looking for, Miss Natasha Privsek."

"That is good news inspector."

"According to the records from Ljubljana airport, Miss Privsek took a flight to Venice on the 21st February at 9:45am."

Wallace waited for her to carry on, but he soon realised that the Dutchwoman had finished speaking.

"So you will now be concentrating the search for Miss Privsek in northern Italy inspector?"

"That is correct Inspector Wallace, and now I wish you good afternoon."

"Yes right, good afternoon to you Inspector Dryker."

Wallace replaced the receiver and called out, "Jack, get in here will you?" A few moments later Jack Terry walked into the office.

"Ah there you are Jack, I have just received a call from Interpol, and apparently Natasha flew out of Ljubljana over a week ago on a flight to Italy."

"Which part of Italy, guv?"

"Northern Italy, Venice to be exact, but Inspector Dryker isn't the best conversationalist we have ever heard, is she? So we will just have to wait for the Interpol agency to get back in touch again."

"If you ask me guv, they only seem to be feeding us a few scraps to keep us sweet, so how about sending me to Venice?"

"Yes I can just see the Super signing the authorisation now Jack."

*

Two days after Harry Bernard's Funeral, Lynda Harker was helping her friend Ester to come to terms with the sudden loss of her estranged husband. Ester was sorting through the recently unopened post, there was the usual pile of junk mail, a couple of final demands from the utility companies and a brown creased envelope that had sticky tape holding the flap firmly down. She opened the grubby letter and pulled out a folded piece of paper. When she opened it out there were just six words written down in large printed form.

FOR YOU HARRY MY OLD FRIEND

She looked again into the envelope and withdrew a crisp, sharp edged slip which read,

THE BANK OF GREECE PAYS THE BEARER OF THIS DRAFT SEVEN HUNDRED AND FIFTY THOUSAND EUROS.

Ester gasped as she read it over again to herself. Lynda looked at her and asked if she was all right. At first she never answered then, after regaining some self-control replied, "Yes, sorry, I am fine darling. It's just that I can't quite believe the amount of debt that Harry had accumulated." She carefully placed the banker's draft into her handbag and tried to carry on normally but all the time she was wondering who could have sent this letter to poor Harry, and why he should have been dealt such a cruel hand in life.

CHAPTER TWENTY THREE

Five years had passed since Ted and Natasha had moved into the villa on Erikoussa and their life could not have been more complete, as now they were blessed with two beautiful little boys. Andreas was three and Helios two, and the family had settled long ago into the slow pace of life on the beautiful picturesque island, where happiness had consumed them into their own tiny idyllic world.

It was a warm sunny Tuesday afternoon as Ted and Natasha prepared to leave Erikoussa for Sidari on the mainland. They had to replenish their supplies, something they undertook on a monthly basis. They used the speedboat which Ted had bought from Harris's brother Yannis four years earlier. Natasha freed the boat lines from the jetty and jumped onto their speedboat *Hermes,* pushing off with her foot as she did so.

She made sure that the children's safety lines were secured and clipped onto the chrome rail attached to the front of the wheel housing. This was a favourite time for Andreas and Helios who loved the boat trip, especially when *Hermes* cut through the top of the waves and the spray from the surf would splash over their tiny faces. They would giggle and call out, "Please, more daddy, more," as the sleek hull skipped across the turquoise Ionian sea on their short trip to Sidari.

This excursion was an absolute necessity as the kafenion on Erikoussa was limited to mostly local produce, and shopping in Sidari was the only possible way they could stock up with supplies they couldn't readily buy on Erikoussa. The journey worried Ted and even though so much time had passed. He still remained vigilant, never dropping his guard for a moment and always ready to return to the island.

The monthly visit was the only time he would venture to Kerkyra himself. If they needed to go to Kerkyra town then Natasha would take the small slipper ferry that supplied the northern islands and would take the children along with her as a special treat.

Arriving at Sidari's tiny harbour, they were both astonished to see just how busy the quayside was. Finding a large enough space for *Hermes* would be much more difficult than normal. They saw Yanni standing on the quayside waving to them to go over in his direction.

"Over here my friends, I will make space for my beautiful *Athena*." He called them over in his direction and then helped the couple by parting two hire boats to allow the vessel to gently glide through the gap, bow first, and up to the jetty. Yanni smiled while joking, "Bloody tourists; think they own the place my friends." This was said very much tongue in cheek as Yanni made a very good living from tourism. He took many visitors from Sidari out on day trips around the northern islands on his new glass bottomed boat.

"Ted, Natasha, my friends where have you been, it seems like years since I have seen you?"

"Yanni it was only last month, anyway how are you and thanks for helping us to tie up *Hermes*."

"No problem, it's so nice to see you both and your beautiful children, come I will buy you a beer, yes?"

"Well perhaps a quick one Yanni, only we need to be back on the island and there's lots of shopping to do."

"Ha, you English always in such a hurry, relax my friend, become Greek and enjoy every moment in your life."

They all walked away from the dock and across to the harbour bar, where Yanni ordered two beers and three *Coca-Colas* for Natasha and the boys.

"Now tell me, how is your life on Erikoussa my friends?"

"Wonderful, just wonderful, we can't thank Harris enough for finding Ted the villa."

They sat there for quite a while chatting away while the children played happily on the sand in front of the bar before Ted politely said, "Yanni, as much as we would like to sit here with you all day, we must go and collect our monthly supplies."

"I understand my friends, don't worry, carry on, and maybe I will call at the villa and taste your olive oil sometime, yes?"

"Yanni you will be more than welcome my old friend please do."

"Ted before you go, I noticed you have changed the name of my beautiful boat. In Greece it is deemed bad luck to do such a thing and especially not to give the vessel a female name, you understand?"

"Don't worry Yanni, Natasha and I are not one bit superstitious, anyway Hermes is your God of travel isn't he?"

"Well maybe we will make Greeks out of you one day." They said their goodbyes and left Yanni talking to the bar owner.

Natasha called out to the children, "Come along you two, let's go along the beach and play while daddy goes into town to fetch the shopping." That afternoon was practically warm with hardly a breath of air as Natasha said goodbye to Ted. He kissed them all in turn before setting off towards Sidari town centre and its shopping area.

This was just like any other shopping trip. Ted would go first to the supermarkets for all the heavy supplies, while Natasha would take the children to play on the beach for an hour or so.

"Come along mummy," they called excitedly as they ran off along the seashore chasing their brightly coloured beach ball as it bounced and rolled on in the afternoon breeze. She followed closely behind watching them happily playing in the warm July sunshine. They were approaching the only part of the beach Natasha disliked, with it's array of sun beds laid out in lines, almost military in fashion.

Sidari is one of Kerkyra's most popular tourist locations and this day the beach was full of people of all shapes and sizes, some tanned beautifully, while others were sun burnt to a dangerous degree. There were also the new arrivals who looked out of place with their pale pasty city complexions. In this category was a middle aged man who sat reading a newspaper with his legs hanging either side of the brightly coloured sun bed, she had only noticed him after Andreas had kicked his ball over in the man's direction.

"Andreas," she called out, but her son was too occupied in retrieving his beach ball to take any notice of his mother. The man peered over the top of his newspaper in a casual manner before then turning another page, glancing across at Natasha momentarily. It was only then that he took notice of the little boy running towards him to retrieve the ball, which had come to rest beside his sun bed. Smiling at the child, he picked the ball up and tossed it gently towards him, and then continued to read his newspaper.

Natasha had recognised him instantly, but she prayed he hadn't realised who she was. Taking hold of both children she quickly walked back along the beach towards the harbour, telling the children that daddy was waiting for them, and begging them to hurry and not daring to look back. When she reached the first turning off the beach that led into the town, she began to panic, now desperate to find Ted, knowing exactly which shop he would be in. Was she being pursued? Had he recognised her? All these thoughts were spinning out of control in her turbulent mind. Natasha let go of Andrea's hand as she stopped to pick Helios up, who by this time was weeping and begging his mother to let them play on the beach. Ignoring his tantrums she took hold of Andreas's hand again and continued frantically on to find Ted.

Turning right onto the square she passed the church of St Nicolas, just as the papas came out onto the plaza. He stared in her direction almost disapprovingly, but she turned her head away and continued out of the square and into the main street knowing she was only one hundred metres or so from Sconto's supermarket, and only a short distance now until she would have to break the terrible news to him. At that very moment Andreas tripped and fell, pulling his mother down onto her knees. Helios clung on desperately as she hit the hard path but somehow she still managed to hold on to Helios. By this time he was screaming as Natasha got back to her feet, pulling Andreas up again, as he sobbed dreadfully beside her.

"Mummy my knee, please mummy stop." This tranquil shopping trip had turned into a nightmare. Tourists were asking if they could help. Ignoring them all, she carried on, with both her own and Andrea's knees bleeding badly. All she wanted to do was to find Ted and break the dreadful news. Now everyone seemed to be staring in her direction as if she was some sort of mad woman, as she dragged the distressed little boy behind her. Soon she was entering the supermarket and she felt the icy coolness from the air conditioning system. She hurriedly walked the length of the store, looking between the shelving hoping to see him. Wanting to shout out his name, she knew she couldn't for the fear that she would bring even more attention to herself.

Where was he? She spotted him at the far corner of the store pushing his trolley along and eyeing the shelves, she more or less ran across the back of the shop. He turned and instantly knew something was dreadfully wrong. Natasha was so exhausted she was finding it really hard to speak, but Ted got the gist of what she was telling him. He abandoned the half filled trolley, lifted up both of his frightened children into his arms and they walked out of the store without looking back. Now they were back onto the main street avoiding eye contact with anyone, before turning down towards the harbour. Helios sobbed as he asked his father if could go and fetch his ball. He didn't answer his little boy, but Natasha answered for him.

"Not now Helios please. I will buy you a new ball, don't worry darling." Without looking back along the beach they carried on to the harbour quayside where *Hermes* was moored. She strapped the children into their tiny life jackets and Ted started the boat's engine while Natasha parted the two hire boats from either side and they slowly left the mooring. Once outside the harbour walls Ted opened up the throttle and the Mercury engine roared away, but not in the direction of Erikoussa. They headed to the east and Acharavi. They never looked or spoke to each other as Natasha sat comforting her two children. While staring out to sea and in the direction the boat was heading, it wouldn't have done any good to have talked to Ted, because both of their minds were in a complete quandary. When he realised the boat was out of sight of Sidari, only then did he steer *Hermes* to the north and to Erikoussa.

Many days of worry passed but Ted was constantly walking the grounds or staring out to sea, transfixed by every boat that arrived at the tiny harbour. Their everyday life was consumed by the thought that perhaps they could lose everything and their dream may well come to an abrupt end. It was late afternoon on 31st July, Ted was dressed only in his shorts as he tightened the lines from the jetty to *Hermes*. He heard the distinctive sound of the port police launch, its engine roaring away in the distance. He was used to the sound because this vessel and it's crew of eight were regular visitors to the taverna in the harbour, where they would sit drinking coffee and chatting to the locals for around an hour, before leaving to continue their patrol around the entire coastline of Kerkyra and it's surrounding islands.

Ted moved away from the jetty and was now awaiting their imminent arrival into the tiny harbour. He didn't have to wait long until the sleek grey patrol boat, now with it's motor idling, cruised around the outside of the huge boulder breakwater which had been built to protect the local fishing boats from the worst of the Ionian sea's winter storms. He looked on as they slowly entered the harbour until they disappeared out of sight behind the rocky headland. Ten minutes or so of scrambling around the rocky outcrop, he arrived at a vantage point high above the waterfront. This gave him a perfect view of the quayside below, and in particular the crew's favourite taverna, Demos.

He observed them as they tied the patrol boat to the taverna jetty helped by Spiro, one of the local fishermen. He was always keen to keep on the right side of the port police who, after all, had all power when it came to the licensing of fishing vessels, net sizes and other important documentation on Kerkyra. Only one man remained on board in the wheelhouse as the rest of crew were now sat in the sunshine outside the taverna laughing and joking with Demos. They seemed to be acting quite normally and no different to any other day. Reassured, Ted slipped away and back towards the villa.

Natasha was bathing the children when Ted entered the coolness of the house. He could hear Natasha talking to them in Greek which she had endeavoured to do ever since they were born. She had learned the language herself in her first year of arriving on the tiny island. Ted would speak to them in English, and only English, so this way the children were learning both languages very easily. He poured himself a drink and walked outside to sit by the pool and tried to relax.

Sometime later he heard the police patrol boat open up her engines and roar off into the distance. He leaned back and gazed up into the blue sky, his mind still mesmerised with the daunting fear that he could lose everything, including his beautiful wife and children. That is, if the person Natasha had seen really had been this Inspector Wallace who just happened to be holidaying on the beach at Sidari. If he had recognised Natasha, it wouldn't be too long before every inch of Kerkyra, and in particular it's remote northern islands, would be searched, leaving no stone unturned until they found them.

When Natasha eventually found him, he was still agonising with their situation and her approach startled him momentarily.

"There you are darling. I have been worried about you how long have you been sitting out here."

"Come and sit beside me Natasha." She sat down next to him and he placed his arm around her shoulders and told her how worried he was about losing her and the children.

"But it's been nearly a week now and nothing out of the ordinary has happened."

"I know Natasha, but we will have to make contingency plans for every eventuality, as we just might have to leave in a hurry."

"Where would we go darling, surely we couldn't just leave all this behind?"

"We may not have a choice Natasha."

"But my darling, where on earth would we go to? Nowhere could be safer than Erikoussa."

"Malta springs to mind, yes Malta, they certainly wouldn't expect us to reach Malta undetected."

"How would we possibly be able to travel to Malta unnoticed. Surely the police will have Kerkyra airport and ferry terminal under surveillance if they suspect you are on the island?"

"No I am afraid you don't understand Natasha, we will be leaving on *Hermes*." Natasha pushed herself angrily away from him before turning towards him again.

"For God's sake Ted, have you taken leave of your senses? We can't possibly risk the lives of our children."

"Please listen to me Natasha, and a look at this map." He picked up one of the boat's many charts of the Adriatic and Ionian Sea, which he had been studying earlier that day.

"Look darling, let me show you. The heel of Italy is just 75 miles away and we have three tanks on board *Hermes*. This gives us plenty of fuel to reach the Italian coast. There we could refuel the boat at Porto Di Lucca, before travelling around the southern coast line, refuelling again at the small port of Capo Rizzio." He pointed at the map as she looked on.

"But Ted you can't be serious, it is still a very long way."

"Please hear me out my darling," he continued, "then after we have refuelled we then steer the short distance to Sicily and finally refuelling again at Portopalo on the southern tip of the island. From there Malta would be within easy reach for *Hermes,* and certainly well in range, being only a further 80 miles away."

"Ted you can't be really serious, suggesting we use our boat, surely?"

"Yes, I certainly am suggesting that my darling. She is a very sturdy vessel, besides I have made much longer journeys in smaller boats than this."

"Ted the children, what about our beautiful children?"

"Look Natasha, they will be fine. I love my children as you do, and of course I wouldn't put them in any uncalculated situation, you must know that. Anyway, if this is to be the worst case scenario, then we will have little choice, believe me. Let us just hope this Inspector Wallace has left Kerkyra none the wiser, and then perhaps we can resume some sort of normality."

The following morning at 9:00am Ted slipped *Hermes* from her mooring and set off around to the harbour to top up her three fuel tanks. Nothing had seemed to have changed apart from his own self recognised paranoia. There were no police, just that lovely atmosphere he enjoyed so much and wouldn't want to lose. He passed the time of day with Spiro, as he squeezed the trigger on the fuel line.

"Fishing trip is it, my friend?"

"No Spiro, I am afraid not. I just wanted to fill the tanks before the government puts the price up once again."

"Ha you English, always so prudent, this is why you have all the best houses on the island." He laughed again and wished Ted a good morning. Ted left the boat tied up alongside Spiro's small wooden jetty and walked around to the harbour taverna to speak to Demos over a coffee, hoping he would have the latest gossip from the mainland for him.

"Kalimera Demos."

"Ted, where have you been my friend?"

"As you know only too well Demos, it is a very busy time at the villa." He ordered his favourite Greek coffee and nodded to a couple of the passing locals. Demos brought the coffee over and sat down beside him, as was his routine with all the local people who lived on Erikoussa and frequented his small establishment.

"So your villa is looking good Ted yes, and your olives, you have strimmed under yes?"

"Yes, all done Demos."

"Always remember the Beebe Ted." He hadn't a clue what Demos was talking about.

"Beebe, Demos what are you telling me?"

"Snakes my friend, always remember to wear long trousers, not like some of your other countrymen I have seen over on the mainland, wearing only shorts, crazy yes?"

"I couldn't agree more with you Demos, but don't you worry, I have all the appropriate equipment."

"I suppose Sidari is still as busy with all it's tourists?" Ted asked knowing Demos taverna was a melting pot of gossip on the island.

"Well my friend Petros was over there yesterday and he was surprised to see so many police." Ted placed his cup down onto the table.

"Police you say, and did Petros say what they were up to Demos?"

"Well according to Andreas at the Sconto supermarket, they are searching for someone." Ted hoped Demos hadn't noticed his body language had changed to the reaction of the news as he tried to remain calm.

"Demos, did Andreas say, who they were looking for?"

"Yes, he seems to think they must have mistaken Kerkyra for the likes of Marbella, something about gangsters hiding out in the hills or maybe even on one of the islands, crazy yes." Ted's heart had already sunk as Demos laughed and then continued, "Why the hell would gangsters ever want come to Kerkyra? Maybe the police believe the Mafiosi are amongst us my friend." Ted stood, trying not to show Demos the way he was really feeling and wished him good morning, telling him he would see him soon.

He steered *Hermes* slowly out the tiny harbour waving goodbye to Demos as he passed by his taverna, then quickly accelerating around to the villa jetty, probably for the last time. He ran up the steps calling out to Natasha. She was standing by the door by the time he made it up to the villa.

"What on earth's wrong Freddy?"

"It's the police Natasha, they are searching Sidari and the surrounding area, and soon they will be on the island looking for us."

"Oh no, my God, what the hell shall we do?"

"There is only one thing we can do Natasha, so please find all the food and drink that you can, and take it down to the jetty. Where are the children?"

"There are both asleep, but are you sure Freddy we have to leave?"

"Natasha listen to me, we have no choice if we want to stay free. Leave the children for now and help me load the boat."

For the next two hours they loaded *Hermes* with every item he thought would come in useful. Ted had always been a well organised man and now it was paying off. His tool box was packed with every conceivable piece of equipment to help him overcome every eventuality. On the forward section of the bow he had rigged up the canvas sleeping area that was designed for the boat. There Natasha and the children could stay dry if the weather turned inclement or shaded from the sun and, of course, sleep if they wanted to.

It was a warm and sticky early August evening and the sun was getting ready to set into the clear turquoise sea. To the east Ted noticed the backdrop of cotton wool like cumulus clouds, hanging high over the distant mountains of Albania. He had lived here now for long enough to know the weather in this part of the world could develop very quickly, catching even the most experienced sailors out and exposing them to high winds and violent summer thunder storms. He rushed back into the villa, opened up the safe, and took out a small leather bound case which contained the rest of the cash he had received for the tiara from Frakas. He knew there was more than enough left for them to start all over again, hopefully in Malta or even Gozo.

With the children now on board, Natasha was comforting them. She told them they were all going on a great adventure, lovingly smiling at her two little boys. Deep down her thoughts were full of anxiety as she strapped them in turn into their life jackets and then finally clipped their safety lines to the rail on the wheelhouse bulkhead. She stood and turned to look back towards the villa. At that point it all became too much for her, and the tears she had held back ran down her now troubled face.

Ted started the engine before freeing the lines from the jetty and they gently left the mooring at around 11:30pm. He never looked back at the villa, he just couldn't bear the thought of leaving behind all they had achieved over the past five years or so. His mind was concentrating on the job in hand in order to save his family from the humiliation that would surely follow if he was captured. He pointed the bow in the direction of north-east and slowly cruised along the coast he knew so well. They rounded the northern tip of Erikoussa then, opening up the throttle, headed due west, passing the island of Othoni on the north side and Mathraki to the south. Ted steered the boat between the islands and out into the open sea.

Hermes felt slightly unlike its normal buoyant self and Ted was surprised it wasn't handling the swell as well as it usually did. He still had plenty of confidence in his boat and did not expect to have too many problems in making their first destination, as long as the weather remained good. He was sure it only felt strange because of the sheer amount of weight he had bestowed. Confident that as the fuel levels dropped later on into the journey, the weight ratio would trim the boat, allowing it to have more of a cutting edge, and subsequently it would ride the swell much better.

An hour passed and the reassurance he had in his vessel began to wane the further *Hermes* proceeded away from the relative safety of the shallower waters around Kerkyra. Half of an hour later the swell increased and caused the boat to rise high up onto the crest of the wave only then to descend steeply into the dark trough before the cycle repeated itself. Ted was more worried now for the family's safety; he questioned himself as to whether he had been too hasty in his decision to leave and place his beautiful family in this dangerous predicament. They were no more than five miles off the coast of Kerkyra and if the swell increased to any further extent he could see the possibility of the boat capsizing, or at the very least taking on water.

This terrifying thought entered his mind on numerous occasions over the next long hour. Should he turn around and head for the safety of one of the islands? Trying to turn in this swell could easily capsize such a small vessel so he would just pray that the conditions didn't deteriorate any further. If they did he would have to lighten the load *Hermes* was carrying.

He had estimated the distance from Erikoussa to the Italian coast as 75 miles and it would take them approximately nine hours at their current speed, but there were many dangers to overcome apart from the elements. The biggest danger of all would be the huge ships that ply their trade up and down the busy Italian coast line. Of course there would be the enormous ferries crossing from the Ionian Sea into the Adriatic and then on to Brindisi or Bari, so he was going to have to be observant if they were going to make the crossing safely. For the first time in his life Ted was truly frightened. He looked down into the canvas cabin where Natasha and the two children were trying to sleep and realised that he had probably been panicked into leaving. This just wasn't like him. He had never doubted himself before, but now his mind was turbulent with terrible thoughts that he was making a great mistake by putting his family through such an ordeal as this.

Again he questioned his decision making. Should he have waited and found out exactly who the police had been searching for on Kerkyra? Then the thought of prison entered his mind and of being locked away for the rest of his life, no longer able to embrace the only woman he had truly loved and his beautiful children. He couldn't stomach the thought of losing them. He wasn't going to change his mind, he couldn't, he had little option if they were ever going to be happy again.

He looked back towards Kerkyra and saw the silhouette of the island slowly slipping away, before he turned again to concentrate on the open sea ahead of them. His mind squared knowing there would be no going back.

Over the next four hours the small vessel ploughed through the swell and Kerkyra and it's northern islands had all but disappeared. Now he could only make out the tops of the mountains which were picked out by the full moon rising in the eastern sky. The state of the sea hadn't deteriorated any further but in the far distance, to the west over the Albania Mountains, he noticed frequent lightening. He wasn't too worried as it was quite common at this time of year, and it reminded him of the summer harvest lightening back in England. Peering down into the canvas cabin again, he could see both of the children were now fast asleep. Natasha, in turn, stared up at him. He could see, even in the moonlight, the anxiety etched on her face. But she then gave him a reassuring smile and he smiled back, mouthing the words, don't worry my darling.

Ted leaned forward over the wheel and placed his hand down onto the securing clip which held Natasha and the children's safety lines, giving them a reassuring tug. After noticing the fuel gauge was showing a quarter of a tank, he knew it was time to turn the valve between tank one and two to enable the fuel to keep flowing from the second tank. Locking the steering to due west, he lifted the rear seat and leaned forward to find the valve before turning it anti-clockwise to allow the fuel to flow. He unlocked the steering again and looked down at the fuel gauge, realising quickly that one third of their petrol had already been used.

His next task was to take a look at the charts. He took the plastic bag from under the wheel housing cabinet and tried his best to read the unfolded chart with the help of a small torch held in his mouth. He worked out that they were on the right course and, according to his calculations, in two hours time they would be approaching the halfway point.

The next two hours went by very slowly for him, his only consolation being to see that Natasha and the children were now fast asleep again. His worst fear, something he had dreaded, the wind was beginning to turn. It was blowing much warmer air in from the south and this would make the journey even more difficult. He knew that, at this time of year, southerly winds usually brought storms. Minute by minute the wind strengthened and he was finding it much harder now to stay on course. The windswept waves battered against the port-side of their small vessel. Natasha was now awake and the children looked restless, she stood up and held onto the wheelhouse rail.

"What's happening Freddy?" She was having difficulty making herself heard over the sound of the wind.

"The wind direction has changed, it's now blowing from the south," he said, struggling to steer and keep on course, as he shouted over the wind noise.

"Do you think we should turn around and go back darling?"

"We can't, the weather looks even worse to the east. Don't worry we will be fine." His voice now rose even higher above the sound of the howling wind. "We are over halfway now and should soon see the lighthouse, just off the Italian coast at Faro.

Go back to the children and hold on to the sheet ropes because it's going to get even rougher of that I am sure. We will get through this, believe me Natasha." She looked slightly more reassured he thought as she sat back down with the children, or was he just kidding himself? Several moments later he felt the first spot of rain on his face. It hadn't rained for at least three months and now, tonight of all nights, the summer weather had decided to break down.

Pulling out his oil skin jacket and leggings from underneath the port-side locker, he made himself ready for the worst that the elements could throw at him. He checked the fuel gauge once more and the reading was as he thought it would be, just under half a tank. Soon he would have to open the second valve to allow the fuel to flow from the final tank. He looked down at the compass to check his course as he knew they would soon approach the main shipping lanes. With visibility deteriorating very quickly he felt much more concerned for his family than he had shown to Natasha. He leaned over and wiped the starboard light, before repeating the same operation on the port-side. He then closed the throttle down a notch or two and cleared the moisture from his face, wishing now he had taken his own advice and turned back when they still had the chance to do so.

The ever increasing wind howled through the slackened sheet lines which held the canvas cabin protecting his now vulnerable family. Looking down anxiously, he was surprised to see that Natasha had somehow dropped off to sleep again. He once again questioned his own sanity on the wisdom of bringing the three people that he worshipped so much into such a dangerous environment. What sort of person had he turned into? He had had a wonderful family once before, until Jackie's business folded and their marriage collapsed under the financial strain of it all. She had then broken his heart by taking their children, Molly and Alistair, to the States, leaving him to live alone on his army pension.

Yes, he could still write to them both, and she always said he could visit them any time he wanted to, but now she had remarried some wealthy property tycoon and he had turned into someone he barely recognised. He was deep in thought, then he glimpsed out the corner of his eye the outline of a large freighter bearing down on them.

"Dear God almighty," was the blood curdling scream that came from the depths of his inner soul, and one of spine chilling proportions as he desperately tried to turn *Hermes*. He just managed to bring the boat around, but not before the freighter's huge bow wave smashed into their tiny craft, lifting it violently up and sideways before crashing back down again. It threw Natasha and the children off their beds and onto the deck. He was powerless to help them as every sinew in his body strained to stop his vessel from overturning. Just as he regained some control, *Hermes* continued to be sucked in by the irresistible force of a whirlpool like action as it received a glancing blow from the freighter's side. He hung on desperately to the wheel, but had no further influence over his tiny vessel. He was now completely incapable of controlling their destiny. All he could do was shout out franticly for his family to hold on.

Natasha and the children were screaming as she hysterically held on to the little boys, although no one would have heard their cries from the ship high above them as the crew were oblivious to their plight. He prayed to God and their only hope was that they would be released from the ship's grip that was now holding *Hermes*. The tiny vessel violently scraped down the whole length of the freighters side as he cried out again in absolute desperation.

"Please God Almighty help us?" At that very moment he was struck on the back of his head by one of the ships loose trailing heavy lines. It sent him sprawling across the tiny vessel and over the side. Natasha screamed out his name as she had tried to stop him but it was no use. It all seemed to have happened in terrifying slow motion, and Ted was gone. She cried out his name again before falling back, helplessly gripping onto her children. It was only a matter of seconds before the freighter spat *Hermes* out and into her wake like some disregarded jetsam. She tied to stand by grabbing hold of her safety line and desperately pulling herself towards the wheel housing. Her face was twisted with the pain she was feeling, and her broken voice screamed out into the dark night, "Freddy, Freddy, my darling where are you?" Only the cruel heartless wind answered her pleas as she crawled back to the tearful children. Soaked and battered by the relentless weather, the tears of agony streamed down her face. She held the two terrified children tightly as they lay on the windswept deck, in total despair of the enormity of their situation.

A few moments later she thought she heard him calling, but surely it could only be the wind playing trickery with her mournful thoughts as her delirious grief-stricken body screamed out for God's help once again. "Natasha help me, help me." This time she managed to stand and once more she held desperately on to the wheelhouse. Looking around she saw nothing but the stern lights of the ship disappearing into the murkiness of that appalling night. She must have been hearing things. Slumping to her knees, she prayed out loud.

"Dear God, please bring him back."

"Natasha, Natasha, help me." She looked and there he was some 50 metres away, desperately trying to swim towards the boat. She crawled across the deck to the rear locker and took out the thin safety line with its small ball attached to one end. Holding on firmly with one hand, she launched the line towards him, repeating the operation over and over again, but all the time he was moving further and further away from her. She could tell he was becoming weaker. Finally she summoned up all the strength left in her traumatic body and launched the line; it landed a metre in front of him. He knew this was his last chance and he frantically reached out his arm at full stretch. He managed to grab the line with one hand before gradually pulling himself, with one hand over the other, closer and closer to his distraught family. Natasha tried to help but all her energy was spent and it was only because of his strength and for his family's preservation that he was able to haul himself along the line until he reached their tiny vessel. Adrenalin kicked in again as she helped him, expending the last drop of any energy she had left. Between them both, their efforts paid off as they managed to haul him on board. He embraced them all before collapsing onto the sodden deck.

As soon as he recovered a little strength, he made his way to the stern and found the engine had been totally swamped by the freighters bow wave, disabling the Mercury more or less immediately it had crashed into *Hermes*. He quickly realised that he had to get the engine started to get them clear of this disastrous position he had got them into. If he couldn't fire up the engine, he knew they were still in mortal danger from the shipping lanes and that they would be left floating helplessly somewhere between Greece and Italy. Their destiny was in the lap of the Gods.

Freddy asked Natasha to keep a lookout as he urgently tried to fire up the Mercury engine. The job wasn't made easy by the fact that he had to stand on the foot plate on the stern of the boat as the sea lapped up and over his waist while the waves tossed the tiny boat around like a cork in a bowl. He struggled to change the two wet spark-plugs hoping this would be enough to start up the swamped outboard. Climbing back over the rear seats, he turned the key. Although the engine turned over it still wouldn't quite start. The fear that now played on his mind, and one he had been dreading, was that maybe the fuel had been contaminated by the water entering the tank lockers. He tried again, still nothing. Lifting the rear seat cover he knelt down to look into the tank bay and found that two of the three tanks were covered in water. His heart sunk at the realisation they would not be able to continue their journey and make landfall in Italy.

He connected the last remaining tank to the fuel line and tried once more, turning the key. It was a wonderful sound when the Mercury leaped back into life. "Thank God Natasha," he shouted out loud above the prevailing wind, which now seemed to have eased slightly. Looking towards the east he could see that the visibility had also improved, much to his relief. The *Rolex* on his wrist read 4:00am and in another thirty minutes or so the sun would be rising. Very reluctantly, he turned *Hermes* the only possible way he could to save his family and headed slowly back towards Erikoussa.

CHAPTER TWENTY FOUR

Jack Terry looked on slightly bemused as his boss walked into the serious crimes office.

"Bloody hell guv, didn't your misses take any suntan cream with you?"

"Yes, yes, very funny Jack."

"Ha, there you are Inspector Wallace." Chief Superintendant Bendery walked into the room.

"Good God Wallace, what's happened to your face man?"

"Sunburn I'm afraid to say sir."

"Haven't you heard of suntan lotion inspector? Anyway perhaps we can make better progress on the Harker case now you're back." Terry looked up at old Bendover and muttered an expletive under his breath. Wallace saw Jack's lips move slightly but he hoped Bendery hadn't heard him.

"Well actually sir, I have only just walked into the office so I haven't had a chance to speak to DS Terry yet. Has there been some sort of a development then after all this time? It must be well over five years now since Interpol lost track of Bromley and Natasha Privsek?"

"Well inspector, perhaps I will leave DS Terry to fill you in with the details. I'll call back later this afternoon." With that Chief Superintendant Bendery left the room.

"Pratt."

"Jack, you can't talk that way about the chief super, even when we know he is. Anyway, come on then spill the beans?"

"Right guv, I have had a couple of conversations with Interpol since you have been away and they have, along with the Hungarian police, found Lynda Harker's tiara."

"Good God Jack, I'm amazed, after all this time. I would have thought it would have been broken up years ago?"

"So would I guv, but apparently not. The Hungarian police discovered the tiara for sale on the black market in Budapest.

Apparently, some known Hungarian villain called Frakas was arrested in Athens along with three others, who were finally tracked down on some Greek island or other."

"Out of interest Jack, which Greek island?"

"Just a minute guv, I will get the file out." Wallace stood up, walked over to the window and waited in expectancy for his DS to give him the name. "Here we are guv. I can't pronounce it properly but, Kerkyra or Kerkar, something like that anyway."

"For Christ sake Jack, I have just spent the last three weeks on Kerkyra."

"I thought you told us you were going on holiday to Corfu guv?"

"Corfu is the English name for Kerkyra."

"Well bugger me, what a coincidence, the fact that you were on Kerkyra at the same time." Wallace walked across to his desk, sat down again and leaned back in his chair, seemingly deep in thought.

"Are you okay guv?"

"Do you think you could fetch me a coffee Jack, only something has just occurred to me, which I can't quite believe?"

"What the hell is it, because you look like you have just seen a ghost?" Jack poured his boss a coffee from the glass percolator and sat down opposite his DI.

"Interpol Jack, have they any idea to the whereabouts of Bromley?"

"I am afraid not, you see this Frakas chap apparently has been dealing on the black market in European and Egyptian antiquities for some time, and the Greek authorities have evidently had an arrest warrant out for him for years."

Jack hesitated and asked, "Are you sure you're all right guv, only you seem miles away?"

"No, I am fine really Jack, carry on."

"The strange thing about this guv, is that the tiara this villain Frakas was trying to pass off as a genuine Hungarian antiquity was actually a fake."

"So had Frakas had a copy of Lynda Harker's tiara made, and then tried to sell it as the original?"

"No. You see, the tiara that she handed over as the ransom, was in fact a fake all a long." Now Wallace was flabbergasted for the second time in only a matter of a few minutes.

"That's not all. Take a look at this file the Hungarian police sent to Interpol." DS Terry passed his boss a brown envelope, emptying it's contents onto his desk. He studied the A4 sheets for some considerable time, his eyes lifting up every so often to stare at Jack momentarily, before continuing to read on. He then expressed himself in a manner of utter disbelief.

"Good God Jack, have you interviewed Lynda Harker about this revelation yet?"

"No guv, I thought you might like to take this interview yourself. I have informed her that we will be calling on them tomorrow morning at 10:30, on a matter of some importance."

"Well done Jack. I will look forward to seeing her reaction for myself."

"Just what I thought you would say guv."

At 10:30am the next day as arranged, Inspector Wallace and Detective Sergeant Jack Terry were standing in the Harker's family drawing room, anxious to interview Lynda.

"Would you like to sit down gentlemen?"

"If you don't mind madam, we would rather stand."

"Oh dear inspector, that sounds ominous, what on earth is wrong?"

"Well madam, we have been informed by Interpol that the piece of jewellery, known as the Keszthely tiara, has been located in Budapest, after the Hungarian police raided a known criminal's property."

"That's wonderful news Inspector Wallace. I must go and tell Jonathan right away. I won't be a moment, he is only in his study."

"If you don't mind Mrs Harker, there is something else we would like to discuss with you first." She sat down again.

"What is it inspector, you are worrying me now?" Wallace turned towards Jack and nodded for him to carry on.

"Mrs Harker, did you know that the tiara you handed over all those years ago to your husband's kidnappers was in fact a fake?"

At first she turned her head nervously to one side as if she was contemplating her answer, then she stood and walked over to the window, appearing to look outside, as she replied, "In fact, yes I did know that." Both detectives once again looked at each other.

Wallace then asked, "So there isn't any Hungarian jewellery of historical significance then madam which, I think you told us, was valued at four to five million pounds?" She came back over to the sofa and sat down again, now looking even more anxious than she had been a few moments ago.

"Yes inspector, the jewellery most defiantly exists. Please let me explain."

"Indeed, please do madam," Wallace rebuffed. Both officers were now intrigued and looking forward to her explanation.

"Inspector, that day I drove to my bank in Market Wellen High Street, in order to meet the terrible demands of Jonathan's abductors, was the first time I had been to the safety deposit box since daddy died. It was only when I opened the box and looked inside, that I remembered the words he whispered to me on his death bed. You see inspector, there were two bags inside the box. One of red velvet containing the genuine tiara of Keszthely and a further gold bag with the fake tiara. Although I say fake, in fact this piece of jewellery is also very valuable. It has two rows of genuine cut diamonds across its top mounting, but I am afraid the rest of the tiara is made up of coloured glass mounted in silver."

"Have you any idea of the value of this so called fake tiara madam?"

"It is probably worth in the region of 60 to 80 thousand pounds as a rough guess."

"Mrs Harker, could you tell us when you were last in the bank vault, previous to that visit?"

"I couldn't say for sure, but I was only a child of, I suppose, eight or nine years."

"To the best of your knowledge, did your father visit the vault regularly?"

"I really don't know the answer to that question Inspector Wallace. Until my father told me on his death bed, I had no idea what his safety deposit box contained."

"Mrs Harker, you told us at the start of our enquiries that your father had passed on this family heirloom to you?"

"Yes, that is correct inspector."

"Then you went on to explain that this precious piece of jewellery, you called the Keszthely tiara, had been in your family for generations. Is that correct madam?"

"That is also correct." Wallace walked across the room to the window and peered outside at the rainwater channelling grooves into the gravel driveway, before returning to ask, "Mrs Harker, if you wouldn't mind, would you ask your husband to join us?"

"Very well inspector. I will go and find him for you." With that she left the room. Wallace looked at the drawing room clock. It was 10:55am. A few moments later both Jonathan and Lynda walked into the room.

"Good morning gentlemen." Jonathan offered.

"Good morning sir. Please would you both like to sit down." Wallace motioned towards their sofa.

"That sounds rather disquieting Inspector Wallace."

"Please sir, if you don't mind." Jonathan and Lynda sat waiting in anticipation at what the police officer was about to reveal to them, as Wallace had the look of a man who was about to deliver only bad news.

"Mrs Harker, from the information you have given us, regarding what you describe as your family's heirloom which your late father claims to have been handed down through several generations of his family was, I am afraid, actually stolen by him." Lynda stood up.

"That is absolutely outrageous Inspector Wallace, and I very much resent such a claim."

"Please sit down madam if you don't mind," Wallace asked politely, yet firmly. Jonathan placed his arm around his wife's shoulders looking bewildered.

Wallace then continued, "As I was about to say, the Hungarian police, along with Interpol, believe the tiara which your family have locked away in your bank vault, truly belongs to the Hungarian Government."

"That can't possibly be true inspector?" she strongly protested.

"I am afraid that it is madam. The piece of jewellery, known throughout Eastern Europe as the Keszthely tiara, was actually stolen from Keszthely Castle, which was also known as the Royal Palace, in the August of 1939." Wallace was now quoting from an email sent by Interpol to his office. Lynda was deemed speechless by the revelations Wallace was now describing.

"Your father, apparently worked at the Royal Palace as a clerk and was a trusted member of their staff, but he disappeared shortly after the jewellery went missing. According to the local police records of the time, he was thought to have left Hungary and escaped to the west before the onset of the Second World War." Lynda looked totally devastated by the statement Inspector Wallace was reading out. She turned to her husband and demanded they must be wrong.

"My father was a well respected gentleman, not some common thief, you know that Jonathan." DS Terry carried on after receiving the nod from his boss.

"Entry records have your father, Mrs Harker, disembarking the Boulogne ferry at the port of Folkstone as a refugee on 30th October of that same year."

"That can't be right sergeant." Lynda intervened again, "My father and his family have lived in the UK for the last century?"

"I am sorry Mrs Harker, but according to these documents, your father's parents and his brothers and sisters, were all deported from Hungary and perished in the holocaust, after the Nazis' occupation of Hungary in 1944."

Jonathan asked Inspector Wallace, "What does all this now mean in regards to the ownership of the tiara?"

"It is quite simple sir, it will have to be confiscated and returned to the Hungarian Government."

"What about the so called fake inspector, surely that must belong to my wife?"

"Well I would imagine they will hold on to that also sir, as the copy was also stolen along with the original." Lynda now sat looking away from the two officers, devastated by the morning's events.

"I am sorry to give you further bad news, but we have been in touch with your bank Mrs Harker, and they have been instructed that, for the time being, there will be no access to your safety deposit box or your personal accounts. I'm afraid all your assets have been frozen until the investigation has been completed." Wallace walked over to the window before turning to face the bemused couple.

"Mrs Harker, the tiara you took away from your bank was, as you know, a fake, or copy if you like. Mr Wicks, your bank manager, has informed us that if you had tried to take away the original, he assures us the bank vault alarms would have been activated by a microchip attached to the tiara and you would not have been allowed to leave the building. You see Mrs Harker, as I think you already know, Sedgwick House and the surrounding land are all mortgaged on the value of the genuine tiara."

Wallace asked Jack to carry on with the interview. The DS opened a large envelope and withdrew two A4 pieces of official looking paper.

"Mrs Harker, yesterday we received a copy of a historical manuscript from the Keszthely Castle Museum, near Budapest. These seventeen century parchments describe the history of the Keszthely tiara and, according to the Royal Palace's scribes of the time, no one has ever profited from owning the tiara. It was thought to have bestowed only misfortune to anyone who came into contact with the precious object, so much so that the tiara was thought to have been cursed by the then Hungarian Royal family and locked away. A copy of the tiara was made and only worn on ceremonial occasions until it was stolen along with the original by your father in 1939."

Lynda sat with her head bowed, holding Jonathan's hand in a vice like grip, listening to the police officer's revelations, in a state of obvious shock.

"The extraordinary fact is Mrs Harker, no one would have been any the wiser regarding your father's indiscretions if your husband hadn't been abducted." Wallace and Terry left the couple sitting on their sofa to reflect on their shocking disclosure. The two officers let themselves out.

CHAPTER TWENTY FIVE

Natasha, Ted and the children soon settled once more into their daily island life style, the locals being none the wiser to their dreadful night at sea. Although not forgotten, the whole terrible incident was firmly put to the back of their minds. It was now September and Ted as always was busy caring for the olive trees and rolling out the black plastic netting, ready for the winter's harvest. Life seemed good again, now that they had decided they would take life as it came. There would be no more running away at the first sign of the police visiting the area or from any gossip from the mainland. Their whole attitude would be more relaxed and they would live life one day at a time, never thinking too much about tomorrow, or to be waiting for a knock on the door for the rest of their days.

The island was much quieter now as most of the summer tourists had already left. The pretty harbour was peaceful once more, looking even more beautiful now that the hire boats had been put away for the winter. It was early one Saturday evening that Ted had arranged for the family to have dinner at the harbour side taverna. It was a wonderfully warm evening for the time of year, with only a hint of breeze gently blowing off the sea, as they made polite conversation while sitting with Demos the owner.

"More wine for you my friends, yes?"

"Yes please Demos, and could you bring the children some of your wife's home made ginger beer."

Demos filled Ted and Natasha's glasses with his own rosé from a large gold coloured tin jug. Helios and Andreas were happily watching a couple of local children sitting with their legs dangling over the quayside. They were fishing for small fry using a long baited line. Every now and then they would excitedly run back to their parents to tell them how many fish were in the children's bucket.

"Demos, could we see the menu please."

"Okay my friends, no problem, but you should know by now the menu is in my head." He laughed in his usual jovial manner and his round weather beaten face lit up with the broadest of smiles.

"So my friends, what would you like to eat this evening?"

Before Ted could answer, Demos stood and walked into the taverna, telling them he would bring them the freshest fish in the whole of Greece. Ten or so Greek minutes later he came back with a huge meze. The tray was covered with every Greek delicacy, including Ted's favourite miniature cheese pies.

"You enjoy this first my friends, and then I bring fresh fish caught by my brother, only one or maybe less than one hour ago okay?" They thanked him warmly for the wonderful food as they admired the tastes of Greece on a plate. They realised just how lucky they were to have so much; two beautiful children; and to be living on this idyllic island where the local people had not only accepted them, but welcomed the whole family with open arms.

Ted placed his hand on top of Natasha's, and gazing into her wonderful dark melting eyes, he said, "Natasha I love you so very much, always remember that." She looked around before saying, "I love you too my darling Freddy." Their glasses came together to toast each other's love and they were so very happy as they watched the sun disappear over the top of the island.

Ted had called the children to the table and they were now sitting, listening to their parents talking and laughing, along with Demos who was telling many jokes.

"You are so lucky Demos, to have been born on such a beautiful island, I hope you realise this?"

"Yes of course, my friends. I pray every day to Artemis, Goddess of the wilderness, for giving me so such good fortune."

Their laughs could be heard all around the harbour, as Demos poured them more wine. Natasha was sitting holding Helios, and was looking in the direction of the narrow lane that meandered down the steep hill from the old part of the village, when she noticed a couple walking arm in arm down towards the harbour.

"Demos who are those people coming down the lane from the village, I thought all the tourists had left?"

He stood so he could see over the top of Ted, then turned to Natasha saying, "Ha these two people, my friends, are the last holidaymakers left on Erikoussa, they stay at villa Julia for one week and only arrived yesterday."

"Well let us hope the weather stays fine for them Demos." As usual Demos was on good form, making the children laugh by telling them stories of the island in the days long before tourism.

"I bring more wine yes?" He stood and went into the taverna, just as the new tourist couple walked in by the side entrance and sat down at a table close to the bar.

"Don't you think it is time we got the children home and to bed now my darling?" Natasha asked.

"Well if you say so Natasha. I suppose it is quite late, but it has been such a wonderful evening I don't want it to end." Never one to leave his wine, he poured the remains of the tin jug into his glass. "I will just finish this darling and then we will go."

Natasha gazed across the table her eyes filled with love and said, "Thank you my darling for giving us all such a wonderful home on this the most delightful of islands, and please, can we stay here forever?"

"Yes of course my beautiful Natasha, this is where we belong, our own Ionian paradise." Demos was busy with his new customers as Ted and Natasha stood up. Ted motioned to Demos that the money for the meal was on the table. Demos waved back in his usual Greek dismissive way, as they both called out to him, "Kalinichta Demos."

"Kalinichta my friends, see you tomorrow yes."

"Here we go children." Ted lifted Andreas while Natasha already had Helios snuggled up in her arms fast asleep. After wishing Demos goodnight again, they began to happily walk away from the taverna. The sound of the police patrol boat surprised them as it rounded the boulder breakwater and slowly entered the harbour. 'Strange,' Ted thought. He had never seen this vessel arrive here so late in the evening, and why hadn't he heard the roar from its powerful engines as it approached. They both stood curiously watching the patrol boat for a moment, Andreas waving at the crew as they walked off again, before they took the children home to their beds thinking nothing more of it.

Without warning, the whole area was illuminated by the vessels powerful search lights. They stood holding the children, trying to protect their eyes from the dazzling glare. This was followed quickly by a blast from a loudspeaker, telling them to turn towards the taverna and stay where they were.

Natasha was already in tears as they obeyed the orders from the serious sounding police officer, knowing there was little else they could do. Two port police officers were standing directly behind them with their sub-machine guns trained onto their targets. Andreas began to cry calling out for his mummy, but all Ted could do was tell him to be a good boy and everything would be all right. He gently kissed the little boy's forehead.

Inside the taverna, Demos stood by the bar, shocked by the dramatic change of atmosphere. The new tourist couple, who only a few moments before were seemingly enjoying their meal, were now walking towards Ted and Natasha.

The stern looking woman made a beeline towards Natasha and Helios woke startled by the woman's voice as she turned towards the tall grey haired man and asked, "Is this Natasha Privsek Inspector Wallace?" Wallace seemed to be considering his answer as Natasha turned to look at Ted who was now holding Andreas as if he would never let him go. Their helpless expressions said everything they needed to. Then she looked across in Wallace's direction, his demeanour, she thought, almost troubled as he uttered the words, "Yes, Chief Inspector Dryker, I am afraid to say, this is her."

EPILOGUE

Eighteen months later Fredrick Edward Bromley was found guilty on two accounts: One for the murder of Antony Miles, for which he was sentenced to 20 years; and two, for the planning and kidnapping of Jonathan Harker, to which he was sentenced a further eight years, both sentences were to run concurrently.

Natasha Privsek was sentenced to six years suspended, after having spent the last 18 months held on remand.

Susan Walters was sentenced to five years for her part in the kidnapping of Jonathan Harker.

After being released Natasha was reunited with her children, who had spent the last 18 months with her sister in Slovenia. No evidence could be found to prove that the villa was purchased with the stolen money from the kidnapping, and three months later Natasha returned home to the villa on Erikoussa, where she and her children continue to live to this day.

Jonathan and Lynda Harker had Sedgwick House reprocessed and now live a more modest life in North London where Jonathan has resumed his career as a lawyer.